(PENGUIN CLASSICS)RED

Can a book save lives? This one can.

Penguin Classics have inspired the imaginations of millions of readers all over the world, transforming the way people think and feel for ever. And now that we've partnered with (PRODUCT)^RED™ to bring you our selection of some of the best stories ever written as (PENGUIN CLASSICS)^RED editions, books are going to help save lives too.

Penguin will be contributing 50% of our profits from these (PENGUIN CLASSICS)^RED editions to the Global Fund to help eliminate AIDS in Africa.

So far, 4 million lives have been reached by the Global Fund-financed programmes supported by (RED)™. These programmes provide antiretroviral drugs, HIV rapid test kits, HIV-related training for medical and counselling staff, and Prevention of Mother to Child Transmission (or PMTCT) treatments. Not one penny is taken out of the Global Fund for overheads, so every single pound goes straight to the people who need help, and straight to keeping them alive so that they can go on taking care of their families, living their lives and changing their own worlds.

Buy a piece of great literature and do something great.

PENGUIN CLASSICS IS A PROUD PARTNER OF (PRODUCT)^RED™

ANTON CHEKHOV

The Lady with the Little Dog

AND OTHER STORIES

Translated and with Notes by
RONALD WILKS

PENGUIN BOOKS

PENGUIN CLASSICS

Published by the Penguin Group
Penguin Books Ltd, 80 Strand, London WC2R ORL, England
Penguin Group (USA) Inc., 375 Hudson Street, New York, New York 10014, USA
Penguin Group (Canada), 90 Eglinton Avenue East, Suite 700, Toronto, Ontario, Canada M4P 2Y3
(a division of Pearson Penguin Canada Inc.)
Penguin Ireland, 25 St Stephen's Green, Dublin 2, Ireland (a division of Penguin Books Ltd)
Penguin Group (Australia), 250 Camberwell Road, Camberwell, Victoria 3124, Australia
(a division of Pearson Australia Group Pty Ltd)
Penguin Books India Pvt Ltd, 11 Community Centre, Panchsheel Park, New Delhi – 110 017, India
Penguin Group (NZ), 67 Apollo Drive, Rosedale, North Shore 0632, New Zealand
(a division of Pearson New Zealand Ltd)
Penguin Books (South Africa) (Pty) Ltd, 24 Sturdee Avenue, Rosebank, Johannesburg 2196, South Africa

Penguin Books Ltd, Registered Offices: 80 Strand, London WC2R ORL, England

www.penguin.com

This edition published in Penguin Classics 2002
This (P E N G U I N CLASSICS)^RED edition published 2010
1

Translation and editorial material © Ronald Wilks, 2002
'The House with the Mezzanine', 'Ionych', 'The Lady with the Little Dog' and
'Disturbing the Balance' newly translated 2002. 'Peasants', 'Man in a Case',
'Gooseberries', 'About Love', 'In the Ravine' and 'The Bishop' first published 1982,
pre-existing translations © Ronald Wilks, 1982. 'My Life' first published 1985,
pre-existing translation © Ronald Wilks, 1985. 'A Visit to Friends' and 'The Bride'
first published 1986, pre-existing translations © Ronald Wilks, 1986

Printed in Great Britain by Clays Ltd, St Ives plc

ISBN: 978–0–141–19547–6

www.greenpenguin.co.uk

Contents

The House with the Mezzanine

(AN ARTIST'S STORY)

I

About six or seven years ago I was staying in a district of T—province, on the estate of a young landowner by the name of Belokurov – a very early riser who sported a peasant jerkin, drank beer in the evenings and who was always complaining to me that no one, anywhere, really appreciated him. He had a cottage in the garden, while I lived in the old manor house, in a vast colonnaded ballroom which, apart from the wide sofa on which I slept and a table where I played patience, was devoid of furniture. Even in calm weather there was always a peculiar droning in the ancient Amos stoves[1] and during thunderstorms the whole house shook as if it were splitting into small pieces. It was rather frightening, especially at night when the ten big windows were suddenly all aglow in the lightning.

Doomed to perpetual idleness, I didn't do a thing and would gaze for hours on end through the windows at the sky, birds, avenues; I would read everything that came with the post – and I slept. Sometimes I would go out and wander around until late evening.

Once, as I was returning home, I happened to stray into the grounds of a manor house that was unfamiliar to me. The sun was already sinking and the evening shadows lay across the flowering rye. Two rows of closely planted, towering fir trees stood like solid, unbroken walls, forming a handsome, sombre avenue. I easily climbed the fence and walked down the avenue, slipping on pine needles that lay about two inches deep on the ground. It was quiet and dark – only high up in the tree tops a vivid golden light quivered here and there and transformed spiders' webs into shimmering rainbows. The smell of resin from the firs was almost stifling. Then I turned into a long avenue of lime trees. And here too all was neglect and age. Last year's leaves rustled sadly underfoot and in the dusk shadows lurked between the trees. In the old fruit orchard to the right an oriole sang feebly, reluctantly, most probably because he too was old. But then the limes ended. I went past a white house with a terrace and a kind of mezzanine or attic storey – and suddenly a vista opened up: a courtyard, a large pond with bathing place, a clump of green willows, and a village on the far bank, with a slender, tall bell-tower whose cross glittered in the setting sun. For one fleeting moment I felt the enchantment of something very close and familiar to me, as though I had once seen this landscape as a child,

At the white stone gates that led from the courtyard into open country – sturdy, old-fashioned gates surmounted by lions – two young girls were standing. One of them – the elder, who was slim, pale and very pretty, with a mass of auburn hair and a small stubborn mouth – wore a stern expression and hardly looked at me. But the other girl, still very young – no more than seventeen or eighteen – similarly slim and pale, with large mouth and big eyes, looked at me in astonishment as I passed by. She said something in English and seemed embarrassed. And it seemed that I had long known these two charming faces. I returned home with the feeling that it had all been a lovely dream.

Soon afterwards when I was strolling with Belokurov one day around noon by the house, a light sprung carriage suddenly drove into the yard, rustling over the grass: in it was one of the girls – the elder. She was collecting money for some villagers whose houses had burnt down. Without looking at us she gave a serious, detailed report about how many houses had burnt down in the village of Siyanov, how many women and children had been left homeless and what immediate measures the relief committee (to which she now belonged) was proposing to take. After getting us to sign the list she put it away and immediately started saying goodbye.

'You've quite forgotten us, Pyotr Petrovich,' she told Belokurov as she gave him her hand. 'Please come and see us – and if Monsieur

N— (she mentioned my name) would like to see some admirers of his work and fancies paying us a visit, Mama and I would be really delighted.' I bowed.

When she had driven off Pyotr Petrovich started telling me about her. He said that the girl was of good family and that her name was Lidiya Volchaninov. The estate on which she lived with her mother and sister – like the large village on the other side of the pond – was called Shelkovka. Her father had once held an important post in Moscow and was a high-ranking civil servant when he died. Although they were very well-off, the Volchaninovs never left their estate, summer or winter. Lidiya taught in their own rural school in Shelkovka, at a monthly salary of twenty-five roubles. She spent nothing else besides this money on herself and was proud of earning her own living.

'An interesting family,' said Belokurov. 'We'll go and visit them one day if you like. They'd be delighted to see you.'

One day after dinner (it was some sort of holiday) we remembered the Volchaninovs and went over to see them at Shelkovka. The mother and her two daughters were at home. Yekaterina Pavlovna, the mother, obviously once very pretty but now plump for her age, sad, short-winded and absent-minded, tried to entertain me with talk about painting. Having learnt from her daughter that I might be coming to see them at Shelkovka she hurriedly mentioned two or three of my landscapes that she had seen at Moscow exhibitions, and now she asked me what I wanted to express in them. Lidiya – or Lida as she was called at home – talked more to Belokurov than to me. Serious and unsmiling, she asked him why he wasn't on the local council and had so far never attended a single meeting.

'It's not right!' she said reproachfully. 'It's not right. You should be ashamed of yourself.'

'That's true, perfectly true,' her mother agreed. 'It's just not right!'

'The whole district is under Balagin's thumb,' Lida continued, turning to me. 'He himself is chairman of the council, he's handed out all the jobs in the district to his nephews and sons-in-law, and he does just what he likes. We must take a stand. The young people must form a pressure group, but you can see for yourself what our young people are like. You ought to be ashamed of yourself, Pyotr Petrovich!'

While we were discussing the local council, Zhenya, the younger sister, said nothing. She never took part in serious conversations: in that family she wasn't considered grown-up at all – just as if she were a little girl they called her Missy, the name she had given her governess as a child. The whole time she kept looking at me inquisitively and when I was examining the photographs in the album she explained: 'That's Uncle . . . that's my godfather . . .' and she ran her finger over the photographs, touching me with her shoulder like a child, so that I had a close view of her delicate, undeveloped bosom, her slender shoulders, her plait and her slim, tight-belted waist.

We played croquet and tennis, strolled in the garden, drank tea, after which we had a leisurely supper. After that vast, empty colonnaded ballroom I somehow felt at home in that small, cosy house where there were no oleographs on the walls and where the servants were spoken to politely. Thanks to Lida and Missy, everything seemed so pure and youthful: it was all so civilized. Over supper Lida again talked to Belokurov about the council, about Balagin and school libraries. She was a vivacious, sincere girl with strong views. And it was fascinating listening to her, although she said a lot, and in a loud voice – perhaps because that was how she was used to speaking in school. On the other hand my friend Pyotr Petrovich, who still retained the student habit of turning everything into an argument, spoke boringly, listlessly and longwindedly – he was obviously most anxious to appear advanced and clever. He waved his arms about and upset a sauceboat with his sleeve, so that a large pool of gravy formed on the tablecloth. But I was the only one who seemed to notice it.

It was quiet and dark when we returned.

'Good breeding isn't that you don't upset gravy on tablecloths, but that you don't notice when someone else does it,' sighed Belokurov. 'Yes, they're a splendid, cultured family. I'm out of touch with refined people – ever so badly out of touch! Nothing but work, work, work!'

He spoke of all the work involved in being a model farmer. But I thought to myself: what an unpleasant, lazy fellow! Whenever he spoke about anything serious he would laboriously drag out his words with a great deal of 'er's and 'erring'. And he worked as he spoke – slowly, always late, always missing deadlines. I had little confidence in his efficiency, if only because he carried around for weeks on end in his pockets the letters I'd given him to post.

'The hardest thing,' he muttered as he walked beside me, 'is not having your work appreciated by anyone! You get no thanks at all!'

I I

I became a regular visitor at the Volchaninovs. Usually I would sit on the bottom step of the terrace, depressed by feelings of dissatisfaction with myself, regretting that my life was passing so quickly, so uninterestingly. I kept thinking how marvellous it would be if I could somehow tear my heart, which felt so heavy, out of my chest. Just then they were talking on the terrace and I could hear the rustle of dresses, the sound of someone turning over pages in a book. I soon became used to Lida receiving the sick and handing out books during the day. Often she would go off to the village with a parasol over her bare head, while in the evenings she would hold forth in a loud voice about councils and schools. Whenever the conversation turned to serious matters, that slim, pretty, invariably severe young lady with her small, finely modelled mouth, would coldly tell me:

'That's of no interest to you.'

I did not appeal to her at all. She did not like me because I was a landscape painter who did not portray the hardships of the common people in my canvases and because – so she thought – I was indifferent to all her deepest beliefs. I remember, when I was once travelling along the shores of Lake Baikal[2] I met a young Buryat[3] girl on horseback, wearing a smock and cotton trousers. I asked her to sell me her pipe, but while we were talking she looked contemptuously at my European face and hat. All of a sudden she became tired of

5

talking and galloped off, uttering wild yells. And in the same way Lida looked down on me, because we were from different worlds. She didn't express her dislike openly, but I could sense it. Sitting on the bottom step of the terrace I felt irritated and told her that dishing out treatment to peasants without being a doctor was a fraud: it was easy enough to play the Good Samaritan when one had five thousand acres of one's own.

But her sister Missy didn't have a care in the world. Like me, she lived a life of complete idleness. The moment she got up in the morning she would take a book and sit reading in a deep armchair on the terrace with her feet barely touching the ground; or she would escape with her book to the lime-tree avenue, or go beyond the gates into the open fields. She would read all day long, eagerly poring over her book and one could only tell from her occasionally tired and glazed look, and her extreme pallor, how taxing this really was for her. When I came she would blush slightly on seeing me, put down her book, look into my face with her big eyes and tell me enthusiastically what had been happening – for example, that the chimney in the servants' quarters had caught fire, or that a workman had hooked a large fish in the pond. On weekdays she usually went around in a brightly coloured blouse and navy blue skirt. We would go for walks together, pick cherries for jam or go boating and whenever she jumped up to reach the cherries or plied the oars her thin, delicate arms showed through her full sleeves. Occasionally, I would sketch while she stood beside me, looking on admiringly.

One Sunday at the end of July I went over to the Volchaninovs at about nine in the morning and I walked through the park, keeping as far as I could away from the house, looking for white mushrooms which were plentiful that summer and putting down markers so that I could return later with Zhenya to pick them. A warm breeze was blowing. I saw Zhenya and her mother, both in bright Sunday dresses, coming back from church. Zhenya was holding onto her hat in the wind. Then I could hear them having breakfast on the terrace.

For a carefree person like myself, forever trying to find an excuse for his perpetual idleness, these Sunday mornings on our estates in summer always had a particular charm. When the green garden, still wet with dew, gleams in the sun and seems to be rejoicing; when there is the scent of mignonette and oleander by the house; when the young people have just returned from church and are having breakfast in the garden; when everyone is dressed so charmingly and is so gay; when you know that all these healthy, well-fed, handsome people will be doing nothing all day long – then one wishes life to be always like that. And these were my thoughts as I walked through the garden, ready to wander just like this, idly and aimlessly, all day, all summer.

Zhenya came out with a basket and she looked as if she knew or sensed she would find me in the garden. We gathered mushrooms and when she asked me something she would go on ahead, so that she could see my face.

'There was a miracle in our village yesterday,' she said. 'That lame Pelageya's been ill the whole year, no doctors or medicine did her any good. But yesterday an old woman recited a spell and she got better.'

'That's nothing much,' I said. 'You shouldn't look for miracles only among the sick and old women. Isn't health a miracle? And life itself? Anything we can't understand is a miracle.'

'But aren't you scared of things you don't understand?'

'No, I face up to phenomena I don't understand boldly and I don't allow myself to be intimidated. I'm on a higher level than them. Man should consider himself superior to lions, tigers, stars – to everything in nature – even those things he doesn't understand and thinks of as miraculous. Otherwise he's not a man but a mouse, afraid of everything.'

Zhenya thought that, as I was an artist, I must know a great deal and could accurately guess what I didn't know. She wanted me to lead her into the realm of the eternal and beautiful, into that loftier world in which, she fancied, I was quite at home. And she spoke to me of God, of immortality, of the miraculous. I refused to admit that I and my imagination would perish for ever after death. 'Yes, people are immortal. Yes, eternal life awaits us,' I replied. And she listened and believed – and she did not ask for proof.

When we were going back to the house she suddenly stopped and said: 'Lida's a remarkable person, isn't she? I love her dearly and I would readily sacrifice my life for her. But tell me,' Zhenya continued, touching my sleeve with her finger, 'tell me why you're always arguing with her? Why do you get so exasperated?'

'Because she's in the wrong.'

Zhenya shook her head and tears came into her eyes. 'I just don't understand,' she murmured.

Lida had just returned from somewhere and she stood by the front porch, crop in hand, graceful and beautiful in the sunlight; she was giving orders to one of the workmen. Talking very loudly, she hurriedly saw two or three patients and then, with a preoccupied, busy look, marched through the rooms, opening one cupboard after the other, after which she went up to the attic storey. For a long time they looked for her, to tell her dinner was ready, and by the time she came down we were already finishing our soup. I remember and cherish all these little details and I vividly remember the whole of that day, although it wasn't particularly eventful. After dinner Zhenya lay in a deep armchair reading, while I sat on the bottom step of the terrace. We said nothing. The sky was overcast and a fine drizzle had set in. It was hot, the wind had long dropped and it seemed the day would never end. Yekaterina Pavlovna came out onto the terrace with a fan – she looked half asleep.

'Oh, Mama!' Zhenya said, kissing her hand. 'It's not healthy sleeping during the day.'

They adored each other. When one went into the garden, the other would be standing on the terrace looking towards the trees, calling out: 'Hullo, Zhenya!' or 'Mama, where are you?' They always prayed together, both shared the same faith and they understood one another perfectly, even when they said nothing. And they both had the same attitude towards people. Yekaterina Pavlovna also took to me in no time at all and when I didn't appear for two or three days she would send someone over to inquire if I was well. She would also gaze admiringly at my sketches and would rattle away about all the latest news – just as readily as Missy; and she often confided family secrets to me.

She revered her elder daughter. Lida never made up to her and would only discuss serious matters with her. She lived a life apart and for her mother and sister she was godlike, something of an enigma, just like an admiral who never leaves his cabin.

'Our Lida's a remarkable person, isn't she?' her mother would often say.

And now, as the drizzle came down, we talked about Lida.

'She's a remarkable person,' her mother said, adding in a muted, conspiratorial tone as she glanced anxiously over her shoulder: 'You don't find many like her. Only I'm getting rather worried, you know. The school, the dispensaries, books – all that's most commendable, but why go to such extremes? After all, she's twenty-three, it's time she thought seriously about herself. What with all those books and dispensaries her life will be over before she even notices it . . . it's time she got married.'

Pale from reading, her hair in disarray, Zhenya raised her head a little, looked at her mother and said as if to herself: 'Mama, everything depends on God's will.'

And once again she buried herself in her book.

Belokurov arrived in his peasant jerkin and embroidered smock. We played croquet and tennis. And then, after dark, we enjoyed a leisurely supper. Again Lida talked about schools and that Balagin, who had the whole district under his thumb. As I left the Volchaninovs that evening I took away with me an impression of a long, idle day – and the sad realization that everything in this world comes to an end, however long it may appear. Zhenya saw us to the gates and, perhaps because she had spent the whole day with me from morning to night, I felt that without her everything was such a bore and I realized how dear this whole charming family was to me. And for the first time that summer I had the urge to paint.

'Tell me, why do you lead such a boring, drab life?' I asked Belokurov as we went back. 'My own life is boring, difficult, monotonous, because I'm an artist. I'm an odd kind of chap; since I was young I've been plagued by feelings of hatred, by frustration with myself, by lack of belief in my work. I've always been poor, I'm a vagrant. But as for you – you're a normal, healthy man, a landowner, a squire. So why do you lead such a boring life? Why do you take so little from it? For instance, why have you never fallen in love with Lida or Zhenya?'

'You're forgetting that I love another woman,' Belokurov replied.

He was talking of his companion Lyubov Ivanovna, who lived in the cottage with him. Every day I saw that plump, podgy, self-important woman – rather like a fattened goose – strolling around the garden in a traditional beaded folk costume, always carrying a parasol. The servants were always calling her in for a meal, or for tea. Three years ago she had rented one of the holiday cottages and had simply stayed on to live with Belokurov – for ever, it seemed. She was about ten years older than him and ruled him with a rod of iron – so much so that he had to ask permission whenever he wanted to go somewhere. She often sobbed in a deep, masculine voice and then I would send word that I would move out of the flat if she didn't stop. And stop she did.

When we were back Belokurov sat on my couch with a pensive frown, while I paced the room, feeling a gentle excitement, as if I were in love. I wanted to talk about the Volchaninovs.

'Lida could only fall in love with a council worker who is as devoted as she is to hospitals and schools,' I said. 'Oh, for a girl like her one would not only do welfare work but even wear out a pair of iron boots, like the girl in the fairy-tale! And there's Missy. Isn't she charming, this Missy!'

Belokurov embarked on a long-winded discussion about the malady of the age – pessimism – dragging out those 'er's. He spoke confidently and his tone suggested that I was quarrelling with him. Hundreds of miles of bleak, monotonous, scorched steppe can never be so utterly depressing as someone who just sits and chatters away – and you have no idea when he's going to leave you in peace.

'Pessimism or optimism have nothing to do with it,' I said, irritably. 'The point is, ninety-nine people out of a hundred have no brains.'

Belokurov took this personally and left in a huff.

III

'The prince is staying in Malozyomovo and sends his regards,' Lida told her mother. She had just come in from somewhere and was removing her gloves. 'He had many interesting things to tell us . . . He promised to raise the question of a clinic for Malozyomovo with the council again, but stressed that there was little hope.' Turning to me she said: 'I'm sorry, I keep forgetting that kind of thing's of no interest to you.'

This really got my back up.

'Why isn't it interesting?' I asked, shrugging my shoulders. 'You don't want to know my opinion, but I assure you that the question interests me a great deal.'

'Really?'

'Yes, really. In my opinion they don't need a clinic at Malozyomovo.'

My irritation was infectious. She looked at me, screwed up her eyes and asked: 'What do they need then? Landscape paintings?'

'They don't need landscapes either. They don't need anything.'

She finished taking off her gloves and unfolded the paper that had just been collected from the post office. A minute later she said quietly, as if trying to control herself: 'Last week Anna died in childbirth. If there'd been a clinic near her she'd be alive now. And I really do think that our fine gentlemen landscape painters should have some opinions on that score.'

'I have very definite views on that score, I assure you,' I replied – and she hid behind her paper as if she didn't want to listen. 'To my mind, with things as they are, clinics, schools, libraries, dispensaries only serve to enslave people. The peasants are weighed down by a great chain and instead of breaking this chain you're only adding new links – that's what I think.'

She raised her eyes and smiled ironically as I continued, trying to catch the main thread of my argument:

'What matters is not Anna dying in childbirth, but that all these peasant Annas, Mavras and Pelageyas toil away from dawn to dusk and that this unremitting labour makes them ill. All their lives they go in fear and trembling for their sick and hungry children, dreading death and illness. All their lives they're being treated for some illness. They fade away before their time and die in filth and stench. And as their children grow up it's the same old story. And so the centuries pass and untold millions of people live worse than animals, wondering where their next meal will come from, hounded by constant fear. The whole horror of their situation is that they have no time to think of their souls, no time to remember that they were created in the image and likeness of their Creator. Famine, irrational fears, unceasing toil – these are like avalanches, blocking all paths to spiritual activity, which is precisely what distinguishes man from beast and makes life worth living. You come to their aid with hospitals and schools, but this doesn't free them from their shackles: on the contrary, you enslave them even more since, by introducing fresh prejudices you increase the number of their needs – not to mention the fact that they have to pay the council for their plasters and books – and so they have to slave away even harder.'

'I'm not going to argue with you,' Lida said, putting down her paper. 'I've heard it all before. But I'll say one thing: you can't just sit twiddling your thumbs. True, we're not the saviours of humanity and perhaps we make lots of mistakes, but we are doing what we can and we are right. The loftiest, most sacred task for any civilized man is to serve his neighbours – and we try to serve them as best we can. You don't like it, but there's no pleasing everyone.'

'True, Lida, that's true,' her mother said.

In Lida's presence she was always rather timid, glancing nervously at her when she spoke and afraid of saying something superfluous or irrelevant. And she never contradicted her:

'True, Lida, that's true,' she always agreed.

'Teaching peasants to read and write, books full of wretched maxims and sayings, clinics, cannot reduce either ignorance or the death-rate, just as the light from your windows cannot illuminate this huge garden,' I said. 'You contribute nothing by meddling in these people's lives, you're simply creating new needs and even more reasons for them to slave away.'

'Oh, God! Surely something has to be done,' Lida said irritably and from her tone I gathered that she considered my arguments trivial and beneath contempt.

'The people must be freed from heavy physical work,' I said. 'We must lighten their yoke, they must have breathing-space, so that they don't have to spend all their lives at the stove, wash-tub and in the fields, so that they have time to think of their souls, of God and thus develop their spiritual lives. Man's true vocation is the life of the spirit, the constant search for truth, for the meaning of life. Liberate them from this rough, brutish labour, let them feel they are free – then you'll see what a farce these dispensaries and books really are. Once a man recognizes his true vocation, only religion, science, art can satisfy him – not all this nonsense of yours.'

'Free them from labour!' Lida laughed. 'Can that be possible?'

'It can. You must take some of their labour on your own shoulders. If all of us town and country dwellers unanimously agreed to divide among ourselves the labour that is normally expended by humanity on the satisfaction of its physical needs, then each of us would probably have to work no more than two or three hours a day. Just imagine if all of us, rich and poor, worked only two or three hours a day and had the rest of the time to ourselves. Imagine if we invented labour-saving machines and tried to reduce our needs to the absolute minimum so as to be less dependent on our bodies and to be able to work even less. We would harden ourselves and our children so that they would no longer fear hunger or cold. We wouldn't be constantly worrying about their health, unlike Anna, Mavra and Pelageya. Imagine if we no longer doctored ourselves, didn't maintain dispensaries, tobacco factories, distilleries – how much more leisure time we'd finally have at our disposal! All of us, working together, would be able to devote our leisure to science and art. Just as peasants sometimes mend roads, working as a community, so all of us, as one big community, would search for the truth and the meaning of life: and the truth would be discovered very quickly, man would rid himself of this constant, agonizing, oppressive fear of death – and even from death itself – of that I'm convinced.'

'But you're contradicting yourself,' Lida said. 'You keep going on about science and art, yet you yourself reject literacy.'

'The kind of literacy, when a man has nothing else to read except pub signs and sometimes books he doesn't understand, has been with us since Ryurik's[4] time. Gogol's Petrushka's[5] been able to read for absolutely ages, whereas our villages are exactly the same as they were in Ryurik's time. It isn't literacy that we need, but freedom to develop our spiritual faculties as widely as possible. We don't need schools – we need universities.'

'And you reject medicine as well?'

'Yes. Medicine might be necessary for the study of diseases as natural phenomena, but not for their treatment. If you want to cure people you shouldn't treat the illness but its cause. Take away the main cause – physical labour – and there won't be any more diseases. I don't recognize the healing arts,' I continued excitedly. 'Genuine science and art don't strive towards temporary, personal ends, but towards the universal and eternal: they seek truth and the meaning of life, they seek God, the soul. But if you reduce them to the level of everyday needs, to the mundane, to dispensaries and libraries, they only complicate life and make it more difficult. We have loads of doctors, pharmacists, lawyers, lots of people who can read and write, but there's a complete lack of biologists, mathematicians, philosophers and poets. One's entire intellect, one's entire spiritual energy has been used up satisfying transient, temporary needs. Scholars, writers and artists are working away – thanks to them life's comforts increase with every day. Our physical needs multiply, whereas the truth is still far, far off and man still remains the most predatory and filthy of animals and everything conspires towards the larger part of mankind degenerating and losing its vitality. In such conditions an artist's life has no meaning and the more talented he is the stranger and more incomprehensible his role, since, on closer inspection, it turns out that, by supporting the existing order, he's working for the amusement of this rapacious, filthy animal. I don't want to work . . . and I *shan't*! I don't need a thing, the whole world can go to hell!'

'Missy dear, you'd better leave the room,' Lida told her sister, evidently finding my words harmful for such a young girl.

Zhenya sadly looked at her sister and mother and went out.

'People who want to justify their own indifference usually come out with such charming things,' Lida said. 'Rejecting hospitals and schools is easier than healing people or teaching.'

'That's true, Lida, that's true,' her mother agreed.

'Now you're threatening to give up working,' Lida continued. 'It's obvious you value your painting very highly! But let's stop arguing. We'll never see eye to eye, since I value the most imperfect of these libraries or dispensaries – of which you spoke so contemptuously just now – more highly than all the landscapes in the world.' Turning to her mother she immediately continued in an entirely different tone of voice: 'The prince has grown much thinner, he's changed dramatically since he was last with us. They're sending him to Vichy.'[6]

She told her mother about the prince to avoid talking to me. Her face was burning and to hide her agitation she bent low over the table as if she were short-sighted, and pretended to be reading the paper. My company was disagreeable for them. I said goodbye and went home.

IV

It was quiet outside. The village on the far side of the pond was already asleep. Not a single light was visible, only the pale reflections of the stars faintly glimmered on the water. Zhenya stood motionless at the gates with the lions, waiting to see me off.

'Everyone's asleep in the village,' I told her, trying to make out her face in the gloom – and I saw those dark, mournful eyes fixed on me. 'The innkeeper and horse thieves are peacefully sleeping, while we respectable people quarrel and annoy one another.'

It was a sad August night – sad because there was already a breath of autumn in the air. The moon was rising, veiled by a crimson cloud and casting a dim light on the road and the dark fields of winter corn along its sides. There were many shooting stars. Zhenya walked along the road by my side, trying not to see the shooting stars, which frightened her for some reason.

'I think you're right,' she said, trembling from the damp night air. 'If people would only work together, if they could give themselves up to the life of the spirit they would soon know everything.'

'Of course, we're superior beings and if in fact we did recognize the full power of human genius and lived only for some higher end, then in the long run we'd all come to be like gods. But that will never happen – mankind will degenerate and not a trace of genius will remain.'

When we could no longer see the gates Zhenya stopped and hurriedly shook hands with me.

'Good night,' she said with a shudder. Only a thin blouse covered her shoulders and she huddled up from the cold. 'Please come tomorrow!'

I was horrified at the prospect of being left alone and felt agitated and unhappy with myself and others. And I too tried not to look at the shooting stars.

'Please stay a little longer,' I said. 'Please do!'

I loved Zhenya. I loved her – perhaps – for meeting me and seeing me off, for looking so tenderly and admiringly at me. Her pale face, her slender neck, her frailty, her idleness, her books – they were so moving in their beauty! And what about her mind? I suspected that she was extremely intelligent. The breadth of her views enchanted me, perhaps because she thought differently from the severe, pretty Lida, who disliked me. Zhenya liked me as an artist. I had won her heart with my talent and I longed to paint for her alone. I dreamt of her as my little queen who would hold sway with me over these trees, fields, this mist, sunset, over this exquisite, magical nature where I had so far felt hopelessly lonely and unwanted.

'Please stay a little longer,' I asked. 'Please stay!'

I took off my coat and covered her chilled shoulders. Afraid that she might look silly and unattractive in a man's coat, she threw it off – and then I embraced her and started showering her face, shoulders and arms with kisses.

'Till tomorrow!' she cried.

For about two minutes after that I could hear her running. I didn't feel like going home and I had no reason for going there anyway. I stood and reflected for a moment and then slowly made my way back to have another look at that dear, innocent old house that seemed to be staring at me with its attic windows as if they were all-comprehending eyes. I walked past the terrace and sat down on a bench in the darkness under the old elm by the tennis court. In the windows of the attic storey where she slept a bright light suddenly shone, turning soft green when the lamp was covered with a shade. Shadows stirred. I was full of tenderness, calm and contentment – contentment because I had let myself be carried away and had fallen in love. And at the same time I was troubled by the thought that only a few steps away Lida lived in one of the rooms of that house – Lida, who disliked and possibly even hated me. I sat waiting for Zhenya to come out. I listened hard and people seemed to be talking in the attic storey.

About an hour passed. The green light went out and the shadows vanished. The moon stood high now over the house and illuminated the sleeping garden, the paths. Dahlias and roses in the flowerbeds in front of the house were clearly visible and all of them seemed the same colour. It became very cold. I left the garden, picked up my coat from the path and unhurriedly made my way home.

Next day, when I arrived at the Volchaninovs after dinner, the French windows into the garden were wide open. I sat for a while on the terrace, expecting Zhenya to appear any minute behind the flowerbed by the tennis court, or on one of the avenues – or her voice to come from one of the rooms. Then I went through the drawing-room and dining-room. There wasn't a soul about. From the dining-room I walked down a long corridor to the hall and back. In the corridor there were several doors and through one of them I could hear Lida's voice.

'God sent a crow . . .' she was saying in a loud, deliberate voice – probably dictating – 'God sent a crow a piece of cheese[7] . . . Who's there?' she suddenly called out, hearing my footsteps.

'It's me.'

'Oh, I'm sorry, but I can't come out now. I'm busy with Dasha.'

'Is Yekaterina Pavlovna in the garden?'

'No. She went this morning with my sister to her aunt's in Penza. This winter they'll probably go abroad,' she added after a pause.

'Go-od se-ent a crow a pi-iece of che-eese. Have you written that down?'

I went into the hall and stared vacantly at the pond and the village. And I could hear her voice: 'A pi-iece of che-eese . . . Go-od sent the crow . . .'

And I left the grounds the same way I had first come: from the courtyard into the garden, past the house, then along the lime-tree avenue. Here a boy caught up with me and handed me a note.

'I've told my sister everything and she insists we break up,' I read. 'I could never upset her by disobeying. May God grant you happiness. I'm sorry. If you only knew how bitterly Mama and I are crying.'

Then came the dark fir avenue, the broken-down fence. On that same field where once I had seen the flowering rye and heard the quails calling, cows and hobbled horses were now grazing. Here and there on the hills were the bright green patches of winter corn. A sober, humdrum mood came over me and I felt ashamed of all I had said at the Volchaninovs. And I was as bored as ever with life. When I got home I packed and left for St Petersburg that same evening.

I never saw the Volchaninovs again. Not long ago, however, I met Belokurov on the train when I was travelling to the Crimea. He was still wearing that peasant jerkin and embroidered smock, and when I inquired about his health he replied that he was well – thank you very much! We started talking. He had sold his estate and bought a smaller one in Lyubov Ivanovna's name. He told me Lida was still living in Shelkovka and teaching in the school. Gradually she'd managed to gather around her a circle of congenial spirits, a pressure group, and at the last local election they'd 'blackballed' Balagin, who up to then had his hands on the whole district. As for Zhenya, Belokurov only told me that she wasn't living at home and that he didn't know where she was.

I'm already beginning to forget that old house with the mezzanine and only occasionally, when I'm painting or reading, do I suddenly remember – for no apparent reason – that green light in the window;

or the sound of my footsteps as I walked home across the fields at night, in love, rubbing my hands in the cold. And even more rarely, when I am sad at heart and afflicted with loneliness, do I have dim memories. And gradually I come to feel that I haven't been forgotten either, that she is waiting for me and that we'll meet again . . .

Missy, where are you?

Peasants

Nikolay Chikildeyev, a waiter at the Slav Fair[1] in Moscow, was taken ill. His legs went numb and it affected his walk so much that one day he stumbled and fell down as he was carrying a tray of peas and ham along one of the passages. As a result, he had to give up his job. Any money he and his wife had managed to save went on medical expenses, so they now had nothing to live on. He got bored without a job, so he decided it was probably best to return to his native village. It's easier being ill at home – and it's cheaper; they don't say 'there's no place like home' for nothing.

It was late in the afternoon when he reached his village, Zhukovo. He had always remembered his old home from childhood as a cheerful, bright, cosy, comfortable place, but now, as he entered the hut, he was actually scared when he saw how dark, crowded and filthy it was in there. Olga, his wife, and his daughter, Sasha, who had travelled back with him, stared in utter bewilderment at the huge neglected stove (it took up nearly half the hut), black with soot and flies – so many flies! It was tilting to one side, the wall-beams were all askew, and the hut seemed about to collapse any minute. Instead of pictures, labels from bottles and newspaper cuttings had been pasted over the wall next to the icons. This was *real* poverty! All the adults were out reaping. A fair-haired, dirty-faced little girl of about eight was sitting on the stove, so bored she didn't even look up as they came in. Down below, a white cat was rubbing itself on the fire-irons. Sasha tried to tempt it over: 'Here Puss, here!'

'She can't hear you,' the little girl said, 'she's deaf.'

'How's that?'

'They beat her.'

From the moment they entered the hut, Nikolay and Olga could see the kind of life they led there. But they didn't make any comment, threw their bundles onto the floor and went out into the street without a word. Their hut was third from the end and seemed the poorest and oldest. The second hut was not much better, while the last one – the village inn – had an iron roof and curtains, was unfenced and stood apart from the others. The huts formed a single row and the whole peaceful, sleepy little village, with willows, elders and ash peeping out of the yards, had a pleasant look.

Beyond the gardens, the ground sloped steeply down to the river, like a cliff, with huge boulders sticking out of the clay. Paths threaded their way down the slope between the boulders and pits dug out by the potters, and bits of brown and red clay piled up in great heaps. Down below a bright green, broad and level meadow opened out – it had already been mown and the village cattle were grazing on it. The meandering river with its magnificent leafy banks was almost a mile from the village and beyond were more broad pastures, cattle, long strings of white geese, and then a similar steep slope on its far side. At the top stood a village, a church with five 'onion' domes, with the manor house a little further on.

'What a lovely spot!' Olga said, crossing herself when she saw the church. 'Heavens, so much open space!'

Just then the bells rang for evensong (it was Saturday evening). Two little girls, who were carrying a bucket of water down the hill, looked back at the church to listen to them.

'It'll be dinner time at the Slav Fair now,' Nikolay said dreamily.

Nikolay and Olga sat on the edge of the cliff, watching the sun go down and the reflections of the gold and crimson sky in the river, in the church windows, in the air all around, which was gentle, tranquil, pure beyond description – such air you never get in Moscow.

But after the sun had set and the lowing cows and bleating sheep had gone past, the geese had flown back from the far side of the river and everything had grown quiet – that gentle light faded from the air and the shades of evening swiftly closed in.

Meanwhile the old couple – Nikolay's parents – had returned. They were skinny, hunchbacked, toothless and the same height. Marya and Fyokla, his sisters-in-law, who worked for a landowner on the other side of the river, had returned too. Marya – the wife of his brother Kiryak – had six children, while Fyokla (married to Denis, who was away on military service) had two. When Nikolay came into the hut and saw all the family there, all those bodies large and small sprawling around on their bunks, cradles, in every corner; when he saw how ravenously the old man and the woman ate their black bread, dipping it first in water, he realized that he had made a mistake coming here, ill as he was, without any money and with his family into the bargain – a real blunder!

'And where's my brother Kiryak?' he asked when they had greeted each other.

'He's living in the forest, working as a nightwatchman for some merchant. Not a bad sort, but he can't half knock it back!'

'He's no breadwinner!' the old woman murmured tearfully. 'Our men are a lousy lot of drunkards, they don't bring their money back home! Kiryak's a drinker. And the old man knows the way to the pub as well, there's no harm in saying it! The Blessed Virgin must have it in for us!'

They put the samovar on especially for the guests. The tea smelt of fish, the sugar was grey and had been nibbled at, and cockroaches ran all over the bread and crockery. The tea was revolting, just like the conversation, which was always about illness and how they had no money. But before they even managed to drink the first cup a loud, long drawn out, drunken cry came from outside.

'Ma-arya!'

'Sounds like Kiryak's back,' the old man said. 'Talk of the devil.'

Everyone went quiet. And a few moments later they heard that cry again, coarse and drawling, as though it was coming from under the earth.

'Ma-arya!'

Marya, the elder sister, turned pale and huddled closer to the stove, and it was somehow strange to see fear written all over the face of that strong, broad-shouldered woman. Suddenly her daughter

– the same little girl who had been sitting over the stove looking so apathetic – sobbed out loud.

'And what's the matter with you, you silly cow?' Fyokla shouted at her – she was strong and broad-shouldered as well. 'I don't suppose he's going to kill you.'

Nikolay learnt from the old man that Marya didn't live in the forest, as she was scared of Kiryak, and that whenever he was drunk he would come after her, make a great racket and always beat her mercilessly.

'Ma-arya!' came the cry – this time right outside the door.

'Please, help me, for Christ's sake, my own dear ones . . .' Marya mumbled breathlessly, panting as though she had just been dropped into freezing water. 'Please protect me . . .'

Every single child in the hut burst out crying, and Sasha gave them one look and followed suit. There was a drunken coughing, and a tall man with a black beard and a fur cap came into the hut. As his face was not visible in the dim lamplight, he was quite terrifying. It was Kiryak. He went over to his wife, swung his arm and hit her across the face with his fist. She was too stunned to cry out and merely sank to the ground; the blood immediately gushed from her nose.

'Should be ashamed of yourself, bloody ashamed!' the old man muttered as he climbed up over the stove. 'And in front of guests. A damned disgrace!'

But the old woman sat there without saying a word, all hunched up, and seemed to be thinking; Fyokla went on rocking the cradle. Clearly pleased at the terrifying effect he had on everyone, Kiryak seized Marya's hand, dragged her to the door and howled like a wild animal, so that he seemed even more terrifying. But then he suddenly saw the guests and stopped short in his tracks.

'Oh, so you've arrived . . .' he muttered, letting go of his wife. 'My own brother, with family and all . . .'

He reeled from side to side as he said a prayer in front of the icon, and his drunken red eyes were wide open. Then he continued, 'So my dear brother's come back home with his family . . . from Moscow. The great capital, that is, Moscow, mother of cities . . . Forgive me . . .'

He sank down on a bench by the samovar and started drinking tea, noisily gulping from a saucer, while no one else said a word. He drank about ten cups, then slumped down on the bench and started snoring.

They prepared for bed. As Nikolay was ill, they put him over the stove with the old man. Sasha lay down on the floor, while Olga went into the barn with the other women.

'Well, dear,' Olga said, lying down on the straw next to Marya. 'It's no good crying. You've got to grin and bear it. The Bible says: "But whosoever shall smite thee on thy right cheek, turn to him the other also . . ."[2] Yes, dear!'

Then she told her about her life in Moscow, in a whispering, singsong voice, about her job as a maid in some furnished flats.

'The houses are very big there and built of stone,' she said. 'There's ever so many churches – scores and scores of them, my dear, and them that live in the houses are all gentlefolk, so handsome and respectable!'

Marya replied that she had never been further than the county town, let alone Moscow. She was illiterate, did not know any prayers – even 'Our Father'. Both she and Fyokla, the other sister-in-law, who was sitting not very far away, listening, were extremely back-ward and understood nothing. Neither loved her husband. Marya was frightened of Kiryak and whenever he stayed with her she would tremble all over. And he stank so much of tobacco and vodka she nearly went out of her mind. If anyone asked Fyokla if she got bored when her husband was away, she would reply indignantly, 'to hell with him!' They kept talking a little longer and then fell silent . . .

It was cool and they could not sleep because of a cock crowing near the barn for all it was worth. When the hazy blue light of morning was already filtering through every chink in the woodwork, Fyokla quietly got up and went outside. Then they heard her running off somewhere, her bare feet thudding over the ground.

II

Olga went to church, taking Marya with her. Both of them felt cheerful as they went down the path to the meadow. Olga liked the wide-open spaces, while Marya sensed that her sister-in-law was someone near and dear to her. The sun was rising and a sleepy hawk flew low over the meadows. The river looked gloomy, with patches of mist here and there. But a strip of sunlight already stretched along the hill on the far side of the river, the church shone brightly and crows cawed furiously in the manor house garden.

'The old man's all right,' Marya was telling her, 'only Grannie's very strict and she's always on the warpath. Our own bread lasted until Shrovetide, then we had to go and buy some flour at the inn. That put her in a right temper, said we were eating too much.'

'Oh, what of it, dear! You just have to grin and bear it. As it says in the Bible: "Come unto me, all ye that labour and are heavy laden."'[3]

Olga had a measured, singsong voice and she walked like a pilgrim, quick and bustling. Every day she read out loud from the Gospels, like a priest, and there was much she did not understand. However, the sacred words moved her to tears and she pronounced 'if whomsoever' and 'whither' with a sweet sinking feeling in her heart. She believed in God, the Holy Virgin and the saints. She believed that it was wrong to harm anyone in the wide world – whether they were simple people, Germans, gipsies or Jews – and woe betide those who were cruel to animals! She believed that all this was written down in the sacred books and this was why, when she repeated words from the Bible – even words she did not understand – her face became compassionate, radiant and full of tenderness.

'Where are you from?' Marya asked.

'Vladimir.[4] But my parents took me with them to Moscow a long time ago, when I was only eight.'

They went down to the river. On the far side a woman stood at the water's edge, undressing herself.

'That's our Fyokla,' Marya said, recognizing her. 'She's been going across the river to the manor house to lark around with the men. She's a real tart and you should hear her swear – something wicked!'

Fyokla, who had black eyebrows and who still had the youthfulness and strength of a young girl, leapt from the bank into the water, her hair undone, threshing the water with her legs and sending out ripples in all directions.

'A real tart!' Marya said again.

Over the river was a rickety wooden-plank footbridge and right below it shoals of large-headed chub swam in the pure, clear water. Dew glistened on green bushes which seemed to be looking at themselves in the river. A warm breeze was blowing and everything became so pleasant. What a beautiful morning! And how beautiful life could be in this world, were it not for all its terrible, never-ending poverty, from which there is no escape! One brief glance at the village brought yesterday's memories vividly to life – and that enchanting happiness, which seemed to be all around, vanished in a second.

They reached the church. Marya stopped at the porch, not daring to go in, or even sit down, although the bells for evening service would not ring until after eight. So she just kept standing there.

During the reading from the Gospels, the congregation suddenly moved to one side to make way for the squire and his family. Two girls in white frocks and broad-brimmed hats and a plump, pink-faced boy in a sailor suit came down the church. Olga was very moved when she saw them and was immediately convinced that these were respectable, well-educated, fine people. But Marya gave them a suspicious, dejected look, as though they were not human beings but monsters who would trample all over her if she did not get out of the way. And whenever the priest's deep voice thundered out, she imagined she could hear that shout again – *Ma-arya!* – and she trembled all over.

III

The villagers heard about the newly arrived visitors and a large crowd was already waiting in the hut after the service. Among them were the Leonychevs, the Matveichevs and the Ilichovs, who wanted news of their relatives working in Moscow. All the boys from Zhukovo who could read or write were bundled off to Moscow to be waiters or bellboys (the lads from the village on the other side of the river just became bakers). This was a longstanding practice, going back to the days of serfdom when a certain peasant from Zhukovo called Luka Ivanych (now a legend) had worked as a barman in a Moscow club and only took on people who came from his own village. Once these villagers had made good, they in turn sent for their families and fixed them up with jobs in pubs and restaurants. Ever since then, the village of Zhukovo had always been called 'Loutville' or 'Lackeyville' by the locals. Nikolay had been sent to Moscow when he was eleven and he got a job through Ivan (one of the Matveichevs), who was then working as an usher at the Hermitage Garden Theatre.[5] Rather didactically Nikolay told the Matveichevs, 'Ivan was very good to me, so I must pray for him night and day. It was through him I became a good man.'

Ivan's sister, a tall old lady, said tearfully, 'Yes, my dear friend, we don't hear anything from him these days.'

'Last winter he was working at Aumont's,[6] but they say he's out of town now, working in some suburban pleasure gardens. He's aged terribly. Used to take home ten roubles a day in the summer season. But business is slack everywhere now, the old boy doesn't know what to do with himself.'

The woman looked at Nikolay's legs (he was wearing felt boots), at his pale face and sadly said, 'You're no breadwinner, Nikolay. How can you be, in your state!'

They all made a fuss of Sasha. She was already ten years old, but she was short for her age, very thin and no one would have thought she was more than seven, at the very most. This fair-haired girl with her big dark eyes and a red ribbon in her hair looked rather comical among the others, with their deeply tanned skin, crudely cut hair and their long faded smocks – she resembled a small animal that had been caught in a field and brought into the hut.

'And she knows how to read!' Olga said boastfully as she tenderly looked at her daughter. 'Read something, dear!' she said, taking a Bible from one corner. 'You read a little bit and these good Christians will listen.'

The Bible was old and heavy, bound in leather and with well-thumbed pages; it smelt as though some monks had come into the hut. Sasha raised her eyebrows and began reading in a loud, singing voice, 'And when they were departed, behold, the angel of the Lord . . . appeareth to Joseph in a dream, saying, "Arise, and take the young child and his mother." '[7]

' "The young child and his mother" ,' Olga repeated and became flushed with excitement.

' "And flee into Egypt . . . and be thou there until I bring thee word . . ." '

At the word 'until', Olga broke down and wept. Marya looked at her and started sobbing, and Ivan's sister followed suit. Then the old man had a fit of coughing and fussed around trying to find a present for his little granddaughter. But he could not find anything and finally gave it up as a bad job. After the reading, the neighbours went home, deeply touched and extremely pleased with Olga and Sasha.

When there was a holiday the family would stay at home all day. The old lady, called 'Grannie' by her husband, daughters-in-law and grandchildren, tried to do all the work herself. She would light the stove, put the samovar on, go to milk the cows and then complain she was worked to death. She kept worrying that someone might eat a little too much or that the old man and the daughters-in-law might have no work to do. One moment she would be thinking that she could hear the innkeeper's geese straying into her kitchen garden from around the back, and she would dash out of the hut with a long stick and stand screaming for half an hour on end by her cabbages that were as withered and stunted as herself; and then she imagined a crow was stalking her chickens and she would rush at it, swearing for all she was worth. She would rant and rave from morning to night and very often her shouting was so loud that people stopped in the street.

She did not treat the old man with much affection and called him 'lazy devil' or 'damned nuisance'. He was frivolous and unreliable and wouldn't have done any work at all (most likely he would have sat over the stove all day long, talking) if his wife hadn't continually prodded him. He would spend hours on end telling his son stories about his enemies and complaining about the daily insults he had apparently to suffer from his neighbours. It was very boring listening to him.

'Oh yes,' he would say, holding his sides. 'Yes, a week after Exaltation of the Cross,[8] I sold some hay at thirty copecks a third of a hundredweight, just what I wanted . . . Yes, very good business. But one morning, as I was carting the hay, keeping to myself, not interfering with anyone . . . it was my rotten luck that Antip Sedelnikov, the village elder, comes out of the pub and asks: "Where you taking that lot, you devil . . . ?" and he gives me one on the ear.'

Kiryak had a terrible hangover and he felt very ashamed in front of his brother.

'That's what you get from drinking vodka,' he muttered, shaking his splitting head. 'Oh God! My own brother and sister-in-law! Please forgive me, for Christ's sake. I'm so ashamed!'

For the holidays they bought some herring at the inn and made soup from the heads. At midday they sat down to tea and went on drinking until the sweat poured off them. They looked puffed out with all that liquid and after the tea they started on the soup, everyone drinking from the same pot. Grannie had what was left of the herring.

That evening a potter was firing clay on the side of the cliff. In the meadows down below, girls were singing and dancing in a ring. Someone was playing an accordion. Another kiln had been lit across the river and the girls there were singing as well and their songs were soft and melodious in the distance. At the inn and round about, some peasants were making a great noise with their discordant singing and they swore so much that Olga could only shudder and exclaim, 'Oh, good heavens!'

She was astonished that the swearing never stopped for one minute and that the old men with one foot in the grave were the ones who swore loudest and longest. But the children and the young girls were obviously used to it from the cradle and it did not worry them at all.

Now it was past midnight and the fires in the pottery kilns on both sides of the river had gone out. But the festivities continued in the meadow below and at the inn. The old man and Kiryak, both drunk, joined arms and kept bumping into each other as they went up to the barn where Olga and Marya were lying.

'Leave her alone,' the old man urged Kiryak. 'Let her be. She doesn't do any harm . . . it's *shameful* . . .'

'Ma-arya!' Kiryak shouted.

'Leave her alone . . . it's sinful . . . she's not a bad woman.'

They both paused for a moment near the barn, then they moved on.

'I lo-ove the flowers that bloom in the fields, oh!'[9] the old man suddenly struck up in his shrill, piercing tenor voice. 'Oh, I do lo-ove to pick the flo-owers!'

Then he spat, swore obscenely and went into the hut.

IV

Grannie stationed Sasha near her kitchen garden and told her to watch out for stray geese. It was a hot August day. The geese could have got into the garden from round the back, but now they were busily pecking at some oats near the inn, peacefully cackling to each other. Only the gander craned his neck, as though he were looking out for the old woman with her stick. The other geese might have come up from the slope, but they stayed far beyond the other side of the river and resembled a long white garland of flowers laid out over the meadow.

Sasha stood there for a few moments, after which she felt bored. When she saw that the geese weren't coming, off she went down the steep slope. There she spotted Motka (Marya's eldest daughter), standing motionless on a boulder, looking at the church. Marya had borne thirteen children, but only six survived, all of them girls – not a single boy among them; and the eldest was eight. Motka stood barefooted in her long smock, in the full glare of the sun which burnt down on her head. But she did not notice it and seemed petrified. Sasha stood next to her and said as she looked at the church, 'God lives in churches. People have icon lamps and candles, but God has little red, green and blue lamps that are just like tiny eyes. At night-time God goes walking round the church with the Holy Virgin and Saint Nikolay . . . tap-tap-tap. And the watchman is scared stiff!' Then she added, mimicking her mother, 'Now, dear, when the Day of Judgement comes, every church will be whirled off to heaven!'

'Wha-at, with their be-ells too?' Motka asked in a deep voice, dragging each syllable.

'Yes, bells and all. On the Day of Judgement, all good people will go to paradise, while the wicked ones will be burnt in everlasting fire, for ever and ever. And God will tell my mother and Marya, "You never harmed anyone, so you can take the path on the right that leads to paradise." But he'll say to Kiryak and Grannie, "You go to the left, into the fire. And all those who ate meat during Lent must go as well."'

She gazed up at the sky with wide-open eyes and said, 'If you look at the sky without blinking you can see the angels.'

Motka looked upwards and neither of them said a word for a minute or so.

'Can you see them?' Sasha asked.

'Can't see nothing,' Motka said in her deep voice.

'Well, *I* can. There's tiny angels flying through the sky, flapping their wings and going buzz-buzz like mosquitoes.'

Motka pondered for a moment as she looked down at the ground and then she asked, 'Will Grannie burn in the fire?'

'Yes, she will, dear.'

From the rock down to the bottom, the slope was gentle and smooth. It was covered with soft green grass which made one feel like touching it or lying on it. Sasha lay down and rolled to the bottom. Motka took a deep breath and, looking very solemn and deadly serious, she lay down too and rolled to the bottom; on the way down her smock rode up to her shoulders.

'That was great fun,' Sasha said rapturously.

They both went up to the top again for another roll, but just then they heard that familiar, piercing voice again. It was really terrifying! That toothless, bony, hunchbacked old woman, with her short grey hair fluttering in the wind, was driving the geese out of her kitchen garden with a long stick, shouting, 'So you had to tread all over my cabbages, blast you! May you be damned three times and rot in hell, you buggers!'

When she saw the girls, she threw the stick down, seized a whip made of twigs, gripped Sasha's neck with fingers as hard and dry as stale rolls, and started beating her. Sasha cried out in pain and fear, but at that moment the gander, waddling along and craning its neck, went up to the old woman and hissed at her. When it returned to the flock all the females cackled approvingly. Then the old woman started beating Motka and her smock rode up again. With loud sobs and in utter desperation, Sasha went to the hut to complain about it. She was followed by Motka, who was crying as well, but much more throatily and without bothering to wipe the tears away. Her face was so wet it seemed she had just drenched it with water.

'Good God!' Olga said in astonishment when they entered the hut. 'Holy Virgin!'

Sasha was just about to tell her what had happened when Grannie started shrieking and cursing. Fyokla became furious and the hut was filled with noise. Olga was pale and looked very upset as she stroked Sasha's head and said consolingly, 'It's all right, it's nothing. It's sinful to get angry with your grandmother. It's all right, my child.'

Nikolay, who by this time was exhausted by the never-ending shouting, by hunger, by the fumes from the stove and the terrible stench, who hated and despised poverty, and whose wife and daughter made him feel ashamed in front of his parents, sat over the stove with his legs dangling and turned to his mother in an irritable, plaintive voice: 'You can't beat her, you've no right at all!'

'You feeble little man, rotting away up there over the stove,'

Fyokla shouted spitefully. 'What the hell's brought you lot here, you parasites!'

Both Sasha and Motka and all the little girls, who had taken refuge in the corner, over the stove, behind Nikolay's back, were terrified and listened without saying a word, their little hearts pounding away.

When someone in a family has been terribly ill for a long time, when all hope has been given up, there are horrible moments when those near and dear to him harbour a timid, secret longing, deep down inside, for him to die. Only children fear the death of a loved one and the very thought of it fills them with terror. And now the little girls held their breath and looked at Nikolay with mournful expressions on their faces, thinking that he would soon be dead. They felt like crying and telling him something tender and comforting.

He clung to Olga, as though seeking protection, and he told her softly, tremulously, 'My dear Olga, I can't stand it any more here. All my strength has gone. For God's sake, for Christ's sake, write to your sister Claudia and tell her to sell or pawn all she has. Then she can send us the money to help us get out of this place.'

He went on in a voice that was full of yearning: 'Oh God, just one glimpse of Moscow is all I ask! If only I just could *dream* about my dear Moscow!'

When evening came and it was dark in the hut, they felt so depressed they could hardly speak. Angry Grannie sat dipping rye crusts in a cup and sucking them for a whole hour. After Marya had milked the cow she brought a pail of milk and put it on a bench. Then Grannie poured it into some jugs, without hurrying, and she was visibly cheered by the thought that as it was the Fast of the Assumption[10] (when milk was forbidden) no one would go near it. All she did was pour the tiniest little drop into a saucer for Fyokla's baby. As she was carrying the jugs with Marya down to the cellar, Motka suddenly started, slid down from the stove, went over to the bench where the wooden cup with the crusts was standing and splashed some milk from the saucer over them.

When Grannie came back and sat down to her crusts, Sasha and Motka sat watching her from the stove, and it gave them great pleasure to see that now she had eaten forbidden food during Lent and would surely go to hell for it. They took comfort in this thought and lay down to sleep. As Sasha dozed off she had visions of the Day of Judgement; she saw a blazing furnace, like a potter's kiln, and an evil spirit dressed all in black, with the horns of a cow, driving Grannie into the fire with a long stick, as *she* had driven the geese not so long ago.

V

After ten o'clock, on the eve of the Feast of the Assumption, the young men and girls who were strolling in the meadows down below suddenly started shouting and screaming and came running back to the village. People who were sitting up on the hill, on the edge of the cliff, could not understand at first what had happened.

'Fire! Fire!' came the desperate cry from below. 'We're on fire!'

The people up above looked round and were confronted by the most terrifying, extraordinary sight: on the thatched roof of one of the huts at the end of the village a pillar of fire swirled upwards, showering sparks everywhere like a fountain. The whole roof turned into a mass of bright flames and there was a loud crackling. The moonlight was dimmed by the glare and the whole village became enveloped in a red, flickering light. Black shadows stole over the ground and there was a smell of burning. The villagers had come running up the hill, were all out of breath and could not speak for trembling; they jostled each other and kept falling down, unable to see properly in that sudden blinding light and not recognizing one another. It was terrifying, particularly with pigeons flying around in the smoke above the fire, while down at the inn (they had not heard about the fire) the singing and accordion-playing continued as if nothing had happened.

'Uncle Semyon's hut's on fire!' someone shouted in a loud, rough voice.

Marya was dashing around near the hut, crying and wringing her hands and her teeth chattered – even though the fire was some distance away, at the far end of the village.

Nikolay emerged in his felt boots and the children came running out in their little smocks. Some of the villagers banged on an iron plate by the police constable's hut, filling the air with a loud clanging; this incessant, unremitting sound made your heart ache and made you go cold all over.

Old women stood holding icons.

Sheep, calves and cows were driven out into the street from the yards; trunks, sheepskins and tubs were carried outside. A black stallion, normally kept apart from the herd – it had a tendency to kick and injure the others – was set loose and galloped once or twice through the village, whinnying and stamping, and then suddenly stopped near a cart and lashed out with its hind legs.

And the bells were ringing out in the church on the other side of the river. Near the blazing hut it was hot and so light that the tiniest blade of grass was visible.

Semyon, a red-haired peasant with a large nose, wearing a waistcoat and with his cap pulled down over his ears, was sitting on one of the trunks they had managed to drag out. His wife was lying face downwards moaning in despair. An old man of about eighty, shortish, with an enormous beard – rather like a gnome – and who was obviously in some way connected with the fire (although he came from another village), was pacing up and down without any hat, carrying a white bundle. A bald patch on his head glinted in the light of the fire. Antip Sedelnikov, the village elder – a swarthy man with the black hair of a gipsy – went up to the hut with an axe and, for some obscure reason, knocked out the windows, one after the other. Then he started hacking away at the front steps.

'Get some water, you women!' he shouted. 'Bring the fire-engine! And be quick about it!'

A fire-engine was hauled up by the same villagers who had just been drinking and singing at the inn. They were all dead drunk and kept stumbling and falling over; all of them had a helpless look and they had tears in their eyes.

The village elder, who was drunk as well, shouted, 'Get some water, quick!'

The women and girls ran down to the bottom of the hill, where there was a spring, dragged up the full buckets and tubs, emptied them into the fire-engine and ran down again. Olga, Marya, Sasha and Motka all helped. The women and little boys helped to pump the water, making the hosepipe hiss, and the village elder began by directing a jet into the doorway, then through the windows, regulating the flow with his finger, which made the water hiss all the more.

'Well done, Antip!' the villagers said approvingly. 'Come on now!'

Antip climbed right into the burning hall from where he shouted, 'Keep on pouring. Try your best, you good Christians, on the *occasion of such an unhappy event.*'

The villagers crowded round and did nothing – they just gazed at the fire. No one had any idea what to do – no one was capable of doing anything – and close by there were stacks of wheat and hay, piles of dry brushwood, and barns. Kiryak and old Osip, his father, had joined in the crowd, and they were both drunk. The old man turned to the woman lying on the ground and said – as though trying to find some excuse for his idleness – 'Now don't get so worked up! The hut's insured, so don't worry!'

Semyon turned to one villager after the other, telling them how the fire had started.

'It was that old man with the bundle, him what worked for General Zhukov . . . used to cook for him, God rest his soul. Along he comes this evening and says, "Let me stay the night, please." Well, we had a drink or two . . . the old girl started messing around with the samovar to make the old man a cup of tea and she put it in the hall before the charcoal was out. The flames shot straight up out of the pipe and set the thatched roof alight, so there you are! *We* nearly went up as well. The old man's cap was burnt, a terrible shame.'

Meanwhile they banged away at the iron plate for all they were worth and the bells in the church across the river kept ringing. Olga ran breathlessly up and down the slope. As she looked in horror at the red sheep, at the pink doves fluttering around in the smoke, she was lit up by the fierce glow. The loud clanging had the effect of a sharp needle piercing her heart and it seemed that the fire would never go out, that Sasha was lost . . . And when the ceiling in the hut collapsed with a loud crash, the thought that the whole village was bound to burn down now made her feel weak and she could not carry any more water. So she sat on the cliff, with the buckets at her side. Nearby, a little lower down, women were sitting and seemed to be wailing for the dead.

But just then some labourers and men from the manor across the river arrived in two carts, together with a fire-engine. A very young student came riding up in his unbuttoned white tunic. Axes started hacking away, a ladder was propped against the blazing framework and five men clambered up it at once, with the student leading the way. His face was red from the flames and he shouted in a hoarse, rasping voice, in such an authoritative way it seemed putting fires out was something he did every day. They tore the hut to pieces beam by beam, and they tore down the cowshed, a wattle fence and the nearest haystack.

Stern voices rang out from the crowd: 'Don't let them smash the place up. Stop them!'

Kiryak went off towards the hut with a determined look and as though intending stopping the newly arrived helpers from breaking the whole place up. But one of the workmen turned him round and hit him in the neck. There was laughter and the workman hit him again. Kiryak fell down and crawled back to the crowd on all fours.

Two pretty girls, wearing hats – they were probably the student's sisters – arrived from across the river. They stood a little way off, watching the fire. The beams that had been pulled down had stopped burning, but a great deal of smoke still came from them. As he manipulated the hose, the student directed the jet at the beams, then at the peasants and then at the women fetching the water.

'Georges!' the girls shouted, in anxious, reproachful voices. 'Georges!'

The fire was out now and only when they started going home did the villagers notice that it was already dawn and that everyone had that pale, slightly swarthy look which always seems to come in the early hours of the morning, when the last stars have faded from the sky. As they went their different ways, the villagers laughed and made fun of General Zhukov's cook and his burnt hat. Already they wanted to turn the fire into a joke – and they even seemed sorry that it was all over so quickly.

'You were a very good fireman,' Olga told the student. 'You should come to Moscow where we live, there's a fire every day.'

'You don't say, you're from *Moscow*?' one of the young ladies asked.

'Oh yes. My husband worked at the Slav Fair. And this is my daughter.'

She pointed to Sasha, who went cold all over and clung to her.

'She's from Moscow as well, miss.'

The two girls said something in French to the student and he gave Sasha a twenty-copeck piece. When old Osip saw it, there was a sudden flicker of hope on his face.

'Thank God there wasn't any wind, sir,' he said, turning to the student, 'or everything would have gone up before you could say knife.' Then he lowered his voice and added timidly, 'Yes, sir, and you ladies, you're good people . . . it's cold at dawn, could do with warming up . . . Please give me a little something for a drink . . .'

They gave him nothing and he sighed and slunk off home. Afterwards Olga stood at the top of the slope and watched the two carts fording the river and the two ladies and the gentleman riding across the meadow – a carriage was waiting for them on the other side.

When she went back into the hut she told her husband delightedly, 'Such fine people! And so good-looking. Those young ladies were like little cherubs!'

'They can damned well go to hell!' murmured sleepy Fyokla, in a voice full of hatred.

VI

Marya was unhappy and said that she longed to die. Fyokla, on the other hand, found this kind of life to her liking – for all its poverty, filth and never-ending bad language. She ate whatever she was given, without any fuss, and slept anywhere she could and on whatever she happened to find. She would empty the slops right outside the front door, splashing them out from the steps, and she would walk barefoot through the puddles into the bargain. From the very first day she had hated Olga and Nikolay, precisely because they did not like the life there.

'We'll see what you get to eat here, my posh Moscow friends,' she said viciously. 'We'll see!'

One morning, right at the beginning of September, the healthy, fine-looking Fyokla, her face flushed with the cold, brought two buckets of water up the hill. Marya and Olga were sitting at the table drinking tea.

'Tea *and* sugar!' Fyokla said derisively. 'Real ladies!' she added, putting the buckets down. 'Is it the latest fashion, then, drinking tea every day? Careful you don't burst with all that liquid inside you.' She gave Olga a hateful look and went on, 'Stuffed your fat mug all right in Moscow, didn't you, you fat cow!'

She swung the yoke and hit Olga on the shoulders; this startled the sisters-in-law so much all they could do was clasp their hands and say, 'Oh, God!'

Then Fyokla went down to the river to do some washing and she swore so loudly the whole way there, they could hear her back in the hut.

The day drew to a close and the long autumn evening set in. In the hut they were winding silk – everyone, that is, except Fyokla, who had gone across the river.

The silk was collected from a nearby factory and the whole family earned itself a little pocket money – twenty copecks a week.

'We were better off as serfs,' the old man said as he wound the silk. 'You worked, ate, slept – everything had its proper place. You had cabbage soup and kasha[11] for your dinner and again for supper. You had as many cucumbers and as much cabbage as you liked and you could eat to your heart's content, if you felt like it. And they were stricter then, everyone knew his place.'

Only one lamp was alight, smoking and glowing dimly. Whenever anyone stood in front of it, a large shadow fell across the window and one could see the bright moonlight. Old Osip took his time as he told them all what life was like before the serfs were emancipated;[12] how, in those very same places where life was so dull and wretched now, they used to ride out with wolfhounds, borzois and skilled hunters.[13] There would be plenty of vodka for the peasants during the *battue*. He told how whole cartloads of game were taken to Moscow for the young gentlemen, how badly behaved peasants were flogged or sent away to estates in Tver,[14] while the good ones were rewarded. Grannie had stories to tell as well. She remembered simply everything. She told of her mistress, whose husband was a drunkard and a rake and whose daughters all made absolutely disastrous marriages; one married a drunkard, another a small tradesman in the town, while the third eloped (with the help of Grannie, who was a girl herself at the time). In no time at all they all died of broken hearts (like their mother) and Grannie burst into tears when she recalled it all.

Suddenly there was a knock at the door and everyone trembled.

'Uncle Osip, put me up for tonight, please!'

In came General Zhukov's cook – a bald, little old man, the same cook whose hat had been burnt. He sat down, listened to the conversation and soon joined in, reminiscing and telling stories about the old days. Nikolay sat listening with his legs dangling from the stove and all he wanted to know was what kind of food they used to eat in the days of serfdom. They discussed various kinds of rissoles, cutlets, soups and sauces. The cook, who had a good memory as well, mentioned dishes that were not made any more. For example, there was some dish made from bulls' eyes called *morning awakening*.

'Did they make cutlets *à la maréchale* then?' Nikolay asked.

'No.'

Nikolay shook his head disdainfully and said, 'Oh, you miserable apology for a cook!'

The little girls who were sitting or lying on the stove looked down without blinking. There seemed to be so many of them, they were like cherubs in the clouds. They liked the stories, sighed, shuddered and turned pale with delight or fear. Breathlessly they listened to Grannie's stories, which were the most interesting, and they were too frightened to move a muscle. All of them lay down to sleep without saying a word. The old people, excited and disturbed by the stories, thought about the beauty of youth, now that it was past: no matter what it had *really* been like, they could only remember it as bright, joyful and moving. And now they thought of the terrible chill of death – and for them death was not far away. Better not to think about it! The lamp went out. The darkness, the two windows sharply outlined in the moonlight, the silence and the creaking cradle somehow reminded them that their lives were finished, nothing could bring them back. Sometimes one becomes drowsy and dozes off, and suddenly someone touches you on the shoulder, breathes on your cheek and you can sleep no longer, your whole body goes numb, and you can think of nothing but death. You turn over and death is forgotten; but then the same old depressing, tedious thoughts keep wandering around your head – thoughts of poverty, cattle fodder, about the higher price of flour and a little later you remember once again that your life has gone, that you can never relive it.

'Oh God!' sighed the cook.

Someone was tapping ever so gently on the window – that must be Fyokla. Olga stood up, yawning and whispering a prayer as she opened the door and then drew the bolt back in the hall. But no one came in and there was just a breath of chill air from the street and the sudden bright light of the moon. Through the open door she could see the quiet, deserted street and the moon itself sailing across the heavens.

Olga called out, 'Who is it?'

'It's me,' came the answer, 'it's me.'

Fyokla was standing near the door, pressing close to the wall, and she was stark naked. She was trembling with the cold and her teeth chattered. In the bright moonlight she looked very pale, beautiful and strange. The shadow and the brilliant light playing over her skin struck Olga particularly vividly and those dark eyebrows and firm young breasts were very sharply outlined.

'It was them beasts on the other side of the river, they stripped me naked and sent me away like this . . .' she muttered. 'I've come all the way home without nothing on . . . stark naked . . . Give me some clothes.'

41

'Come into the hut!' Olga said softly and she too started shivering. 'I don't want the old people to see me!'

But in actual fact Grannie had already become alarmed and was grumbling away, while the old man asked, 'Who's there?'

Olga fetched her own smock and skirt and dressed Fyokla in them. Then they both tiptoed into the hut, trying not to bang the doors.

'Is that you, my beauty?' Grannie growled angrily when she realized who it was. 'You little nightbird, want a nice flogging, do you?'

'It's all right, it's all right, dear,' Olga whispered as she wrapped Fyokla up.

Everything became quiet again. They always slept badly in the hut, every one of them would be kept awake by obsessive, nagging thoughts – the old man by his backache, Grannie by her worrying and evil mind, Marya by her fear and the children by itching and hunger.

And now their sleep was as disturbed as ever and they kept tossing and turning, and saying wild things; time after time they got up for a drink of water.

Suddenly Fyokla started bawling in her loud, coarse voice, but immediately tried to pull herself together and broke into an intermittent sobbing which gradually became fainter and fainter until it died away completely. Now and again the church on the other side of the river could be heard striking the hour, but in the most peculiar way: first it struck five and then three.

'Oh, my God!' sighed the cook.

It was hard to tell, just by looking at the windows, whether the moon was still shining or if dawn had already come. Marya got up and went outside. They could hear her milking the cow in the yard and telling it, 'Ooh, keep still!' Grannie went out as well. Although it was still dark in the hut, by now every object was visible.

Nikolay, who had not slept the whole night, climbed down from the stove. He took his tailcoat out of a green trunk, put it on, smoothed the sleeves as he went over to the window, held the tails for a moment and smiled. Then he carefully took it off, put it back in the trunk and lay down again.

Marya returned and started lighting the stove. Quite clearly she was not really awake yet and she was still coming to as she moved around. Most probably she had had a dream or suddenly remembered the stories of the evening before, since she said, 'No, *freedom*[15] is best,' as she sensuously stretched herself in front of the stove.

VII

The 'gentleman' arrived – this was how the local police inspector was called in the village. Everyone knew a week beforehand exactly when and why he was coming. In Zhukovo there were only forty households, but they were so much in arrears with their taxes and rates that over two thousand roubles were overdue.

The inspector stopped at the inn. There he 'imbibed' two glasses of tea and then set off on foot for the village elder's hut, where a crowd of defaulters was waiting for him. Antip Sedelnikov, the village elder, despite his lack of years (he had only just turned thirty) was a very strict man and always sided with the authorities, although he was poor himself and was always behind with his payments. Being the village elder obviously amused him and he enjoyed the feeling of power and the only way he knew to exercise this was by enforcing strict discipline. At village meetings everyone was scared of him and did what he said. If he came across a drunk in the street or near the inn he would swoop down on him, tie his arms behind his back and put him in the village lock-up. Once he had even put Grannie there for swearing when she was deputizing for Osip at a meeting and he kept her locked up for twenty-four hours. Although he had never lived in a town or read any books, somehow he had managed to accumulate a store of various clever-sounding words and he loved using them in conversation, which made him respected, if not always understood.

When Osip entered the elder's hut with his rent book, the inspector – a lean old man with long grey whiskers, in a grey double-breasted jacket – was sitting at a table in the corner near the stove, writing something down. The hut was clean and all the walls were gay and colourful with pictures cut out of magazines. In the most conspicuous place, near the icons, hung a portrait of Battenberg,[16] once Prince of Bulgaria. Antip Sedelnikov stood by the table with his arms crossed.

'This one 'ere owes a hundred and nineteen roubles, your honour,' he said when it was Osip's turn. ''E paid a rouble before Easter, but not one copeck since.'

The inspector looked up at Osip and asked, 'How come, my dear friend?'

'Don't be too hard on me, your honour,' Osip said, getting very worked up, 'just please let me explain, sir. Last summer the squire from Lyutoretsk says to me, "Sell me your hay, Osip, sell it to me . . ." Why not? I had about a ton and a half of it, what the women mowed in the meadows . . . well, we agreed the price . . . It was all very nice and proper.'

He complained about the elder and kept turning towards the other peasants as though summoning them as witnesses. His face became red and sweaty and his eyes sharp and evil-looking.

'I don't see why you're telling me all this,' the inspector said. 'I'm asking *you* why you're so behind with your rates. It's *you* I'm asking. None of you pays up, so do you think *I'm* going to be responsible!'

'But I just can't!'

'These words have no *consequences*, your honour,' the elder said. 'In actual fact those Chikildeyevs belong to the *impecunious* class. But if it please your honour to ask the others, the whole reason for it is vodka. And they're real troublemakers. They've no *comprehension*.'

The inspector jotted something down and told Osip in a calm, even voice, as though asking for some water, 'Clear off!'

Shortly afterwards he drove away and he was coughing as he climbed into his carriage. From the way he stretched his long, thin back one could tell that Osip, the elder and the arrears at Zhukovo were no more than dim memories, and that he was now thinking about something that concerned him alone. Even before he was half a mile away, Antip Sedelnikov was carrying the samovar out of the Chikildeyevs' hut, pursued by Grannie, who was shrieking for all she was worth, 'I won't let you have it, *I won't*, blast you!'

Antip strode along quickly, while Grannie puffed and panted after him, nearly falling over and looking quite ferocious with her hunched back. Her shawl had slipped down over her shoulders and her grey hair, tinged with green, streamed in the wind. Suddenly she stopped and began beating her breast like a real rebel and shouted in an even louder singsong voice, just as though she were sobbing, 'Good Christians, you who believe in God! Heavens, we've been trampled on! Dear ones, we've been persecuted. Oh, please help us!'

'Come on, Grannie,' the elder said sternly, 'time you got some sense into that head of yours!'

Life became completely and utterly depressing without a samovar in the Chikildeyevs' hut. There was something humiliating, degrading in this deprivation, as though the hut itself were in disgrace. It wouldn't have been so bad if the elder had only taken the table, all the benches and pots instead – then the place wouldn't have looked so bare as it did now. Grannie yelled, Marya wept and the little girls looked at her and wept too. The old man felt guilty and sat in one corner, his head downcast and not saying a word. Nikolay did not say a word either: Grannie was very fond of him and felt sorry for him, but now all compassion was forgotten as she suddenly attacked him with a stream of reproaches and insults, shaking her fists right under his nose. He was to blame for everything, she screamed. And in actual fact, why had he sent them so little, when in his letters he had boasted that he was earning fifty roubles a month at the Slav Fair? And why did he have to come with his family? How would they pay for the funeral if he died here . . . ? Nikolay, Olga and Sasha made a pathetic sight.

The old man wheezed, picked his cap up and went off to see the elder. Already it was getting dark. Antip Sedelnikov was soldering something near the stove, puffing his cheeks out. The air was heavy with fumes. His skinny, unwashed children – they were no better than the Chikildeyev children – were playing noisily on the floor, while his ugly, freckled, pot-bellied wife was winding silk. It was a wretched, miserable family – with the exception of Antip, who was handsome and dashing. Five samovars stood in a row on a bench. The old man offered a prayer to Battenberg and said, 'Antip, have pity on us, give us the samovar back, for Christ's sake!'

'Bring me three roubles – then you can have it back.'

'I haven't got them!'

Antip puffed his cheeks out, the fire hummed and hissed and its light gleamed on the samovars. The old man rumpled his cap, pondered for a moment and said, 'Give it back!'

The dark-faced elder looked jet-black, just like a sorcerer. He turned to Osip and said in a rapid, stern voice, 'It all depends on the magistrate. At the administrative meeting on the 26th inst. you can announce your grounds for dissatisfaction, orally or in writing.'

Osip did not understand one word of this, but he seemed satisfied and went home.

About ten days later the inspector turned up again, stayed for an hour and then left. About this time the weather was windy and cold. The river had frozen over long ago, but there still hadn't been any snow and everyone was miserable, as the roads were impassable. On one holiday, just before evening, some neighbours dropped in at Osip's for a chat. The conversation took place in the dark – it was considered sinful to work, so the fire had not been lit. There was a little news – most of it unpleasant: some hens had been confiscated from two or three households that were in arrears and taken to the council offices where they died, since no one bothered to feed them. Sheep were confiscated as well – they were taken away with their legs tied up and dumped into a different cart at every village; one died. And now they were trying to decide who was to blame.

'The local council, who else?' Osip said.

'Yes, of course, it's the council.'

The council was blamed for everything – tax arrears, victimization, harassment, crop failures, although not one of them had any idea what the function of the council was. And all this went back to the times when rich peasants who owned factories, shops and inns had served as councillors, became dissatisfied, and cursed the council when they were back in their factories and inns. They discussed the fact that God hadn't sent them any snow: firewood had to be moved, but it was impossible to drive or walk because of all the bumps in the road. Fifteen or twenty years ago – or even earlier – the local gossip in Zhukovo was much more interesting. In those times every old man looked as though he was hiding some secret, knew something, and was waiting for something. They discussed deeds with golden seals, allotments and partition of land, hidden treasure and they were always hinting at something or other. But now the people of Zhukovo had no secrets at all: their entire lives were like an open book, which anyone could read and all they could talk about was poverty, cattle feed, lack of snow . . .

They fell silent for a while: then they remembered the hens and the sheep and tried to decide whose fault it was.

'The council's!' Osip exclaimed gloomily. 'Who else's!'

VIII

The parish church was about four miles away, at Kosogorovo, and the people only went there when they really had to – for christenings, weddings or funerals. For ordinary prayers they went to the church across the river. On saints' days (when the weather was fine) the young girls put on their Sunday best and crowded along to Mass, making a very cheerful picture as they walked across the meadows in their yellow and green dresses. But when the weather was bad everyone stayed at home. Pre-Communion services were held in the parish church. The priest fined anyone who had not prepared for Communion during Lent fifteen copecks as he went round the huts at Easter with his cross.

The old man didn't believe in God, for the simple reason that he rarely gave him a moment's thought. He admitted the existence of the supernatural, but thought that it could only affect women. Whenever anyone discussed religion or the supernatural with him, or questioned him, he would reluctantly reply as he scratched himself, 'Who the hell knows!'

The old woman believed in God, but only in some vague way. Everything in her mind had become mixed up and no sooner did she start meditating on sin, death and salvation, than poverty and everyday worries took charge and immediately she forgot what she had originally been thinking about. She could not remember her prayers and it was usually in the evenings, before she went to bed, that she stood in front of the icons and whispered, 'to the Virgin of Kazan, to the Virgin of Smolensk, to the Virgin of the Three Arms . . .'

Marya and Fyokla would cross themselves and prepare to take the sacrament once a year, but they had no idea what it meant. They hadn't taught their children to pray, had told them nothing about God and never taught them moral principles: all they did was tell them not to eat forbidden food during fast days. In the other families it was almost the same story: hardly anyone believed in God or understood anything about religion. All the same, they loved the Bible dearly, with deep reverence; but they had no books, nor was there anyone to read or explain anything to them. They respected Olga for occasionally reading to them from the Gospels, and spoke to her and Sasha very politely.

Olga often went to festivals and services in the neighbouring villages and the county town, where there were two monasteries and twenty-seven churches. Since she was rather scatterbrained, she tended to forget all about her family when she went on these pilgrimages. Only on the journey home did she suddenly realize, to her great delight, that she had a husband and daughter, and then she would smile radiantly and say, 'God's been good to me!'

Everything that happened in the village disgusted and tormented her. On Elijah's Day[17] they drank, on the Feast of the Assumption they drank, on the day of the Exaltation of the Cross they drank. The Feast of the Intercession was a parish holiday in Zhukovo, and the men celebrated it by going on a three-day binge. They drank their way through fifty roubles of communal funds and on top of this they had a whip-round from all the farms for some vodka. On the first day of the Feast, the Chikildeyevs slaughtered a sheep and ate it for breakfast, lunch and dinner, consuming vast quantities, and then the children got up during the night for another bite. During the entire three days Kiryak was terribly drunk – he drank everything away, even his cap and boots, and he gave Marya such a thrashing that they had to douse her with cold water. Afterwards everyone felt ashamed and sick.

However, even in Zhukovo or 'Lackeyville', a truly religious ceremony was once celebrated. This was in August, when the icon of the Life-giving Virgin was carried round the whole district, from one village to another. The day on which the villagers at Zhukovo expected it was calm and overcast. Right from the morning the girls, in their Sunday best, had left their homes to welcome the icon and towards evening it was carried in procession into the village with the church choir singing and the bells in the church across the river ringing out loud. A vast crowd of villagers and visitors filled the street; there was noise, dust and a terrible crush . . . The old man, Grannie and Kiryak all held their hands out to the icon, looked at it hungrily and cried out tearfully, 'Our Protector, holy Mother!'

It was as though everyone suddenly realized that there wasn't just a void between heaven and earth, that the rich and the strong had not grabbed everything yet, that there was still someone to protect them from slavery, crushing, unbearable poverty – and that infernal vodka.

'Our Protector, holy Mother!' Marya sobbed. 'Holy Mother!'

But the service was over now, the icon was taken away and everything returned to normal. Once again those coarse drunken voices could be heard in the pub.

Only the rich peasants feared death, and the richer they became, the less they believed in God and salvation – if they happened to donate candles or celebrate Mass, it was only for fear of their departure from this world – and just to be on the safe side. The peasants who weren't so well off had no fear of death.

Grannie and the old man had been told to their faces that their lives were over, that it was time they were gone, and they did not care. They had no qualms in telling Fyokla, right in front of Nikolay, that when he died her husband Denis would be discharged from the army and sent home. Far from having any fear of death, Marya was only sorry that it was such a long time coming, and she was glad when any of her children died.

Death held no terrors for them, but they had an excessive fear of all kinds of illness. It only needed some trifle – a stomach upset or a slight chill – for the old woman to lie over the stove, wrap herself up and groan out loud, without stopping, 'I'm dy-ing!' Then the old man would dash off to fetch the priest and Grannie would receive the last sacrament and extreme unction. Colds, worms and tumours that began in the stomach and worked their way up to the heart were everyday topics. They were more afraid of catching cold than anything else, so that even in summer they wrapped themselves in thick clothes and stood by the stove warming themselves. Grannie loved medical treatment and frequently went to the hospital, telling them there that she was fifty-eight, and not seventy: she reasoned if the doctor knew her real age he would refuse to have her as a patient and would tell her it was time she died, rather than have hospital treatment. She usually left early in the morning for the hospital, taking two of the little girls with her, and she would return in the evening, cross and hungry, with drops for herself and ointment for the little girls. Once she took Nikolay with her; he took the drops for about two weeks afterwards and said they made him feel better.

Grannie knew all the doctors, nurses and quacks for twenty miles around and she did not like any of them. During the Feast of the Intercession, when the parish priest went round the huts with his cross, the lay reader told her about an old man living near the town prison, who had once been a medical orderly in the army and who knew some very good cures. He advised her to go and consult him, which Grannie did. When the first snows came she drove off to town and brought a little old man back with her: he was a bearded, Jewish convert to Christianity who wore a long coat and whose face was completely covered with blue veins. Just at that time some jobbing tradesmen happened to be working in the hut – an old tailor with terrifying spectacles was cutting a waistcoat from some old rags and two young men were making felt boots from wool. Kiryak, who had been given the sack for drinking and lived at home now, was sitting next to the tailor mending a horse collar. It was cramped, stuffy and evil-smelling in the hut. The convert examined Nikolay and said that he should be bled, without fail.

He applied the cupping glasses, while the old tailor, Kiryak and the little girls stood watching – they imagined that they could actually see the illness being drawn out of Nikolay. And Nikolay also watched the cup attached to his chest slowly filling with dark blood and he smiled with pleasure at the thought that something was really coming out.

'That's fine,' the tailor said. 'Let's hope it does the trick, with God's help.'

The convert applied twelve cups, then another twelve, drank some tea and left. Nikolay started shivering. His face took on a pinched look, like a clenched fist, as the women put it; his fingers turned blue. He wrapped himself tightly in a blanket and a sheepskin, but he only felt colder. By the time evening came he was very low. He asked to be laid on the floor and told the tailor to stop smoking. Then he fell silent under his sheepskin and passed away towards morning.

IX

What a long harsh winter it was!

By Christmas their own grain had run out, so they had to buy flour. Kiryak, who was living at home now, made a dreadful racket in the evening, terrifying everyone, and in the mornings he was tormented by self-disgust and hangovers; he made a pathetic sight. Day and night a hungry cow filled the barn with its lowing, and this broke Grannie and Marya's hearts. And, as though on purpose, the frosts never relented in their severity and snowdrifts piled up high. The winter dragged on: a real blizzard raged at Annunciation and snow fell at Easter.

However, winter finally drew to an end. At the beginning of April it was warm during the day and frosty at night – and still winter hadn't surrendered. But one warm day did come along at last and it gained the upper hand. The streams flowed once more and the birds began to sing again. The entire meadow and the bushes near the river were submerged by the spring floods and between Zhukovo and the far side there was just one vast sheet of water with flocks of wild duck flying here and there. Every evening the fiery spring sunset and rich luxuriant clouds made an extraordinary, novel, incredible sight – such clouds and colours that you would hardly think possible seeing them later in a painting.

Cranes flashed past overhead calling plaintively, as though inviting someone to fly along with them. Olga stayed for a long while at the edge of the cliff watching the flood waters, the sun, the bright church which seemed to have taken on a new life, and tears poured down her face; a passionate longing to go somewhere far, far away, as far as the eyes could see, even to the very ends of the earth, made her gasp for breath. But they had already decided to send her back to Moscow as a chambermaid and Kiryak was going with her to work as a hall porter or at some job or other. Oh, if only they could go soon!

When everything had dried out and it was warm, they prepared for the journey. Olga and Sasha left at dawn, with rucksacks on their backs, and both of them wore bast shoes. Marya came out of the hut to see them off. Kiryak wasn't well and had to stay on in the hut for another week. Olga gazed at the church for the last time and thought about her husband. She did not cry, but her face broke out in wrinkles and became ugly, like an old woman's. During that winter she had grown thin, lost her good looks and gone a little grey. Already that pleasant appearance and agreeable smile had been replaced by a sad, submissive expression that betrayed the sorrow she had suffered and there was something blank and lifeless in her, as though she were deaf. She was sorry to leave the village and the people there. She remembered them carrying Nikolay's body and asking for prayers to be said at each hut, and how everyone wept and felt for her in her sorrow. During the summer and winter months there were hours and days when these people appeared to live worse than cattle, and life with them was really terrible. They were coarse, dishonest, filthy, drunk, always quarrelling and arguing amongst themselves, with no respect for one another and living in mutual fear and suspicion. Who maintains the pubs and makes the peasants drunk? The peasant. Who embezzles the village, school and parish funds and spends it all on drink? The peasant. Who robs his neighbour, sets fire to his house and perjures himself in court for a bottle of vodka? Who is the first to revile the peasant at district council and similar meetings? The peasant. Yes, it was terrible living with these people; nevertheless, they were still human beings, suffering and weeping like other people and there was nothing in their lives which did not provide some excuse: killing work which made bodies ache all over at night, harsh winters, poor harvests, overcrowding, without any help and nowhere to find it. The richer and stronger cannot help, since they themselves are coarse, dishonest and drunk, using the same foul language. The most insignificant little clerk or official treats peasants like tramps, even talking down to elders and churchwardens, as though this is their right. And after all, could one expect help or a good example from the mercenary, greedy, dissolute, lazy people who come to the village now and then just to insult, fleece and intimidate the peasants? Olga recalled how pathetic and downtrodden the old people had looked when Kiryak was taken away for a flogging that winter . . . and now she felt sorry for all these people and kept glancing back at the huts as she walked away.

Marya went with them for about two miles and then she made her farewell, prostrating herself and wailing out loud, 'Oh, I'm all alone again, a poor miserable wretch . . .'

For a long time she kept wailing, and for a long time afterwards Olga and Sasha could see her still kneeling there, bowing as though someone were next to her and clutching her head, while the rooks circled above.

The sun was high now and it was warm. Zhukovo lay far behind. It was very pleasant walking on a day like this. Olga and Sasha soon forgot both the village and Marya. They were in a gay mood and everything around was a source of interest. Perhaps it was an old burial mound, or a row of telegraph poles trailing away heaven knows where and disappearing over the horizon, with their wires humming mysteriously. Or they would catch a glimpse of a distant farmhouse, deep in foliage, with the smell of dampness and hemp wafting towards them and it seemed that happy people must live there. Or they would see a horse's skeleton lying solitary and bleached in a field. Larks poured their song out untiringly, quails called to each other and the corncrake's cry was just as though someone was tugging at an old iron latch.

By noon Olga and Sasha reached a large village. In its broad street they met that little old man who had been General Zhukov's cook. He was feeling the heat and his sweaty red skull glinted in the sun. Olga and the cook did not recognize one another at first, but then they both turned round at once, realized who the other was and went their respective ways without a word. Olga stopped by the open windows of a hut which seemed newer and richer than the others, bowed and said in a loud, shrill singsong voice, 'You good Christians, give us charity, for the sake of Christ, so that your kindness will bring the kingdom of heaven and lasting peace to your parents . . .'

'Good Christians,' Sasha chanted, 'give us charity for Christ's sake, so that your kindness, the kingdom of heaven . . .'

[The following two chapters have been taken from incomplete MSS fragments that have survived in draft form; see also note on pp. 332–3.]

X

Olga's sister, Klavdiya Abramovna, lived in a narrow side-street near Patriarch's Ponds,[18] in a wooden, two-storey house. On the ground floor was a laundry and the entire upper floor was rented by an elderly spinster, a quiet and unassuming gentlewoman, who lived off the income from rooms she in turn rented out. When you went into the dark hall you would find two doors, one on the right, one on the left. One of them opened into the tiny room where Klavdiya Abramovna lived with Sasha; the other room was rented by a typesetter. Then there was a sitting-room, with couch, armchairs, a lamp with shade, pictures on the walls – all thoroughly proper, except that a smell of linen and steam came from the laundry and all day long one could hear singing from down below. The sitting-room, from which there was access to three flats, was used by all the tenants. In one of these flats lived the landlady, in another the old footman

Ivan Makarych Matveyevich, a native of Zhukovo, who had found Nikolay a job. A large barn lock was suspended by rings on his white, well-thumbed door. Behind the third door lived a young, skinny, eagle-eyed, thick-lipped woman with three children who were constantly crying. On church holidays a monastery priest visited her; all day she normally went around in only a skirt, uncombed and unwashed, but when she was expecting her priest she would put on a nice silk dress and curl her hair.

In Klavdiya Abramovna's little place there wasn't room to swing a cat, as they say. There were a bed, chest of drawers, a chair – and nothing else – but still it was cramped. However, the room was kept neat and tidy, and Klavdiya Abramovna called it her 'boudoir'. She was extremely pleased with her surroundings, particularly with the objects on her chest of drawers: mirror, powder, scent bottles, lipstick, tiny boxes, ceruse and every single luxury that she considered an essential accessory of her profession and on which she spent almost everything she earned. And there were also framed photographs in which she appeared in various poses. There was one of herself with her postman husband, with whom she lived just one year before leaving him, since she felt no vocation for family life. She was photographed, like most women of her sort, with a fringe curled like a lamb's forelock, in military uniform with drawn sabre, and as a page astride a chair, which made her thighs, sheathed in woollen tights, lie flat over the chair like two fat boiled sausages. And there were male portraits – these she called her visitors and she couldn't name all of them. Here our friend Kiryak made an appearance: he was photographed full height, in a black suit he had borrowed for the occasion.

Klavdiya Abramovna had been in the habit of going to masked balls and to Filippov's[19] and she spent entire evenings on Tversky Boulevard.[20] As the years passed she gradually became a stay-at-home and now that she was forty-two she very rarely had visitors – there were just a few friends from earlier days who visited her for old time's sake. They, alas, had aged too and visits became increasingly rare, because every year their number dwindled. The only new visitor was a very young man without a moustache. He would enter the hall quietly, sullenly – like a conspirator – with the collar of his school coat turned up, endeavouring to avoid being seen from the sitting-room. Later, when he left, he would place a rouble on the chest of drawers.

For days on end Klavdiya Abramovna would stay at home doing nothing. But in good weather she would sometimes stroll down the Little Bronny[21] and Tversky, her head proudly held high, feeling that she was a solid and imposing lady. Only when she looked in at the chemist's to ask in a whisper if they had any ointment for wrinkles or red hands did she show any sign of shame. In the evenings she would sit in her little room with the lamp unlit, waiting for someone to come. And between ten and eleven o'clock – this happened rarely, only once or twice a week – you could hear someone quietly going up or down stairs, rustling at the door as he looked for the bell. The door would open, a muttering would be heard and a stout, old, ugly and usually bald visitor would gingerly enter the hall and Klavdiya Abramovna would hurriedly take him to her room. She adored good visitors. For her there was no nobler or worthier being. To receive a good visitor, to treat him tactfully, to respect and please him, was a spiritual necessity, a duty, her happiness and pride. She was incapable of refusing a visitor or failing to make him welcome, even when fasting in preparation for Communion.

When she was back from the country Olga lodged Sasha with her for the time being, her mother supposing that while the girl was little she would not understand if she happened to see something bad. But now Sasha was thirteen and the time had really come to find alternative accommodation for her; but she and her aunt had grown attached to each other and now it was hard to separate them. In any event, there was nowhere to take Sasha to, since Olga herself was sheltering in the corridor of an establishment with furnished rooms, where she slept on some chairs. Sasha would spend the day with her mother, or out in the street, or downstairs in the laundry: she spent the nights on her aunt's floor, between the bed and chest of drawers, and if a visitor came she would go and sleep in the entrance hall.

In the evenings she loved going to Ivan Makarych's place of work and watching the dancing from the kitchen. There was always music and it was cheerful and noisy, with a tasty smell of food around the cook and washers-up. Grandpa Ivan Makarych would give her tea or ice-cream and pass her assorted titbits that he brought back into the kitchen on plates and dishes. One evening in late autumn, after returning from Ivan Makarych, she brought a little parcel containing a chicken leg, a piece of sturgeon and a slice of cake. Auntie was already in bed.

'Auntie dear,' Sasha said sadly. 'I've brought you something to eat.'

They lit the lamp. Sitting up in bed, Klavdiya Abramovna started eating. Sasha looked at her curlers, which made her look dreadful, at her withered, aged shoulders. She looked long and sadly, as if she were seeing a sick woman; suddenly tears flowed down her cheeks.

'Auntie dear,' she said in a trembling voice. 'Auntie dear, this morning the laundry girls were saying that when you're old you'll end up begging in the streets and that you'll die in hospital. It's not true, Auntie, it's *not* true,' Sasha continued, sobbing now. 'I won't leave you, I'll feed you, I won't let you go into hospital.'

Klavdiya Abramovna's chin quivered and tears shone in her eyes. But she immediately took hold of herself and with a stern look she told Sasha: 'You shouldn't listen to laundry girls!'

XI

In the 'Lisbon' furnished rooms the tenants were gradually quietening down. There was the smell of burning from extinguished lamps and the lanky attendant was already stretched out on some chairs in the corridor. Olga took off her white ribboned cap and her apron, covered her head with a kerchief and went off to see Sasha and Klavdiya Abramovna at Patriarch's Ponds. Every day from morning to late evening she was busy working at the 'Lisbon' rooms and was rarely able to visit her family – and then only at night. Her work took up all her time, leaving her without a single free minute, so that since her return from the country she had not once gone to church.

She hurried to show Sasha the letter she had received from Marya in the village. In it there were only greetings – and complaints of poverty, of grief, and that the old folk were still alive and getting fed without doing any work. But for some reason these crooked lines, where every letter resembled a cripple, held a special, hidden charm and besides those greetings and complaints she also read of the warm clear days in the country now, of quiet fragrant evenings when you could hear the church clock striking the hour on the other side of the river. She could visualize the village cemetery where her husband lay. The green graves breathed peace and one envied the dead – such space, such open expanses! And the strange thing was, when they had lived in the country she had dearly wished to go to Moscow, but now it was the opposite and she longed for the country.

Olga woke Sasha. Alarmed and afraid that the whispers and light might disturb someone, she read her the letter twice. Then they both went down the dark, evil-smelling stairs and left the house. Through the wide open windows they could see the laundry girls ironing. Two girls were standing outside the gates, smoking. Olga and Sasha hurried down the street, discussing what a good idea it would be to save up two roubles and send them to the village: one for Marya and one to pay for memorial prayers over Nikolay's grave.

'Oh, I've had to put up with so much lately!' Olga was saying, clasping her hands. 'We'd only just started dinner, my sweet, when all of a sudden in comes Kiryak, like a bolt from the blue, drunk as a lord! "Give me some money, Olga!" he says. And he shouts and stamps his feet. "Give me some – now!" But where was I to get money from? I don't get any wages, I just live on what nice gents give me – that's all my wealth! But he wouldn't listen: "Give me some!" The tenants look out of their rooms, the boss comes – it was real punishment – and the shame of it! I begged thirty copecks from the students and gave them to him. He left . . . All day long I've been walking around whispering: "Soften his heart, O Lord." That's what I've been whispering.'

It was quiet in the streets. Now and then a night cab drove past, and somewhere far off, most probably in the pleasure gardens, the band was still playing and you could hear the vague crackle of fireworks.

Man in a Case

Two men who had come back very late from a hunting expedition had to spend the night in a barn belonging to Prokofy, the village elder, at the edge of Mironositskoye. They were Ivan Ivanych, the vet, and Burkin, the schoolteacher. The vet had a rather strange double-barrelled surname – Chimsha-Gimalaysky – that did not suit him at all, and everyone simply called him Ivan Ivanych. He lived on a stud farm near the town and had come on the expedition just to get some fresh air, while Burkin, the teacher, regularly stayed every summer with a local count and his family, and knew the area very well.

They were still awake. Ivan Ivanych, who was tall and thin, with a long moustache, was sitting outside the door, smoking his pipe in the full light of the moon. Burkin was lying on the hay inside, invisible in the dark.

They were telling each other different stories and happened to remark on the fact that Mavra, the village elder's wife, a healthy, intelligent woman, had never left her native village in her life, had never seen a town or a railway, had been sitting over her stove for the past ten years and would only venture out into the street at night.

'And what's so strange about that!' Burkin said. 'There's so many of these solitary types around, like hermit crabs or snails, they are, always seeking safety in their shells. Perhaps it's an example of atavism, a return to the times when our ancestors weren't social animals and lived alone in their dens. Or perhaps it's simply one of the many oddities of human nature – who knows? I'm not a scientist and that kind of thing's not really my province. I only want to say that people like Mavra are not unusual. And you don't have to look far for them – take a certain Belikov, for example, who died two months ago in my home town. He taught Greek at the same high school. Of course, you must have heard of him. His great claim to fame was going around in galoshes, carrying an umbrella even when it was terribly warm, and he invariably wore a thick, padded overcoat. He kept this umbrella in a holder and his watch in a grey chamois leather pouch. And the penknife he used for sharpening pencils had its own little case. His face seemed to have its own cover as well, as he always kept it hidden inside his upturned collar. He wore dark glasses, a jersey, stuffed his ears with cottonwool and always had the top up when he rode in a cab. Briefly, this man had a compulsive, persistent longing for self-encapsulation, to create a protective cocoon to isolate himself from all external influences. The real world irritated and frightened him and kept him in a constant state of nerves. Perhaps, by forever praising the past and what never even happened, he was trying to justify this timidity and horror of reality. The ancient languages he taught were essentially those galoshes and umbrella in another guise, a refuge from everyday existence.

'"Oh, Greek is so melodious, so beautiful," he would say, savouring his words. And as if to prove his point he would screw his eyes up, raise one finger and pronounce the word: *Anthropos*.

'Belikov tried to bury his thoughts inside a rigid case. Only official regulations and newspaper articles, in which something or other was prohibited, had any meaning for him. For him, only rules forbidding students to be out in the streets after nine in the evening or an article outlawing sexual intercourse were unambiguous and authoritative: the thing was prohibited – and that was that! But whenever anything was allowed and authorized, there was something dubious, vague and equivocal lurking in it. When a dramatic society or a reading-room, or a tea-shop in town, was granted a licence, he would shake his head and softly say, "That's all very well, of course, but there *could* be trouble!"

'The least infringement, deviation, violation of the rules reduced him to despair, although you may well ask what business was it of his *anyway*? If a fellow-teacher was late for prayers, or if news of some schoolboy mischief reached his ears, or if he spotted a schoolmistress out late at night with an officer, he would get very heated and say over and over again, "There *could* be trouble." At staff meetings he really got us down with his extreme caution, his suspiciousness and his positively encapsulated notions about current wretched standards of behaviour in boys' and girls' schools, about the terrible racket students made in class and once again he would say, "Oh dear, what if the authorities got to hear? Oh, there *could* be trouble! Now, what if we expelled that Petrov in the second form and Yegorov in the fourth?" Well then, what with all his moaning and whining, what with those dark glasses and that pale little face (you know, it was just like a ferret's), he terrorized us so much that we had to give in. Petrov and Yegorov were given bad conduct marks, put in detention and finally were both expelled. He had the strange habit of visiting us in our digs. He would call in on some teacher and sit down without saying a word, as though he were trying to spy something out. After an hour or two he would get up and go. He called it "maintaining good relations with my colleagues". These silent sessions were clearly very painful for him and he made them only because he felt it was his duty to his fellow-teachers. All of us were scared of him, even the Head. It was quite incredible really, since we teachers were an intelligent, highly respectable lot, brought up on Turgenev and Shchedrin.[1] And yet that miserable specimen, with that eternal umbrella and galoshes, kept the whole school under his thumb for fifteen whole years! And not only the school, but the whole town! Our ladies gave up their Saturday amateur theatricals in case he found out about them. And the clergy were too frightened to eat meat or play cards when he was around. Thanks to people like Belikov, the people in this town have lived in fear of *everything* for the last ten or fifteen years. They are frightened of talking out loud, sending letters, making friends, reading books, helping the poor or teaching anyone to read and write . . .'

Ivan Ivanych wanted to say something and coughed, but first he lit his pipe, peered up at the moon and said in a slow deliberate voice, 'Yes, those intelligent, decent people had read their Shchedrin and Turgenev, their Henry Buckles[2] and so on . . . , but still they gave in and put up with it. That's exactly my point.'

Burkin continued, 'Belikov and I lived in the same house and on the same floor. His room was right opposite mine and we saw a lot of each other. I knew his private life intimately. At home it was the same story: dressing-gown, night-cap, shutters, bolts, and a whole series of various prohibitions and restrictions – and all those "There *could* be trouble"s. Fasting was bad for you and as he couldn't touch meat on days forbidden by the church – or people might say Belikov didn't observe fasts – he would eat perch cooked in animal fat, food that couldn't be faulted, being neither one thing nor the other. He didn't have any female servants for fear people might "think the wrong thing", but he had a male cook, Afanasy, an old, drunken sixty-year-old half-wit, who had once been a batman in the army and who could knock up a meal of sorts. This Afanasy was in the habit of standing at the door with arms folded, always muttering the same old thing with a profound sigh, "There's been an awful lot of *that* about lately!"'

'Belikov's bedroom was small, like a box in fact, and the bed was a four-poster. He would pull the blankets right up over his head when he got into it. The room was hot and stuffy, the wind would rattle the bolted doors and make the stove hum. Menacing sighs would drift in from the kitchen. He was terrified under those blankets, afraid of the trouble there *could* be, afraid that Afanasy might cut his throat, afraid of burglars. Then all night long he would have night-mares and, when we left for school together in the morning, he would look pale and depressed. Obviously the thought of that crowded school for which he was heading terrified him, deeply repelled his whole being – even walking next to me was an ordeal for this lone wolf. "The students are terribly noisy in class," he would tell me, as if seeking an excuse for his low spirits. "It's simply *shocking*."

'And this teacher of Greek, this man in his case, nearly got married once, believe it or not.'

Ivan Ivanych took a quick look into the barn and said, 'You must be joking!'

'Oh, yes, he nearly got married, strange as it may seem. A new history and geography master was appointed, a Ukrainian called

Mikhail Savvich Kovalenko. He came here with his sister Barbara. He was young, tall, dark-skinned and had enormous hands. From his face you could tell he had a deep bass voice, the kind that really seems to come booming straight out of a barrel. The sister wasn't what you might call young, though – about thirty, I'd say – and like her brother she was tall, with the same figure, dark eyebrows and red cheeks – in short, not the spinsterish type but a real beauty, always bright and jolly, singing Ukrainian songs and roaring with laughter. The least thing sent her into fits of loud laughter. I remember now, the first time we really got to know the Kovalenkos was at the Head's name-day party. Among all those stiff, intensely boring pedagogues (they only went to parties because they had to) we suddenly saw this new Aphrodite rising from the foam. She walked hands on hips, laughing, singing, dancing. She sang "Breezes of the South Are Softly Blowing"[3] with great feeling and followed one song with another, enchanting all of us – even Belikov. "Ukrainian is like classical Greek in its softness and agreeable sonority," he said with a sugary smile as he sat down next to her.

'She was flattered and she gave him a stirring lecture about life on her farm down in Gadyach[4] where Mama lived, where they grew such marvellous pears and melons and *pubkins*: Ukrainians like calling pumpkins "pubkins", that's the way they talk there. And they made borsch with sweet little red beets, "Oh, *so* delicious – *frightfully* tasty!"

'We listened, and listened, and suddenly the same thought dawned on all present. "They'd make a very nice couple," the Head's wife told me quietly.

'For some reason this reminded us that our Belikov wasn't married and we wondered why we hadn't thought of it before, why we had completely overlooked this most important part of his life. What did he think of women, how would he answer this vital question? We hadn't been at all interested before – perhaps we couldn't bring ourselves to believe that this man who could wear galoshes in all kinds of weather, who slept in a four-poster, could be capable of loving.

' "He's well over forty and she's thirty," the Head's wife went on. "I think she'd accept him."

'Oh, the stupid, trivial things boredom makes us provincials do! And all because we can never get anything right. For example, why this sudden impulse to marry off our dear Belikov – surely not the ideal husband! The Head's wife, the inspector's wife and all the mistresses who taught at the high school suddenly brightened up, looked prettier even, as if they had discovered a purpose in life. The Head's wife took a box at the theatre and who do we see sitting next to her but a radiant, happy Barbara, holding some kind of fan, with Belikov at her side, so small and hunched up you'd have thought he'd been dragged from his house with a pair of tongs. If I gave a party, the ladies would absolutely insist on my inviting both Belikov and Barbara. Briefly, the wheels had been set in motion. It turned out that Barbara wasn't against marriage. Living with her brother wasn't very cheerful and apparently they'd argue and squabble for days on end. Just picture the scene for yourself: Kovalenko, that lanky, healthy boor walking down the street in his embroidered shirt, a tuft of hair falling onto his forehead from under his cap. In one hand a bundle of books, in the other a thick knobbly stick. Then his sister following close behind, loaded with books as well.

'"But Mikhail, you haven't read it!" she says in a loud, argumentative voice. "I'm telling you, I swear it's the truth, you've *never* read it!"

'"And I'm telling you that I *have*!" Kovalenko thunders back, banging his stick on the pavement.

'"Goodness gracious, Mikhail dear, don't lose your temper. It's only a matter of *principle* we're arguing about!"

'"But I'm telling you I *have* read it!" Kovalenko shouts, even louder.

'And when they had visitors they'd be at each other's throats again. She must have been fed up with that kind of life and wanted her own little place – and then of course there was her age. She couldn't pick or choose any more, so anyone would do, even a Greek teacher. In fact most of the young ladies here aren't too choosy, as long as they find a husband. Anyway, Barbara began to show a decided liking for Belikov.

'And what about Belikov? He'd behave just the same at Kovalenko's as he did with us. He would go and sit down and say nothing, while Barbara would sing "Breezes of the South" for him or gaze at him thoughtfully with her dark eyes, or suddenly break into loud peals of laughter.

'In love affairs and above all in marriage a little persuasion plays a large part. Everyone, his colleagues and their wives, tried to persuade Belikov to get married – there was nothing else for him to live for. We all congratulated him and tried to look serious, and came out with such banal remarks as "marriage is a serious step". Barbara was good-looking and interesting. What's more, the daughter of a privy councillor, with a farm in the Ukraine. But most important, she was the first woman ever to treat Belikov with any warmth or affection. This turned his head and he made up his mind that he really should get married.'

'Now *that* would have been the best time to relieve him of his galoshes and umbrella,' Ivan Ivanych muttered.

'But can you imagine, that proved impossible,' Burkin said. 'He put Barbara's portrait on his desk and kept coming to see me and chatting about her, about family life, about marriage being a serious step. He often visited the Kovalenkos, but he did not change his way of life one jot. In fact, it was the reverse, and his decision to get married had a rather morbid effect on him. He grew thin and pale and seemed to withdraw even further into his shell.

' "I like Barbara," he told me, with a weak, wry little smile, "and I know that everyone should get married . . . but hm . . . it's all been so *sudden* . . . I must think about it . . ."

' "Why?" I asked. "Just go ahead, that's all there is to it."

' "No, marriage is a serious step, one has carefully to consider the impending duties and responsibilities – you never know – in case there's trouble. I'm so worried I can't sleep at all. And to be honest, I'm scared. She and her brother have peculiar ideas, they have a strange way of talking, you know, and they're a bit too smart. You can get married and before long find yourself mixed up in something – you never know."

'So he didn't propose, but kept putting it off, much to the annoyance of the Head's wife and all the ladies. He continually weighed up the "impending duties and responsibilities" and at the same time went for a walk with Barbara nearly every day, perhaps because he thought he should do that in his position, and kept calling on me to discuss family life. Most likely he would have proposed in the long run and we would have had another of those unnecessary, stupid marriages – thousands of them are made every day, the fruit of boredom and having nothing to do – if a *kolossalische Skandal* hadn't suddenly erupted. Here I must say that Barbara's brother had taken a violent dislike to Belikov from the start, he just couldn't stand him.

'"I just don't understand," he told us, shrugging his shoulders, "how you can stomach that ugly little sneak. Really, gentlemen, how *can* you live in this place! The air is foul, stifling. Call yourselves pedagogues, teachers? You're lousy bureaucrats and this isn't a temple of learning, it's more like a police station and it has the sour stink of a sentrybox. No, my friends, I'm hanging on just a bit longer, then it's off to the farm to catch crayfish and teach the peasants. Yes, I'll be gone while you'll be here with your Judas, blast his guts!"

'Or he'd laugh out loud until the tears flowed – first in that deep bass, then in a thin squeaky tone. "Why does he hang around my room, what's he after? He just sits and gapes," he'd say, helplessly spreading his hands out.

'He even thought up a nickname for Belikov – Mr Creepy-Crawly.⁵ Naturally we didn't tell him his sister intended marrying this Mr Creepy-Crawly. Once, when the Head's wife hinted how nice it would be if his sister settled down with such a reliable, universally respected person as Belikov, he frowned and growled, "That's nothing to do with me. She can marry a viper if she wants. I don't go poking my nose into other people's business."

'Now listen to what happened next. Some practical joker drew a caricature of Belikov walking in his galoshes, his umbrella open, the bottoms of his trousers rolled up, and Barbara on his arm. Underneath was the caption *The Lovesick Anthropos*. It caught him to a tee, amazing. The artist must have worked many a long night, as all the teachers at the boys' and girls' high schools, as well as lecturers at the theological college *and* local civil servants – they all got a copy. So did Belikov, and it had the most depressing effect on him.

'Next Sunday, the first of May, we left the house together. All the teachers and their pupils had arranged to meet first at the school and then go out of town for a walk in the woods. Off we went, with Belikov looking green and gloomier than a storm cloud.

'"What wicked, evil people there are!" he said, his lips trembling. I really felt sorry for him. Then, as we were on our way, Kovalenko suddenly came bowling along on a bicycle, followed by his sister, also on one – she was flushed and looked worn out, but still cheerful and happy.

'"We're going on ahead!" she shouted. "What wonderful weather, oh, *frightfully* wonderful!"

'And they both disappeared from view. Belikov changed colour from green to white and he looked stunned. He stopped, looked at me and asked, "Would you mind telling me what's going on? Are my eyes deceiving me? Do you think it's proper for high school teachers, for *ladies*, to ride bicycles?"

'"What's improper?" I said. "Let them cycle to their hearts' content!"

'"What are you saying!" he shouted, amazed at my indifference. "What *do* you mean?" He was so shocked he wouldn't go any further and turned back home.

'All next day he kept nervously rubbing his hands together and quivering, and from his face we could see he wasn't well. He stayed away from school – for the first time in his life. And he didn't eat any lunch. Towards evening he put some warmer clothes on, although it was a perfect summer's day, and he plodded off to the Kovalenkos. Barbara had gone out, only her brother was home.

'"Please take a seat," Kovalenko muttered coldly. He was scowling and looked sleepy – he'd just been taking a nap after his meal and was in a terrible mood.

'After sitting for ten minutes without a word, Belikov began: "I've come to get something off my chest. I'm deeply upset. Some comedian has produced a cartoon in which myself and another person – close to both of us – are made to look silly. I consider it my duty to assure you that in no way am I involved, that I have never given grounds for such ridicule. On the contrary I have invariably conducted myself as a person of the highest integrity."

'Kovalenko boiled up inside, and said nothing. Belikov waited and then continued in a soft, sad voice, "And there's something else. I've been teaching for a long time, you're only just beginning, and I consider it my duty, as a senior colleague, to give you some words of warning. You ride a bicycle: that's a pastime which is utterly improper for a tutor of young people."

' "How so?" Kovalenko asked in his deep voice.

' "Do I need to make it any clearer, Mikhail Savvich, don't you get my meaning? If teachers start riding bicycles, what are we to expect from the pupils? That they'll take to walking on their heads, I dare say! There's nothing in the school rules that states it's allowed, so that means you *can't*. I was horrified yesterday! When I saw your sister, my eyes went dim. A woman or young girl on a *bicycle* — that's shocking!"

' "What exactly do you want?"

' "Only one thing, Mikhail Savvich. To warn you. You're a young man, with your future before you and you should watch your behaviour *very* carefully. You don't obey the rules, oh, no! You wear an embroidered shirt, you're always carrying books in the street, and now there's the bicycle. The Head will get to hear all about your sister and yourself cycling, then the governors . . . That's not very nice, is it?"

' "If my sister and I go cycling that's no one else's business," Kovalenko said, turning purple. "And if anyone starts poking his nose into my private and personal affairs I'll tell him to go to hell!"

'Belikov turned white and got up. "If you take that tone with me I must conclude this conversation. And I beg you never to use such expressions about the authorities in my presence. You should have some respect for authority."

' "Did I say anything nasty about them?" Kovalenko said, looking at him angrily. "Now, please leave me alone. I'm an honest man and I don't want to talk to the likes of you. I hate sneaks."

'Belikov fidgeted nervously and hastily put his coat on. Horror was written all over his face. This was the first time *anyone* had been so rude to him.

'"You're entitled to say what you like," he said, going out onto the landing. "But I must warn you: it's possible someone has overheard us and in case our conversation is misinterpreted and in case there's trouble, I shall be obliged to report the contents to the Head . . . the main points anyway. That is my duty."

'"Report it? Go ahead and report it then!"

'Kovalenko grabbed him by the collar from behind and pushed him. Belikov slid down the stairs, his galoshes thudding as he fell. The stairs were steep and high, but he safely reached the bottom, got up and felt his nose to see if his glasses were intact. But just as he was sliding down, in had come Barbara, with two young ladies. They stood at the bottom and watched him: this was the end. He would rather have broken his neck or both legs than become such a laughing-stock, I do believe. Now it would be all over town, and the Head and the governors would get to hear . . . oh, *now* there would be trouble – there'd be a new cartoon and he would finish up having to resign . . .

'Barbara recognized him when he was on his feet, and when she saw his ridiculous expression, his crumpled coat, his galoshes, she didn't understand what had happened – she thought he had fallen down the stairs accidentally – she couldn't stop herself breaking into fits of loud laughter that could be heard all over the house.

'And these echoing peals of laughter marked the end of everything: of the courtship and Belikov's earthly existence. He couldn't hear what Barbara was saying, he saw nothing. As soon as he got home he removed her portrait from the table. Then he lay down, never to rise again.

'Three days later Afanasy came and asked me if we should send for the doctor, as "something was wrong with the master". I went to see Belikov. He was lying in his curtained bed, with a blanket over him and he didn't speak. He just replied "yes" or "no" to any question, saying nothing else. While he lay there, Afanasy (looking gloomy, frowning and sighing deeply) fussed round him, reeking of vodka.

'A month later Belikov died. All of us went to the funeral – that is, everyone from the two schools and the theological college. Then, as he lay in his coffin, his face looked gentle and pleasant – even cheerful – just as if he were rejoicing that at last he had found a container from which he would never emerge. Yes, he had achieved his ideal! The weather had turned wet and miserable – in his honour it seemed – and we all wore galoshes and carried umbrellas. Barbara was with us and she burst into tears when the coffin was lowered. I've noticed that Ukrainian women can only cry or laugh, there's no happy medium.

'I must confess burying a man like Belikov was a great pleasure. On the way back from the cemetery we all assumed modest, pious expressions, no one wanted to betray the pleasure he felt. It was the same feeling we had long, long ago when our parents went out and we would run round the garden for an hour or so, revelling in perfect freedom. Freedom, oh freedom! Doesn't the slightest hint, the faintest hope of its possibility lend wings to the soul?

'We were all in an excellent mood when we returned from the cemetery. However, hardly a week passed and we were in the same old rut again. Life was just as harsh, tiring and senseless, not exactly prohibited by the school rules, but not really allowed either. Things didn't improve. Belikov was indeed dead and buried, but how many of these encapsulated men are still left, and how many are yet to come!'

'Yes, that's just my point!' Ivan Ivanych said, lighting his pipe.

The teacher came out of the barn. He was short, plump, completely bald, with a black beard that nearly reached his waist. He had two dogs with him.

'Just look at that moon!' he said, looking up.

It was already midnight. To his right, the whole village could be clearly seen, with the long road stretching into the distance for about three miles. Everything was buried in a deep, peaceful slumber. Not a sound or movement anywhere and it was hard to believe that nature could be so silent. When you see a broad village street on a moonlit night, its huts, hayricks and sleeping willows, your heart is filled with tranquillity and finds sanctuary from its toil, worries and sorrows in this calm and in the shadows of night. It becomes gentle, sad and beautiful, and it seems that the very stars are looking down on it with love and tenderness, that all evil has vanished from the world and that happiness is everywhere. To the left, at the edge of the village, the open fields began; they could be seen stretching into the distance, right up to the horizon, and over all that vast moonlit expanse there was neither movement nor sound.

'Yes, that's just my point,' Ivan Ivanych repeated. 'Isn't living in a crowded, stuffy town, writing documents nobody really needs, playing cards, the same as being in some kind of case? And spending our whole lives with idlers, litigants, stupid ladies of leisure, talking and hearing all kinds of rubbish – isn't that living in a case? If you like, I'll tell you another very edifying story.'

'No, it's time we got some sleep,' Burkin said. 'It can wait till tomorrow.'

The two men went into the barn and lay down on the hay. They had only just covered themselves and were dozing off when suddenly they could hear the patter of light footsteps. Someone was walking near the barn. The steps passed, stopped, then came the same patter. The dogs growled.

'That's Mavra,' Burkin said.

The footsteps died away.

'People are such liars,' Ivan Ivanych said as he turned over, 'and you're called a fool for putting up with their lies. Suffering insults, humiliation, lacking the courage to declare that you're on the side of honest, free people, lying yourself, smiling – all this for a slice of bread, a snug little home of your own, a lousy clerical job not worth a damn! No, I can't live this kind of life any more!'

'Come on, that's another story, Ivan Ivanych,' the teacher said. 'Let's go to sleep.'

And ten minutes later, Burkin was fast asleep. But Ivan Ivanych kept tossing and turning, and sighing. Then he got up, went outside again, sat in the doorway and lit his pipe.

Gooseberries

The sky had been overcast with rain clouds since early morning. The weather was mild, and not hot and oppressive as it can be on dull grey days when storm clouds lie over the fields for ages and you wait for rain which never comes. Ivan Ivanych, the vet, and Burkin, a teacher at the high school, were tired of walking and thought they would never come to the end of the fields. They could just make out the windmills at the village of Mironositskoye in the far distance – a range of hills stretched away to the right and disappeared far beyond it. They both knew that the river was there, with meadows, green willows and farmsteads, and that if they climbed one of the hills they would see yet another vast expanse of fields, telegraph wires and a train resembling a caterpillar in the distance. In fine weather they could see even as far as the town. And now, in calm weather, when the whole of nature had become gentle and dreamy, Ivan Ivanych and Burkin were filled with love for those open spaces and they both thought what a vast and beautiful country it was.

'Last time we were in Elder Prokofy's barn, you were going to tell me a story,' Burkin said.

'Yes, I wanted to tell you about my brother.'

Ivan Ivanych heaved a long sigh and lit his pipe before beginning his narrative; but at that moment down came the rain. Five minutes later it was simply teeming. Ivan Ivanych and Burkin were in two minds as to what they should do. The dogs were already soaked through and stood with their tails drooping, looking at them affectionately.

'We must take shelter,' Burkin said. 'Let's go to Alyokhin's, it's not very far.'

'All right, let's go there.'

They changed direction and went across mown fields, walking straight on at first, and then bearing right until they came out on the high road. Before long, poplars, a garden, then the red roofs of barns came into view. The river glinted, and then they caught sight of a wide stretch of water and a white bathing-hut. This was Sofino, where Alyokhin lived.

The mill was turning and drowned the noise of the rain. The wall of the dam shook. Wet horses with downcast heads were standing by some carts and peasants went around with sacks on their heads. Everything was damp, muddy and bleak, and the water had a cold, malevolent look. Ivan Ivanych and Burkin felt wet, dirty and terribly uncomfortable. Their feet were weighed down by mud and when they crossed the dam and walked up to the barns near the manor house they did not say a word and seemed to be angry with each other.

A winnowing fan was droning away in one of the barns and dust poured out of the open door. On the threshold stood the master himself, Alyokhin, a man of about forty, tall, stout, with long hair, and he looked more like a professor or an artist than a landowner. He wore a white shirt that hadn't been washed for a very long time, and it was tied round with a piece of rope as a belt. Instead of trousers he was wearing underpants; mud and straw clung to his boots. His nose and eyes were black with dust. He immediately recognized Ivan Ivanych and Burkin, and was clearly delighted to see them.

'Please come into the house, gentlemen,' he said, smiling, 'I'll be with you in a jiffy.'

It was a large house, with two storeys. Alyokhin lived on the ground floor in the two rooms with vaulted ceilings and small windows where his estate managers used to live. They were simply furnished and smelled of rye bread, cheap vodka and harness. He seldom used the main rooms upstairs, reserving them for guests. Ivan Ivanych and Burkin were welcomed by the maid, who was such a beautiful young woman that they both stopped and stared at each other.

'You can't imagine how glad I am to see you, gentlemen,'

Alyokhin said as he followed them into the hall. 'A real surprise!' Then he turned to the maid and said, 'Pelageya, bring some dry clothes for the gentlemen. I suppose I'd better change too. But I must have a wash first, or you'll think I haven't had one since spring. Would you like to come to the bathing-hut while they get things ready in the house?'

The beautiful Pelageya, who had such a dainty look and gentle face, brought soap and towels, and Alyokhin went off with his guests to the bathing-hut.

'Yes, it's ages since I had a good wash,' he said as he undressed. 'As you can see, it's a nice hut. My father built it, but I never find time these days for a swim.'

He sat on one of the steps and smothered his long hair and neck with soap; the water turned brown.

'Yes, I must confess . . .' Ivan Ivanych muttered, with a meaning-ful look at his head.

'Haven't had a wash for ages,' Alyokhin repeated in his embarrass-ment and soaped himself again; the water turned a dark inky blue.

Ivan Ivanych came out of the cabin, dived in with a loud splash and swam in the rain, making broad sweeps with his arms and sending out waves with white lilies bobbing about on them. He swam right out to the middle of the reach and dived. A moment later he popped up somewhere else and swam on, continually trying to dive right to the bottom.

'Oh, good God,' he kept saying with great relish. 'Good God . . .'

He reached the mill, said a few words to the peasants, then he turned and floated on his back in the middle with his face under the rain. Burkin and Alyokhin were already dressed and ready to leave, but he kept on swimming and diving.

'Oh, dear God,' he said. 'Oh, God!'

'Now that's enough,' Burkin shouted.

They went back to the house. Only when the lamp in the large upstairs drawing-room was alight and Burkin and Ivan Ivanych, wearing silk dressing-gowns and warm slippers, were sitting in armchairs and Alyokhin, washed and combed now and with a new frock-coat on, was walking up and down, obviously savouring the warmth, cleanliness, dry clothes and light shoes, while his beautiful Pelageya glided silently over the carpet and gently smiled as she served tea and jam on a tray – only then did Ivan Ivanych begin his story. It seemed that Burkin and Alyokhin were not the only ones who were listening, but also the ladies (young and old) and the officers, who were looking down calmly and solemnly from their gilt frames on the walls.

'There are two of us brothers,' he began, 'myself – Ivan Ivanych – and Nikolay Ivanych, who's two years younger. I studied to be a vet, while Nikolay worked in the district tax office from the time he was nineteen. Chimsha-Gimalaysky, our father, had served as a private, but when he was promoted to officer we became hereditary gentlemen and owners of a small estate. After he died, this estate was sequestrated to pay off his debts, but despite this we spent our boyhood in the country free to do what we wanted. Just like any other village children, we stayed out in the fields and woods for days and nights, minded horses, stripped bark, went fishing, and so on . . . As you know very well, anyone who has ever caught a ruff or watched migrating thrushes swarming over his native village on cool clear autumn days can never live in a town afterwards and he'll always hanker after the free and open life until his dying day. My brother was miserable in the tax office. The years passed, but there he stayed, always at the same old desk, copying out the same old documents and obsessed with this longing for the country. And gradually this longing took the form of a definite wish, a dream of buying a nice little estate somewhere in the country, beside a river or a lake.

'He was a kind, gentle man and I was very fond of him, but I could never feel any sympathy for him in this longing to lock himself away in a country house for the rest of his life. They say a man needs only six feet of earth,[1] but surely they must mean a corpse – not a *man*! These days they seem to think that it's very good if our educated classes want to go back to the land and set their hearts on a country estate. But in reality these estates are only that same six feet all over again. To leave the town and all its noise and hubbub, to go and shut yourself away on your little estate – that's no life! It's selfishness, laziness, a peculiar brand of monasticism that achieves nothing. A man needs more than six feet of earth and a little place in the country, he needs the whole wide world, the whole of nature, where there's room for him to display his potential, all the manifold attributes of his free spirit.

'As he sat there in his office, my brother Nikolay dreamt of soup made from his own home-grown cabbages, soup that would fill the whole house with a delicious smell; eating meals on the green grass; sleeping in the sun; sitting on a bench outside the main gates for hours on end and looking at the fields and woods. Booklets on agriculture and words of wisdom from calendars were his joy, his favourite spiritual nourishment. He liked newspapers as well, but he only read property adverts – for so many acres of arable land and meadows, with "house, river, garden, mill, and ponds fed by running springs". And he had visions of garden paths, flowers, fruit, nesting-boxes for starlings, ponds teeming with carp – you know the kind of thing. These visions varied according to the adverts he happened to see, but for some reason, in every single one, there *had* to be gooseberry bushes. "Life in the country has its comforts," he used to say. "You can sit drinking tea on your balcony, while your ducks are swimming in the pond . . . it all smells so good and um . . . there's your gooseberries growing away!"

'He drew up a plan for his estate and it turned out exactly the same every time: (a) manor house; (b) servants' quarters; (c) kitchen garden; (d) gooseberry bushes. He lived a frugal life, economizing on food and drink, dressing any-old-how – just like a beggar – and putting every penny he saved straight into the bank. He was terribly mean. It was really painful to look at him, so I used to send him a little money on special occasions. But he would put that in the bank too. Once a man has his mind firmly made up there's nothing you can do about it.

'Years passed and he was transferred to another province. He was now in his forties, still reading newspaper adverts and still saving up. Then I heard that he'd got married. So that he could buy a country estate with gooseberry bushes, he married an ugly old widow, for whom he felt nothing and only because she had a little money tucked away. He made her life miserable too, half-starved her and banked her money into his own account. She'd been married to a postmaster and was used to pies and fruit liqueurs, but with her second husband she didn't even have enough black bread. This kind of life made her wither away, and within three years she'd gone to join her maker. Of course, my brother didn't think that *he* was to blame – not for one minute! Like vodka, money can make a man do the most peculiar things. There was once a merchant living in our town who was on his deathbed. Just before he died, he asked for some honey, stirred it up with all his money and winning lottery tickets, and swallowed the lot to stop anyone else from laying their hands on it. And another time, when I was inspecting cattle at some railway station, a dealer fell under a train and had his leg cut off. We took him to the local casualty department. The blood simply gushed out, a terrible sight, but all he did was ask for his leg back and was only bothered about the twenty roubles he had tucked away in the boot. Scared he might lose them, I dare say!'

'But that's neither here nor there,' Burkin said.

'When his wife died,' Ivan continued, after a pause for thought, 'my brother started looking for an estate. Of course, you can look around for five years and still make the wrong choice and you finish up with something you never even dreamt of. So brother Nikolay bought about three hundred acres, with manor house, servants' quarters and a park, on a mortgage through an estate agent. But there wasn't any orchard, gooseberries or duck pond. There *was* a river, but the water was always the colour of coffee because of the brickworks on one side of the estate and a bone-ash factory on the other. But my dear Nikolay didn't seem to care. He ordered twenty gooseberry bushes, planted them out and settled down to a land-owner's life.

'Last year I visited him, as I wanted to see what was going on. In his letter my brother had called his estate "Chumbaroklov Patch" or "Gimalaysky's". One afternoon I turned up at "Gimalaysky's". It was a hot day. Everywhere there were ditches, fences, hedges, rows of small fir trees and there seemed no way into the yard or anywhere to leave my horse. I went up to the house, only to be welcomed by a fat ginger dog that looked rather like a pig. It wanted to bark, but it was too lazy. Then a barefooted, plump cook – she resembled a pig as well – came out of the kitchen and told me the master was having his after-lunch nap. So I went to my brother's room and there he was sitting up in bed with a blanket over his knees. He'd aged, put on weight and looked very flabby. His cheeks, nose and lips stuck out and I thought any moment he was going to grunt into his blanket, like a pig.

'We embraced and wept for joy, and at the sad thought that once we were young and now both of us were grey, and that our lives were nearly over. He got dressed and led me on a tour of the estate.

' "Well, how's it going?" I asked.

' "All right, thank God. It's a good life."

'No longer was he the poor, timid little clerk of before, but a real squire, a *gentleman*. He felt quite at home, being used to country life by then and he was enjoying himself. He ate a great deal, took proper baths, and he was putting on weight. Already he was suing the district council and both factories, and he got very peeved when the villagers didn't call him "sir". He paid great attention to his spiritual wellbeing (as a gentleman should) and he couldn't dispense charity nice and quietly, but had to make a great show of it. And what did it all add up to? He doled out bicarbonate of soda or castor oil to his villagers – regardless of what they were suffering from – and on his name-day held a thanksgiving service in the village, supplying vodka in plenty, as he thought this was the right thing to do. Oh, those horrid pints of vodka! Nowadays your fat squire drags his villagers off to court for letting their cattle stray on his land and the very next day (if it's a high holiday) stands them all a few pints of vodka. They'll drink it, shout hurray and fall at his feet in a drunken stupor. Better standards of living, plenty to eat, idleness – all this makes us Russians terribly smug. Back in his office, Nikolay had been too scared even to voice any opinions of his own, but now he was expounding the eternal verities in true ministerial style: "Education is essential, but premature as far as the common people are concerned" or "Corporal punishment, generally speaking, is harmful, but in certain cases it can be useful and irreplaceable". And he'd say,

"I know the working classes and how to handle them. They *like* me, I only have to lift my little finger and they'll do *anything* for me."

'And he said all this, mark you, with a clever, good-natured smile. Time after time he'd say "we *gentlemen*" or "speaking as *one of the gentry*". He'd evidently forgotten that our grandfather had been a peasant and our father a common soldier. Even our absolutely ridiculous surname, Chimsha-Gimalaysky, was melodious, distinguished and highly agreeable to his ears now.

'But it's myself I'm concerned with, not him. I'd like to tell you about the change that came over me during the few hours I spent on his estate. Later, when we were having tea, his cook brought us a plateful of gooseberries. They weren't shop gooseberries, but home-grown, the first fruits of the bushes he'd planted. Nikolay laughed and stared at them for a whole minute, with tears in his eyes. He was too deeply moved for words. Then he popped one in his mouth, looked at me like an enraptured child that has finally been given a long-awaited toy and said, "Absolutely delicious!" He ate some greedily and kept repeating, "So tasty, you *must* try one!"

'They were hard and sour, but as Pushkin says: "Uplifting illusion is dearer to us than a host of truths."[2] This was a happy man whose cherished dreams had clearly come true, who had achieved his life's purpose, had got what he wanted and was happy with his lot – and himself. My thoughts about human happiness, for some peculiar reason, had always been tinged with a certain sadness. But now, seeing this happy man, I was overwhelmed by a feeling of despondency that was close to utter despair. I felt particularly low that night. They made up a bed for me in the room next to my brother's. He was wide awake and I could hear him getting up, going over to the plate and helping himself to one gooseberry at a time. And I thought how many satisfied, happy people really do exist in this world! And what a powerful force they are! Just take a look at this life of ours and you will see the arrogance and idleness of the strong, the ignorance and bestiality of the weak. Everywhere there's unspeakable poverty, overcrowding, degeneracy, drunkenness, hypocrisy and stupid lies . . . And yet peace and quiet reign in every house and street. Out of fifty thousand people you won't find one who is prepared to shout

out loud and make a strong protest. We see people buying food in the market, eating during the day, sleeping at night-time, talking nonsense, marrying, growing old and then contentedly carting their dead off to the cemetery. But we don't hear or see those who suffer: the real tragedies of life are enacted somewhere behind the scenes. Everything is calm and peaceful and the only protest comes from statistics – and they can't talk. Figures show that so many went mad, so many bottles of vodka were emptied, so many children died from malnutrition. And clearly this kind of system is what people need. It's obvious that the happy man feels contented only because the unhappy ones bear their burden without saying a word: if it weren't for their silence, happiness would be quite impossible. It's a kind of mass hypnosis. Someone ought to stand with a hammer at the door of every happy contented man, continually banging on it to remind him that there are unhappy people around and that however happy *he* may be at the time, sooner or later life will show him its claws and disaster will overtake him in the form of illness, poverty, bereavement and there will be no one to hear or see him. But there isn't anyone holding a hammer, so our happy man goes his own sweet way and is only gently ruffled by life's trivial cares, as an aspen is ruffled by the breeze. All's well as far as *he's* concerned.

'That night I realized that I too was happy and contented,' Ivan Ivanych went on, getting to his feet. 'I too had lectured people over dinner – or out hunting – on how to live, on what to believe, on how to handle the common people. And I too had told them that knowledge is a shining lamp, that education is essential, and that plain reading and writing is good enough for the masses, for the moment. Freedom is a blessing, I told them, and we need it like the air we breathe, but we must wait for it patiently.'

Ivan Ivanych turned to Burkin and said angrily, 'Yes, that's what I used to say and now I'd like to know *what* is it we're waiting for? I'm asking you, *what?* What is it we're trying to prove? I'm told that nothing can be achieved in five minutes, that it takes time for any kind of idea to be realized; it's a gradual process. But who says so? And what is there to prove he's right? You refer to the natural order of things, to the law of cause and effect. But *is* there any law or order in a state of affairs where a lively, thinking person like myself should have to stand by a ditch and wait until it's choked with weeds, or silted up, when I could quite easily, perhaps, leap across it or bridge it? I ask you again, what are we waiting for? Until we have no more strength to live, although we long to and *need* to go on living?

'I left my brother early next morning and ever since then I've found town life unbearable. I'm depressed by peace and quiet, I'm scared of peering through windows, nothing makes me more dejected than the sight of a happy family sitting round the table drinking tea. But I'm old now, no longer fit for the fray, I'm even incapable of hating. I only feel sick at heart, irritable and exasperated. At night my head seems to be on fire with so many thoughts crowding in and I can't get any sleep . . . Oh, if only I were young again!'

Ivan Ivanych paced the room excitedly, repeating, 'If only I were young again!'

Suddenly he went up to Alyokhin and squeezed one hand, then the other. 'Pavel Konstantinych,' he pleaded, 'don't go to sleep or be lulled into complacency! While you're still young, strong and healthy, never stop doing good! Happiness doesn't exist, we don't need any such thing. If life has *any* meaning or purpose, you won't find it in happiness, but in something more rational, in something greater. Doing good!'

Ivan Ivanych said all this with a pitiful, imploring smile, as though pleading for himself.

Afterwards all three of them sat in armchairs in different parts of the room and said nothing. Ivan Ivanych's story satisfied neither Burkin nor Alyokhin. It was boring listening to that story about some poor devil of a clerk who ate gooseberries, while those generals and ladies, who seemed to have come to life in the gathering gloom, peered out of their gilt frames. For some reason they would have preferred discussing and hearing about refined people, about ladies. The fact that they were all sitting in a drawing-room where every-thing – the draped chandeliers, the armchairs, the carpets underfoot – indicated that those same people who were now looking out of their frames had once walked around, sat down and drunk their tea there . . . and with beautiful Pelageya moving about here without a sound – all this was better than any story.

Alyokhin was dying to get to bed. That morning he had been up and about very early (before three) working on the farm, and he could hardly keep his eyes open. However, he was frightened he might miss some interesting story if he left now, so he stayed. He didn't even try to fathom if everything that Ivan Ivanych had just been saying was clever, or even true: he was only too glad that his guests did not discuss oats or hay or tar, but things that had nothing to do with his way of life, and he wanted them to continue . . .

'But it's time we got some sleep,' Burkin said, standing up. 'May I wish you all a very good night!'

Alyokhin bade them good night and went down to his room, while his guests stayed upstairs. They had been given the large room with two old, elaborately carved beds and an ivory crucifix in one corner. These wide, cool beds had been made by the beautiful Pelageya and the linen had a pleasant fresh smell.

Ivan Ivanych undressed without a word and got into bed. Then he muttered, 'Lord have mercy on us sinners!' and pulled the blankets over his head. His pipe, which was lying on a table, smelt strongly of stale tobacco and Burkin was so puzzled as to where the terrible smell was coming from that it was a long time before he fell asleep.

All night long the rain beat against the windows.

About Love

Next day they had delicious pies, crayfish and mutton chops for lunch, and during the meal Nikanor, the cook, came upstairs to inquire what the guests would like for dinner. He was a man of medium height, puffy-faced and with small eyes. He was so close-shaven his whiskers seemed to have been plucked out and not cut off with a razor.

Alyokhin told his guests that the beautiful Pelageya was in love with the cook. However, since he was a drunkard and a brawler, she didn't want to marry him; but she did not object to 'living' with him, as they say. He was a very devout Christian, however, and his religious convictions would not allow him to 'set up house' with her. So he insisted on marriage and would not hear of anything else. He cursed her when he was drunk and even beat her. When he was like this, she would hide upstairs and sob, and then Alyokhin and his servants would not leave the house in case she needed protecting. They began to talk about love.

Alyokhin started: 'What makes people fall in love and why couldn't Pelageya fall for someone else, someone more suited to her mentally and physically, instead of that ugly-mug Nikanor (everyone round here calls him ugly-mug), since *personal* happiness is so important in love? It's a mystery, and you can interpret it which way you like. Only one indisputable truth has been said about love up to now, that it's a "tremendous mystery", and everything else that's been written or said about it has never provided an answer and is just a reformulation of problems that have always remained unsolved. One theory that might, on the face of it, explain one case, won't explain a dozen others. Therefore, in my opinion, the best way is to treat each case individually, without making generalizations. In doctors' jargon, you have to "isolate" each case.'

'Absolutely true,' Burkin said.

'Decent Russians like ourselves have a passion for problems that have never been solved. Usually, love is poeticized, beautified with roses and nightingales, but we Russians have to flavour it with the "eternal problems" – and we choose the most boring ones at that.

'When I was still studying in Moscow I had a "friend", a dear lady who'd be wondering how much I'd allow her every month and how much a pound of beef was while I held her close. And *we* never stop asking ourselves questions when we love: is it honourable or dishonourable, clever or stupid, how will it all end, and so on. Whether that's a good thing or not, I don't know, but I do know that it cramps your style, doesn't provide any satisfaction and gets on your nerves.'

It looked as if he wanted to tell us a story. It's always the same with people living on their own – they have something that they are only too pleased to get off their chests. Bachelors living in town go to the public baths and restaurants just to talk to someone, and sometimes they tell the bath attendants or waiters some very interesting stories. Out in the country they normally pour out their hearts to their guests. Through the windows we could only see grey skies now and trees dripping with rain – in this kind of weather there was really nowhere to go and nothing else to do except listen to stories.

'I've been living and farming in Sofino for quite a long time now – since I left university, in fact,' Alyokhin began. 'I was never brought up to do physical work and I'm an "armchair" type by inclination. When I first came to this estate they were up to their eyes in debts. But since my father had run up these debts partly through spending so much on my education, I decided to stay and work on the estate until the debts were paid off. That was my decision and I started working here – not without a certain degree of aversion, I must confess. The soil's not very fertile round here, and to avoid farming at a loss you have to rely on serfs or hire farm labourers, which more or less comes to the same thing. Or else you have to run your own estate peasant-style, which means you yourself and all your family have to slave away in the fields. There's no two ways about it. But then I didn't have time for subtleties: I didn't leave a square inch of soil unturned, I rounded up all the peasants and their wives from neighbouring villages and we all worked like mad. I did the ploughing, sowing and reaping myself, which was a terrible bore and it made me screw my face up in disgust, like the starving village cat forced to eat cucumbers in some kitchen garden. I was all aches and pains and I'd fall asleep standing up. From the very beginning I thought that I'd have no trouble at all combining this life of slavery with my cultural activities. All I had to do, so I thought, was keep to some settled routine. So I installed myself in the best rooms up here, had coffee and liqueurs after lunch and dinner, and took the *European Herald*[1] with me to bed. But our parish priest, Father Ivan, turned up and polished off all my liqueurs at one sitting. And the *European Herald* ended up with his daughters, since during the summer, especially when we were harvesting, I never made it to my own bed but had to sleep in a barn, on a sledge, or in a woodman's hut somewhere, so what time was there for reading? Gradually I moved downstairs, had meals with the servants – they were all that was left of my earlier life of luxury – the same servants who had waited on my father and whom I did not have the heart to dismiss.

'In my early years here I was made honorary justice of the peace. This meant occasional trips into town, taking my seat at the sessions and local assizes, and this made a break for me. When you're stuck in a place like this for two or three months at a stretch – especially in the winter – you end up pining for your black frock-coat. I saw frock-coats – and uniforms and tailcoats as well – at the assizes. They were all lawyers, educated men there, people I could talk to. After sleeping on a sledge or eating with the servants it was the height of luxury sitting in an armchair, with clean underwear, light boots, and a watch-chain on your chest!

'They gave me a warm welcome in town and I eagerly made friends. The most significant, and frankly, the most pleasant, of these friendships was with Luganovich, vice-president of the assizes. Both of you know him, he's a most delightful man. Now, all this was about the time of that famous arson case. The questioning went on for two days and we were exhausted. Luganovich took a look at me and said, "Do you know what? Come and have dinner at my place."

'This was right out of the blue, as I didn't know him at all well, only through official business, and I'd never been to his house. I went to my hotel room for a quick change and went off to dinner. Now I had the chance to meet Luganovich's wife, Anna Alekseyevna. She was still very young then, not more than twenty-two, and her first child had been born six months before. It's all finished now and it's hard for me to say exactly what it was I found so unusual about her, what attracted me so much, but at the time, over dinner, it was all so clear, without a shadow of doubt: here was a young, beautiful, kind, intelligent, enchanting woman, unlike any I'd met before. Immediately I sensed that she was a kindred spirit, someone I knew already, and that her face, with its warm clever eyes, was just like one I had seen before when I was a little boy, in an album lying on my mother's chest of drawers.

'At the trial four Jews had been convicted of arson and conspiracy – in my opinion, on no reasonable grounds at all. I became very heated over dinner, felt bad and I can't remember even now what I said, only that Anna Alekseyevna kept shaking her head and telling her husband, "Dmitry, how *can* they do this?"

'Luganovich was a good man, one of those simple, open-hearted people who are firmly convinced that once you have a man in the dock he *must* be guilty, and that a verdict can only be challenged in writing, according to the correct legal procedure, and *never* during dinner or private conversation. "*We* haven't set anything alight," he said softly, "so *we* won't have to stand trial or go to prison."

'Both husband and wife plied me with food and drink. Judging from little details – the way they made coffee together and their mutual understanding that needed no words – I concluded that they were living peacefully and happily, and that they were glad to have a guest. After dinner there were piano duets. When it grew dark I went back to the hotel. All of this was at the beginning of spring. I spent the whole of the following summer in Sofino without emerging once and I was too busy even to think of going into town. But I could not forget that slender, fair-haired woman for one moment.

Although I made no conscious effort to think about her, she seemed to cast a faint shadow over me.

'In late autumn there was a charity show in town. I took my seat in the governor's box, where I'd been invited during the interval, and there was Anna Alekseyevna sitting next to the governor's wife. Once again I was struck by that irresistible, radiant beauty, by those tender, loving eyes, and once again I felt very close to her.

'We sat side by side, then we went into the foyer where she told me, "You've lost weight. Have you been ill?"

'"Yes, I've rheumatism in my shoulder and I sleep badly when it rains."

'"You look quite exhausted. When you came to dinner in the spring you seemed younger, more cheerful. You were very lively then and said some most interesting things. I was even a little taken with you, I must confess. For some reason I often thought about you during the summer and when I was getting ready for the theatre I had a feeling I might see you today." And she burst out laughing.

'"But now you seem to have no energy," she repeated. "It ages you."

'Next day I had lunch with the Luganoviches. Afterwards they drove out to their country villa to make arrangements for the winter, and I went with them. I came back to town with them and at midnight I was having tea in those peaceful domestic surroundings, in front of a roaring fire, while the young mother kept slipping out to see if her little girl was sleeping. Afterwards I made a point of visiting the Luganoviches whenever I came to town. We grew used to one another and I usually dropped in unannounced, like one of the family.

'That soft drawling voice I found so attractive would come echoing from one of the far rooms: "Who's there?"

'"It's Pavel Konstantinych," the maid or nanny would reply.

'Then Anna Alekseyevna would appear with a worried look and every time she'd ask me the same question, "Why haven't you been to see us? Is anything wrong?"

'The way she looked at me, the delicate, noble hand she offered me, the clothes she wore in the house, her hairstyle, her voice and footsteps always made me feel that something new, out of the ordinary and important had happened in my life. We'd have long conversations – and long silences – immersed in our own thoughts. Or she would play the piano for me. If she was out, I'd stay and wait, talk to the nanny, play with the baby, or lie on the sofa in the study and read the papers. When Anna Alekseyevna came back I'd meet her in the hall, take her shopping and for some reason I'd always carry it so devotedly and exultantly you'd have thought I was a little boy.

'You know the story about the farmer's wife who had no worries until she went and bought a pig. The Luganoviches had no worries, so they made friends with me. If I was away from town for long, they thought I must be ill or that something had happened to me and they would get terribly worked up. And they were concerned that an educated man like myself, speaking several languages, didn't use his time studying or doing literary work and could live out in the wilds, forever turning round like a squirrel on a wheel and slaving away without a penny to show for it. They sensed that I was deeply unhappy and that if I spoke, laughed or ate, it was only to hide my suffering. Even at cheerful times, when I was in good spirits, I knew they were giving me searching looks. They were particularly touching when I really was in trouble, when some creditor was chasing me, or when I couldn't pay some bill on time. Both of them would stay by the window whispering, and then the husband would come over to me, looking serious, and say, "Pavel Konstantinych, if you're a bit short, my wife and I *beg* you not to think twice about asking us!"

'And his ears would turn red with excitement. Often, after a whispering session at the window, he would come over to me, ears flushed, and say, "My wife and I *beg* you to accept this little gift."

'And he'd give me cufflinks, a cigarette case or a table-lamp. In return, I'd send them some poultry, butter or flowers from the country. They were quite well-off, by the way, both of them. In my younger days I was always borrowing and wasn't too fussy where the money came from, taking it wherever I could get it. But for nothing in the world would I have borrowed from the Luganoviches. The very idea!

'I was unhappy. Whether I was at home, out in the fields, in the barn, I couldn't stop thinking about *her*, and I tried to unravel the mystery of that young, beautiful, clever woman who had married an uninteresting man, who could almost be called old (he was over forty) and had borne his children. And I tried to solve the enigma of that boring, good-natured, simple-minded fellow, with his insufferable common sense, always crawling up to the local stuffed shirts at balls and soirées, a lifeless, useless man whose submissive, indifferent expression made you think he'd been brought along as an object for sale, a man who believed, however, that he had the right to be happy and to be the father of *her* children. I never gave up trying to understand why she was fated to meet him, and not me, why such a horrible mistake should have to occur in *our* lives.

'Every time I went into town I could tell from her eyes that she had been waiting for me, and she would admit that from the moment she'd got up she'd had some kind of premonition that I would be coming. We had long talks and there were long silences, and we didn't declare our love, but concealed it jealously, timidly, fearing anything that might betray our secret to each other. Although I loved her tenderly, deeply, I reasoned with myself and tried to guess what the consequences would be if we had no strength to combat it. It seemed incredible that my gentle, cheerless love could suddenly rudely disrupt the happy lives of her husband and children – of that whole household in fact, where I was so loved and trusted. Was I acting honourably? She would have gone away with me, but where could I take her? It would have been another matter if my life had been wonderful and eventful – if, for example, I'd been fighting to liberate my country, or if I'd been a famous scholar, actor or artist. But I'd only be taking her away from an ordinary, pedestrian life into one that was just the same, just as prosaic, even more so, perhaps. And just how long would we stay happy? What would become of her if I was taken ill, or died? Or if we simply stopped loving each other?

'And she seemed to have come to the same conclusion. She had been thinking about her husband, her children, and her mother, who loved her husband like a son. If she were to let her feelings get the better of her, then she would have to lie or tell the whole truth, but either alternative would have been equally terrible and distressing for someone in her position. And she was tormented by the question: would her love make me happy, wouldn't she be complicating a life which was difficult enough already, brimful of all kinds of unhappiness? She thought that she was no longer young enough for me and that she wasn't hard-working or energetic enough to start a new life with me. Often she told her husband that I should marry some nice clever girl who would make a good housewife and be a help to me. But immediately she would add that it would be a hard job finding someone answering to that description in *that* town.

'Meanwhile the years passed. Anna Alekseyevna already had two children. Whenever I called on the Luganoviches the servants welcomed me with smiles, the children shouted that Uncle Pavel Konstantinych had arrived and clung to my neck. Everyone was glad. They didn't understand what was going on deep down inside me and they thought that I too shared their joy. All of them considered me a most noble person, and both parents and children felt that the very personification of nobility was walking around the house, and this lent a very special charm to their attitude towards me, as if my being there made their lives purer and finer. I would go to the theatre with Anna Alekseyevna – we always used to walk. We would sit side by side in the stalls, shoulders touching, and as I took the opera glasses from her I felt that she was near and dear to me, that she belonged to me, that we couldn't live without each other. But through some strange lack of mutual understanding we would always say goodbye and part like strangers when we left the theatre. In that town they were already saying God knows what about us, but there wasn't one word of truth in it.

'Later on, Anna Alekseyevna visited her mother and sister more often. She started to have fits of depression when she realized her life was unfulfilled, ruined, and she had no desire to see either her husband ·or the children. She was already having treatment for a nervous disorder.

'We didn't say one word to each other and she seemed strangely irritated with me when other people were around. She'd quarrel with everything I said, and if I was having an argument she would always take the other person's side. If I dropped something she would coldly say, "Congratulations." If I left my opera glasses behind when we went to the theatre she'd say afterwards, "I *knew* that you'd forget them."

'Whether for better or for worse, there's nothing in this life that doesn't come to an end sooner or later. The time to part finally came when Luganovich was made a judge in one of the western provinces. They had to sell the furniture, horses and the villa. When we drove out to the villa and turned round for a last glimpse of the garden and the green roof, everyone felt sad and it was then I realized the time had come to say farewell – and not only to a simple villa. On the advice of her doctor they decided to send Anna Alekseyevna to the Crimea, while soon afterwards Luganovich would take the children with him to the western province.

'A large crowd of us went to see Anna Alekseyevna off. She had already said goodbye to her husband and children, and the train was about to leave at any moment. I rushed to her compartment to put a basket that she'd almost forgotten onto the luggage-rack. Now it was time to say farewell. When our eyes met we could hold ourselves back no longer. I embraced her and she pressed her face to my chest and the tears just flowed. As I kissed her face, shoulders and hands that were wet with tears – oh, how miserable we both were! – I declared my love and realized, with a searing pain in my heart, how unnecessary, trivial and illusory everything that had stood in the way of our love had been. I understood that with love, if you start theorizing about it, you must have a nobler, more meaningful starting-point than mere happiness or unhappiness, sin or virtue, as they are commonly understood. Otherwise it's best not to theorize at all.

'I kissed her for the last time, pressed her hand and we parted for ever. The train was already moving. I took a seat in the next compartment, which was empty, and cried until the first stop, where I got out and walked back to Sofino.'

While Alyokhin was telling his story the rain had stopped and the sun had come out. Burkin and Ivan Ivanych went onto the balcony, from which there was a wonderful view of the garden and the river, gleaming like a mirror now in the sunlight. As they admired the view they felt sorry that this man, with those kind, clever eyes, who had just told his story so frankly, was really turning round and round in his huge estate like a squirrel in a cage, showing no interest in academic work or indeed anything that could have made his life more agreeable. And they wondered how sad that woman's face must have been when he said goodbye on the train and kissed her face and shoulders. Both of them had met her in town and in fact Burkin had even known her and thought she was beautiful.

A Visit to Friends

(A STORY)

A letter arrived one morning.

Kuzminki, June 7th

Dear Misha,

You've completely forgotten us, please come and visit us soon, we so want to see you. Come today. We beg you, dear sir, on bended knees! Show us your radiant eyes!

Can't wait to see you,

Ta and Va

The letter was from Tatyana Alekseyevna Losev, who had been called 'Ta' for short when Podgorin was staying at Kuzminki ten or twelve years ago. But who was this 'Va'? Podgorin recalled the long conversations, the gay laughter, the love affairs, the evening walks and that whole array of girls and young women who had once lived at Kuzminki and in the neighbourhood. And he remembered that open, lively, clever face with freckles that matched chestnut hair so well – this was Varvara Pavlovna, Tatyana's friend. Varvara Pavlovna had taken a degree in medicine and was working at a factory somewhere beyond Tula.[1] Evidently she had come to stay at Kuzminki now.

'Dear Va!' thought Podgorin, surrendering himself to memories. 'What a wonderful girl!'

Tatyana, Varvara and himself were all about the same age. But he had been a mere student then and they were already marriageable girls – in their eyes he was just a boy. And now, even though he had become a lawyer and had started to go grey, all of them still treated him like a youngster, saying that he had no experience of life yet.

He was very fond of them, but more as a pleasant memory than in actuality, it seemed. He knew little about their present life, which was strange and alien to him. And this brief, playful letter too was something quite foreign to him and had most probably been written after much time and effort. When Tatyana wrote it her husband Sergey Sergeich was doubtlessly standing behind her. She had been given Kuzminki as her dowry only six years before, but this same Sergey Sergeich had already reduced the estate to bankruptcy. Each time a bank or mortgage payment became due they would now turn to Podgorin for legal advice. Moreover, they had twice asked him to lend them money. So it was obvious that they either wanted advice or a loan from him now.

He no longer felt so attracted to Kuzminki as in the past. It was such a miserable place. That laughter and rushing around, those cheerful carefree faces, those rendezvous on quiet moonlit nights – all this had gone. Most important, though, they weren't in the flush of youth any more. Probably it enchanted him only as a memory, nothing else. Besides Ta and Va, there was someone called 'Na', Tatyana's sister Nadezhda, whom half-joking, half-seriously they had called his fiancée. He had seen her grow up and everyone expected him to marry her. He had loved her once and was going to propose. But there she was, twenty-three now, and he still hadn't married her.

'Strange it should turn out like this,' he mused as he reread the letter in embarrassment. 'But I can't *not* go, they'd be offended.'

His long absence from the Losevs lay like a heavy weight on his conscience. After pacing his room and reflecting at length, he made a great effort of will and decided to go and visit them for about three days and so discharge his duty. Then he could feel free and relaxed – at least until the following summer. After lunch, as he prepared to leave for the Brest Station, he told his servants that he would be back in three days.

It was two hours by train from Moscow to Kuzminki, then a twenty-minute carriage drive from the station, from which he could see Tatyana's wood and those three tall, narrow holiday villas that Losev (he had entered upon some business enterprise in the first years of his marriage) had started building but had never finished. He had been ruined by these holiday villas, by various business projects, by frequent trips to Moscow, where he used to lunch at the Slav Fair[2] and dine at the Hermitage,[3] ending up in Little Bronny Street[4] or at a gipsy haunt named Knacker's Yard, calling this 'having a fling'. Podgorin liked a drink himself – sometimes quite a lot – and he associated with women indiscriminately, but in a cool, lethargic way, without deriving any pleasure. It sickened him when others gave themselves up to these pleasures with such zest. He didn't understand or like men who could feel more free and easy at the Knacker's Yard than at home with a respectable woman, and he felt that any kind of promiscuity stuck to them like burrs. He didn't care for Losev, considering him a boring, lazy, old bungler and more than once had found his company rather repulsive.

Just past the wood, Sergey Sergeich and Nadezhda met him.

'My dear fellow, why have you forgotten us?' Sergey Sergeich asked, kissing him three times and then putting both arms round his waist. 'You don't feel affection for us any more, old chap.'

He had coarse features, a fat nose and a thin, light-brown beard. He combed his hair to one side to make himself look like a typical simple Russian. When he spoke he breathed right into your face and when he wasn't speaking he'd breathe heavily through the nose. He was embarrassed by his plumpness and inordinately replete appearance and would keep thrusting out his chest to breathe more easily, which made him look pompous.

In comparison, his sister-in-law Nadezhda seemed ethereal. She was very fair, pale-faced and slim, with kind, loving eyes. Podgorin couldn't judge as to her beauty, since he'd known her since she was a child and grown used to the way she looked. Now she was wearing a white, open-necked dress and the sight of that long, white bare neck was new to him and not altogether pleasant.

'My sister and I have been waiting for you since morning,' she said. 'Varvara's here and she's been expecting you, too.'

She took his arm and suddenly laughed for no reason, uttering a faint cry of joy as if some thought had unexpectedly cast a spell over her. The fields of flowering rye, motionless in the quiet air, the sunlit wood – they were so beautiful. Nadezhda seemed to notice these things only now, as she walked at Podgorin's side.

'I'll be staying about three days,' he told her. 'I'm sorry, but I just couldn't get away from Moscow any earlier.'

'That's not very nice at all, you've forgotten we exist!' Sergey Sergeich said, reproaching him good-humouredly. '*Jamais de ma vie!*' he suddenly added, snapping his fingers. He had this habit of suddenly blurting out some irrelevance, snapping his fingers in the process. He was always mimicking someone: if he rolled his eyes, or nonchalantly tossed his hair back, or adopted a dramatic pose, that meant he had been to the theatre the night before, or to some dinner with speeches. Now he took short steps as he walked, like an old gout-ridden man, and without bending his knees – he was most likely imitating someone.

'Do you know, Tanya wouldn't believe you'd come,' Nadezhda said. 'But Varvara and I had a funny feeling about it. I somehow *knew* you'd be on that train.'

'*Jamais de ma vie!*' Sergey Sergeich repeated.

The ladies were waiting for them on the garden terrace. Ten years ago Podgorin – then a poor student – had given Nadezhda coaching in maths and history in exchange for board and lodging. Varvara, who was studying medicine at the time, happened to be taking Latin lessons from him. As for Tatyana, already a beautiful mature girl then, she could think of nothing but love. All she had desired was love and happiness and she would yearn for them, forever waiting for the husband she dreamed of night and day. Past thirty now, she was just as beautiful and attractive as ever, in her loose-fitting peignoir and with those plump, white arms. Her only thought was for her husband and two little girls. Although she was talking and smiling now, her expression revealed that she was preoccupied with other matters. She was still guarding her love and her rights to that love and was always on the alert, ready to attack any enemy who might want to take her husband and children away from her. Her love was very strong and she felt that it was reciprocated, but jealousy and fear for her children were a constant torment and prevented her from being happy.

After the noisy reunion on the terrace, everyone except Sergey Sergeich went to Tatyana's room. The sun's rays did not penetrate the lowered blinds and it was so gloomy there that all the roses in a large bunch looked the same colour. They made Podgorin sit down in an old armchair by the window; Nadezhda sat on a low stool at his feet. Besides the kindly reproaches, the jokes and laughter that reminded him so clearly of the past, he knew he could expect an unpleasant conversation about promissory notes and mortgages. It couldn't be avoided, so he thought that it might be best to get down to business there and then without delaying matters, to get it over and done with and then go out into the garden, into fresh air.

'Shall we discuss business first?' he said. 'What's new here in Kuzminki? Is something rotten in the state of Denmark?'[5]

'Kuzminki is in a bad way,' Tatyana replied, sadly sighing. 'Things are so bad it's hard to imagine they could be any worse.' She paced the room, highly agitated. 'Our estate's for sale, the auction's on 7 August. Everywhere there's advertisements, and buyers come here – they walk through the house, looking . . . Now anyone has the right to go into my room and look round. That may be legal, but it's humiliating for me and deeply insulting. We've no funds – and there's nowhere left to borrow any from. Briefly, it's shocking!'

She stopped in the middle of the room, the tears trickling from her eyes, and her voice trembled as she went on, 'I swear, I swear by all that's holy, by my children's happiness, I can't live without Kuzminki! I was born here, it's my home. If they take it away from me I shall never get over it, I'll die of despair.'

'I think you're rather looking on the black side,' Podgorin said. 'Everything will turn out all right. Your husband will get a job, you'll settle down again, lead a new life . . .'

'How *can* you say that!' Tatyana shouted. Now she looked very beautiful and aggressive. She was ready to fall on the enemy who wanted to take her husband, children and home away from her, and this was expressed with particular intensity in her face and whole figure. 'A new life! I ask you! Sergey Sergeich's been busy applying for jobs and they've promised him a position as tax inspector somewhere near Ufa[6] or Perm[7] – or thereabouts. I'm ready to go anywhere. Siberia even. I'm prepared to live there ten, twenty years, but I must be certain that sooner or later I'll return to Kuzminki. I can't live without Kuzminki. I can't, and I won't!' She shouted and stamped her foot.

'Misha, you're a lawyer,' Varvara said, 'you know all the tricks and it's your job to advise us what to do.'

There was only one fair and reasonable answer to this, that there was nothing anyone could do, but Podgorin could not bring himself to say it outright.

'I'll . . . have a think about it,' he mumbled indecisively. 'I'll have a think about it . . .'

He was really two different persons. As a lawyer he had to deal with some very ugly cases. In court and with clients he behaved arrogantly and always expressed his opinion bluntly and curtly. He was used to crudely living it up with his friends. But in his private, intimate life he displayed uncommon tact with people close to him or with very old friends. He was shy and sensitive and tended to beat about the bush. One tear, one sidelong glance, a lie or even a rude gesture was enough to make him wince and lose his nerve. Now that Nadezhda was sitting at his feet he disliked her bare neck. It palled on him and even made him feel like going home. A year ago he had happened to bump into Sergey Sergeich at a certain Madame's place in Little Bronny Street and he now felt awkward in Tatyana's company, as if *he* had been the unfaithful one. And this conversation about Kuzminki put him in the most dreadful difficulties. He was used to having ticklish, unpleasant questions decided by judge or jury, or by some legal clause, but faced with a problem that he personally had to solve he was all at sea.

'You're our friend, Misha. We all love you as if you were one of the family,' Tatyana continued. 'And I'll tell you quite candidly: all our hopes rest in you. For heaven's sake, tell us what to do. Perhaps we could write somewhere for help? Perhaps it's not too late to put the estate in Nadezhda's or Varvara's name? What shall we do?'

'Please save us, Misha, *please*,' Varvara said, lighting a cigarette. 'You were always so clever. You haven't seen much of life, you're not very experienced, but you have a fine brain. You'll help Tatyana. I know you will.'

'I must think about it . . . perhaps I can come up with something.'

They went for a walk in the garden, then in the fields. Sergey Sergeich went too. He took Podgorin's arm and led him on ahead of the others, evidently intending to discuss something with him – probably the trouble he was in. Walking with Sergey Sergeich and talking to him were an ordeal too. He kept kissing him – always three kisses at a time – took Podgorin's arm, put his own arm round his waist and breathed into his face. He seemed covered with sweet glue that would stick to you if he came close. And that look in his eyes which showed that he wanted something from Podgorin, that he was about to ask him for it, was really quite distressing – it was like having a revolver aimed at you.

The sun had set and it was growing dark. Green and red lights appeared here and there along the railway line. Varvara stopped and as she looked at the lights she started reciting:

> The line runs straight, unswerving,
> Through narrow cuttings,
> Passing posts, crossing bridges,
> While all along the verges,
> Lie buried so many Russian workers![8]

'How does it go on? Heavens, I've forgotten!'

> In scorching heat, in winter's icy blasts,
> We laboured with backs bent low.

She recited in a magnificent deep voice, with great feeling. Her face flushed brightly, her eyes filled with tears. This was the Varvara that used to be, Varvara the university student, and as he listened Podgorin thought of the past and recalled his student days, when he too knew much fine poetry by heart and loved to recite it.

> He still has not bowed his hunched back
> He's gloomily silent as before . . .

But Varvara could remember no more. She fell silent and smiled weakly, limply. After the recitation those green and red lights seemed sad.

'Oh, I've forgotten it!'

But Podgorin suddenly remembered the lines — somehow they had stuck in his memory from student days and he recited in a soft undertone,

> The Russian worker has suffered enough,
> In building this railway line.
> He will survive to build himself
> A broad bright highway
> By the sweat of his brow . . .
> Only the pity is . . .

' "The pity is," ' Varvara interrupted as she remembered the lines,

> that neither you nor I
> Will ever live to see that wonderful day.

She laughed and slapped him on the shoulder.

They went back to the house and sat down to supper. Sergey Sergeich nonchalantly stuck a corner of his serviette into his collar, imitating someone or other. 'Let's have a drink,' he said, pouring some vodka for himself and Podgorin. 'In our time, we students could hold our drink, we were fine speakers and men of action. I drink your health, old man. So why don't you drink to a stupid old idealist and wish that he will die an idealist? Can the leopard change his spots?'

Throughout supper Tatyana kept looking tenderly and jealously at her husband, anxious lest he ate or drank something that wasn't good for him. She felt that he had been spoilt by women and exhausted by them, and although this was something that appealed to her, it still distressed her. Varvara and Nadezhda also had a soft spot for him and it was obvious from the worried glances they gave him that they were scared he might suddenly get up and leave them. When he wanted to pour himself a second glass Varvara looked angry and said, 'You're poisoning yourself, Sergey Sergeich. You're a highly strung, impressionable man — you could easily become an alcoholic. Tatyana, tell him to remove that vodka.'

On the whole Sergey Sergeich had great success with women. They loved his height, his powerful build, his strong features, his idleness and his tribulations. They said that his extravagance stemmed only from extreme kindness, that he was impractical because he was an idealist. He was honest and high-principled. His inability to adapt to people or circumstances explained why he owned nothing and didn't have a steady job. They trusted him implicitly, idolized him and spoilt him with their adulation, so that he himself came to believe that he really was idealistic, impractical, honest and upright, and that he was head and shoulders above these women.

'Well, don't you have something good to say about my little girls?' Tatyana asked as she looked lovingly at her two daughters – healthy, well-fed and like two fat buns – as she heaped rice on their plates. 'Just take a good look at them. They say all mothers can never speak ill of their children. But I do assure you I'm not at all biased. My little girls are quite remarkable. Especially the elder.'

Podgorin smiled at her and the girls and thought it strange that this healthy, young, intelligent woman, essentially such a strong and complex organism, could waste all her energy, all her strength, on such uncomplicated trivial work as running a home which was well managed anyway.

'Perhaps she knows best,' he thought. 'But it's so boring, so stupid!'

> Before he had time to groan
> A bear came and knocked him prone,[9]

Sergey Sergeich said, snapping his fingers.

They finished their supper. Tatyana and Varvara made Podgorin sit down on a sofa in the drawing-room and, in hushed voices, talked about business again.

'We must save Sergey Sergeich,' Varvara said, 'it's our moral duty. He has his weaknesses, he's not thrifty, he doesn't put anything away for a rainy day, but that's only because he's so kind and generous. He's just a child, really. Give him a million and within a month there'd be nothing left, he'd have given it all away.'

'Yes, that's so true,' Tatyana said and tears rolled down her cheeks. 'I've had a hard time with him, but I must admit he's a wonderful person.'

Both Tatyana and Varvara couldn't help indulging in a little cruelty, telling Podgorin reproachfully, 'Your generation, though, Misha, isn't up to much!'

'What's all this talk about generations?' Podgorin wondered. 'Surely Sergey Sergeich's no more than six years older than me?'

'Life's not easy,' Varvara sighed. 'You're always threatened with losses of some kind. First they want to take your estate away from you, or someone near and dear falls ill and you're afraid he might die. And so it goes on, day after day. But what can one do, my friends? We must submit to a Higher Power without complaining, we must remember that nothing in this world is accidental, everything has its final purpose. Now you, Misha, know little of life, you haven't suffered much and you'll laugh at me. Go ahead and laugh, but I'm going to tell you what I think. When I was passing through a stage of deepest anxiety I experienced second sight on several occasions and this completely transformed my outlook. Now I know that nothing is contingent, everything that happens in life is necessary.'

How different this Varvara was, grey-haired now, and corseted, with her fashionable long-sleeved dress – this Varvara twisting a cigarette between long, thin, trembling fingers – this Varvara so prone to mysticism – this Varvara with such a lifeless, monotonous voice. How different she was from Varvara the medical student, that cheerful, boisterous, adventurous girl with the red hair!

'Where has it all vanished to?' Podgorin wondered, bored with listening to her. 'Sing us a song, Va,' he asked to put a stop to that conversation about second sight. 'You used to have a lovely voice.'

'That's all long ago, Misha.'

'Well, recite some more Nekrasov.'

'I've forgotten it all. Those lines I recited just now I happened to remember.'

Despite the corset and long sleeves she was obviously short of money and had difficulty making ends meet at that factory beyond Tula. It was obvious she'd been overworking. That heavy, monotonous work, that perpetual interfering with other people's business and worrying about them – all this had taken its toll and had aged her. As he looked at that sad face whose freshness had faded,

Podgorin concluded that in reality it was *she* who needed help, not Kuzminki or that Sergey Sergeich she was fussing about so much.

Higher education, being a doctor, didn't seem to have had any effect on the woman in her. Just like Tatyana, she loved weddings, births, christenings, interminable conversations about children. She loved spine-chilling stories with happy endings. In newspapers she only read articles about fires, floods and important ceremonies. She longed for Podgorin to propose to Nadezhda – she would have shed tears of emotion if that were to happen.

He didn't know whether it was by chance or Varvara's doing, but Podgorin found himself alone with Nadezhda. However, the mere suspicion that he was being watched, that they wanted something from him, disturbed and inhibited him. In Nadezhda's company he felt as if they had both been put in a cage together.

'Let's go into the garden,' she said.

They went out – he feeling discontented and annoyed that he didn't know what to say, she overjoyed, proud to be near him, and obviously delighted that he was going to spend another three days with them. And perhaps she was filled with sweet fancies and hopes. He didn't know if she loved him, but he did know that she had grown used to him, that she had long been attached to him, that she considered him her teacher, that she was now experiencing the same kind of feelings as her sister Tatyana once had: all she could think of was love, of marrying as soon as possible and having a husband, children, her own place. She had still preserved that readiness for friendship which is usually so strong in children and it was highly probable that she felt for Podgorin and respected him as a friend and that she wasn't in love with *him*, but with her dreams of a husband and children.

'It's getting dark,' he said.

'Yes, the moon rises late now.'

They kept to the same path, near the house. Podgorin didn't want to go deep into the garden – it was dark there and he would have to take Nadezhda by the arm and stay very close to her. Shadows were moving on the terrace and he felt that Tatyana and Varvara were watching him.

'I must ask your advice,' Nadezhda said, stopping. 'If Kuzminki is sold, Sergey Sergeich will leave and get a job and there's no doubt that our lives will be completely changed. I shan't go with my sister, we'll part, because I don't want to be a burden on her family. I'll take a job somewhere in Moscow. I'll earn some money and help Tatyana and her husband. You *will* give me some advice, won't you?'

Quite unaccustomed to any kind of hard work, now she was inspired at the thought of an independent, working life and making plans for the future – this was written all over her face. A life where she would be working and helping others struck her as so beautifully poetic. When he saw that pale face and dark eyebrows so close he remembered what an intelligent, keen pupil she had been, with such fine qualities, a joy to teach. Now she probably wasn't simply a young lady in search of a husband, but an intelligent, decent girl, gentle and soft-hearted, who could be moulded like wax into anything one wished. In the right surroundings she might become a truly wonderful woman!

'Well, why *don't* I marry her then?' Podgorin thought. But he immediately took fright at this idea and went off towards the house. Tatyana was sitting at the grand piano in the drawing-room and her playing conjured up bright pictures of the past, when people had played, sung and danced in that room until late at night, with the windows open and birds singing too in the garden and beyond the river. Podgorin cheered up, became playful, danced with Nadezhda and Varvara, and then sang. He was hampered by a corn on one foot and asked if he could wear Sergey Sergeich's slippers. Strangely, he felt at home, like one of the family, and the thought 'a typical brother-in-law' flashed through his mind. His spirits rose even higher. Looking at him the others livened up and grew cheerful, as if they had recaptured their youth. Everyone's face was radiant with hope: Kuzminki was saved! It was all so very simple in fact. They only had to think of a plan, rummage around in law books, or see that Podgorin married Nadezhda. And that little romance was going well, by all appearances. Pink, happy, her eyes brimming with tears in anticipation of something quite out of the ordinary, Nadezhda whirled round in the dance and her white dress billowed, revealing her small pretty legs in flesh-coloured stockings. Absolutely delighted, Varvara took Podgorin's arm and told him quietly and meaningly, 'Misha, don't run away from happiness. Grasp it while you can. If you wait too long you'll be running when it's too late to catch it.'

Podgorin wanted to make promises, to reassure her and even he began to believe that Kuzminki was saved – it was really so easy.

'"And thou shalt be que-een of the world",'[10] he sang, striking a pose. But suddenly he was conscious that there was nothing he could do for these people, absolutely nothing, and he stopped singing and looked guilty.

Then he sat silently in one corner, legs tucked under him, wearing slippers belonging to someone else.

As they watched him the others understood that nothing could be done and they too fell silent. The piano was closed. Everyone noticed that it was late – it was time for bed – and Tatyana put out the large lamp in the drawing-room.

A bed was made up for Podgorin in the same little outhouse where he had stayed in the past. Sergey Sergeich went with him to wish him goodnight, holding a candle high above his head, although the moon had risen and it was bright. They walked down a path with lilac bushes on either side and the gravel crunched underfoot.

> Before he had time to groan
> A bear came and knocked him prone,

Sergey Sergeich said.

Podgorin felt that he'd heard those lines a thousand times, he was sick and tired of them! When they reached the outhouse, Sergey Sergeich drew a bottle and two glasses from his loose jacket and put them on the table.

'Brandy,' he said. 'It's a Double-O. It's impossible to have a drink in the house with Varvara around. She'd be on to me about alcoholism. But we can feel free here. It's a fine brandy.'

They sat down. The brandy was very good.

'Let's have a really good drink tonight,' Sergey Sergeich continued, nibbling a lemon. 'I've always been a gay dog myself and I like having a fling now and again. That's a *must*!'

But the look in his eyes still showed that he needed something from Podgorin and was about to ask for it.

'Drink up, old man,' he went on, sighing. 'Things are really grim at the moment. Old eccentrics like me have had their day, we're finished. Idealism's not fashionable these days. It's money that rules and if you don't want to get shoved aside you must go down on your knees and worship filthy lucre. But I can't do that, it's absolutely sickening!'

'When's the auction?' asked Podgorin, to change the subject.

'August 7th. But there's no hope at all, old man, of saving Kuzminki. There's enormous arrears and the estate doesn't bring in any income, only losses every year. It's not worth the battle. Tatyana's very cut up about it, as it's her patrimony of course. But I must admit I'm rather glad. I'm no country man. My sphere is the large, noisy city, my element's the fray!'

He kept on and on, still beating about the bush and he watched Podgorin with an eagle eye, as if waiting for the right moment.

Suddenly Podgorin saw those eyes close to him and felt his breath on his face.

'My dear fellow, please save me,' Sergey Sergeich gasped. '*Please* lend me two hundred roubles!'

Podgorin wanted to say that he was hard up too and he felt that he might do better giving two hundred roubles to some poor devil or simply losing them at cards. But he was terribly embarrassed – he felt trapped in that small room with one candle and wanted to escape as soon as possible from that breathing, from those soft arms that grasped him around the waist and which already seemed to have stuck to him like glue. Hurriedly he started feeling in his pockets for his notecase where he kept money.

'Here you are,' he muttered, taking out a hundred roubles. 'I'll give you the rest later. That's all I have on me. You see, I can't refuse.' Feeling very annoyed and beginning to lose his temper he went on. 'I'm really far too soft. Only please let me have the money back later. I'm hard up too.'

'Thank you. I'm so grateful, dear chap.'

'And please stop imagining that you're an idealist. You're as much an idealist as I'm a turkey-cock. You're simply a frivolous, indolent man, that's all.'

Sergey Sergeich sighed deeply and sat on the couch.

'My dear chap, you *are* angry,' he said. 'But if you only knew how hard things are for me! I'm going through a terrible time now. I swear it's not myself I feel sorry for, oh no! It's the wife and children. If it wasn't for my wife and children I'd have done myself in ages ago.' Suddenly his head and shoulders started shaking and he burst out sobbing.

'This really is the limit!' Podgorin said, pacing the room excitedly and feeling really furious. 'Now, what can I do with someone who has caused a great deal of harm and then starts sobbing? These tears disarm me, I'm speechless. You're sobbing, so that means you must be right.'

'Caused a great deal of harm?' Sergey Sergeich asked, rising to his feet and looking at Podgorin in amazement. 'My dear chap, what are you saying? Caused a great deal of harm? Oh, how little you know me. How little you understand me!'

'All right then, so I don't understand you, but please stop whining. It's revolting!'

'Oh, how little you know me!' Sergey Sergeich repeated, quite sincerely. 'How little!'

'Just take a look at yourself in the mirror,' Podgorin went on. 'You're no longer a young man. Soon you'll be old. It's time you stopped to think a bit and took stock of who and what you are. Spending your whole life doing nothing at all, forever indulging in empty, childish chatter, this play-acting and affectation. Doesn't it make your head go round – aren't you sick and tired of it all? Oh, it's hard going with you! You're a stupefying old bore, you are!'

With these words Podgorin left the outhouse and slammed the door. It was about the first time in his life that he had been sincere and really spoken his mind.

Shortly afterwards he was regretting having been so harsh. What was the point of talking seriously or arguing with a man who was perpetually lying, who ate and drank too much, who spent large amounts of other people's money while being quite convinced that he was an idealist and a martyr? This was a case of stupidity, or of deep-rooted bad habits that had eaten away at his organism like an illness past all cure. In any event, indignation and stern rebukes were useless in this case. Laughing at him would be more effective. One good sneer would have achieved much more than a dozen sermons!

'It's best just ignoring him,' Podgorin thought. 'Above all, not to lend him money.'

Soon afterwards he wasn't thinking about Sergey Sergeich, or about his hundred roubles. It was a calm, brooding night, very bright. Whenever Podgorin looked up at the sky on moonlit nights he had the feeling that only he and the moon were awake – everything else was either sleeping or drowsing. He gave no more thought to people or money and his mood gradually became calm and peaceful. He felt alone in this world and the sound of his own footsteps in the silence of the night seemed so mournful.

The garden was enclosed by a white stone wall. In the right-hand corner, facing the fields, stood a tower that had been built long ago, in the days of serfdom. Its lower section was of stone; the top was wooden, with a platform, a conical roof and a tall spire with a black weathercock. Down below were two gates leading straight from the garden into the fields and a staircase that creaked underfoot led up to the platform. Under the staircase some old broken armchairs had been dumped and they were bathed in the moonlight as it filtered through the gate. With their crooked upturned legs these armchairs seemed to have come to life at night and were lying in wait for someone here in the silence.

Podgorin climbed the stairs to the platform and sat down. Just beyond the fence were a boundary ditch and bank and further off were the broad fields flooded in moonlight. Podgorin knew that there was a wood exactly opposite, about two miles from the estate, and he thought that he could distinguish a dark strip in the distance. Quails and corncrakes were calling. Now and then, from the direction of the wood, came the cry of a cuckoo which couldn't sleep either.

He heard footsteps. Someone was coming across the garden towards the tower.

A dog barked.

'Beetle!' a woman's voice softly called. 'Come back, Beetle!'

He could hear someone entering the tower down below and a moment later a black dog – an old friend of Podgorin's – appeared on the bank. It stopped, looked up towards where Podgorin was sitting and wagged its tail amicably. Soon afterwards a white figure rose from the black ditch like a ghost and stopped on the bank as well. It was Nadezhda.

'Can you see something there?' she asked the dog, glancing upwards.

She didn't see Podgorin but probably sensed that he was near, since she was smiling and her pale, moonlit face was happy. The tower's black shadow stretching over the earth, far into the fields, that motionless white figure with the blissfully smiling, pale face, the black dog and both their shadows – all this was just like a dream.

'Someone *is* there,' Nadezhda said softly.

She stood waiting for him to come down or to call her up to him, so that he could at last declare his love – then both would be happy on that calm, beautiful night. White, pale, slender, very lovely in the moonlight, she awaited his caresses. She was weary of perpetually dreaming of love and happiness and was unable to conceal her feelings any longer. Her whole figure, her radiant eyes, her fixed happy smile, betrayed her innermost thoughts. But he felt awkward, shrank back and didn't make a sound, not knowing whether to speak, whether to make the habitual joke out of the situation or whether to remain silent. He felt annoyed and his only thought was that here, in a country garden on a moonlit night, close to a beautiful, loving, thoughtful girl, he felt the same apathy as on Little Bronny Street: evidently this type of romantic situation had lost its fascination, like *that* prosaic depravity. Of no consequence to him now were those meetings on moonlit nights, those white shapes with slim waists, those mysterious shadows, towers, country estates and characters such as Sergey Sergeich, and people like himself, Podgorin, with his icy indifference, his constant irritability, his inability to adapt to reality and take what it had to offer, his wearisome, obsessive craving for what did not and never could exist on earth. And now, as he sat in that tower, he would have preferred a good fireworks display, or some moonlight procession, or Varvara reciting Nekrasov's *The Railway* again. He would rather another woman was standing there on the bank where Nadezhda was: this other woman would have told him something absolutely fascinating and new that had nothing to do with love or happiness. And if she did happen to speak of love, this would have been a summons to those new, lofty, rational aspects of existence on whose threshold we are perhaps already living and of which we sometimes seem to have premonitions.

'There's no one there,' Nadezhda said.

She stood there for another minute or so, then she walked quietly towards the wood, her head bowed. The dog ran on ahead. Podgorin could see her white figure for quite a long time. 'To think how it's all turned out, though . . .' he repeated to himself as he went back to the outhouse.

He had no idea what he could say to Sergey Sergeich or Tatyana the next day or the day after that, or how he would treat Nadezhda. And he felt embarrassed, frightened and bored in advance. How was he going to fill those three long days which he had promised to spend here? He remembered the conversation about second sight and Sergey Sergeich quoting the lines:

> Before he had time to groan
> A bear came and knocked him prone.

He remembered that tomorrow, to please Tatyana, he would have to smile at those well-fed, chubby little girls – and he decided to leave.

At half past five in the morning Sergey Sergeich appeared on the terrace of the main house in his Bokhara dressing-gown and tasselled fez. Not losing a moment, Podgorin went over to him to say goodbye.

'I have to be in Moscow by ten,' he said, looking away. 'I'd completely forgotten I'm expected at the Notary Public's office. Please excuse me. When the others are up please tell them that I apologize. I'm dreadfully sorry.'

In his hurry he didn't hear Sergey Sergeich's answer and he kept looking round at the windows of the big house, afraid that the ladies might wake up and stop him going. He was ashamed he felt so nervous. He sensed that this was his last visit to Kuzminki, that he would never come back. As he drove away he glanced back several times at the outhouse where once he had spent so many happy days. But deep down he felt coldly indifferent, not at all sad.

At home the first thing he saw on the table was the note he'd received the day before: 'Dear Misha,' he read. 'You've completely forgotten us, please come and visit us soon.' And for some reason he remembered Nadezhda whirling round in the dance, her dress billowing, revealing her legs in their flesh-coloured stockings . . .

Ten minutes later he was at his desk working – and he didn't give Kuzminki another thought.

Ionych

When visitors to the county town of S— complained of the monotony and boredom of life there, the local people would reply, as if in self-defence, that the very opposite was the case, that life there was in fact extremely good, that the town had a library, a theatre, a club, that there was the occasional ball and – finally – that there were intelligent, interesting and agreeable families with whom to make friends. And they would single out the Turkins as the most cultivated and gifted family.

This family lived in its own house on the main street, next door to the Governor's. Ivan Petrovich Turkin, a stout, handsome, dark-haired man with sideburns, would organize amateur theatricals for charity – and he himself played the parts of elderly generals, when he would cough most amusingly. He had a copious stock of funny stories, riddles and proverbs, was a great wag and humorist, and you could never tell from his expression whether he was serious or joking. His wife, Vera Iosifovna, a thin, attractive woman with pince-nez, wrote short stories and novels which she loved reading to her guests. Their young daughter Yekaterina Ivanovna played the piano. In short, each Turkin had some particular talent. The Turkins were convivial hosts and cheerfully displayed their talents to their guests with great warmth and lack of pretension. Their large stone house was spacious, and cool in summer. Half of its windows opened onto a shady old garden where nightingales sang in spring. When they had visitors the clatter of knives came from the kitchen and the yard would smell of fried onion – all of which invariably heralded a lavish and tasty supper.

And no sooner had Dr Dmitry Ionych Startsev been appointed local medical officer and taken up residence at Dyalizh, about six miles away, then he too was told that — as a man of culture — he simply *must* meet the Turkins. One winter's day he was introduced to Ivan Petrovich in the street. They chatted about the weather, the theatre, cholera — and an invitation followed. One holiday in spring (it was Ascension Day), after seeing his patients, Startsev set off for town to relax a little and at the same time to do a spot of shopping. He went there on foot, without hurrying himself (as yet he had no carriage and pair), and all the way he kept humming: ''Ere I had drunk from life's cup of tears.'[1]

In town he dined, took a stroll in the park, and then he suddenly remembered Ivan Petrovich's invitation and decided to call on the Turkins and see what kind of people they were.

'Good day — if you please!' Ivan Petrovich said, meeting him on the front steps. 'Absolutely, overwhelmingly delighted to see such a charming visitor! Come in, I'll introduce you to my good lady wife. Verochka,' he went on, introducing the doctor to his wife, 'I've been telling him that he has no right at all under Roman law to stay cooped up in that hospital — he should devote his leisure time to socializing. Isn't that so, my sweet?'

'Please sit here,' Vera Iosifovna said, seating the guest beside her. 'You are permitted to flirt with me. My husband's as jealous as Othello, but we'll try and behave so that he doesn't notice a thing.'

'Oh, my sweet little chick-chick!' Ivan Petrovich muttered tenderly, planting a kiss on her forehead. 'You've timed your visit to perfection!' he added, turning once more to his guest. 'My good lady wife's written a real whopper of a novel and she's going to read it out loud this evening.'

'Jean, my pet,' Vera Iosifovna told her husband. '*Dites que l'on nous donne du thé.*'

Startsev was introduced to Yekaterina Ivanovna, an eighteen-year-old girl who was the image of her mother — and just as thin and attractive. Her waist was slim and delicate, and her expression was still that of a child. And her youthful, already well-developed, beautiful, healthy bosom hinted at spring, true spring. Then they had tea with jam, honey, chocolates, and very tasty pastries that simply melted in one's mouth.

Towards evening more guests began to arrive and Ivan Petrovich would look at them with his laughing eyes and say: 'Good evening – if you please!'

Then they all sat in the drawing-room with very serious expressions, and Vera Iosifovna read from her novel, which began: 'The frost was getting harder . . .' The windows were wide open and they could hear the clatter of knives in the kitchen; the smell of fried onion drifted over from the yard . . . To be sitting in those soft armchairs was highly relaxing and the lamps winked so very invitingly in the twilight of the drawing-room; and now, on an early summer's evening, when the sound of voices and laughter came from the street and the scent of lilac wafted in from outside, it was difficult to understand all that claptrap about how the frost was getting harder and 'the setting sun was illuminating with its cold rays the lonely wayfarer crossing a snowy plain'. Vera Iosifovna read how a beautiful young countess established schools, hospitals and libraries in her village and how she fell in love with a wandering artist. She read of things that never happen in real life. All the same, it was pleasantly soothing to hear about them – and they evoked such serene and delightful thoughts that one was reluctant to get up.

'Not awfully baddish!' Ivan Petrovich said softly.

One of the guests, whose thoughts were wandering far, far away as he listened, remarked: 'Yes . . . indeed . . .'

One hour passed, then another. In the municipal park close by a band was playing and a choir was singing. For five minutes after Vera Iosifovna had closed her manuscript everyone sat in silence listening to the choir singing 'By Rushlight', a song that conveyed what really happens in life and what was absent from the novel.

'Do you have your works published in magazines?' Startsev asked Vera Iosifovna.

'No,' she replied. 'I don't publish them anywhere . . . I hide away what I've written in a cupboard. And why publish?' she explained. 'It's not as if we need the money.'

And for some reason everyone sighed.

'And now, Pussycat, play us something,' Ivan Petrovich told his daughter.

They raised the piano lid and opened some music that happened to be lying there ready. Yekaterina Ivanovna sat down and struck the keys with both hands. And then she immediately struck them again, with all her might – and again and again. Her shoulders and bosom quivered, relentlessly she kept hammering away in the same place and it seemed that she had no intention of stopping until she had driven those keys deep into the piano. The drawing-room was filled with the sound of thunder. Everything reverberated – floor, ceiling, furniture. Yekaterina Ivanovna played a long, difficult, monotonous passage that was interesting solely on account of its difficulty. As Startsev listened he visualized large boulders rolling from the top of a high mountain, rolling and forever rolling – and he wanted the rolling to quickly stop. And at the same time, Yekaterina Ivanovna, her face pink from the exertion, strong and brimful of energy, with a lock of hair tumbling onto her forehead, struck him as most attractive. And how pleasant and refreshing it was, after a winter spent in Dyalizh among patients and peasants, to be sitting in that drawing-room, to be looking at that young, exquisite and most probably innocent creature, to be listening to those deafening, tiresome, yet civilized sounds.

'Well, Pussycat! You've really excelled yourself today!' Ivan Petrovich said with tears in his eyes, rising to his feet when his daughter had finished. ' "Die now Denis, you'll never write better!" '[2]

They all surrounded and congratulated her, expressed their admiration and assured her that it was a long, long time since they had heard such a performance, while she listened in silence, faintly smiling – and triumph was written all over her figure.

'Wonderful! Excellent!' Startsev exclaimed too, yielding to the general mood of enthusiasm.

'Where did you study music?' he asked Yekaterina. 'At the Conservatoire?'

'No, I'm still only preparing for it, but in the meantime I've been having lessons with Madame Zavlovsky.'

'Did you go to the local high school?'

'Oh no!' intervened Vera Iosifovna. 'We engaged private tutors. At high school or boarding-school, you must agree, one could meet with bad influences. A growing girl should be under the influence of her mother and no one else.'

'I'm going to the Conservatoire all the same,' Yekaterina retorted.

'No, Pussycat loves her Mama. Pussycat's not going to upset Mama and Papa, is she?'

'I *will* go, I *will*!' replied Yekaterina half-joking, acting like a naughty child and stamping her little foot.

Over supper Ivan Petrovich was able to display his talents. He told funny stories, laughing only with his eyes; he joked, he set absurd riddles and solved them himself, perpetually talking in his own weird lingo that had been cultivated by lengthy practice in the fine art of wit and which had evidently become second nature to him by now:

'A real whopper! – not awfully baddish! – thanking you most convulsively!'

But that was not all. When the guests, replete and contented, crowded in the hall, sorting out their coats and canes, Pavlushka the footman (or Peacock as he was nicknamed), a boy of about fourteen with cropped hair and chubby cheeks, kept bustling around them.

'Now, Peacock, perform!' Ivan Petrovich told him.

Peacock struck a pose and raised one arm aloft.

'Die, wretched woman!' he declaimed in tragic accents. And everyone roared with laughter.

'Most entertaining!' thought Startsev as he went out into the street. He called at a restaurant and drank some beer before setting off for Dyalizh. All the way he kept humming: 'Thy voice for me is dear and languorous.'[3]

After a six-mile walk he went to bed, not feeling in the least tired: on the contrary, he felt that he could have walked another thirteen miles with the greatest pleasure.

'Not awfully baddish!' he remembered as he dozed off. And he burst out laughing.

II

Startsev had always been intending to visit the Turkins again, but he was so overloaded with work in the hospital that it was impossible to find a spare moment. This way more than a year passed in hard work and solitude. But one day someone from town brought him a letter in a light blue envelope.

Vera Iosifovna had long been suffering from migraine but recently, when Pussycat had been scaring her every day by threatening to go off to the Conservatoire, the attacks had become much more frequent. Every doctor in town called on the Turkins, until finally it was the district doctor's turn. Vera Iosifovna wrote him a touching letter, begging him to come and relieve her sufferings. So Startsev went and subsequently became a very frequent visitor at the Turkins' – very frequent. In point of fact, he did help Vera Iosifovna a little and she told all her friends that he was an exceptional, a truly wonderful doctor. But it was no longer the migraine that brought Startsev to the Turkins'.

He had the day off. Yekaterina Ivanovna finished her interminable, tiresome piano exercises, after which they all sat in the dining-room for a long time drinking tea, while Ivan Petrovich told one of his funny stories. But then the front door bell rang and Ivan Petrovich had to go into the hall to welcome some new visitor. Startsev took advantage of the momentary distraction and whispered to Yekaterina Ivanovna in great agitation:

'Don't torment me, for Christ's sake. I beg you! Let's go into the garden.'

She shrugged her shoulders as if at a loss to understand what he wanted from her; still, she got up and went out.

'You usually play the piano for three or four hours at a time,' he said as he followed her, 'then you sit with your mama, so I have no chance to talk to you. Please spare me a mere quarter of an hour. I beg you!'

Autumn was approaching and all was quiet and sad in the old garden; dark leaves lay thick on the paths. Already the evenings were drawing in.

'I haven't seen you the whole week,' Startsev continued. 'If you only knew what hell I've been through! Let's sit down. Please listen to what I have to say.'

Both of them had their favourite spot in the garden – the bench under the broad, old maple. And now they sat down on this bench.

'What do you want?' Yekaterina Ivanovna asked in a dry, matter-of-fact tone.

'I haven't seen you the whole week. It's been so long since I heard you speak. I passionately want to hear your voice, I *thirst* for it! Please speak.'

She captivated him by her freshness, by that naïve expression of her eyes and cheeks. Even in the way she wore her dress he saw something exceptionally charming, touching in its simplicity and innocent grace. And at the same time, despite her naïveté, she struck him as extremely intelligent and mature for her age. With someone like her he could discuss literature, art – anything he liked in fact; he could complain to her about life, about people, although during serious conversations she would sometimes suddenly start laughing quite inappropriately and run back to the house. Like almost all the young ladies of S— she read a great deal (on the whole the people of S— read very little and they said in the local library that if it weren't for girls and young Jews they might as well close the place down). This pleased Startsev immeasurably and every time they met he would excitedly ask her what she had been reading over the past few days and he would listen enchanted when she told him.

'What did you read that week we didn't meet?' he asked her now. 'Tell me, I beg you.'

'I read Pisemsky.'[4]

'And what precisely?'

'*A Thousand Souls*,' Pussycat replied. 'And what a funny name Pisemsky had: Aleksey Feofilaktych!'

'But where are you going?' Startsev cried out in horror when she suddenly got up and went towards the house. 'I must talk to you . . . there's something I must explain . . . Please stay, for just five minutes! I implore you!'

She stopped as if she wanted to say something. Then she awkwardly thrust a little note into his hand and ran off into the house, where she sat down at the piano again.

'Be at the cemetery tonight at eleven o'clock by the Demetti tomb,' read Startsev.

'Well, that's really rather silly,' he thought, collecting himself. 'Why the *cemetery*? What for?'

Pussycat was obviously playing one of her little games. Who in their right mind would want to arrange a rendezvous at night in a cemetery, miles from town, when they could easily have met in the street or the municipal park? And did it become him, a district doctor, an intelligent, respectable person, to be sighing, receiving billets-doux, hanging around cemeteries, doing things so silly that even schoolboys would laugh at them these days! What would his colleagues say if they found out?

These were Startsev's thoughts as he wandered around the tables at the club. But at half past ten he suddenly upped and went to the cemetery.

He now had his own carriage and pair – and a coachman called Panteleymon, who wore a velvet waistcoat. The moon was shining. It was quiet and warm but autumn was in the air. Near the abattoirs in one of the suburbs dogs were howling. Startsev left his carriage in a lane on the edge of town and walked the rest of the way to the cemetery. 'Everyone has his peculiar side,' he thought. 'Pussycat's rather weird too and – who knows? – perhaps she's not joking and she'll turn up.' And he surrendered to this feeble, vain hope – and it intoxicated him.

For a quarter of a mile he walked over the fields. The cemetery[5] appeared in the distance as a dark strip – like a forest or large garden. The white stone wall, the gates came into view . . . In the moonlight he could read on the gates: 'The hour is coming when . . .'[6] Startsev passed through a wicket-gate and what first caught his eye were the white crosses and tombstones on either side of a wide avenue and the black shadows cast by them and the poplars. All around, far and wide, he could see black and white, and the sleepy trees lowered their branches over the white beneath them. It seemed lighter here than in the open fields. The paw-like leaves of the maples stood out sharply against the yellow sand of the avenues and against the gravestones, while inscriptions on monuments were clearly visible. Immediately Startsev was struck by what he was seeing for the first time in his life and what he would probably never see again: a world that was unlike any other, a world where the moonlight was so exquisite and soft it seemed to have its cradle here; a world where there was no life – no, not one living thing – but where, in every dark poplar, in every grave, one sensed the presence of some secret that promised peaceful, beautiful, eternal life. From those stones and faded flowers, mingling with the smell of autumnal leaves, there breathed forgiveness, sadness and peace.

All around was silence. The stars looked down from the heavens in profound humility and Startsev's footsteps rang out so sharply, so jarringly here. Only when the chapel clock began to strike and he imagined himself dead and buried here for ever did he have the feeling that someone was watching him and for a minute he thought that here was neither peace nor tranquillity, only the mute anguish of non-existence, of stifled despair . . .

Demetti's tomb was in the form of a shrine surmounted by an angel. An Italian opera company had once passed through S— and one of the female singers had died. She had been buried here and they had erected this monument. No longer was she remembered in town, but the lamp over the entrance to the shrine reflected the moonlight and seemed to be burning.

No one was there. And how could anyone think of coming here at midnight? But Startsev waited – and as if the moonlight were kindling his desires he waited passionately, imagining kisses and embraces. He sat by the monument for about half an hour, then he wandered along side-paths, hat in hand, waiting and reflecting how many women and young girls who had once been beautiful and enchanting, who had loved and burnt at night with passion, who had yielded to caresses, lay buried here. And in effect, what a terrible joke Nature plays on man – and how galling to be conscious of it!

These were Startsev's thoughts – and at the same time he wanted to shout out loud that he yearned for love, that he was waiting for love and that he must have it at all costs. Now he no longer saw slabs of white marble, but beautiful bodies; he saw figures coyly hiding in the shadows of the trees. He felt their warmth – and this yearning became all too much to bear . . .

And then, just as if a curtain had been lowered, the moon vanished behind the clouds and suddenly everything went dark. Startsev had difficulty finding the gate – all around it was dark, the darkness of an autumn night. Then he wandered around for an hour and a half, looking for the lane where he had left the carriage and pair.

'I'm so exhausted I can barely stand,' he told Panteleymon. And as he happily settled down in the carriage he thought: 'Oh, I really ought to lose some weight!'

III

Next evening he went to the Turkins' to propose to Yekaterina Ivanovna. But it happened to be an inconvenient time, since Yekaterina Ivanovna was in her room with her hairdresser having her hair done. That evening she was going to a dance at the club.

So once again he was condemned to a tea-drinking session in the dining-room. Noticing that his guest was bored and in a thoughtful mood Ivan Petrovich took some small pieces of paper from his waistcoat pocket and read out a comical letter from a German estate manager, that 'all the machinations on the estate were ruinated' and that 'all the proprieties had collapsed'.

'I bet they'll come up with a good dowry,' Startsev thought, listening absent-mindedly.

After a sleepless night he was in a state of stupor, just as if he had been given some sweetly cloying sleeping draught. His feelings were confused, but warm and joyful – and at the same time a cold, obdurate, small section of his brain kept reasoning: 'Stop before it's too late! Is she the right kind of wife for you? She's spoilt, capricious, she sleeps until two in the afternoon. But you're a sacristan's son, a country doctor . . .'

'Well, what of it?' he thought. 'It doesn't matter.'

'What's more, if you marry her,' continued the small voice, 'her family will make you give up your country practice and you'll have to move to town.'

'What of it?' he thought. 'Nothing wrong with living in town. And there'll be a dowry, we'll set up house together . . .'

At last in came Yekaterina Ivanovna, wearing a ball gown, décolletée, looking very pretty and elegant. Startsev couldn't admire her enough and such was his delight that he was at a loss for words and could only look on and smile.

She began to make her farewells and he stood up – there was nothing more for him to stay for – saying that it was time he went home as his patients were waiting.

'Well, it can't be helped, you'd better go,' said Ivan Petrovich. 'At the same time you could give Pussycat a lift to the club.'

Outside it was drizzling and very dark, and only from Panteleymon's hoarse cough could they tell where the carriage was. They put the hood up.

'Such a fright will set you alight,' Ivan Petrovich said, seating his daughter in the carriage. 'If you lie – it's as nice as pie . . . ! Off you go now. Goodbye – if you please!'

They drove off.

'Last night I went to the cemetery,' Startsev began. 'How unkind, how heartless of you!'

'You went to the cemetery?'

'Yes, I went and waited for you until two o'clock. It was sheer hell.'

Delighted to have played such a cunning trick on the man who loved her, and that she was the object of such fervent passion, Yekaterina Ivanovna burst out laughing – and then she suddenly screamed with terror, for just then the horses turned sharply through the club gates, making the carriage lurch violently. Startsev put his arms around Yekaterina Ivanovna's waist as she clung to him in her fright.

He could not control himself and kissed her lips and chin passionately, holding her in an even tighter embrace.

'That will do!' she said curtly.

A moment later she was gone from the carriage and the policeman standing at the lighted entrance to the club shouted at Panteleymon in a very ugly voice:

'What yer stopped there for, you oaf! Move on!'

Startsev went home but he soon returned. Wearing borrowed coat and tails and a stiff white cravat which somehow kept sticking up as if wanting to slide off his collar, he sat at midnight in the club lounge and told Yekaterina Ivanovna in passionate terms:

'Oh, those who have never loved – how little do they know! I think that no one has ever truly described love – and how could anyone describe that tender, joyful, agonizing feeling! Anyone who has but once experienced it would never even think of putting it into words! But what's the point of preambles and descriptions? Why this superfluous eloquence? My love has no bounds. I'm asking you, begging you,' Startsev at last managed to say, 'to be my wife!'

'Dmitry Ionych,' Yekaterina Ivanovna said with a very serious expression after pausing for thought, 'Dmitry Ionych, I'm most grateful for the honour and I respect you, but . . .' She stood up and continued standing. 'I'm sorry, I cannot be your wife. Let's talk seriously. As you know, Dmitry Ionych, I love art more than anything in the world. I'm mad about music, I simply adore it. I've dedicated my whole life to it. I want to be a concert pianist. I want fame, success, freedom. But you want me to go on living in this town, to carry on with this empty, useless life that's become quite unbearable for me. To be your *wife* . . . oh no, I'm sorry! One must always aspire towards some lofty, brilliant goal, but family life would tie me down for ever. Dmitry Ionych' (at this she produced a barely perceptible smile since, when saying Dmitry Ionych the name Aleksey Feofilaktych came to mind), 'Dmitry Ionych, you're a kind, honourable, clever man, you're the best of all . . .' (here her eyes filled with tears), 'I feel for you with all my heart, but . . . but you must understand . . .'

And to avoid bursting into tears she turned away and walked out of the lounge.

Startsev's heart stopped pounding. As he went out of the club into the street the first thing he did was tear off that stiff cravat and heave a deep sigh of relief. He felt rather ashamed and his pride was hurt

– he had not expected a refusal. And he just could not believe that all his dreams, yearnings and hopes had led to such a stupid conclusion, as if it were all a trivial little play performed by amateurs. And he regretted having felt as he did, he regretted having loved – so much so that he came close to sobbing out loud or walloping Panteleymon's back as hard as he could with his umbrella.

For three days he could not put his mind to anything, he could neither sleep nor eat. But when the rumour reached him that Yekaterina Ivanovna had gone to Moscow to enrol at the Conservatoire he calmed down and carried on with his life as before.

Later, when he occasionally recalled how he had wandered around the cemetery or had driven all over town in search of coat and tails, he would stretch lazily and say: 'Really! All that fuss!'

IV

Four years passed. Startsev now had a large practice in town. Every morning he hastily saw patients at his surgery in Dyalizh, then he drove to see his patients in town – no longer conveyed by carriage and pair, but by three horses abreast – and with bells! He would come home late at night. He had filled out, put on weight and he was reluctant to walk anywhere, as he had become short-winded. And Panteleymon had filled out too, and the more his girth expanded the more mournfully he sighed and complained of his bitter lot: all that driving was too much for him!

Startsev visited many different houses and met many people, but he did not strike up a close friendship with anyone. The townspeople's conversations, attitude to life, even their appearance, irritated him. Gradually, experience had taught him that as long as one only played cards or enjoyed a meal with any resident of that town, then that person would be inoffensive, good-natured and even quite intelligent. But the moment one started a conversation about something that was inedible, such as politics or science, then the other person would either be stumped or give vent to such absurd and vicious ideas that one could only give it up as a bad job and make one's exit. Whenever Startsev tried to start a conversation, even with a citizen of liberal views – for example, concerning the immense progress that humanity was making, thank God, and that, given time, it would be able to dispense with passports or the death penalty – he would be greeted with distrustful, sidelong glances and asked: 'In that case, anyone could cut the throat of anyone he wanted to in the street, couldn't he?' And whenever he had supper or tea in company and ventured to say that one had to work hard, that life was impossible without hard work, everyone took it as a personal insult, got angry and launched into the most tiresome disputations. Yet these townspeople did nothing, absolutely nothing, and they were interested in nothing. So Startsev avoided conversations (it was impossible to think of anything to discuss with them), confining himself to eating and playing whist with them. Whenever he happened to be in a house where there was some family celebration and he was invited to stay for supper, he would sit down and eat in silence, staring blankly at his plate. And everything they happened to be discussing struck him as uninteresting, unfair, stupid; but despite his irritation and exasperation he remained silent. These stony silences and his habit of staring at his plate earned him the name 'Snooty Pole' in that town, although he had never been Polish.

He shunned diversions such as the theatre and concerts, but took great pleasure in playing whist every evening, until two o'clock in the morning. But there was one other diversion to which he became gradually, imperceptibly drawn. This was in the evenings, when he took from his pockets the banknotes he had earned from his practice – and his pockets often happened to be stuffed with seventy roubles' worth of yellow or green notes that reeked of perfume, vinegar, incense and train oil. When he had amassed a few hundred he would take them to the Mutual Credit Bank and pay them into his current account.

During the entire four years after Yekaterina Ivanovna's departure for Moscow he visited the Turkins only twice, at the invitation of Vera Iosifovna, whom he was still treating for migraine. Every summer Yekaterina Ivanovna would come to stay with her parents but as things turned out he did not see her even once.

But four years had now passed. One calm, warm morning he was brought a letter at the hospital, in which Vera Iosifovna wrote that she missed him very much and begged him to come and see her without fail and relieve her sufferings – that day happened to be her birthday. There was a PS: 'I join in Mama's request. K.'

Startsev thought for a while and that evening he drove over to the Turkins'.

'Ah, good evening – if you please!' Ivan Petrovich greeted him. Only his eyes were smiling. '*Bonjourez-vous!*'

Vera Iosifovna had aged considerably and her hair was white now. She shook Startsev's hand, and sighed affectedly.

'Doctor!' she exclaimed. 'You don't want to flirt with me, you never call on us, so I must be too old for you. But my young daughter's arrived, perhaps she'll have more luck!'

And Pussycat? She had grown thinner, paler, prettier and shapelier. But now she was a fully-fledged Yekaterina Ivanovna and not a Pussycat. Gone were that freshness and expression of childlike innocence. And in her look and manners there was something new, a hesitancy and air of guilt, as if here, in the Turkins' house, she no longer felt at home.

'It's been simply ages!' she said, offering Startsev her hand – and her heart was visibly pounding. Peering into his face intently, quizzically, she continued: 'How you've put on weight! You've acquired a tan, you've matured, but on the whole you haven't changed very much.'

And even now he liked her – very much so. But something was lacking, or there was something superfluous – he himself couldn't put his finger on it, but it prevented him from feeling as he did before. He did not like her pallor, her new expression, that weak smile, her voice. And a little later he didn't like her dress, or the armchair she was sitting in; something about the past, when he had nearly married her, displeased him. He recalled his love, those dreams and hopes that had disturbed him four years before, and he felt uncomfortable.

They had tea and cakes. Then Vera Iosifovna read her novel out loud – about things that never happen in real life – and Startsev listened, looked at her grey handsome head and waited for her to finish.

'A mediocrity is not someone who's no good at writing stories,' he thought. 'It's someone who writes them but can't keep quiet about it.'

'Not awfully baddish!' Ivan Petrovich commented.

Then Yekaterina Ivanovna played the piano long and noisily, and when she had finished there followed lengthy expressions of gratitude and admiration.

'Lucky I didn't marry her,' thought Startsev.

She glanced at him and was evidently waiting for him to suggest going out into the garden, but he said nothing.

'Let's have a little talk,' she said, going over to him. 'How are you getting on? What's your news? How are things? All this time I've been thinking of you,' she continued nervously. 'I wanted to write to you, to come and see you in Dyalizh myself. In fact I actually decided to come but I changed my mind. Heaven knows what you think of me now. I've been so excited waiting for you today. For heaven's sake, let's go into the garden.'

They went into the garden and sat down on the bench under the old maple, as they had done four years before. It was dark.

'Well, how are things?' Yekaterina Ivanovna asked.

'All right, I get by,' Startsev replied.

And he could think of nothing more to say. They both fell silent.

'I'm so excited,' Yekaterina Ivanovna said, covering her face with her hands, 'but don't take any notice. I *so* enjoy being at home. I'm so glad to see everyone and it takes getting used to. So many memories! I thought we'd be talking non-stop, until the early hours.'

And now he saw her face close up, her sparkling eyes; and here, in the darkness, she looked younger than in the room and even her former childlike expression seemed to have returned. And in fact she gazed at him with naïve curiosity, as if she wanted to have a closer look, to understand the man who had once loved her so passionately, so tenderly, so unhappily. Her eyes thanked him for that love. And he recalled everything that had happened, down to the very last detail – how he had wandered around the cemetery, how he had gone home exhausted towards morning; and suddenly he felt sad and he regretted the past. A tiny flame flickered in his heart.

'Do you remember when I gave you a lift that evening to the club?' he asked. 'It was raining then, and dark . . .'

The flame was still flickering in his heart and he felt the urge to speak, to complain about life . . .

'Oh!' he sighed. 'You ask me how things are, what kind of lives we lead here? Well, we don't lead any kind of life. We grow old, get fat, go to seed. Day after day life drags on in its lacklustre way, no impressions, no thoughts . . . During the day I make money, in the evening there's the club and the company of cardsharpers, alcoholics and loudmouths whom I cannot stand. So what's good about it?'

'But there's your work, a noble purpose in life. You used to love talking about your hospital. I was rather strange then, I imagined myself as a great pianist. Now all young women play the piano and I played like everyone else and there was nothing special about me. I'm as much a concert pianist as Mama's a writer. Of course, I didn't understand you then, but afterwards, in Moscow, I often thought of you. In fact, I thought of nothing else. What bliss to be a country doctor, to help the suffering, to serve the common people! What utter bliss!' Yekaterina repeated rapturously. 'Whenever I thought of you in Moscow you struck me as idealistic, lofty . . .'

He stood up to go back to his house. She took hold of his arm.

'You are the best person I've ever known in my life,' she went on. 'We'll see each other, we'll talk, won't we? *Promise* me. I'm no concert pianist, I've no illusions about myself and when you're with me I shall neither play nor talk about music.'

Three days later Peacock brought him a letter from Yekaterina Ivanovna.

'You never come and see us. Why?' she wrote. 'I'm afraid that you don't feel the same towards us any more. I'm afraid – and this thought alone terrifies me. Please set my mind at rest, *please* come and tell me that everything's all right. I *must* talk to you. Your Y.T.'

After reading this letter he pondered for a moment and then he told Peacock:

'Tell them, dear chap, that I can't come today, I'm too busy. Tell them I'll come and see them in about three days.'

But three days passed, a week passed and still he, didn't go. Once, when he was driving past the Turkins' house, he remembered that he really should call on them, if only for a few minutes, but on reflection he decided against it.

And he never visited the Turkins again.

V

Several years have passed. Startsev has put on even more weight, grown flabby, has difficulty breathing and walks with his head thrown back. When he drives along in his carriage with three-horse team and bells, puffy and red-faced, and Panteleymon, likewise puffy and red-faced, with fleshy neck, sits on the box with his straight, seemingly wooden arms thrust forward, shouting at passers-by 'Keep to the right!', the effect is truly awe-inspiring and it seems that here comes a pagan god and no ordinary mortal. He has an enormous practice in town, he has no time for relaxation, and now he owns an estate, and two houses in town: he's looking for a third house that would bring in more income and whenever they talk of some house up for auction at the Mutual Credit Bank, then, without standing on ceremony, he marches right into the house, goes through all the rooms, ignoring half-naked women and children, who look at him in fear and trembling, pokes every door with his stick and says:

'Is this the study? Is this the bedroom? And what's *this*?'

And he breathes heavily and wipes the sweat from his brow.

He has much to preoccupy him, but he still doesn't give up his place on the local council. Greed has triumphed and he always wants to be everywhere at the right time. He's called simply Ionych in Dyalizh and in town. 'Where's old Ionych going?' or 'Shall we invite Ionych to a committee meeting?' they say.

Probably because his throat is bloated his voice has changed and become reedy and harsh. His personality has changed too: he's heavy-going now, irritable. When he sees patients he normally gets angry and impatiently bangs his stick on the floor.

'Please reply to the question! Don't argue!' he shouts in his jarring voice. In fact, he's a real lone wolf. Life is a bore, nothing interests him.

The whole time he lived in Dyalizh his love for Pussycat was his only joy and probably his last. He plays whist every evening at the club and then he sits on his own at the big table and has supper. He's waited upon by Ivan, the oldest and most venerable club servant. He's served the Lafite No. 17 and every single person there – the senior members and the footmen – knows his likes and dislikes and does his utmost to please him, otherwise he might suddenly lose his temper and start banging his stick on the floor.

When he has supper he turns round from time to time and joins in some conversation: 'Who are you talking about? Eh? *Who?*'

And when someone at a neighbouring table happens to start discussing the Turkins he asks: 'Which Turkins do you mean? The ones whose daughter plays the piano?'

And that's all one can say about him.

And the Turkins? Ivan Petrovich hasn't aged, hasn't changed one bit and he's joking and telling his funny stories as always. And Vera Iosifovna reads her novels to her guests as eagerly as ever, with warmth and unpretentiousness. Pussycat plays the piano every day, for hours at a time. She has aged noticeably, suffers from ill health and every autumn she goes to the Crimea with her mother. When he sees them off at the station, Ivan Petrovich wipes the tears from his eyes as the train pulls out.

'Goodbye – if you please!' he shouts.

And he waves his handkerchief.

My Life

I

'I'm only keeping you on out of respect for your esteemed father,' the manager told me. 'Otherwise I'd have sent you flying long ago.'

I replied, 'You flatter me too much, sir, in supposing I'm capable of flight.'

Then I heard him say 'Take this gentleman away from here, he's getting on my nerves.'

Two days later I was dismissed, which meant I'd had nine different jobs since the time I'd reached adulthood – to the great chagrin of my father, the town architect. I had worked in various government departments, but all nine jobs had been exactly the same and involved sitting on my backside, copying, listening to idiotic, cheap remarks and waiting for the sack.

When I arrived at Father's, he was deep in his armchair and his eyes were closed. His gaunt, wasted face, with that bluish-grey shadow where he shaved (he looked like an elderly Catholic organist), expressed humility and resignation. Without acknowledging my greeting, or opening his eyes, he told me, 'If my beloved wife, your mother, were alive today, the kind of life you lead would be a constant torment for her. I see the workings of Divine Providence in her untimely death. I'm asking you, you miserable wretch,' he went on, opening his eyes, 'to tell me what I should do with you.'

When I was younger, my relatives and friends had known what to do with me: some advised me to volunteer for military service, some told me to get a job in a chemist's shop, while others said I should work in a telegraph office. But now that I had turned twenty-five (I was even going a little grey at the temples) and had been in the army, had worked in a chemist's shop and in a telegraph office, it seemed that I had exhausted all earthly possibilities, and so they stopped advising me and merely sighed or shook their heads.

'Who do you think you are?' Father continued. 'At your age young men already have a sound position in life, but just take a look at yourself, you common riff-raff, living off your father!'

As usual, he went on about the young people of today being doomed by their atheism, materialism and inflated opinions of themselves, and about the need to ban amateur theatricals, as they distracted young people from their religion and their duties.

'Please hear me out,' I said morosely, fearing the worst from this conversation. 'What you call "position in society" is nothing but the privileges bestowed by capital and education. But the poor and uneducated earn their living by manual labour and I see no reason why I should be any exception.'

'When you talk about manual labour you sound so stupid and trite,' Father said irritably. 'Can't you get this into your thick head, you dim-wit, that there's something besides brute strength inside you. You have the divine spirit, the sacred fire which sets you miles apart from an ass or a reptile and makes you akin to the sublime! The finest people needed thousands of years to produce that fire. General Poloznev, your great-grandfather, fought at Borodino.[1] Your grandfather was a poet, public orator, marshal of the gentry. Your uncle's a teacher. And lastly, I, your father, am an architect! So all the Poloznevs have preserved this divine fire, only for you to put it out!'

'Please be fair,' I said. 'Millions of people do manual work.'

'Well, let them! They're fit for nothing else! Anyone can do manual work, even a downright idiot or criminal. It's the distinguishing mark of slaves and barbarians, whereas the sacred fire is granted only to the few!'

There was no point in talking any more. Father worshipped himself and could only be convinced by what he himself said. What's more, I knew very well that his pompous attitude to manual labour was not founded on thoughts of sacred flames so much as on a secret fear that I might become a labourer and thus make myself the talk of the town. However, the main thing was that all my contemporaries had graduated long ago and were doing well, and that the son of the manager of the State Bank was already quite an important civil servant, whereas I, an only son, was a nobody! It was useless continuing this disagreeable conversation, but I sat there feebly protesting in the hope that he would understand what I meant. After all, the problem was simple and clear enough – how was I to earn my living? But simplicity went unnoticed as Father trotted out those sickly phrases about Borodino, the sacred fire, my grandfather – a forgotten poet who wrote bad, meretricious verse at some time. I felt insulted – being called dim-wit and brainless fool was highly insulting. But how I wanted to be understood! In spite of everything I loved my father and sister. My childhood habit of asking them for advice had become so deeply rooted in me that I could never shake it off. Whether I was right or wrong, I was always afraid of upsetting them, afraid that Father was so excited now that his skinny neck had turned red and that he might have a stroke.

'Sitting in a stuffy room,' I said, 'copying, competing with a typewriter, is shameful and insulting for a man of my age. What does all *that* have to do with sacred flames?'

'But it's still brain work,' Father said. 'However, that's enough for now, we must stop this conversation. In any case, I'm warning you: if you don't go back to the office and if you persist in these contemptible inclinations of yours, then my daughter and I will cast you from our hearts. I'll disinherit you, I swear to God I will!'

In all sincerity and to demonstrate the unquestionable purity of the motives by which I wished to be guided all my life I replied, 'The question of my inheritance is of no importance to me. I renounce it in advance.'

Quite contrary to what I was expecting, these words hurt Father deeply. He turned crimson.

'Don't you dare talk to me like that, you fool!' he shouted in a thin, shrill voice. 'You ignorant lout!'

Swiftly and deftly, in his usual practised way, he slapped me twice in the face. 'You're forgetting yourself!'

When Father beat me as a child I had to stand to attention, hands to my sides and look him in the face. And now, whenever he beat me, I would panic completely, stand to attention and try to look him in the face, just as though I were a small child again. Father was old and very thin, but those slender muscles must have been as tough as leather straps, as he really hurt me.

I staggered back into the hall, where he grabbed his umbrella and struck me several times on the head and shoulders. Just then my sister opened the drawing-room door to see what the noise was about, but immediately turned away with a look of horror and pity, without a word in my defence.

I remained unshakeable in my determination not to return to the office, and in my intention to start a new life as a working man. All I had to do was choose a job, and this didn't seem particularly difficult, since I thought that I was terribly strong, had great stamina and was therefore equal to the most arduous work. A workman's life lay ahead of me, with all its monotony, hunger, stench and grim surroundings. And there was the constant worry of having enough to live on. Returning from work on Great Dvoryansky Street, I might still envy Dolzhikov the engineer, who worked with his brain. Who knows? But now the thought of these future misfortunes cheered me up. At one time I used to dream of intellectual work, imagining myself as a teacher, doctor or writer, but my dreams never came true. My liking for intellectual pleasures such as the theatre and reading had grown into a passion, but I cannot say whether I had any flair for brain work. At school I had an utter aversion to Greek and I had to be taken out of the fourth form; for a long time I was coached by private tutors who tried to get me into the fifth. Then I worked in different government departments, spending most of the day doing absolutely nothing: this, I was told, constituted brain work. My school and office work called for neither mental effort, nor talent, nor any particular ability or creative energy. It was just mechanical. I consider that type of brain work beneath manual labour. I despise it and do not think that it could justify an idle life of leisure for one minute, since it's only a sham, another form of idleness. Probably I never knew what real brain work was.

Evening set in. We lived in Great Dvoryansky Street, the town's main thoroughfare, where our *beau monde* strolled in the evenings for want of a decent municipal park. This delightful street was a partial substitute for a park, since poplars (particularly sweet-smelling after rain) grew along both sides; acacias, tall lilac bushes, wild cherries and apple trees hung out over fences and railings. The May twilight, the soft green leaves and shadows, the scent of lilac, the droning beetles, the silence, the warmth – spring returns every year, but how fresh, how marvellous everything seemed nonetheless! I would stand by the gate watching the promenaders. I had grown up with most of them and got up to mischief with them when we were children. But they would most likely be startled at the sight of me now, as I was poorly, unfashionably dressed. People called my very narrow trousers and large, clumsy boots 'macaroni on floats'. Moreover, I had a bad name in that town because I had no social status and frequently played billiards in low pubs. Perhaps another reason was that I'd twice been hauled off to the police station, although I'd done absolutely nothing.

Someone was playing the piano in the engineer Dolzhikov's flat in the large house opposite. It was growing dark and stars twinkled in the sky. Along came Father with my sister on his arm, wearing that old top-hat with its broad, upturned brim and acknowledging the bows of passers-by as he slowly walked past.

'Just look!' he was saying to my sister, pointing at the sky with the same umbrella he had struck me with. 'Just look at that sky! Even the smallest star is a world of its own! How insignificant is man compared with the universe!'

His tone suggested that he liked being insignificant and found it exceedingly flattering. What a bungler he was! Unfortunately, he was our only architect and not one decent house had been built in the town for the past fifteen or twenty years that I could remember. When he was commissioned to design a house, he usually drew the ballroom and drawing-room first. Just as boarding-school girls, long ago, could dance only if they began from where the stove was, so his creative ideas could only develop by starting from the ballroom and drawing-room. He would add a dining-room, nursery, study –

all of them linked by doors. Inevitably, they turned into corridors, each room having two or even three doors too many. He must have had a vague, extremely confused and stunted creative imagination. Always sensing that something was missing, he would resort to different kinds of extensions, lumping one on top of the other. I can still see those narrow entrance-halls, narrow little passages and small, crooked staircases leading onto mezzanines where you could not stand up straight, with three enormous steps instead of a floor, like shelves in a bath-house. And the kitchen was invariably underneath the main house, with vaulted ceilings and brick floors. The façades had a stubborn, harsh look; their lines were stiff, timid, and the roofs were low, squashed-looking. It seemed that the squat, dumpy chimneys just had to be capped with wire cowls and squeaky black weathervanes. The houses that Father built were almost identical – somehow they vaguely put me in mind of his top-hat and the forbidding, rigid lines of the back of his neck. As time passed the town grew used to Father's ineptitude: it took root and became established as the ruling style.

Father also introduced this style into my sister's life. To start with, he called her Cleopatra, just as he had called me Misail. When she was a little girl he would scare her by talking about the stars, about the sages of antiquity and our ancestors, explaining the concepts of life and duty in great detail to her. And now that she was twenty-six, he was still at it. Only *he* was allowed to take her arm when they went for a walk and he somehow imagined that sooner or later a respectable young man would turn up and want to marry her out of respect for his moral virtues. She worshipped Father, was afraid of him and thought him exceptionally clever.

It grew quite dark and the street gradually became deserted. The music died away in the house opposite, gates opened wide and a troika jauntily careered off down the street, its bells softly jingling. The engineer and his daughter had gone for a ride. It was time for bed!

I had my own room in the house, but I lived in a little hut joined onto a brick shed probably built as a harness-room at one time, as large spikes were driven into the walls. But now it was no longer needed for storage and for thirty years Father had been stacking only newspapers there. For some obscure reason he had them bound every six months and would not let anyone touch them. Living in that hut I saw much less of Father and his guests and I felt that if I didn't have a proper room and didn't go into the house for dinner every day, that would make Father's remarks about my being a burden seem less hurtful.

My sister was waiting for me. Without Father's knowledge, she had brought me supper – a small piece of cold veal and a slice of bread. In our house people were always going on about 'counting the copecks' or 'taking care of the roubles', and so on. Subjected to all this banal talk, my sister's only concern was how to save money – and as a result we ate badly. After she put the plate on the table she sat down on the bed and burst into tears.

'Misail,' she said, 'what are you doing to us?'

She did not cover her face; tears trickled on to her breast and arms and she looked most despondent. Then she slumped on to the pillow and gave free rein to her tears, shaking all over and sobbing.

'That's another job you've left,' she said. 'Oh, it's absolutely terrible!'

'*Please* try and understand, my dear sister,' I said, and her tears filled me with despair.

And as though on purpose, my lamp ran out of paraffin – it was smoking and about to go out. The old spikes on the walls had a sombre look and their shadows flickered.

'Please spare a thought for us!' my sister said, getting up. 'Father is dreadfully upset, I'm not well and nearly going out of my mind. What will become of you?' she sobbed, holding her hands out. 'I beg you, I implore you, for our dear mother's sake, go back to your job!'

'I can't, Cleopatra,' I said, almost giving in. 'I can't!'

'Why not?' my sister continued. 'Why not? If you couldn't get on with your boss you should have found another job. Why don't you go and work on the railway, for instance? I've just been speaking to Anyuta Blagovo and she tells me they're bound to take you on. She's even promised to put in a word for you. For heaven's sake, Misail, think about it! Think about it, I beg you!'

After a little more discussion I gave in. I told her I'd never given much thought to working on the railway and that I'd try it.

She smiled joyfully through her tears, squeezed my hand – and then she started crying again, unable to stop. I went to get some paraffin from the kitchen.

II

No one in that town had greater enthusiasm for amateur theatricals, concerts and *tableaux vivants* for charity than the Azhogins, who owned a house on Great Dvoryansky Street. They provided the premises for every performance, looked after the organization and took responsibility for all expenses. This rich, landowning family had about eight thousand acres in the district with a splendid manor house, but they had no love for the country and lived in town all year round.

The family consisted of the mother, a tall, thin, refined woman, with short hair, a short blouse and plain skirt in the English style; and three daughters who, instead of being called by their Christian names, were simply known as 'Eldest', 'Middle' and 'Youngest'. All three of them had ugly, sharp chins, were shortsighted and round-shouldered. They dressed just like their mother and had an unpleasant lisp. But in spite of this they insisted on taking part in every performance and were always doing charitable work through their acting, reading or singing. They were very earnest, never smiled and even acted – completely lifelessly – in musical comedies with a businesslike look, as though they were book-keepers at work.

I loved our shows, in particular the frequent, somewhat chaotic, noisy rehearsals, after which we were always given supper. I had no part in selecting the plays or casting – my work was backstage. I painted scenery, copied out parts, prompted, helped with the make-up. I was also entrusted with various sound-effects, such as thunder, nightingales' songs, and so on. As I had no status in society or decent clothes I kept away from everyone at rehearsals, hiding in the darkness of the wings and maintaining a bashful silence.

I painted the scenery – in the Azhogins' brick shed or out in the yard. I was helped by a house-painter or, as he liked to call himself, 'decorating contractor' named Andrey Ivanov. He was about fifty, tall, very thin and pale, with a sunken chest, sunken temples and dark blue patches under his eyes which made him look rather frightening. He suffered from some wasting disease and every spring and autumn people said he was dying, but after a spell in bed he would get up again and declare in a surprised voice 'So, I'm still here, ain't I!'

In the town he was called Radish – people said it was his real name. He loved the theatre as much as I did and the moment he heard rumours of a new show he would drop whatever he was doing and go off to the Azhogins' to paint scenery.

The day after that showdown with my sister I worked from morning to night at the Azhogins'. The rehearsal was due to start at seven p.m., and an hour beforehand all the company assembled in the ballroom; the three sisters, Eldest, Middle and Youngest, walked up and down the stage reading from notebooks. In his long, reddish-brown coat and with a scarf around his neck, Radish stood with his head against the wall, reverently watching the stage. Their mother Mrs Azhogin went up to each of the guests to say something pleasant. She had a way of staring you in the face and speaking softly, as if telling a secret.

'It must be hard work painting scenery,' she said softly, coming over to me. 'I was talking to Madame Mufke about superstitions just now when I saw you come in. Good heavens, I've struggled against superstition all my life! To try and convince the servants how stupid their fears are I always light three candles in my room and start any important business matters only on the thirteenth of the month.'

The daughter of Dolzhikov the engineer arrived. She was a pretty, buxom blonde, dressed in 'Paris fashion' as they described it in the town. She didn't do any acting, but they put a chair for her on the stage during rehearsals and the shows didn't start until she was sitting in the front row, looking radiant and amazing everyone with her dresses. As she came from the capital, she was allowed to pass remarks during rehearsals, which she did with a pleasant, condescending smile, and she obviously thought that our shows were childish games. It was said that she had studied singing at the St Petersburg Conservatoire and had even sung for a winter season in a private opera house. She attracted me very much and at rehearsals or performances I could hardly take my eyes off her.

I had already picked up the notebook for prompting when suddenly my sister appeared. Without taking off her hat and coat she came over to me and said 'Come with me, please.'

I went. Anyuta Blagovo was standing in the doorway backstage. She also wore a hat, with a dark veil. She was the daughter of the deputy judge who had been serving in our town for some time, almost since the day the local court was first set up. Being tall and well built, she was considered indispensable for *tableaux vivants*, and when she represented some fairy, or 'Fame', her face would burn with shame. But she never took part in the plays, just dropping in at rehearsals on some business or other and never entering the hall. And she had obviously looked in only for a moment now.

'Father's been talking about you,' she said dryly, without looking at me and blushing. 'Dolzhikov's promised you a job on the railway. Go and see him tomorrow, he'll be at home.'

I bowed and thanked her for her trouble.

'You can leave that,' she said, pointing to the notebook.

She and my sister went up to Mrs Azhogin and they whispered for a minute or two, looking at me now and again. They were consulting one another about something.

'Indeed,' Mrs Azhogin said quietly as she came over to me and stared me in the face, 'indeed, if this is keeping you from more serious work' (she took the notebook from me) 'you can hand it over to someone else. Don't worry, my dear friend. Off with you now – and good luck.'

I said goodbye and left, feeling rather put out. As I went down the stairs I saw my sister and Anyuta Blagovo hurriedly leaving. They were talking excitedly, most probably about my railway job. My sister never used to come to rehearsals and was probably feeling guilty, afraid that Father might find out that she had been at the Azhogins' without his permission.

Next day, at about half past twelve, I went to see Dolzhikov. A manservant showed me into a very fine room which the engineer used as drawing-room and office. Here everything was soft, elegant and even rather strange for someone like me, unused to such surroundings. There were expensive carpets, huge armchairs, bronzes, pictures, gilt and plush frames. The photographs all over the walls were of very beautiful women with clever, fine faces, in natural poses. From the drawing-room a door led straight onto a balcony overlooking the garden, where I could see lilac, a table laid for lunch, a great number of bottles and a bunch of roses. It smelt of spring, expensive cigars – the true smell of happiness – and everything seemed to be telling me that this man had really lived, worked hard and attained such happiness as is possible in this world. The engineer's daughter was sitting at the writing-table reading the paper.

'Have you come to see Father?' she asked. 'He's having a shower and he'll be down in a moment. Please take a seat.'

I sat down.

'You live opposite, don't you?' she asked after a brief silence.

'Yes.'

'Every day I watch you out of the window, from nothing better to do. I hope it doesn't bother you,' she went on, glancing at the newspaper, 'and I often see you or your sister. She always has such a kind, concentrated expression.'

Dolzhikov came in. He was drying his neck on a towel.

'Papa, this is Monsieur Poloznev,' she said.

'Yes, yes, so Blagovo told me,' he said, turning briskly towards me without offering his hand. 'Now listen, what do you want from me? What job do you think I have for you?'

In a loud voice, as if telling me off, he continued, 'You're a strange lot! Twenty men come here every day, thinking it's an office I'm running here! I have a *railway* to run, gentlemen, and it's damned hard work. I need mechanics, metal workers, navvies, carpenters, well-sinkers, but all you lot can do is sit on your behinds and scribble! You're just writers!'

He exuded that same air of prosperity as his carpets and armchairs. Stout, rosy-cheeked, broad-chested, well-washed, he looked just like a china figure of a coachman in his cotton-print shirt and baggy trousers. He had a rounded, curly beard, a hooked nose, and his eyes were dark, clear, innocent. He didn't have one grey hair on his head.

'What can you do?' he went on. 'Nothing! I'm an engineer and I'm financially secure. But before I was put in charge of this railway I spent years sweating my guts out. I was an engine-driver, then I worked in Belgium for two years as a common greaser. So what work do you think I can give you, young man?'

'Yes, you're right, of course,' I muttered. I was terribly taken aback and could not bear those clear, innocent eyes of his.

'But you can at least work a telegraph, can't you?' he asked after a moment's thought.

'Yes, I've worked in a telegraph office.'

'Hm . . . well, we'll see. Go to Dubechnya² for the time being. I do have someone there, but he's a bloody dead loss.'

'And what will my duties be?' I asked.

'We'll see. Now, off you go for the time being and I'll see to it. Only don't start boozing while you're working for me or come asking for any favours, or you'll be out on your neck!'

He walked away without even a nod. I bowed to him and his daughter, who was reading the paper, and left. I felt so terribly depressed that when my sister asked what kind of reception I'd had at the engineer's I just could not speak one word.

Next morning I rose very early, at sunrise, to go to Dubechnya. Great Dvoryansky Street was absolutely deserted – everyone was still in bed – and my footsteps had a hollow, solitary ring. The dew-covered poplars filled the air with their gentle fragrance. I felt sad and reluctant to leave the town. I loved my birthplace, it seemed so beautiful and warm! I loved the greenery, the quiet sunny mornings, the sound of church bells. But the people I had to live with bored me, were like strangers and at times they disgusted me. I neither liked nor understood them. I could not understand what these sixty-five thousand people were living for or how they made ends meet. I knew that Kimry³ earned its living from boots, that Tula⁴ made samovars and rifles, that Odessa was a port. But I had no idea what our town was or what it produced. The people of Great

Dvoryansky Street, and two other better-class streets, lived off their capital and civil servants' salaries that were paid by the government. But how the remaining eight streets that ran parallel for two miles and disappeared behind the hill coped was always an insoluble mystery to me. It embarrasses me to describe how they lived. No public gardens, no theatre, no decent orchestra. Only young Jewish men went into the town and club libraries, so magazines and new books lay uncut for months. Rich, educated people slept in stuffy, cramped bedrooms on wooden beds crawling with bugs, children were kept in disgustingly dirty rooms called nurseries and even old and respected servants slept on the kitchen floor, covered in rags. On fast days the houses reeked of borsch and on others of sturgeon fried in sunflower oil. They ate nasty food and drank unwholesome water. At the town hall, the governor's, the bishop's – all over the place – they had been talking for years about the town not having good, cheap water and maintained that two hundred thousand should be borrowed from the government to provide a proper supply. The three dozen or so very rich people in town, who had been known to gamble away whole estates at cards, also drank the bad water and were forever talking excitedly about the loan: this was something I just could not understand. It struck me that it would have been simpler for them to lay out the money from their own pockets.

I did not know one honest man in the whole town. My father took bribes, imagining that he was given them out of respect for his moral virtues. If schoolboys wanted to get into a higher class, they boarded with their teachers, who charged them the earth. At recruiting-time the military commander's wife took bribes from the young men, even allowing them to buy her a few drinks, and once she was too drunk to get up off her knees in church. The doctors also took bribes at recruiting-time, while the town medical officer and vet levied a tax on butchers' shops and inns. The local college traded in certificates granting exemption to certain classes; the senior clergy took bribes from the lower and from churchwardens. Anyone making an application at the municipal offices, the citizens' bureau, the health clinic and any other kind of institution was followed as he left by shouts of 'Don't forget to say *thank you*,' which meant going back and handing over thirty or forty copecks. And those who didn't accept bribes – officials from the law department, for example – were arrogant, shook hands with two fingers, and were callous and narrow-minded. They played cards a great deal, drank a lot, and married the rich girls. There was no doubt that they had a harmful, corrupting influence on their surroundings. Only a few young girls gave any hint of moral purity. Most of them had honourable aspirations, were decent and pure of heart. But they had no knowledge of life and believed that bribes were given out of respect for moral virtue. After marrying they let themselves go, aged quickly and were hopelessly swallowed up in the mire of that vulgar, philistine existence.

III

They were building a railway in our district. On Saturday evenings gangs of louts roamed around the town. They were called navvies and the people were scared of them. I often saw one of these brutes, bloody-faced and capless, hauled off to the police station, while material evidence in the form of a samovar or underwear still wet from the washing-line was carried behind. The navvies usually congregated around pubs and markets. They ate, drank and swore and pursued every woman of easy virtue who happened to be passing with piercing whistles. To amuse this starving riff-raff our shopkeepers gave dogs and cats vodka to drink, or tied a paraffin can to a dog's tail and then whistled, making it tear down the street. Squealing in terror from the can clattering after it, the dog would think some dreadful monster was in hot pursuit and ran way out of town, far into the fields, until it dropped exhausted. And there were some dogs in the town that never stopped trembling, their tails permanently between their legs. People said the joke was too much for them and they had gone mad.

The station was being constructed about three miles from town. The engineers were said to have asked for a bribe of fifty thousand roubles if they brought the line right up to the town. But the council was not prepared to pay more than forty and they fell out over the ten thousand. And now the citizens were sorry, because they had to build a road to the station which, according to estimates, would cost a great deal more. Sleepers and rails had already been laid along the whole line and service trains ran, carrying building materials and workmen. The only delay was with the bridges, which Dolzhikov was building, and one or two unfinished stations.

Dubechnya, as the first station was called, was about eleven miles away. I walked there. As the morning sun caught them, the cornfields shone bright green. The countryside was flat and cheerful round about here, and in the distance the station, hillocks and remote farmsteads were clearly outlined. How good it was to be out in the open country! And how I longed to be saturated by this awareness of freedom – if only for one morning – so that I could forget what was happening in town, forget how hungry and poor I was. Nothing was so off-putting as those sharp pangs of hunger, when loftier notions became strangely intermingled with thoughts of buckwheat porridge, mutton chops and fried fish. There I was standing in the fields looking up at a skylark hovering motionless in the air, hysterically pouring out its song, while all I could think was 'Some bread and butter would be nice!' Or I would sit by the roadside with my eyes closed, to rest and to listen to the wonderful sounds of May – when suddenly I'd recall the smell of hot potatoes. In general, for someone so tall and strongly built as myself, I wasn't getting enough to eat and therefore my overriding sensation during the day was one of hunger. Perhaps it was because of this that I understood so well why many people work just for their daily bread and can talk only of food.

At Dubechnya the inside of the station was being plastered and an upper wooden storey added to the pumping-house. It was hot, there was a smell of slaked lime and the workmen idly wandered around piles of wooden shavings and rubble. A pointsman was sleeping near his hut and the sun beat right into his face. There wasn't a single tree. The telegraph wires, with hawks perched on them here and there, hummed faintly. Not knowing what to do I wandered among the heaps of rubbish and remembered the engineer's reply when I asked what my duties would be: '. . . we'll see'. But what was there to see in this wilderness? The plasterers talked about a foreman and a certain Fedot Vasilyev. It was all foreign to me and I became more and more depressed – a physical depression when you are conscious of your arms, legs and massive body, but when you have no idea what to do with them or where to put them.

After wandering about for at least two hours I noticed some telegraph poles stretching away from the station to the right of the track, stopping by a white stone wall about a mile off. The workmen said that the office was over there and at last I understood that that was where I had to report.

It was a very old, long-abandoned country estate. The spongy stone wall, severely weathered, had collapsed in places. The blind wall of one of the outbuildings – which had a rusty roof patched with shiny bits of tin – faced the open country. Through the gates I could see a spacious yard thick with weeds and an old manor house with sun-blinds in the window and a steep roof red with rust. On each side of the house stood the outbuildings, which were identical. One had its windows boarded up, while the other's were open. A line of washing hung nearby and some calves were wandering about. The last telegraph pole stood in the yard with a wire leading from it to a window in the outbuilding with the outward-facing blank wall. The door was open and I went in. A man with dark curly hair and a canvas jacket was sitting at a table by the telegraph apparatus. He gave me a stern, sullen look, but immediately smiled and said, 'Hullo, Better-than-Nothing.'

It was Ivan Cheprakov, an old friend from school who had been expelled from Form Two for smoking. During the autumn we used to catch goldfinches, greenfinches and grosbeaks and sell them in the market early in the morning, while our parents were still asleep. We would lie in wait for flocks of migrant starlings, shooting at them with pellets and then gathering up the wounded. Some of them died in the most terrible torment – to this day I can remember them squeaking at night in the cage in my room. The ones that recuperated were sold and we swore blind that they were males. In the market once I had only one starling left which I had been trying to sell and finally let it go for a mere copeck. 'Still, *it's better than nothing*!' I said, trying to console myself as I put the copeck in my pocket. From that time street urchins and the boys from school nicknamed me 'Better-than-Nothing'. Urchins and shopkeepers still teased me with this name, although no one except me could remember its origin.

Cheprakov wasn't strongly built. He was narrow-chested, round-shouldered and long-legged. His tie was like a piece of string, he had no waistcoat, and his down-at-heel boots were in a worse state than mine. He rarely blinked and always had a look of urgency about him, as though about to grab something.

'Now, wait a jiff,' he said, fidgeting. 'And listen! Now, what was I saying?'

We started talking. I found out that the estate where I now was had been the Cheprakovs' property until recently, and only last autumn had passed into the hands of Dolzhikov, who thought it more profitable to put his money into land than keep it in cash. Already he had bought three sizeable estates in the district on mortgage. At the sale Cheprakov's mother had reserved the right to live in one of the outbuildings for two years and had talked them into giving her son a job in the office.

'It would have surprised me if he hadn't bought it!' Cheprakov said, referring to the engineer. 'He makes so much out of the contractors alone! He fleeces everybody!'

Then he took me off to dinner, having decided, after a great deal of fuss, that I would live with him in the outbuilding and have my meals at his mother's.

'She's very tight-fisted with me,' he said. 'But she won't charge you very much.'

It was very cramped in the small rooms where his mother lived. All of them, even the hall and lobby, were crammed with furniture brought from the big house after the sale of the estate. It was all mahogany and very old-fashioned. Mrs Cheprakov, a very plump, middle-aged woman with slanting Chinese eyes, was sitting in a large armchair at the window knitting a stocking.

She greeted me with great ceremony.

'Mother, this is Poloznev,' Cheprakov said, introducing me. 'He'll be working here.'

'Are you a *gentleman*?' she asked in a strange, unpleasant voice. I thought I could hear fat gurgling in her throat.

'Yes,' I replied.

'Please sit down.'

It was a poor meal. All we had was sour curd pie and milk soup. Yelena Nikiforovna, our hostess, kept winking strangely, first with one eye, then the other. Although she spoke and ate, there was something deathly about her whole body and she even seemed to smell like a corpse. There was scarcely a flicker of life in her, only the dim consciousness that she was a lady, and a landowner, who had once owned serfs, and that she had been a general's wife, whom the servants had to call madam. When these pathetic remnants of life briefly flared up she would tell her son, 'Jean, you're not holding your knife properly.'

Or she would breathe deeply and tell me, with all the affectedness of a hostess anxious to entertain her guest, 'As you know, we've sold the estate. It's a pity, of course, we'd grown so used to it. But Dolzhikov has promised to make Jean stationmaster at Dubechnya, so we shan't be leaving. We'll live in the station, which is really the same as being on the estate. Such a nice man, that engineer! He's very handsome, isn't he?'

Not long before, the Cheprakovs had been living in style, but after the general died everything changed. Mrs Cheprakov started quarrelling with the neighbours and taking people to court. She stopped paying her managers and workmen. She was in perpetual fear of being robbed and in about ten years Dubechnya had become unrecognizable.

Behind the main house was an old garden that had run wild, and it was choked with weeds and bushes. I walked up and down the terrace, which was still firm and beautiful. Through a french window I could see a room with a parquet floor – most probably the drawing-room. The only furniture was an old-fashioned piano and engravings in broad mahogany frames on the walls. All that was left of the flower-beds were peonies and poppies holding their white and bright red heads above the grass. Young maples and elms, gnawed at by cows, grew over the paths, stretching out and crowding one another. The garden was thickly overgrown and seemed impenetrable, but this was only near the house, where there were still poplars, pines and ancient limes, all of the same age and survivors of former avenues. Beyond them, however, the garden had been cleared for mowing hay, and here it was not so damp, one's mouth and eyes were not attacked by cobwebs, and now and then a gentle breeze stirred. The deeper you went into that garden the more it opened out. Here there were wild cherry and plum trees, wide-spreading apple trees disfigured by props and canker. There were such lofty pear trees that it was hard to believe they really were pear trees. This part of the garden was rented to women traders from the town and it was guarded against thieves and starlings by an idiot peasant who lived in a cottage.

As it gradually thinned out the garden became a real meadow sloping down to a river overgrown with green rushes and osiers. Near the mill-dam was a deep pond full of fish. A small mill with a thatched roof angrily hummed away and frogs croaked furiously. Occasionally the mirror-like surface of the water was broken by ripples, water-lilies trembled as lively fish brushed past them. On the far side of the stream was the hamlet of Dubechnya. The calm blue millpond drew one to it, promising cool and rest. And now all this – the millpond, the mill and the pleasant river banks – belonged to the engineer!

And so I started my new job. I received and despatched telegrams, wrote out expense sheets, made fair copies of order forms, claims and reports that were sent to our office by illiterate foremen and workmen. Most of the day I did nothing but pace the room waiting for telegrams. Or I would make a boy sit there and go out into the garden for a walk until he came running to tell me that the telegraph machine was clicking. I had dinner at Mrs Cheprakov's. They hardly ever served meat and we usually had nothing but milk dishes; on fast days such as Wednesday and Friday, they brought out the 'Lenten' pink plates. Mrs Cheprakov was in the habit of always winking and I felt ill at ease whenever I was with her.

As there wasn't enough work in the outbuilding, even for one person, Cheprakov slept or went down with his rifle to the millpond to shoot ducks. In the evenings he would get drunk in the village or at the station, and before going to bed would look at himself in the mirror and shout, 'Hullo, Ivan Cheprakov!'

When drunk he looked very pale, and he kept rubbing his hands and producing a neighing laugh. He would strip and run around the field stark naked for the fun of it. He used to eat flies and said that they had a rather sour taste.

IV

One day, after dinner, he came running breathlessly into the outbuilding and said, 'You'd better get moving, your sister's arrived.'

I went out. A cab from the town was standing at the entrance to the main house. My sister had come with Anyuta Blagovo and a gentleman in a military tunic. As I went closer I recognized him as Anyuta's brother, an army doctor.

'We've come for a picnic!' he said. 'I hope it's all right.'

My sister and Anyuta wanted to ask how I was getting on, but neither spoke and simply stared at me. They could see I didn't like it there and my sister's eyes filled with tears, while Anyuta Blagovo blushed. We went into the garden with the doctor leading the way and exclaiming rapturously, 'What air! My goodness, what air!'

He still looked like a student, he spoke and walked like one, and his grey eyes had the lively, natural, open look of a good student. Next to his tall, beautiful sister he seemed frail and thin. His beard was thin too, as was his pleasant tenor voice. He had been serving somewhere with his regiment and was now home on leave. He said that he was going to St Petersburg in the autumn to sit for his M.D. A family man with a wife and three children, he had married young, when he was a second-year student, and people in the town said he had an unhappy life at home and that he wasn't living with his wife.

'What's the time?' my sister asked anxiously. 'We'll have to be back early. Papa said I could come and see my brother, but only if I'm back by six, without fail.'

'Oh, blow your Papa!' the doctor sighed.

I put the samovar on and we drank our tea on a rug in front of the terrace of the big house. The doctor knelt as he drank out of a saucer, saying that it was sheer bliss. Then Cheprakov fetched a key, opened the french window, and we all went into the house. It was gloomy, mysterious and smelt of fungus. Our footsteps had a hollow ring as if there was a cellar under the floor. The doctor stood at the piano and touched the keys, which replied with a weak, tremulous, rather blurred but melodious chord. He tested his voice and sang a song, frowning and impatiently stamping his foot when he touched a dead key. My sister had forgotten about going home, and excitedly paced the room saying, 'I feel so gay, so very, very gay!'

There was a note of surprise in her voice and it was as if she did not think that she too could be happy. It was the first time I had seen her looking so cheerful. She even looked prettier. In profile she wasn't very pretty, with protruding nose and mouth, so that she always seemed to be blowing. But she had beautiful, dark eyes, a pale, very delicate complexion and a kind, sad look that was most touching. When she spoke she seemed attractive, beautiful even. Both of us took after our mother – we were broad-shouldered, strong, and with great staying-power – but her pallor was that of a sick person. She was always coughing and sometimes I detected in her eyes the look of a person who was seriously ill but who was somehow trying to hide it. There was something child-like, naïve in her gaiety now, as if the child's sense of joy that had been crushed and stifled by our strict upbringing had suddenly awakened in her and was struggling to express itself.

But when evening came and the horses were brought round my sister became quiet and seemed to shrink. She sat down in the carriage like a prisoner in the dock.

When they had driven off and everything became quiet, it struck me that Anyuta Blagovo had not spoken one word to me the whole time.

'An amazing girl!' I thought. 'Wonderful!'

St Peter's Fast arrived and every day we had only Lenten food. Idleness and the uncertainty of my position had brought on a physical depression. Feeling dissatisfied with myself, sluggish and hungry, I lounged around the estate, just waiting until I was in the right mood to leave.

One day, late in the afternoon, when Radish was with us in the outbuilding, Dolzhikov unexpectedly came in, very sunburnt and grey with dust. He had spent three days on his section of the line, had just travelled to Dubechnya on a railway engine and had walked over from the station to see us. While he was waiting for a cab to come from town and collect him, he made a tour of the estate with his manager, giving orders in a loud voice. Then he sat in our building for a whole hour writing letters. While he was there some telegrams came through and he tapped out the answers himself. The three of us stood to attention, not saying a word.

'What a mess!' he said, looking disgustedly at the records. 'In a fortnight's time I'm transferring the office to the station and I just don't know what I'm going to do with you.'

'I'm trying very hard, sir,' Cheprakov said.

'I can see how you're trying. All you can do is draw your wages,' he continued. 'Just because you have people to pull strings for you, you think it's easy to get a quick leg-up. Well, *no one* gets that from me. No one ever bothered about *me*. Before I was in charge of the railway I was an engine-driver. I worked in Belgium as an ordinary greaser. Hey, you, Panteley,' he said, turning to Radish, 'what are you doing here? Getting drunk with this lot, eh?'

For some reason he called all simple labourers Panteley, while he despised people like myself and Cheprakov, calling us scum and drunken pigs behind our backs. On the whole he was hard on his junior clerks, fined them and coolly gave them the sack without any explanation.

At last his carriage arrived. By way of farewell he promised to sack the lot of us in a fortnight and called his manager a blockhead. Then he sprawled back in his carriage and bowled off to town.

'Andrey,' I asked Radish, 'can I work for you?'

'Oh, all right.'

And we went off to town together. When the station and manor house were far behind I asked 'Andrey, why did you come to Dubechnya just now?'

'Firstly, my lads are working on the line, and secondly I went to pay the general's widow the interest I owe her. Last year I borrowed fifty roubles and now I'm paying her a rouble a month.'

The painter stopped and caught hold of one of my coat buttons. 'My dear Misail,' he went on, 'the way I see it is this. An ordinary working man or gent who lends money – even at the very lowest rates – is a villain. The truth cannot dwell in him.'

Thin, pale and terrifying, Radish closed his eyes, shook his head and spoke out, in the solemn voice of a sage, 'Aphids eat grass, rust eats iron – and lies the soul. God save us sinners!'

V

Radish was an impractical person, with no head for business. He took on more work than he could handle, tended to lose his nerve when settling up, and as a result was almost always losing money. He did painting, glazing, wallpapering and even roofing jobs, and I can remember him running around for three days looking for roofers – just because of some miserable little job. He was an excellent workman and sometimes earned as much as ten roubles a day. But for his wish to be boss at all costs, to call himself a contractor, he would have been quite prosperous.

He was paid by the job, while he paid me and the other lads by the day – between seventy copecks and a rouble. When the weather was hot and dry we did different outside jobs, mainly roof painting. I was not used to this kind of work and my feet burnt – I felt I was walking over red-hot flagstones – and when I put my felt boots on my feet were even hotter. But this was only at the beginning; later on I got used to it and everything went as smooth as clockwork.

Now I was living among people who had to do physical work, for whom it was unavoidable and who slaved like carthorses, often without being aware of the moral meaning of work and never using the word 'work' in conversation even. Next to them I felt rather like a carthorse myself. I became ever more aware that what I was doing just had to be done, there was no avoiding it, and this made life easier and freed me from all doubts.

At first I found everything new and absorbing, as if I had been reborn. I could sleep on the ground or go barefoot, which was extremely pleasant. I could stand in a crowd of ordinary people without attracting any bad feeling, and when a cabman's horse fell down in the street I would rush to help pull it up without worrying if my clothes got dirty. Most important, I was earning my own living and wasn't a burden to anyone.

Painting roofs, particularly when we used our own paint, was considered highly profitable, and so even such good workmen as Radish didn't turn their noses up at this rough, tedious work. With skinny, purple legs, he looked like a stork in his short trousers as he walked over the roofs, and I would hear him sigh deeply as he wielded his brush 'Woe, woe unto us sinners!'

He walked over roofs as easily as over the ground. Despite being as pale and sickly as a corpse, he was extraordinarily agile, painting the cupolas and domes of churches just like a young man, without using any scaffolding – only ladders and ropes. It was rather frightening seeing him there, poised aloft, far above the ground, stretching himself to his full height and pronouncing solemnly, on behalf of some person unknown, 'Aphids eat grass, rust eats iron – and lies the soul!'

At times he would ponder something and answer his own thoughts: 'Anything's possible! Anything!'

When I went home from work, everyone sitting on benches near their gates – shop-assistants, errand-boys and their masters – followed me with sneers and abuse. At first this worried me and seemed quite monstrous.

'Better-than-Nothing!' I heard from all sides. 'Got yer paint, botcher!'

No one was so unkind to me as those very people who only recently had themselves been ordinary labourers and earned their living by unskilled labour. When I passed the row of shops, water was 'accidentally' thrown over me near the ironmonger's and once someone even threw a stick at me. A grey-haired old fish merchant once barred my path, eyed me malevolently and said, 'I'm not sorry for you, you fool! It's your father I'm sorry for!'

For some reason my friends were embarrassed if they met me. Some looked on me as a crank or a clown, others were sorry for me, while others did not know how to approach me and I found it difficult to make them out. One day I met Anyuta Blagovo in a side-street near Great Dvoryansky Street. I was on my way to work, carrying two long brushes and a bucket of paint. She flushed when she recognized me.

'Please don't bow to me in the street,' she said, in a nervous, stern, trembling voice, without offering to shake hands, and suddenly tears glistened in her eyes. 'If you really must do this kind of thing, then go ahead, but please try and avoid meeting me in public.'

I had left Great Dvoryansky Street and was living in the suburb of Makarikha with my old nanny Karpovna, a kindly but morose old woman who lived in perpetual fear that something dreadful was about to happen. She was frightened by any kind of dream and even saw evil omens in the bees and wasps that flew into her room. In her opinion my becoming a workman was an evil portent.

'It's all up with you!' she said mournfully, shaking her head. 'You're finished!'

Prokofy the butcher, her adopted son, lived with her in that little house. He was a hulking, clumsy fellow of about thirty, with reddish hair and wiry moustache. Whenever we met in the hall he would not speak and would politely give way to me – if he happened to be drunk he would accord me a full military salute. When he dined in the evenings I could hear him grunting and sighing through the wooden plank partition as he polished off one glass of vodka after the other.

'Ma!' he would call in a low voice.

'What is it?' Karpovna would reply. (She loved her adopted son dearly.) 'What is it, sonny?'

'I'm going to do you a favour, Ma. I'll keep you in your old age, in this vale of tears, and when you die I'll pay all the funeral expenses. I mean it.'

I would be up before dawn every morning and I went early to

bed. We house-painters had good appetites and slept soundly, but for some reason my heart would beat violently at night. I never quarrelled with my workmates. All day long there was an endless torrent of abuse, obscene oaths, and sentiments such as 'Damn your eyes!' or 'Blast your guts!' were typical. However, we were all good friends. The lads suspected I was some kind of religious fanatic and poked good-humoured fun at me, saying that even my own father had disowned me. Then they would tell me that they seldom showed up at church and that many of them hadn't been to confession for ten years. They tried to justify this slackness by saying that painters were the black sheep of humanity.

The other men respected me and looked up to me. They were obviously pleased that I didn't smoke or drink, that I led a quiet, steady life. But they were rather shocked when I didn't help them steal drying oil or join them when they went to ask customers for tips. Stealing employers' oil and paint was common practice among painters and decorators and was not considered a crime. Remarkably, even someone as virtuous as Radish always took some whiting and oil after work, and even respectable old men with their own houses in Makarikha weren't above asking for tips. I would feel angry and ashamed when the lads, at the start or finish of some job, would all go cringing before some little pipsqueak, humbly thanking him for the ten copecks he gave them.

They behaved like sly courtiers to customers and almost every day I was reminded of Shakespeare's Polonius.

'Oh, it looks like rain,' a customer would remark, glancing at the sky.

'Yes, sir, no doubt about it,' the painters would agree.

'On the other hand, those aren't rain clouds. Perhaps it's not going to rain.'

'Oh, no, sir, that's for sure!'

Behind customers' backs their attitude was usually ironical – when they saw a gentleman, for example, sitting on his balcony with a newspaper they would remark, 'Can sit reading his paper all right, but I dare say he's got nothing to eat.'

I never visited my family. When I returned from work I would often find brief, worried notes from my sister, about Father. One day he'd been unusually pensive over dinner and had eaten nothing. Or he'd fallen down. Or he'd locked himself in his room and had not emerged for a long time. News like this worried me and kept me awake. I even used to walk past our house in Great Dvoryansky Street at night, looking into the dark windows and trying to find out if things were all right at home. On Sundays my sister would visit me, but she did this furtively, pretending she had come to see Nanny, not me. If she came into my room she would invariably look very pale, with tear-stained eyes, and she would immediately start crying.

'Father will never get over it!' she said. 'If something should happen to him, God forbid, it will be on your conscience for the rest of your life. It's dreadful, Misail! I beg you, turn over a new leaf, for Mother's sake!'

'My dear sister,' I said, 'how can I turn over a new leaf when I'm convinced that I'm acting according to my conscience? Try and understand that!'

'I know you're obeying your conscience, but why can't you do it differently, without upsetting everyone?'

'Oh, goodness gracious!' the old woman would sigh from behind the door. 'It's all up with you! There's trouble brewing, my dears, there's trouble brewing!'

VI

One Sunday Dr Blagovo paid me an unexpected visit. He was wearing a tunic over his silk shirt and high, patent-leather boots.

'I've come to see you!' he began, pressing my hand like a student. 'Every day I hear things about you and I've been meaning to come and have a heart-to-heart with you, as they say. It's deadly boring in this town. They all seem dead and there's no one you can have a conversation with. God, it's hot!' he went on, taking his tunic off, leaving just his silk shirt. 'My dear chap, please let's talk!'

I myself felt bored and for a long time had been wanting some other company than house-painters. I was genuinely delighted to see him.

'Let me begin,' he said, sitting on my bed, 'by saying how deeply I feel for you and how deeply I respect the kind of life you're leading. You're misunderstood in this town, but there's no one capable of understanding you here. As you know only too well, with one or two exceptions, they're all a lot of pig-faced freaks.[5] Right away, at the picnic, I guessed the kind of person you were. You are a noble, honest person with high principles. I respect you and it's a great honour to shake you by the hand!' he continued rapturously. 'To change your life as drastically and abruptly as you did, you first had to experience a complex emotional crisis. To continue as you are, always true to your convictions, you must try and put your heart and soul into it, day after day, never flagging. And now for a start, tell me if you agree that if you exercised your willpower, effort, all your potential, on something else – on eventually becoming a great scholar or artist – would your life be richer, deeper, more productive, in every respect?'

We kept talking and when we came to the subject of manual labour, I expressed the following opinion: 'The strong should not enslave the weak, the minority must not be parasites on the majority, or leeches, forever sucking their lifeblood. By that I mean – and without exception – everyone, strong or weak, rich or poor, should play his part in the struggle for existence. In this respect there's no better leveller than physical work, with *everyone* being forced to do some.'

'So you think that absolutely everyone must do physical work?' asked the doctor.

'Yes.'

'All right, but supposing everyone, including the cream of humanity – the thinkers and great scholars – played his part in the struggle for existence and wasted his time breaking stones or painting roofs. Wouldn't that be a serious threat to progress?'

'But where's the danger?' I asked. 'Surely progress is all about good deeds and obeying the moral law. If you don't enslave anyone, if you aren't a burden to anyone, what more progress do you need?'

'Look here!' Blagovo said, suddenly flying into a rage and leaping to his feet. 'Really! If a snail in its shell passes its time trying to perfect itself, messing around with moral laws – would you call that progress?'

'Why *messing around*?' I said, taking offence. 'If you stop compelling your neighbour to feed, clothe you, to transport you from place to place, to protect you from your enemies, isn't that progress, in the context of a life founded on slavery? In my opinion, that's progress and perhaps the only kind possible for man, the only kind that is really necessary.'

'There's no limit to the progress that man can make, and this applies all over the world. Any talk of "possible" progress, limited by our needs or short-term considerations, is strange, if you don't mind my saying so.'

'If progress has no limits, as you put it, then its aims are bound to be vague,' I said. 'Imagine living without knowing what for!'

'All right! But this "not knowing" isn't as boring as your "knowing". I climb a ladder called progress, civilization, culture. I keep climbing, not knowing precisely where I'm going, but in fact this wonderful ladder alone makes life worth living. But you know why you are living – so that some people stop enslaving others, so that the artist and the man who mixes his colours both have the same food to eat. But this vulgar, sordid, grey side of life – aren't you revolted, living for that alone? If some insects enslave others, then to hell with them! Let them gobble each other up! But it's not them we should be talking about; they will die and rot anyway, however hard you try to save them from slavery. The Great Unknown which awaits all mankind in the remote future – *that's* what we should be thinking about.'

Blagovo argued heatedly, but I could see that something else was worrying him. 'I don't think your sister's coming,' he said, looking at his watch. 'When she was with us yesterday she said she'd come out here to see you. You keep on and on about slavery . . .' he continued. 'But that's a particular case, isn't it, and mankind solves such problems gradually, as it goes along.'

We talked about gradual development. I said, 'The question

whether to do good or evil is decided by each person by himself, without waiting for mankind to solve the problem gradually. What's more, gradual development cuts two ways. Side by side with the gradual development of humane ideas we can observe the gradual growth of quite different ideas. Serfdom has been abolished,[6] but capitalism flourishes. Notions of freedom are all the rage now, but the majority still feeds, clothes and defends the minority, just as in the times of the Tatars, while it starves, goes naked and unprotected itself. This state of affairs fits in beautifully with any trend or current of opinion you like, since the art of enslavement is also being gradually refined. We don't flog our servants in the stables any more, but we develop refined forms of slavery – at least, we are very good at finding justification for it in isolated instances. Ideas are all right, but if now, at the end of the nineteenth century, it became possible for us to lumber working men with all our more unpleasant bodily functions, then lumber them we would. And then of course we would try and justify ourselves by saying that if the élite – the thinkers and great scholars – wasted their priceless time on these functions, then progress would be seriously jeopardized.'

Just then my sister arrived. Seeing the doctor, she fidgeted nervously, grew flustered and immediately said it was time to go home to Father.

'Now, Cleopatra,' Blagovo urged her, pressing both hands to his heart. 'What can possibly happen to your dear Papa if you stay just half an hour with me and your brother?'

He was quite open with us and was able to infect others with his high spirits. After a moment's deliberation my sister burst out laughing and suddenly cheered up, as she had done on the picnic. We went out into the fields, lay down on the grass and continued our conversation, looking at the town, where every window facing west seemed to have turned bright gold from the setting sun.

Every time my sister subsequently came to see me, Blagovo would turn up, and they greeted each other as if they had met accidentally in my room. As I argued with the doctor, my sister would listen, and her face would take on an ecstatic, deeply affected, inquisitive look. I had the impression that another world was gradually opening up before her, one that she had never even dreamt of and whose meaning she was now trying to fathom. Without the doctor there she was quiet and sad, and if she sometimes cried when she sat on my bed she never told me the reason.

In August Radish ordered us to leave for the railway line. Two days before we had received the command to 'get going' out of that town. Father came to see me. He sat down and wiped his red face without hurrying or looking at me. Then he took a local *Herald* out of his pocket and proceeded to read slowly, emphasizing every word, about how someone – the same age as me – the son of the manager of the State Bank, had been appointed departmental director in a provincial revenue office.

'Just look at yourself now!' he said, folding the paper. 'Beggar! Tramp! Ruffian! Even the working classes and peasants are educated, so they can take their place in life. And you, a Poloznev, for all your distinguished, noble ancestors, are heading straight for the rubbish dump. But I didn't come here to talk to *you*. I've already given you up as a bad job,' he went on in a subdued voice as he stood up. 'I've come to find out where your sister is, you scoundrel. She left the house after dinner, it's getting on for eight and she's still not back. She's started going out fairly often now without telling me. She hasn't the same respect for me – there I can see your evil, rotten influence. Where is she?'

He was holding that umbrella I knew so well and I was at my wits' end. Expecting a beating, I stood to attention. But he saw me glance at the umbrella and this probably put him off.

'Do what you like!' he said. 'You won't have my blessing!'

'Oh dear, oh dear!' Nanny muttered behind the door. 'You poor, stupid wretch. I feel deep down that there's trouble brewing. I can feel it!'

I started work on the railway line. For the whole of August it rained non-stop and it was damp and cold. They could not get the crops in from the fields, and on the big farms, where they used harvesting-machines, the wheat was lying in heaps instead of sheaves – I can remember those miserable heaps growing darker with every day that passed, the wheat germinating in them. It was hard to do any sort of work. The heavy rain ruined everything we tried to do. We weren't allowed to live or sleep in the station buildings, so we took shelter in filthy, damp dug-outs where the navvies had lived during the summer, and I could not sleep at night for the cold and the woodlice crawling across my face and arms. When we were working near the bridges, a whole gang of navvies turned up in the evenings just to give the painters a thrashing – this was a form of sport for them. They beat us, stole our brushes and – to provoke us to a fight – they smeared the railway huts with green paint. To cap it all, Radish started paying us extremely irregularly. All the painting in this section was handed over to some contractor who passed it on to someone else, who handed it on to Radish for a twenty per cent commission. We weren't paid much for the work – and there was that incessant rain. Time was wasted, we were unable to work, but Radish was obliged to pay the men daily. The hungry painters came near to beating him up, called him a swindler, bloodsucker, Judas, while the poor man sighed, held up his hands to heaven in desperation and went time and again to Mrs Cheprakov for money.

VII

A rainy, muddy, dark autumn set in. There was no work around and I would sit at home for days on end without anything to do. Or I would take on different jobs not connected with painting – shifting earth for foundations and getting twenty copecks a day for it. Dr Blagovo had gone to St Petersburg, my sister did not come any more, Radish was at home ill in bed, expecting to die any day.

And the general mood was autumnal. Perhaps it was because I was a working man now that I saw only the seamy side of town life and therefore I could not avoid making discoveries nearly every day that drove me to despair. My fellow citizens, of whom I already had a low opinion, or who appeared to be perfectly decent, now turned out to be contemptible, cruel people, capable of the meanest trick. They swindled simple working men like us, cheated us out of our money, made us wait hours on end in freezing entrance-halls or kitchens, insulted us and treated us very roughly. During the autumn I papered the reading-room and two other rooms at the club. I was paid seven copecks a roll, but I was told to sign for twelve, and when I refused, a handsome gentleman with gold-rimmed spectacles (most probably one of the senior members) told me, 'Just one more word from you and I'll bash your face in, you swine!'

And when a waiter whispered to him that I was the son of Poloznev the architect, he blushed with embarrassment, but immediately recovered and said 'To hell with him!'

At the local shops we workmen were fobbed off with rotten meat, stale flour and weak tea. In church we were shoved around by the police; in hospital we were robbed by junior staff and nurses, and if we didn't have the money to bribe them with, they took revenge by giving us our food on filthy plates. The most junior post office clerk thought he had the right to address us as if we were animals, yelling roughly and insolently: 'Hey, you there, wait! Where do you think you're going?' Even house dogs were hostile and attacked us particularly viciously. However, what startled me more than anything in my new job was the complete lack of fair play – precisely what the common people mean when they say that someone has become a 'lost soul'. Hardly a day passed without some kind of swindle. The merchants who sold us mixing oils, the main contractors, workmen, even customers – they all tried it on. Of course, there was no question of our having any rights, and we always had to beg for the money we had earned as we stood cap in hand at the back door.

I was papering one of the rooms next to the club reading-room. One evening as I was about to leave, the engineer Dolzhikov's daughter came in carrying a pile of books. I bowed.

'Oh, hullo!' she said, immediately recognizing me and holding out her hand. 'So glad to see you.'

She smiled and gave my smock, bucket of paste, the rolls of paper scattered over the floor an inquisitive, puzzled look. I was embarrassed and she felt the same.

'Please forgive me for staring at you,' she said. 'People have told me so much about you, especially Dr Blagovo. He's simply crazy about you. And I've met your sister. She's a charming, likeable girl, but I was unable to convince her that there's nothing terrible about the simple life you're leading. On the contrary, you're the most fascinating man in town now.'

She glanced once again at the bucket of paste and the wallpaper and went on: 'I've asked Dr Blagovo to help us to get to know each other better, but he's obviously forgotten or was too busy. At any rate, we already know each other and I'd be extremely obliged if you dropped in to see me some time. I'm really longing to have a talk with you! I'm a straightforward sort of person,' she continued, holding out her hand to me, 'and I hope you won't feel shy at my place. Father's away in St Petersburg.'

Her dress rustled as she entered the reading-room. It took me a long time to get to sleep after I was home.

During that gloomy autumn some kind soul, who obviously wanted to make my life a little easier, sent me tea, lemons, cakes and roast grouse from time to time. Karpovna said that a soldier always brought the food, but she didn't know who the sender was. The soldier would ask if I was well, if I had a hot meal every day and if I had warm clothes. When the frosts set in, the soldier came over as before, while I was out, with a soft woollen scarf. It had a delicate, very faint smell of perfume and I guessed who my good fairy was. The perfume was lily-of-the-valley, Anyuta Blagovo's favourite.

Towards winter there was more work about and everything cheered up. Radish recovered once more and together we worked in the cemetery chapel, cleaning the iconostasis and scraping it with palette knives before the gilding. It was clean, relaxing work – money for jam, as the lads put it. In one day we could get through a lot of work and besides that the time flew past imperceptibly. There was no swearing, laughter or noisy conversation. The very place encouraged us to be quiet and well-behaved and inspired us with calm, serious thoughts. Immersed in our work, we would stand or sit, as motionless as statues. There was the deathly silence befitting a cemetery and if someone dropped his tool or if the icon-lamp sputtered there was a sharp, resonant, echoing sound, which made us all look round. After a long silence we would hear a humming, just like a swarm of bees — they were reading burial prayers at the porch for an infant, in unhurried, hushed voices. Or the artist who was painting a dove surrounded by stars on a cupola would start softly whistling, then suddenly stop, remembering where he was. Or Radish would answer his own thoughts and sigh 'Anything's possible! Anything!' Or bells would toll slowly and mournfully above our heads and the painters would say that they must be burying some rich man.

I spent the days in that silence, in the church twilight, and on long evenings played billards or sat in the theatre gallery wearing the new woollen suit that I had bought with my wages. The performances and concerts had already started at the Azhogins'. Radish painted the scenery by himself now. He told me the plots of the plays and *tableaux vivants* which he had managed to see at the Azhogins', and I listened enviously. I had a strong urge to go to rehearsals, but I could not bring myself to go to the Azhogins'.

Dr Blagovo arrived a week before Christmas. Once again we argued and in the evenings we played billiards. During the games he would take off his jacket, unbutton his shirt at the front, and for some reason he was always trying to look like some inveterate rake. He did not drink very much, but became very rowdy when he did have a drop, managing to part with twenty roubles in an evening in a low pub like the Volga.

Once again my sister began visiting me. Both she and the doctor seemed surprised every time they happened to meet, but it was obvious from her joyful, guilty face that these meetings were not accidental. One evening the doctor asked me, when we were playing billiards, 'Listen, why don't you call on Mariya Viktorovna? You don't know how clever and charming she is, such a simple, kind soul.'

I told him about the reception I had got from her father in the spring.

'But it's stupid to talk like that!' the doctor laughed. 'There's a world of difference between the father and her! Now, my dear boy, don't offend her, try and call on her some time. What if we both went along tomorrow evening, together? Would you like that?'

He persuaded me. The following evening I put on my new woollen suit and set off, full of apprehension, to see Mariya Viktorovna. The footman didn't seem so snooty and intimidating as before, nor did the furniture look so luxurious as on that morning when I came to ask for a job. Mariya Viktorovna was expecting me and welcomed me like an old friend, shaking my hand firmly and warmly. She was wearing a grey, full-sleeved dress and her hair was done in the style that was called 'dogs' ears' a year later, when it became fashionable in town: it was combed back from the temple, over the ears, which made her face seem broader, and on this occasion she struck me as very like her father, who had a broad red face and an expression rather like a coachman's. She looked beautiful and elegant, but not young – about thirty perhaps, although she was in fact no more than twenty-five.

'That dear doctor, I'm so grateful to him!' she said, asking me to sit down. 'You wouldn't have come to see me if it hadn't been for him. I'm bored to death! Father's gone away and left me alone, and I don't know what to do with myself in this town.'

Then she began questioning me as to where I was working, what my wages were, where I lived.

'Do you earn enough to live on?' she asked.

'Yes.'

'You lucky man!' she sighed. 'I think all the evil in life comes from idleness, boredom, from nothing to exercise your mind on, and that's inevitable when you're used to living off others. Please don't get the idea that I'm just trying to impress. I mean this sincerely. It's not very interesting or pleasant being rich. They say "Make to yourselves friends of the mammon of unrighteousness"[7] because there's no such thing as honest wealth and there never can be.'

She gave the furniture a cold, serious look as if she wanted to make an inventory. Then she went on, 'Comfort and luxury have a magical power. They gradually drag even strong-willed people down. Father and I once lived modestly and simply, but now take a look. It's just unheard of. We get through twenty thousand a year,' she said, shrugging her shoulders. 'In the provinces!'

'Comforts and luxuries should be viewed as the inevitable privilege of capital and education,' I said, 'and it strikes me that the comforts of life can be combined with any type of work, even the hardest and dirtiest. Your father is rich, but he himself says that he once had to work as an engine-driver and ordinary greaser.'

She smiled and sceptically shook her head. 'Papa sometimes eats bread soaked in kvass too,' she said. 'It's just a whim of his!'

At that moment the doorbell rang and she stood up.

'Educated and rich people should work like everyone else,' she went on, 'and everyone should be able to share in the creature comforts. There shouldn't be any privileges. Well, that's enough of the theorizing. Tell me something to cheer me up. Tell me about the house-painters. What are they like? Funny?'

The doctor came in. I started telling them all about the painters, but I was short of conversational practice. This had an inhibiting effect and I talked in the earnest dull voice of an ethnographer. The doctor told some stories too, about workmen's lives. He staggered, wept, knelt and even lay down on the floor to imitate a drunkard. It was an excellent piece of mimicry and Mariya Viktorovna watched him and laughed until the tears came. Then he played the piano and sang in his pleasant, slight tenor voice while Mariya Viktorovna stood nearby choosing the songs and correcting him when he made a mistake.

'I've heard that you sing as well,' I said.

'Yes, she sings "as well"!' the doctor said, horrified. 'She's wonderful, a true artist. And you say she sings "as well". Really, that's a bit much!'

'I used to study it once quite seriously,' she answered, 'but I've given it up now.'

Sitting on a low stool, she told us about her life in St Petersburg and imitated some well-known singers, mimicking their voices and styles. She made a sketch of the doctor in her album and then me. Although she was poor at drawing, she produced good likenesses of us both. She laughed, grew mischievous, pulled faces most charmingly. This suited her better than all her talk of ill-gotten gains. I felt that she had not really meant what she had just said about wealth and comfort, that it was all a kind of masquerade. She was an excellent comic actress. I pictured her next to the young ladies from the town, and even the beautiful, majestic Anyuta Blagovo didn't bear comparison with her. The difference was enormous – like that between a fine, cultivated rose and a wild one.

The three of us had supper together. The doctor and Mariya Viktorovna drank red wine, champagne and then coffee with brandy. They clinked glasses and drank to friendship, intellect, progress, freedom. They didn't get drunk, only went red in the face, and they kept laughing at nothing until the tears flowed. As I didn't want to appear a wet blanket, I drank some red wine too.

'Extremely clever, richly gifted people,' Mariya Viktorovna said, 'know how to live and they go their own way. But average people, like myself, for example, know nothing and can't do anything on their own. All that's left for them is to take note of important social trends and swim along with the tide.'

'But you can't take note of what doesn't exist, can you?' the doctor asked.

'Doesn't exist? We only say that because we can't actually see it.'

'Really? Social trends are an invention of modern literature. We don't have any such trends.'

And an argument started.

'We don't have any profound social currents and we never did,' the doctor said in a loud voice. 'There's just no limit to what this modern literature has invented. It's even thought up these intellectual tillers of the soil, but search any village around here – all you'll find is country bumpkins in their jackets or black frock-coats who can't even write a three-letter word without making four mistakes. In this land of ours cultural life hasn't even begun. There's that same savagery, that same out-and-out boorishness, that same mediocrity that existed five hundred years ago. These trends and currents are a load of piffling, pitiful trash – they're all bound up with lousy little interests! How can you possibly see anything worthwhile in them? If you think you've spotted some important social trend and follow it and devote your life to the latest rage – say freeing insects from slavery, or abstaining from beef rissoles – then I must congratulate you, madam. We must study and study. But as for significant social trends, we're not mature enough for them yet and, to be honest, we understand nothing about them.'

'You don't understand, but I do,' Mariya Viktorovna said. 'Heavens, you're so dreadfully boring this evening!'

'Our job is to study, to try and accumulate as much knowledge as we can, since important social trends are to be found together with knowledge. The future happiness of mankind will proceed from knowledge alone. I drink to learning!'

'One thing is certain: we must reorganize our lives somehow,' Mariya Viktorovna said after a pause for thought. 'Up to now life hasn't been worth living. Let's not talk about it.'

When we left her the cathedral clock was already striking two.

'Did you like her?' the doctor asked. 'She's wonderful, isn't she?'

On Christmas Day we dined at Mariya Viktorovna's and we visited her almost every day during the holidays. We were the only visitors and she was right when she said that she knew no one in town besides myself and the doctor. We spent most of the time in long conversations. Sometimes the doctor brought a book or magazine, from which he read aloud to us. He was in fact the first educated man whom I had met. I'm not qualified to judge how much he knew, but he always let others into what he knew, as he wanted them to benefit from it. When it came to medicine, he was quite unlike any of our town doctors and what he said struck me as novel, something special. I felt that he could have become a real scholar had he wished. And he was perhaps the only man who had any serious influence on me at this time. After our frequent meetings and reading the books he gave me, I felt more and more the need for knowledge that might breathe life into my cheerless labours. Now it seemed strange that I hadn't known before that the whole world consisted of sixty elements, for example, or what oils or paint were made from, and that somehow I had got by without knowing these things. My friendship with the doctor uplifted me morally too. We often argued, and although I usually stuck to my opinions, it was thanks to him that I gradually became aware I just didn't understand everything, and I tried to devise the most stringent moral guidelines, so that my conscience would not be clouded or muddled.

For all that, the doctor, the most educated, the best man in the whole town, was far from perfect. In his manners, in his readiness to argue, in his pleasant tenor voice – even in his friendliness – there was something rather crude and bumptious. Whenever he took his coat off and walked around in his silk shirt, or when he tipped a waiter at a restaurant, I always had the impression that there was something of the barbarian in him, despite his being a cultured man.

One morning, towards Epiphany, he returned to St Petersburg. After dinner my sister came to see me. Without taking off her fur coat or hat she sat silently, very pale, staring at something. She had the shivers and I could see she was fighting against it.

'You must have caught a cold,' I said.

Her eyes filled with tears. She stood up and went over to Karpovna without a word to me, as if I had offended her. Shortly afterwards I heard her bitterly complaining voice: 'Nanny, what have I been living for up to now? What for? Tell me, I've wasted my youth, haven't I? The best years of my life have been spent keeping accounts, pouring tea, counting copecks, entertaining guests, in the conviction that there was nothing better! Please understand, Nanny, I have spiritual needs like anyone else and I want to lead a full life. But all they've done is turn me into a kind of housekeeper! Don't you think that's dreadful?'

She flung the keys through the doorway and they fell clattering to the floor in my room. They were the keys to the sideboard, kitchen cupboard, cellar and china cabinet – keys that Mother had once carried.

'Oh dear, oh dear me!' the old woman said in horror. 'Saints above!'

As she left, my sister came into my room to pick up the keys.

'Forgive me,' she said. 'Something strange has been happening to me recently.'

VIII

One day, in the late evening, I came home from Mariya Viktorovna's to find a young police officer in a new uniform sitting at my table looking through a book.

'At last!' he said, standing up and stretching himself. 'This is the third time I've been. The Governor has ordered you to report to him at precisely nine o'clock tomorrow morning. Without fail.'

After taking a signed statement from me that I would do exactly what the Governor had ordered, he left. The police officer's late visit, plus the unexpected invitation to the Governor's, utterly depressed me. Since early childhood I have always been scared of gendarmes, policemen and court officials, and now I was worried stiff that I might really have committed some crime. I just could not sleep. Nanny and Prokofy were upset too and they couldn't sleep either. And Nanny had earache as well. She kept groaning, and several times she started crying from the pain. Hearing that I was awake, Prokofy gingerly entered my room with a lamp and sat down at the table.

'You should drink some pepper-brandy,' he said after a moment's thought. 'A drink won't never do you harm in this vale of tears. And if Nanny had a drop of that stuff in her ear it would do her the world of good.'

After two o'clock he prepared to leave for the slaughterhouse to fetch some meat. I knew that I wouldn't sleep before morning, so I went with him to kill the time until nine o'clock. We took a lamp with us. Prokofy's assistant Nikolka, a thirteen-year-old boy with blue patches on his face from frostbite – a real bandit from the look of him – urged on his horse in a husky voice as he followed us in a sledge.

'Like as not you'll be punished at the Governor's,' Prokofy told me on the way. 'Governors, archimandrites, officers, doctors – every calling has its own proper way of doing things. But you don't fall into line at all, you won't get away with that.'

The slaughterhouse was beyond the cemetery and up to now I'd only seen it from the distance. It consisted of three gloomy sheds surrounded by a grey fence, and they gave off a suffocating stench when the wind blew from their direction on hot summer days. But it was so dark as we went into the yard we couldn't see them. I kept meeting horses and sledges – either empty or laden with meat. Men were walking around with lamps, cursing and swearing obscenely. Prokofy and Nikolka swore just as badly, and the incessant sound of abuse, coughing and the neighing of horses filled the air.

There was a smell of carcases and dung. It was thawing and snow mingled with the mud – in the darkness I felt I was walking over pools of blood.

When our sledge was fully laden we went off to the butcher's stall in the market. Day was breaking. Cooks with baskets and elderly women in cloaks passed by, one after the other. Cleaver in hand and wearing a blood-stained white apron, Prokofy swore terribly, crossed himself in the direction of the church and shouted all over the market that he was selling his meat at cost price, at a loss even. He gave short weight and short change. Despite seeing this, the cooks were so deafened by his shouting that they offered no protest, apart from calling him swindler and crook. Raising and bringing down that fearful cleaver with a fierce 'Ugh!' every time, he assumed picturesque poses. I was scared that he really might chop off someone's head or hand.

I spent the whole morning at the butcher's and when I finally went to the Governor's my fur coat smelt of meat and blood. I felt that someone had ordered me to go and attack a bear with a spear. I remember that steep staircase with its striped carpet and the young clerk in coat and tails with bright buttons silently pointing towards a door with both hands and then dashing off to announce me. I entered the hall, which was luxurious but cold, and tastelessly furnished. The narrow wall mirrors and bright yellow curtains were particular eyesores. I could see that governors might come and go, but the furnishings stayed the same for ever. The young clerk again pointed at the door with both hands and I went over to a large green table, behind which stood a general with the Order of Vladimir round his neck.

'Mr Poloznev, I asked you to report to me,' he began, holding some letter and opening his mouth wide, like the letter 'O'. 'I asked you to come here so that I can inform you of the following. Your dear respected father has applied both orally and in writing to the Provincial Marshal of the Nobility, requesting him to summon you and make quite clear to you the absolute incompatibility of your behaviour with the title of gentleman, to which class you have the honour to belong. His Excellency Alexander Pavlovich, rightly assuming that your behaviour might lead others into temptation, and finding that mere persuasion on his part might be insufficient and that it was a clearcut case for serious intervention on the part of the authorities, has conveyed his opinion of you in this letter. That opinion I happen to share.'

He said all this softly, respectfully, standing upright as though I were his superior. And there was nothing at all severe in the way he looked at me. His face was flabby, worn, and covered with wrinkles, with bags under the eyes. He dyed his hair and it was impossible to guess his age by looking at him – he could have been forty or sixty.

'I hope,' he went on, 'that you appreciate the tact of honourable Alexander Pavlovich in approaching me privately and not through official channels. I also invited you unofficially and I'm not talking to you as Governor but as a sincere admirer of your father. So, I'm asking you. Either mend your ways and return to those responsibilities befitting your rank. Failing that, to keep yourself out of trouble, go and live somewhere else, where you're not known and where you can do what you like. Otherwise I shall be compelled to take extreme measures.'

He stood surveying me in silence for about thirty seconds, his mouth wide open. 'Are you a vegetarian?'[8] he asked.

'No, sir, I eat meat.'

He sat down and reached for some document. I bowed and left.

It wasn't worth going to work before dinner and I went back home to sleep, but I was unable to because of the unpleasant feelings aroused by the slaughterhouse and the conversation with the Governor. I waited until evening and then went off to Mariya Viktorovna's in a gloomy, troubled frame of mind. I told her that I had been to the Governor's and she looked at me in disbelief. Then she suddenly broke into the kind of loud, cheerful, uninhibited laugh that only good-natured people with a sense of humour can produce.

'If only I could tell them in St Petersburg!' she said, leaning towards the table and nearly collapsing with laughter. 'If only I could tell them in St Petersburg!'

IX

Now we met quite often, about twice a day. Almost every afternoon she came to the cemetery, where she read the inscriptions on crosses and tombstones while waiting for me. Sometimes she would come into the church and stand by me, watching me work. The silence, the painters' and gilders' simple work, Radish's good sense, the fact that outwardly I was no different from the other men and worked just as they did, in waistcoat and old shoes, and the fact that they spoke to me as if I were one of them – all this was new to her and she found it moving. Once when she was there an artist who was high up painting a dove shouted down to me, 'Misail, give me some whiting.'

I carried it up to him, and afterwards, when I was climbing down the rickety scaffolding, she looked at me, moved to tears, and smiling.

'What a dear you are!' she said.

Ever since I was a child I remembered how a green parrot had escaped from its cage in one of the rich men's houses in the town and how it had wandered round the town for a whole month, lazily flying from garden to garden, lonely and homeless. Mariya Viktorovna put me in mind of that bird.

'At the moment I've absolutely nowhere to go besides the cemetery,' she told me laughing. 'I'm bored to death in this town. At the Azhogins' they do nothing but read, sing and babble away; I just can't stand them lately. Your sister keeps to herself, Mademoiselle Blagovo hates me for some reason, and I don't like the theatre. So where can I go?'

When I visited her I smelt of paint and turpentine and my hands were black. She liked this and wanted me to wear only my ordinary working clothes when I called on her. But they made me feel awkward in her drawing-room – it was as if I were in uniform, and therefore I always wore my new woollen suit when I went there. She didn't like this.

'You must admit, you haven't quite got used to your new role,' she told me once. 'You feel awkward and embarrassed in your workman's clothes. Tell me, is it because you've lost confidence in yourself, because you're dissatisfied? This work you've chosen – all this splashing paint around – does that really satisfy you?' she asked, laughing. 'I know that painting makes things prettier, makes them last longer, but surely these things belong to the rich people in town and are really luxuries. Besides, as you yourself said more than once, everyone should earn bread by his labours, whereas you earn money, not bread. Why don't you stick to the literal meaning of what you say? If it's *bread* that you have to earn, then you must plough, sow, reap, thresh, or do something directly connected with agriculture – keeping cows, for example, digging, building log-huts . . .'

She opened a pretty little cupboard near her writing-table and said, 'I've been telling you all this because I want to let you into my secret. *Voilà*. This is my agricultural library. Here are books on arable land, vegetable gardens, orchards, cattle-yards and bee-keeping. I love reading them, and I know all the theory already, in great detail. It's my dream, my cherished wish to go to Dubechnya as soon as March is here. It's wonderful there, fantastic! Don't you agree? For the first year I'll just look around to get the hang of things, but the following year I'll really start work, without sparing myself, as they say. Daddy's promised me Dubechnya and I can do anything I want there.'

Blushing, laughing and excited to the point of tears, she daydreamed aloud about her life at Dubechnya, about how interesting it would be. And I envied her. March wasn't far away, the days were drawing out, thawing snow dripped from the roofs at midday in the bright sun and the smell of spring was in the air. I too longed for the country.

When she said that she was moving to Dubechnya I immediately saw myself left alone in the town, and I felt jealous of her book cupboard and her farming.

I didn't know a thing about farming and I had no love for it. I almost told her that farming was a form of slavery, but I remembered my father having said something of the sort more than once, so I remained silent.

Lent began. Viktor Ivanych, the engineer, whose existence I had just about forgotten, arrived from St Petersburg quite unexpectedly, without even sending a telegram beforehand. When I arrived – in the evening, as usual – there he was, pacing the drawing-room and talking. He had just washed, and with his hair cut short he looked about ten years younger. His daughter was kneeling by his trunks, taking out boxes, scent bottles and books and handing them to Pavel, one of the male servants. When I saw the engineer I couldn't help taking a step backwards, but he stretched both hands out to me and revealed his firm, white, coachman's teeth as he smiled and said, 'So it's him! Here he is! Delighted to see you, Mr Painter! Masha's told me everything; she's been praising you to the skies. I understand you and heartily approve of what you're doing.'

He took me by the arm and continued: 'Being an honest workman is a sight more clear-headed and decent than using up reams of paper and wearing a ribbon in your hat. I used to work in Belgium myself, with these hands you see here, then I was an engine-driver for two years.'

He wore a short jacket and comfortable house-slippers, and he walked with a slight roll, as if he were suffering from gout; he kept rubbing his hands. He hummed, purred softly and squeezed himself from the sheer pleasure of being home again and having taken his beloved shower.

'There's no denying it,' he told me over supper, 'there's no denying it. You are all nice, charming people, but as soon as you try to do any physical work or look after the peasants you end up religious fanatics. Why is it? Now, don't deny it, you belong to some religious sect, don't you? You don't drink vodka, eh? What's that if it isn't belonging to some sect?'

Just to please him I drank some vodka, and some wine too. We tried different cheeses, sausages, pâtés, pickles and various savouries which the engineer had brought with him, and the wines that had arrived while he was abroad. The wines were excellent. Somehow he managed to bring in his wines and cigars duty-free. Someone sent him caviare and smoked sturgeon for nothing; he paid no rent for the flat since the landlord supplied paraffin to the railway. The general impression he and his daughter gave me was that all the best things in life were theirs for the asking and they received them free of charge.

I went on visiting them, but not so enthusiastically as before. The engineer cramped my style and I always felt uncomfortable when he was around. I could not stand those clear, innocent eyes, and his offensive remarks were very tiresome. I was irked by the thought too that only recently I had been under the command of that well-fed, red-faced man and that he had been dreadfully rude to me. True, he put his arm round my waist now, gave me friendly slaps on the shoulder and approved of my way of life, but I sensed that he still despised me for being a mediocrity and he only put up with me for his daughter's sake. I could no longer laugh or say what I wanted, so I became stand-offish, and I was always expecting him to address me as a servant, like Pavel. How my petty provincial pride suffered! I, one of the working masses, a house-painter, visited the rich almost every day, people who lived in a different world, whom the whole town looked on as foreigners. Every day I drank expensive wines at their houses and ate exotic food – my conscience would not come to terms with that! On my way to their place I tried to look gloomy and avoided passers-by and scowled at them as if I really did belong to some religious sect. But when I left the engineer's I was ashamed I had wined and dined so well.

Most of all, I was scared of falling in love. Whether I was walking down the street, working, talking to my workmates, all I could think of was going to see Mariya Viktorovna in the evening, and I would imagine her voice, her laughter, her walk. Before each visit I would stand for a long time in front of Nanny's crooked looking-glass, tying my tie. My woollen suit repelled me. I was going through hell and at the same time I despised myself for taking such trivial things so seriously. When she called out from another room to say that she was not dressed yet and asked me to wait, I could hear her putting on her clothes. This disturbed me and I felt as though the floor were sinking under me. Whenever I saw a woman in the street, even far off, I could not help making comparisons, and then all our women and girls seemed vulgar, ridiculously dressed and without poise. These comparisons aroused the pride in me. Mariya Viktorovna was the best of the lot! And at night I dreamed of both of us.

Once, at supper, both of us, together with the engineer, polished off a whole lobster. Back home I remembered the engineer twice calling me 'My dear young man!' over supper and I realized that they were spoiling me like a huge, wretched stray dog; that they were only amusing themselves with me; and that they would drive me away like a dog when they were bored with me. I was ashamed and hurt – so hurt, I was close to tears, as if someone had insulted me. I looked up at the sky and vowed to put an end to it all.

Next day I didn't go to the Dolzhikovs'. Late that evening (it was quite dark and raining) I strolled along Great Dvoryansky Street looking at the windows. At the Azhogins everyone was in bed – only one light burnt in one of the windows right at the end of the house – that was old Mrs Azhogin embroidering by the light of three candles and imagining she was carrying on the battle against superstition. Our house was dark, but over the road, at the Dolzhikovs', the windows were bright, though I couldn't see inside for the flowers and curtains. I continued to walk up and down the street and was drenched by the cold March rain. I heard Father returning from the club; he knocked on the gate and a minute later a light appeared at one of the windows and I saw my sister hurrying with a lamp and smoothing her thick hair with one hand as she went. Then Father paced the drawing-room, talking and rubbing his hands together, while my sister sat motionless in an armchair thinking and not listening to him.

But then they left the room and the light went out. I looked round at the engineer's house – it was as dark as a well there now. In the gloom and the rain I felt desperately lonely, left to the mercy of fate. I felt that in comparison with my loneliness, my present sufferings, with what lay in store for me, how trivial everything was that I had ever done or wished for, thought or spoken of. Alas, the actions and thoughts of living beings are not nearly as important as their sorrows! Without knowing exactly what I was doing, I tugged as hard as I could at the bell on the Dolzhikovs' gate – and broke it. I ran off in terror down the street like a naughty child, convinced they would come out at once and recognize me. When I stopped to catch my breath at the end of the street all I could hear was falling rain and a nightwatchman, far away, banging on his iron sheet.

For a whole week I stayed away from the Dolzhikovs'. I sold my woollen suit. There was no painting work about and once again I was half-starving, earning ten to twelve copecks a day where I could by doing heavy, nasty work. Wallowing up to my knees in cold mud and using all my strength, I tried to suppress any memories, as if taking revenge on myself for all those cheeses and tinned delicacies the engineer had treated me to. But no sooner did I climb into bed, hungry and wet, than my sinful imagination began to conjure up wonderful, seductive pictures and to my amazement I realized that I was in love, passionately so, and I would drop into a sound, healthy sleep, feeling that all the penal servitude was only making my body stronger.

One evening it snowed – quite out of season – and the wind blew from the north as if winter had returned. When I was home from work I found Mariya Viktorovna sitting in my room. She wore her fur coat, with her hands in a muff.

'Why don't you come any more?' she asked, raising her clever, bright eyes. I was overcome with joy and stood stiffly in front of her, just as I had done before Father when he was about to hit me. She looked into my face and I could see by her eyes that she understood why I was overcome.

'Why don't you come any more?' she repeated. 'Well, as you don't want to, I've come to you instead.'

She stood up and came close to me.

'Don't leave me,' she said, her eyes filling with tears. 'I'm lonely, so terribly lonely!'

She began to cry and hid her face in her muff. 'I'm lonely. Life is so dreadful, really dreadful, and besides you I've no one in the whole wide world. Don't leave me!'

She searched for a handkerchief to dry her eyes and gave me a smile. We said nothing for some time, then I embraced her and kissed her, scratching my cheek on her hatpin until it bled. And we started talking as if we had been close to one another for a long, long time.

X

Two days later she sent me to Dubechnya, and words could not describe how delighted I was. As I walked to the station and later, as I sat in the train, I laughed for no reason and people thought I was drunk. It was snowing and there was frost in the mornings, but the roads were turning brown, and cawing rooks circled above them.

The first thing I wanted was to arrange accommodation for Masha and myself in the outbuilding, opposite Mrs Cheprakov's. But it turned out to have long been the home of pigeons and ducks and it would have been impossible to clean it out without destroying a large number of nests. Whether we liked it or not, we had to move into the bleak rooms with Venetian blinds in the big house. This house was called The Palace by the peasants. It had more than twenty rooms, but the only furniture was a piano and a child's armchair in the attic. Even if Masha had brought all her furniture from the town, we could not have destroyed that bleak, empty, cold atmosphere. I chose three small rooms with windows looking onto the garden, and I was busy from dawn to dusk cleaning them, putting in new window-panes, hanging wallpaper and filling in cracks and holes in the floor. It was easy, pleasant work. Now and then I ran down to the river to see if the ice was breaking up and I kept imagining that the starlings had returned. At night, as I thought of Masha, I felt overjoyed and entranced as I listened to the scurrying rats and the wind sighing and knocking above the ceiling. It sounded as if some old house goblin was coughing up in the attic.

The snow was deep. At the end of March there was another heavy fall, but it thawed quickly, as if by magic. The spring floods surged past and by the beginning of April the starlings were already chattering and yellow butterflies flitted around the garden. It was marvellous weather. Every day, just before evening, I went off to town to meet Masha. And how enjoyable it was walking barefoot along a road that was drying, but still soft! Halfway I would sit down and look at the town, not daring to go nearer. The sight of it disturbed me. I kept wondering how my friends would react once they heard of my love. What would Father say? The thought that my life had become so complicated that I could no longer keep it under control worried me more than anything. Life was carrying me away like a balloon – God knows where. I no longer thought about making ends meet or earning a living. I honestly can't remember what I was thinking about.

When Masha arrived in her carriage, I would sit next to her and we would drive off to Dubechnya, happy and free. At other times, after waiting for the sun to set, I would go home, disconsolate and bored, wondering why she hadn't come. Then suddenly a delightful apparition would greet me at the gate or in the garden – Masha! Later it turned out that she had come by train and had walked from the station. And what a wonderful occasion this used to be! She wore a modest woollen dress and scarf and held a simple umbrella. At the same time, she was tightly corseted and slim, and she wore expensive foreign boots. This was a talented actress playing the part of a small-town housewife. We would inspect the place and try to decide what rooms we would take and plan the paths, kitchen-garden and beehives. Already we had ducks and geese that we loved because they were ours. We had clover, oats, timothy grass, buckwheat and vegetable seeds – all ready for sowing. We spent a long time examining these things and wondering what the harvest would be like. Everything that Masha told me seemed exceptionally clever and fine. This was the happiest time of my life.

Soon after Easter we were married in our parish church at Kuri-lovka, the village about two miles from Dubechnya. Masha wanted everything simple. At her wish the ushers were lads from the village, and one parish clerk did all the singing. We returned from church in a small, shaky trap, which she drove. The only guest from town was my sister, to whom Masha had sent a note a couple of days before the wedding; she wore a white dress and gloves. During the ceremony she cried softly for joy, being deeply touched, and her expression was motherly, infinitely kind. Our happiness had intoxicated her and she smiled continually, as if inhaling heady fumes. Watching her during the service I realized that for her there was nothing finer in the whole world than earthly love. This was what she had always secretly longed for, timidly yet passionately. She kissed and embraced Masha. Not knowing how to express her joy she told her, 'He's a good man, so good!'

Before leaving she changed into her ordinary clothes and led me into the garden to talk to me in private.

'Father's very upset you didn't write,' she said. 'You should have asked for his blessing. But he's actually very pleased with you. He says that this wedding will raise your social status and that, under Masha's influence, you'll take things more seriously. We only talk about you in the evenings, and yesterday he even called you "our Misail". This gave me so much joy. It seems he has a plan of some kind and I think that he wants to show you how magnanimous he can be, by being the first to talk of a reconciliation. Most likely he'll soon be coming to see you here.'

Several times she quickly made the sign of the cross over me and said, 'Well, God bless you. Be happy. Anyuta Blagovo is a very clever girl. She says that your marriage is a fresh ordeal sent by God. Yes, family life is not all bliss, there's suffering too. You can't avoid it.'

Masha and I walked about two miles with her as we saw her off. On our way back we walked quietly and slowly, as if taking a rest. Masha held my arm; I felt easy at heart and I didn't want to talk about love any more. After the wedding we had grown even closer, had become kindred spirits, and it seemed nothing could keep us apart.

'Your sister is a nice person,' Masha said, 'but she looks as if she's been suffering never-ending torments. Your father must be a horrible man.'

I began telling her how my sister and I had been brought up and how our childhood had really been a meaningless ordeal. When she learnt that my father had struck me only recently she shuddered and pressed close to me.

'Don't say any more,' she said. 'It's terrible.'

And now she did not leave me. We lived in three rooms in the big house and in the evenings we bolted the door to the empty part of the house, as if some stranger we feared was living there. I would rise at the crack of dawn and immediately get down to work. I used to mend carts, lay paths in the garden, dig the flowerbeds, paint the roof of the house. When the time for sowing oats came I tried double-ploughing, harrowing. All this I did conscientiously, and did not lag behind our farm labourer. I would become exhausted; the rain and the sharp, cold wind made my face and legs burn, and at nights I dreamed of ploughed land. Working in the fields held no delights for me. I knew nothing about farming and I disliked it – probably because my ancestors had never been tillers of the soil and pure town blood ran in my veins. I loved nature dearly, the fields and meadows and the vegetable gardens. But the wet, ragged peasant turning the earth with his plough and craning his neck as he urged on his wretched horse was for me the embodiment of crude, savage, monstrous strength. As I watched his clumsy movements I could never stop myself thinking of that long-past, legendary life, when man did not know the use of fire. Awesome bulls roaming around the peasant's herd, horses stampeding through the village with pounding hooves – they scared the wits out of me. Any creature that was in the least large, strong and angry, whether a horned ram, a gander or a watchdog, seemed to symbolize that wild, crude strength. This prejudice was particularly strong in bad weather, when heavy clouds hung over the black plough-lands. But most of all, whenever I ploughed or sowed and two or three peasants stood watching me, I did not feel that my work was in any sense indispensable or that I was obliged to do it: I seemed to be merely amusing myself. I preferred working in the yard and I liked nothing better than painting roofs.

I used to walk through the garden and the meadow to our mill. This was rented to Stefan, a handsome, dark-skinned, tough-looking

peasant from Kurilovka, with a thick black beard. He did not like
working the mill, thinking it boring and unprofitable, and he only
lived there to escape from home. He was a saddle-maker and always
had a pleasant smell of tar and leather about him. Not very talkative,
he was lethargic and sluggish. He was always humming, always
sitting on the river bank or in his doorway. Sometimes his wife and
mother-in-law – both pale-faced, languid and meek creatures –
would come over from Kurilovka to see him. They would bow low
and call him 'Mr Stefan Petrovich'. He would not reply with a single
movement or word, but sat by himself on the river bank softly
humming. An hour or so would pass in silence. Then, after whispering
to each other, the mother-in-law and wife would stand up and look
at him for some time, waiting for him to turn round. Then they
would make low curtsies and say 'Goodbye, Stefan Petrovich!' in
their sugary, singsong voices. And then they would leave. Taking
the bundle of rolls or the shirt they had left for him, Stefan would
sigh and wink in their direction.

'Women!' he would say.

The two stones at the mill worked day and night. I helped Stefan
and I enjoyed it. Whenever he went away I willingly took over.

XI

After the fine, warm weather there was a wet spell. Throughout May
it rained and it was cold. The sound of the mill-wheels and the rain
made one feel sleepy and lazy; so did the shaking floor and smell of
flour. My wife appeared twice a day in her short fur jacket and rubber
boots, and she would invariably say the same thing: 'Call this summer!
It's worse than October!'

We would drink tea together, cook porridge, or silently sit for
hours on end waiting for the rain to stop. Once, when Stefan had
gone to the fair, Masha spent the whole night at the mill. When we
got up, there was no telling what the time was, as the whole sky was
dark with rain clouds. But sleepy cocks crowed in Dubechnya and

corncrakes cried in the meadow: it was still very, very early. I went down to the millpond with my wife and hauled out the fish-trap that Stefan had thrown in the previous evening while we were there. One large perch was floundering about and a crayfish angrily stretched its claws upwards.

'Let them go,' Masha said. 'Let them be happy too . . .'

Because we had got up very early and then done nothing, the day seemed extremely long, the longest day in my life. Just before evening Stefan returned and I went back home to the big house.

'Your father came today,' Masha told me.

'Where is he, then?'

'He's gone. I sent him away.'

Seeing me standing there in silence, she realized that I was sorry for Father.

'One must be consistent. I didn't let him in and I sent a message telling him not to trouble himself about coming again.'

A minute later I was through the gates and on my way to sort things out with Father. It was muddy, slippery and cold. For the first time since the wedding I felt sad, and the thought that I was not living as I should flashed through my brain, which was exhausted by the long, grey day. I felt worn out, and gradually I succumbed to faint-heartedness and inertia: I had no desire to move or to think. After a few steps I gave up and went home.

Dolzhikov was standing in the middle of the yard, in a leather coat with hood.

'Where's the furniture?' he shouted. 'There used to be beautiful empire-style things, paintings, vases, but they've collared the lot! To hell with her, I bought the estate *with* the furniture!'

Close by, Moisey, the general's wife's handyman, stood crumpling his cap. He was about twenty-five, thin, pock-marked and with small, cheeky eyes. One cheek was larger than the other, as if he'd been lying on it.

'But, sir, you did buy it without the furniture,' he said sheepishly. 'I do remember that.'

'Shut up!' the engineer shouted, turning crimson and shaking all over. His voice echoed right round the garden.

XII

Whenever I worked in the garden or in the yard, Moisey would stand nearby, hands behind his back, idly and cheekily looking at me with those tiny eyes of his. This irritated me so much that I would leave what I was doing and go away.

Stefan revealed that this Moisey had been the general's wife's lover. I noticed that when people came for money they would first turn to Moisey, and once I saw a peasant, black all over (he was probably a charcoal-burner), prostrating himself in front of him. Sometimes after an exchange of whispers he would hand out the money himself, without telling the mistress, from which I deduced that he did business transactions of his own, on the quiet.

He used to go shooting right under the windows in the garden, filched food from our larders and took horses without our permission. We were furious, and Dubechnya didn't seem to be ours at all. Masha would turn pale.

'Do we have to live with this scum for another eighteen months?' she would ask.

Ivan, the son of the general's wife, was a guard on our railway. During the winter he had grown terribly thin and weak. Just one glass of vodka was enough to make him drunk and he felt the cold if he was out of the sun. He loathed and was ashamed of having to wear a guard's uniform. But it was a profitable job, he thought, since he was able to steal candles and sell them. My new position aroused mixed feelings in him – amazement, envy and the vague hope that he too might be lucky. He followed Masha with admiring eyes, asked what I had for dinner these days. His gaunt, ugly face would take on a sickly, sad expression and he twiddled his fingers as though he could actually touch my good fortune.

'Now, listen, Better-than-Nothing,' he said fussily, constantly relighting his cigarette. He always made a terrible mess wherever he stood, since he wasted dozens of matches on one cigarette. 'Listen, things have reached rock-bottom with me. The worst of it is, every tinpot little subaltern thinks he's entitled to shout "Hey, you, guard!

You over there!" I've just about had enough of hearing all sorts of things in trains, and now I can see that this life stinks! My mother's ruined me! A doctor told me once in a train that if the parents have no morals, then the children turn out drunks or criminals. That's what!'

Once he came staggering into the yard, his eyes wandering aimlessly, his breathing heavy. He laughed, cried and went on as if he was delirious. All I could make out in that gibberish was 'Mother! Where's my mother?', which he said weeping, like a child that has lost its mother in a crowd. I led him into the garden and laid him down under a tree. All day and night Masha and I took it in turns to sit with him. He was in a bad state and Masha looked into his pale, wet face with revulsion.

'Are we really going to have this scum living in our yard another eighteen months? That's horrible, horrible!' she said.

And how much distress the peasants caused us! How many deep disappointments we suffered from the very beginning, in the spring, when we yearned for happiness! My wife was building a school for them. I drew up a plan for a school for sixty boys. The local authorities approved it but advised us to build it at Kurilovka, that large village about two miles away. As it happened, the school at Kurilovka, which was attended by children from four villages, including Dubechnya, was old and cramped and one had to be careful walking over the rotten floorboards. At the end of March Masha was appointed trustee of the Kurilovka school, as she had wished, and at the beginning of April we arranged three meetings where we tried to convince the peasants that their school was cramped and old, and someone from the local council and the inspector of state schools came. They too tried to make the peasants see sense. After each meeting they surrounded us and asked for a barrel of vodka. We felt hot amongst all that crowd and were very soon exhausted. So we went home, feeling dissatisfied and rather embarrassed. In the end the peasants picked a site for the school and had to fetch all the building materials from the town on their own horses. The first Sunday after the spring wheat had been sown, carts left Kurilovka and Dubechnya to fetch bricks for the foundations. The men left as soon as it was light and came back late in the evening – drunk, and complaining what a rotten job it was.

As if to spite us, the cold rainy weather lasted the whole of May. The roads were thick with mud. After returning from town the carts usually entered our yard, and what a dreadful sight this was! A pot-bellied horse would appear at the gates, straddling its forelegs. Before coming into the yard it appeared to bow; then a wet, slimy-looking thirty-foot beam would slide in on a low cart. Wrapped up against the rain, his coat flaps tucked inside his belt, a peasant would stride along beside it, not looking where he was going, and walking straight through the puddles. Another cart laden with planks would appear, then a third carrying a beam, then a fourth. Gradually the space in front of the house would become choked with horses, beams and planks. With heads covered and clothes tucked up, the peasants – both the men and women – would look malevolently at our windows, make a dreadful racket and demand that the lady of the house come out. The swearing was appalling. Moisey would stand to one side and seemed to be revelling in the ignominy of our position.

'We don't want to do any more shifting!' the peasants would shout. 'We're worn out! Let her go and fetch the stuff herself!'

Pale-faced and scared out of her wits at the thought that they might try and break into the house, Masha would send out the money for half a barrel. After that the noise would die down, and, one after the other, the long beams would trundle out of the yard again.

Whenever I went to the building-site my wife grew worried.

'The peasants are in a nasty temper,' she would say. 'They might do something to you. Wait a moment, I'm coming with you.'

We would drive to Kurilovka together and there the carpenters would ask us for a tip. The timber frame was ready; it was time for laying the foundations, but the bricklayers didn't turn up. The carpenters grumbled at the delay. When the bricklayers finally did turn up, they found that there was no sand – for some reason we'd forgotten this would be needed. The peasants took advantage of our desperate situation and asked for thirty copecks a load, although it wasn't more than a few hundred yards from the site to the river, where the sand was taken from. And we needed more than five hundred loads. There was no end to the misunderstandings, swearing and cadging, which exasperated my wife. The foreman-bricklayer – an old man of seventy, by the name of Titus Petrov – would take her by the arm and say, 'Look 'ere! Just you bring me that sand and I'll have ten men 'ere in two ticks and the job'll be done in a couple of days. You see to it!'

The sand was brought; two days, four days, a week went by and still there was a gaping hole where the foundations were to be laid.

'It's enough to drive you insane!' my wife said, terribly agitated. 'What dreadful, really dreadful people!'

While all these arguments were going on, Viktor Ivanych came to see us. He brought some hampers of wine and savouries, took his time over his meal, then lay down on the terrace to sleep, snoring so loudly that the workmen shook their heads and said, 'Now wotcher think of that!'

Masha was never pleased when he came. She didn't trust him, but took his advice nonetheless. When he'd had his after-dinner nap, he would get up in a bad mood and say nasty things about the way we ran the house. Or he would say he was sorry that he'd bought Dubechnya, on which he'd lost so much money. At these moments poor Masha looked quite desperate. While she complained, he would yawn and say that the peasants needed a good thrashing. He called our marriage and life together a farce, a piece of irresponsible self-indulgence.

'It's not the first time she's done something like this,' he told me, referring to Masha. 'Once she imagined she was an opera singer and ran away from me. I looked for her for two months and spent a thousand roubles on telegrams alone, my dear chap.'

He no longer called me 'sectarian' or 'Mr Painter' and he no longer approved of my living as a workman.

'You're a strange one, you are!' he said. 'You're not normal! I'm not one for prophesying, but you'll come to a bad end, you will!'

Masha slept badly at night and was always sitting at our bedroom window, deep in thought.

There was no more laughter at supper, no more of those endearingly funny faces. I felt wretched and when it rained every drop seemed to burrow its way into my heart. I was ready to fall on my knees before Masha and apologize for the weather. Whenever the peasants had a row in the yard, I felt that I was to blame for this as well. I would sit in one place for hours on end, just thinking what a wonderful person Masha was. I loved her passionately and everything she did or said captivated me. She had a liking for quiet, studious work and loved reading and studying for hours on end. Although she knew farming only from books, she amazed all of us with her knowledge. All the advice she gave us was always practical and was always put to good use. Besides this, she had such a fine character, such good taste and good humour – the good humour possessed usually only by very well-bred people.

For a woman like this, with a healthy, practical mind, the chaos in which we were living, with all its petty worries and squabbling, was a real ordeal. This was quite clear to me and I too could not sleep at night, as my brain was still active. Deeply affected by everything, I would toss and turn, not knowing what to do.

I used to gallop off to town to fetch books, papers, sweets and flowers for Masha. I would go fishing with Stefan and stood in the rain for hours on end, up to my neck in cold water, trying to bring variety to our table with a burbot. I would swallow my pride and request the peasants not to make a noise, treat them to vodka, bribe them and make various promises. There was no end to the silly things I did!

Finally the rain stopped and the earth dried out. I would rise at four in the morning and go out into the garden – here there were flowers sparkling with dew, the sounds of birds and insects – and not a cloud in the sky. The garden, the meadows and the river were all beautiful – and then I would remember the peasants, carts, the engineer! Masha and I would drive out into the fields in a racing-trap to look at the oats. She held the reins, with shoulders held high and the wind playing with her hair, while I sat behind.

'Keep to the right!' she would shout to passers-by.

'You're just like a coachman!' I once told her.

'That's quite possible! After all, my grandfather' (the engineer's father) 'was a coachman. Didn't you know?' she asked, turning round. And immediately she began to imitate the way coachmen sing and shout.

'That's great!' I thought as I listened. 'That's great!'

And then I remembered the peasants, carts, the engineer . . .

XIII

Dr Blagovo arrived on a bicycle and my sister became a frequent visitor. Once again we talked about physical labour, progress and that mysterious Unknown awaiting mankind in the remote future. The doctor didn't like farming, since it interfered with our dis-cussions. Ploughing, reaping, grazing calves, he maintained, were not the right work for free men. In time people would delegate all these crude forms of the struggle for survival to animals and machines, while they would devote all their time to scientific research. My sister kept begging us to let her go home early, and if she stayed late or spent the night with us, there was terrible trouble.

'God, what a child you are!' Masha reproached her. 'It's really rather stupid!'

'Yes, it is,' my sister agreed. 'I admit it. But what can I do if I can't control myself? I always think I'm behaving badly.'

During haymaking my whole body ached, since I wasn't used to the work. If I sat on the terrace in the evening chatting I would suddenly fall asleep and everyone would roar with laughter, wake me up and sit me down at the supper table. Even so, I would still be overcome by drowsiness and, as if half-dreaming, I would see lights, faces, plates. I would hear voices without understanding what they said – after that early morning start I had immediately picked up my scythe, or I'd gone off to the building-site and been working there all day long.

On holidays, when I stayed at home, I noticed that my wife and sister were hiding something from me and even seemed to be avoiding me. My wife was as tender with me as before, but she was harbouring some thoughts of her own that she did not wish to reveal to me.

There was no doubt that she was getting increasingly annoyed with the peasants and the life here had become much more difficult for her. But she no longer complained to me. Nowadays she preferred talking to the doctor than to me and I couldn't understand why.

It was the custom in our province, at haymaking and harvest-time, for the workers to come to the big house in the evenings for their vodka treat. Even the young girls would drink a glass. But we did not observe this custom. The reapers and peasant women would stand in our yard until late evening, waiting for some vodka, and then they left swearing. Masha would frown sternly the whole time and say nothing, or else she would whisper irritably to the doctor, 'Savages! Barbarians!'

In the country, newcomers usually meet with an unfriendly, almost hostile reception, like new boys at school. And this was what we got. At first they took us for stupid, simple-minded people who had bought the estate because we did not know what to do with our money. They just laughed at us. Peasants let their cattle graze in our wood, even in the garden; they drove our cows and horses to the village and then came asking for money to repair the damage they had done. The whole village would flock into our yard, noisily maintaining that, when we were cutting the hay, we had trespassed on some fields at some Bysheyevka or Semyonikha or other that did not belong to us. But as we were not yet sure of our exact boundaries we took their word for it and paid the fine. Subsequently it turned out that we had been in the right after all. They stripped lime bark off the trees in our wood. One profiteer from Dubechnya, a peasant trading in vodka without a licence, bribed our workers, and the whole bunch of them played the most dirty tricks on us. They replaced our new cartwheels with old, they made off with the horse collars we used for ploughing and sold them back to us, and so on. But worst of all was what happened at the Kurilovka building-site. The women there stole planks, bricks, tiles and iron at night. The village elder would search their places with witnesses and each one would be fined two roubles at a village meeting. Subsequently the money from the fines was spent on drinks for everyone in the village.

Whenever Masha found out about these things she would angrily tell the doctor or my sister, 'What animals! It's appalling, shocking!'

And more than once I heard her regretting that she had ever taken on the task of building a school.

'Please understand,' the doctor would try and convince her, 'if you build a school and generally do good deeds, it's not for the peasants, but in the interests of culture, it's for the future. And the worse the peasants are, the more reason there is for building a school. Please understand that!'

But there was no conviction in his voice and it struck me that he detested the peasants as much as Masha did.

Masha often went to the mill with my sister and they would both laugh and say that they were going to look at Stefan because he was so handsome. As it turned out, Stefan was taciturn and slow on the uptake only with men; with women he was free and easy and could never stop talking. Once, when I went down to the river for a swim I happened to overhear them. Masha and Cleopatra, in white dresses, were sitting on the river bank in the broad shade of a willow, while Stefan stood nearby with his hands behind his back.

'D'ye think them peasants is human beings?' he asked. 'No, they're not. Begging your pardons, they're wild animals, crooks. What kind of life does a peasant lead? Drinking and eating the cheapest stuff he can get and bawling his head off in the pub. And he can't talk proper, can't be'ave, no manners. He's an ignorant oaf! He wallows in muck, so's his wife, so's his children. He sleeps in his clothes, picks spuds out of the soup with 'is fingers, drinks kvass with black beetles an' all – don't ever trouble hisself to blow 'em away!'

'But he's so dreadfully poor!' my sister interrupted.

'What d'ye mean poor! He's just not well-off; there's all kinds of not being well-off, lady. If someone's in jail, or blind, or hasn't got no legs, you wouldn't wish that on anyone. But if he's free, has 'is wits about him, has eyes and hands, faith in God, what more does he need? It's just pampering hisself, lady. It's ignorance but it ain't poverty. Supposing you honest folk with your fine education tried to help him, out of pity. Why, he's so low he'll spend all the money on drink. Even worse, he'll open a pub 'isself and use your money to cheat his own people with. You mentioned poverty. But does a rich peasant live any better? Begging your pardons, he lives like a pig too. He's a bully, a loudmouth, a blockhead, broader than he's long, with a fat red mug. I'd like to take a swing and bash the bastard's face in. That old Larion from Dubechnya, he's got money, but I'll bet he's as good at stripping the trees in your forest as the poor ones. And he's got a foul mouth, and his children. And as soon as 'e's had a drop too much he'll flop face first into a puddle and fall asleep. They're not worth a light, lady. It's hell living in the same village as them. I'm sick and tired of the village and I thank the Lord above I've enough to eat. I've got clothes, I've served my time in the dragoons, was a village elder for three years and now I'm a free man. I live where I like. I don't want to live in the village and no one can force me. Folk tells me I've a wife, that it's my duty to live in a cottage with my wife. But why? I wasn't taken on as a servant.'

'Tell me, Stefan, did you marry for love?' Masha asked.

'What love can there be in a village?' Stefan replied, smiling. 'If you'd really like to know, lady, it's my second marriage. I'm not from Kurilovka, but Zalegoshch.⁹ I settled in Kurilovka when I got married. I mean to say, my father didn't want to divide the land between us – and there was five of us brothers. So I says my goodbyes and off I goes to a strange village, to my wife's family. But my first wife died young.'

'From what?'

'From being stupid. She used to cry, keep on and on for no reason at all and so she wasted away. She kept drinking herbs to make herself look prettier and it must have damaged her insides. My second wife, the one from Kurilovka – what's special about her? She's a village woman, a peasant, that's all. I felt drawn towards her when the match was being made, and thought she was young, all nice and pure-looking, and it was a clean-living family. Her mother was a Khlyst,¹⁰ drank coffee. Most important, she lived cleanly. So I got married then, and the very next day, when we was sitting down to eat, I asked my mother-in-law for a spoon. She gave me one, but I saw her wiping it with her finger. Well, now, I thought to myself, that's how clean you are! I lived with them for a year and then I left.

Per'aps I should have married a town girl,' he went on after a pause. 'They say a wife is a helpmate to her husband. What do I need a helpmate for? I can help myself. And I'd like you to speak nice and sensibly to me, not all that posh talk. Nice and proper, with feeling. What's life without a good natter!'

Stefan suddenly fell silent and immediately I heard his dull, monotonous humming. That meant he had spotted me.

Masha often went to the mill and she enjoyed talking to Stefan. She liked his company, because he seemed so genuine, so convincing when he cursed those peasants. Whenever she returned from the mill the village idiot who kept watch over the orchard would shout, 'Hey, girl! Hullo, girlie!' And he would bark at her like a dog.

She would stop and look at him closely, as if she had found an answer to her thoughts in that idiot's barking. Most probably it had the same fascination as Stefan's swearing. Some unpleasant news was always waiting for her at home – for example, the village geese had flattened the cabbages in our garden, or Larion had stolen the reins. Smiling and shrugging her shoulders, she would say, 'But what do you expect from such people!?'

She would become highly indignant and things really were beginning to boil up inside her. But I grew used to the peasants and felt drawn more and more to them. They were mostly very nervy, irritable, downtrodden people. They were people whose imagination had been crushed, they were ignorant, with a limited, dull range of interests and were forever thinking about grey soil, grey days, black bread. They were people who tried to be cunning but, like birds, thought that they could get away with hiding only their heads behind a tree. They couldn't count. Twenty roubles would not tempt them to come and help you in the haymaking, but they would turn up for half a barrel of vodka, although the twenty roubles could have bought them four. And there was in fact filth, drunkenness, stupidity and cheating. But for all this, I had the feeling that, on the whole, peasant life had firm, sound foundations. Yes, the peasant did resemble some great clumsy beast as he followed his wooden plough; he did stupefy himself with vodka. But when one took a closer look, he seemed to possess something vital and highly important, something that Masha, for example, and the doctor lacked. What I'm talking about is his belief that truth is the chief thing on earth and that he and the whole nation can be saved only by the truth. Therefore he loves justice more than anything in the world. I used to tell my wife that she couldn't see the glass for the stains on the window-pane. She would either not reply or would hum like Stefan. Whenever that kind, clever woman turned pale with indignation and spoke to the doctor with trembling voice about drunkenness and cheating, she amazed me with the shortness of her memory. How could she forget that her father, the engineer, also drank – drank a great deal – and that the money with which he had bought Dubechnya came from a whole series of brazen, shameless swindles? How could she forget that?

XIV

My sister lived a life of her own too, which she took great pains to hide from me. She and Masha had frequent whispering sessions. Whenever I went up to her she would shrink back and her eyes would take on a guilty, pleading look. Clearly something she feared or was ashamed of was preying on her mind. To avoid meeting me in the garden or being left alone with me she kept close to Masha the whole time. It was only rarely – during dinner – that I had the chance to speak to her.

One evening I was quietly walking through the garden on my way home from the building-site. It had already begun to grow dark. Without noticing me or hearing my footsteps there was my sister, as quiet as a ghost, near an old wide-spreading apple tree. She was dressed in black and was hurrying backwards and forwards in a straight line, always looking at the ground. An apple fell from a tree. She started at the noise, stopped and pressed her hands to her temples. At that moment I went over to her.

A feeling of tender love rushed to my heart as I tearfully held her shoulders and kissed her. For some reason our mother, our childhood, came to mind. 'What's the matter?' I asked. 'You're miserable. I've noticed that for a long time now. Tell me, what's wrong?'

'I'm frightened . . .' she said, trembling.

'What's the matter?' I asked again. 'For God's sake, you can be frank with me!'

'I will be frank, I'll tell you the whole truth. It's so hard, it's agony hiding things from you! Misail, I'm in love,' she went on in a whisper. 'I'm in love, in love . . . I'm happy, but why am I so frightened?'

We heard footsteps and Dr Blagovo, in a silk shirt and topboots, appeared among the trees. Obviously they had a rendezvous, here by the apple tree. The moment she saw him she dashed impulsively over to him with a pained cry, as if he were being taken away from her.

'Vladimir! Vladimir!'

She pressed close to him and hungrily gazed into his eyes. Only then did I notice how thin and pale she had grown recently. This was especially noticeable from that long-familiar lace collar, which now hung more loosely than ever around her long, thin neck. The doctor was taken aback, but quickly recovered, stroked her hair and said, 'Now, now, it's all right. Why are you so nervous? I'm here now, you see.'

We said nothing and sheepishly eyed one another. Then the three of us went off and I heard the doctor telling me, 'Cultural life hasn't begun yet in this country. The old console themselves – even if nothing is happening at the moment, things were happening in the forties and sixties, they say. But these are old men, and you and I are young, our brains aren't afflicted yet with senile decay, therefore we cannot comfort ourselves with such illusions. Russia began in the year AD 862,[11] but civilized Russia, as I understand it, hasn't started yet.'

But I didn't attempt to follow these ideas of his. It was all rather strange. I didn't want to believe that my sister was in love, that here she was walking along arm-in-arm with a stranger, giving him fond looks. My own sister, that neurotic, downtrodden, enslaved creature, loved a married man with children! Something made me feel sorry, but I couldn't pinpoint it. I found the doctor's company somewhat disagreeable, and I had no idea what would become of this love of theirs.

XV

Masha and I drove to Kurilovka for the opening of the school.

'Autumn, autumn, autumn,' Masha said softly as she looked around. 'Summer has passed. The birds have gone, only the willows are green.'

Yes, summer was over. Bright, warm days had set in, but the mornings were chilly, shepherds were wearing their sheepskin coats now and the dew stayed all day on the asters in the garden. We kept hearing plaintive sounds and we couldn't tell if they were shutters groaning on rusty hinges or if the cranes were flying. It made one feel so good, so full of life!

'Summer has passed,' Masha said. 'Now you and I can take stock. We've worked a lot, thought a lot, and we are all the better for it and should feel proud of ourselves. We've improved our own lives, but has our success had any visible effect on the lives around us? Has it been of use to *anyone*? No. Ignorance, personal filthiness, drunkenness, a shockingly high infant mortality rate – everything's just as it ever was. All your ploughing and sowing, my spending money and reading books – this hasn't made anyone's life better. We've worked, indulged in lofty thinking for ourselves alone – that's for sure.'

This kind of argument baffled me and I didn't know what to think.

'We've been sincere from start to finish,' I said, 'and sincere people have right on their side.'

'I don't deny it. We were right in our thinking but wrong in the way we set about things. It was mostly our methods that were wrong, weren't they? You want to be useful to people, but the mere fact of buying an estate rules out any possibility of helping them from the start. What's more, if you work, dress and eat like a peasant, you lend your authority and approval to their heavy clumsy clothes, their dreadful huts and stupid beards. On the other hand, let's suppose you work for a very long time – all your life – so that in the end you achieve some practical results. But what do these amount to? What good are they against elemental forces, such as wholesale ignorance, hunger, cold, degeneracy? They're a mere drop in the ocean! To counter those things you need a different line of attack, one that is powerful, bold, speedy! If you really do want to be useful, then you must abandon your narrow sphere of activity and act directly on the masses! Above all you need noisy, vigorous propaganda. Why is art – music, for example – really so alive, so popular, so powerful? Because the musician or singer influences thousands at the same time. Dear, wonderful art!' she went on, dreamily gazing at the sky. 'Art gives you wings and carries you far, far away! For those who are tired of filth, petty trifling concerns, for those who are confused, outraged, indignant, there is peace and satisfaction only in beauty.'

When we drove towards Kurilovka the weather was bright and joyful. In the farmyards, here and there, they were threshing and there was a smell of rye-straw. Behind some wattle fences was a bright red mountain ash, and wherever one looked every tree was golden or red. The church bells were ringing and icons were being carried to the school. I could hear them singing 'Holy Virgin, Intercessor'.[12] And how clear the air was, how high the pigeons were flying!

The service was held in a classroom. Then the peasants from Kurilovka presented Masha with an icon and those from Dubechnya brought her a large pretzel and a gilt saltcellar. Masha began to sob.

'If we've said something out of turn or been a nuisance, please forgive us,' an old man said as he bowed to us both.

On the way home Masha kept looking around at the school. The green roof that I had painted glistened in the sun and we could see it for a long time afterwards. Masha was now glancing at it in farewell.

XVI

That evening she set off for town. Recently she had been going to town often and spending the night there. When she was away I couldn't work, my head drooped and I felt weak. Our great yard seemed like some bleak, revolting wasteland, and there were angry noises in the garden. Without Masha the house, the trees, the horses were no longer 'ours', as far as I was concerned.

I never left the house, but sat at Masha's table, near the cupboard full of farming books – those old favourites that were needed no longer and which looked at me with such embarrassment. For hours on end, while it struck seven, eight, nine, while the sooty black autumn night crept up to the windows, I would examine her old glove or the pen she always used, or her little scissors. I did nothing and I understood quite clearly that everything I'd done before – ploughing, reaping, felling trees – had only been done because that was her wish. If she had sent me to clean out a deep well, where I would have had to stand waist-deep in water, I would have climbed in without asking myself if it needed cleaning or not. But now, when she was away, Dubechnya struck me as sheer chaos with its ruins, banging shutters, untidiness, and stealing twenty-four hours a day. In that kind of place any sort of work was a waste of time. And why should I work there, why all that worrying about the future, when I felt that the ground was giving way beneath me, that my role here in Dubechnya was played out – in short, when I felt that I was doomed to the same fate as those farming books? It was awful in the lonely hours of the night, when every minute I feared that someone might shout that it was time I left. It wasn't Dubechnya that I regretted, but my own love, whose autumn had clearly arrived. What happiness, to love and be loved! And how dreadful to feel that you're beginning to fall off that lofty tower!

Masha returned from town the following day, towards evening. Something was annoying her, but she tried to hide it and she only inquired why all the winter window-frames had been put in – it was simply stifling, she said. So I took two frames out. We weren't very hungry, but we sat down to supper all the same.

'Go and wash your hands,' my wife said. 'You smell of putty.'

She had brought some new illustrated journals from town and after supper we looked at them together. There were supplements with fashion-plates and patterns. Masha just glanced at them and laid them to one side to have a proper look at later on. But one dress with a wide, smooth, bell-shaped skirt and full sleeves caught her eye and she seriously examined it for about a minute.

'That's not bad,' she said.

'Yes, it would suit you very well!' I said. 'Very well.'

I felt touched as I looked at the dress, admiring that grey blotch only because she liked it.

'A wonderful, charming dress!' I continued, tenderly. 'My beautiful, marvellous Masha! My dear Masha!'

And my tears fell on to the fashion-plate.

'Wonderful Masha!' I muttered. 'My dear, lovely, darling Masha.'

She went to bed, while I stayed up for another hour looking at the illustrations.

'You shouldn't have taken those window-frames out,' she called from the bedroom. 'I hope it won't be cold now. Really, you can feel the draught!'

I read something in the miscellany – about how to make cheap ink and about the largest diamond in the world. And again my attention was caught by that illustration of the dress she had liked and I imagined her at a ball, with fan, bare shoulders, brilliant, splendid, knowing all about music, painting, literature. How small and brief my role in her life seemed!

Our meeting one another, our married life, were only an episode – only one of many to come in the life of this lively, richly talented woman. All the best things in this world, as I've already pointed out, were at her feet, they were hers for nothing. Even ideas and the latest intellectual trends were a source of pleasure for her, bringing variety to her life. I was only the cab-driver, taking her from one infatuation to the other. Now that I was no longer needed, she would fly away, leaving me alone.

As if in answer to my thoughts, a desperate shout suddenly rang out in the yard.

'He-elp!'

It was a thin, female-like voice. As though trying to mimic it, the wind suddenly shrilled in the chimney. Half a minute passed and again I heard that voice through the sound of the wind, but this time it appeared to come from the other end of the yard.

'He-elp!'

'Misail, did you hear that?' my wife asked softly. 'Did you hear?' She came out from her bedroom in her nightdress, her hair hanging loose; peering at the dark window, she listened hard.

'Someone's being murdered!' she said. 'That's the last straw!'

I took my gun and went out. It was very dark outside and the strong wind made it difficult to stand. I walked up to the gates and listened. The trees moaned, the wind whistled and a dog – most likely the village idiot's – lazily howled in the garden. Outside the gates it was pitch-dark, without one light along the railway track. From somewhere just by the outbuilding where the office had been last year, there suddenly came a strangled cry.

'He-elp!'

'Who's there?' I called.

Two men were struggling. One was pushing, the other trying to hold his ground, and both were breathing heavily.

'Let go!' one of them said and I recognized Ivan Cheprakov. So he was the one who had shouted in that shrill, woman's voice. 'Let go, damn you, or I'll bite your hands!' he said.

I recognized the other as Moisey. As I parted them I couldn't resist hitting Moisey twice in the face. He fell, stood up, and then I hit him again.

'That gent wanted to kill me,' he muttered. 'He was trying to get into his mum's chest of drawers. I'd like to have him locked up in the outbuilding, for safety's sake, sir.'

Cheprakov was drunk and didn't recognize me. He breathed heavily, as if filling his lungs before shouting 'He-elp!' again.

I left them and went back into the house. My wife was lying on the bed, fully dressed. I told her what had happened outside and did not even hide the fact that I had hit Moisey.

'It's terrible living in the country,' she said. 'And what a long night, damn it.'

'He-elp!' came the cry again.

'I'll go and separate them,' I said.

'No, let them tear each other's throats out,' she said with a disgusted look.

She glanced up at the ceiling, listening hard, while I sat close by, not daring to speak and feeling that I was to blame for those cries for help outside and for the interminable night.

We said nothing to each other and I waited impatiently for dawn to glimmer at the windows. Masha looked as if she had just come out of a deep sleep and now she was asking herself how such a clever, well-educated, respectable woman like herself could land herself in this wretched, provincial wilderness, among a crowd of insignificant nobodies. How could she lower herself so, fall for one of these people and be his wife for more than six months? I felt that it was all the same if it were me, Moisey or Cheprakov: for her, everything had become identified with that drunken, wild cry for help – myself, our marriage, our farming and the dreadful autumn roads. When she sighed or made herself more comfortable, I could read in her face: 'Oh, please come quickly, morning!'

In the morning she left. I stayed on at Dubechnya for another three days waiting for her. Then I packed all our things into one room, locked it and walked to town. When I rang the engineer's bell it was already evening and the lamps were lit on Great Dvoryansky Street. Pavel told me there was no one at home. Viktor Ivanych had gone to St Petersburg, while Mariya Viktorovna must be at a rehearsal at the Azhogins'. I remember how anxious I felt as I went to the Azhogins', how my heart throbbed and sank as I climbed the stairs and stood for a long time on the landing, not daring to enter that temple of the muses. In the ballroom, candles in groups of three were burning everywhere – on the little table, on the piano and on the stage. The first performance was to be on the thirteenth and the first rehearsal on a Monday, an unlucky day. This was the battle against superstition! All the lovers of drama were already there. The eldest, middle and youngest sisters were walking over the stage, reading their parts from notebooks. Away from everybody stood Radish, his head pressed sideways to the wall as he watched the stage with adoring eyes, waiting for the rehearsal to begin. Everything was still the same!

I went over to greet the mistress of the house when suddenly everyone started crying 'Ssh!' and waving at me to tread softly.

There was silence. They raised the piano lid and a lady sat down and screwed up her shortsighted eyes at the music. Then my Masha walked over to the piano. She was beautifully dressed – but she looked beautiful in a strange new way, not at all like the Masha who had come to see me at the mill that spring.

Why do I love thee, O radiant night?[13]

It was the first time since I had known her that I had heard her sing. She had a fine, rich, powerful voice, and hearing her was like eating a ripe, sweet, fragrant melon. When she finished everyone applauded and she smiled and looked very pleased as she flashed her eyes, turned over the music and smoothed her dress. She was like a bird that has finally broken out of its cage and preens its wings in freedom. Her hair was combed behind her ears and she looked aggressive, defiant, as if she wanted to challenge us all or shout at us, as though we were horses, 'Whoa, my beauties!'

And at that moment she must have looked very like her grandfather, the coachman.

'So you're here as well?' she said, giving me her hand. 'Did you hear me sing? What do you think of it?' And without waiting for a reply she went on, 'You've timed it very well. Tonight I'm leaving for St Petersburg, just for a short stay. Is that all right with you?'

At midnight I took her to the station. She embraced me tenderly – most probably out of gratitude for not bothering her with useless questions, and she promised to write. For a long time I held and kissed her hands, barely able to keep back my tears and without saying a single word to her.

After she had gone I stood looking at the receding lights and fondled her in my imagination.

'My dear Masha, my wonderful Masha,' I said softly.

I stayed the night at Karpovna's in Makarikha. In the morning, Radish and I upholstered some furniture for a rich merchant who was marrying his daughter to a doctor.

XVII

On Sunday my sister came for tea.

'I'm reading a lot now,' she said, showing me some books that she had borrowed from the public library on her way. 'I must thank your wife and Vladimir, they've made me aware again. They've saved me and made me feel like a human being. Up to now I couldn't sleep at night for worrying – "Oh, we've used too much sugar this week! Oh, I mustn't put too much salt on the cucumbers!" I don't sleep now, but I've other thoughts on my mind. It's sheer torture to think how stupidly, spinelessly I've spent half my life. I despise my past, I'm ashamed of it, and now I consider Father my enemy. Oh, how grateful I am to your wife! And Vladimir? He's such a wonderful man! They've opened my eyes.'

'That's no good, not sleeping,' I said.

'So you think I'm ill? Not one bit. Vladimir listened to my chest and told me I'm perfectly healthy. But it's not my health that's the problem, that's not so important . . . Tell me, am I right in what I'm doing?'

She needed moral support, that was clear. Masha had gone, Dr Blagovo was in St Petersburg, and except myself there was no one in town to tell her that she was right. She stared at me, trying to read my innermost thoughts, and if I was thoughtful or silent in her company, she would take it personally and become miserable. I had to be on my guard the whole time and whenever she asked me if she was right, I would hurriedly reply that she was and that I had great respect for her.

'Did you know? I've been given a part at the Azhogins',' she continued. 'I want to act. I want to live, to drain the cup of life. I've no talent at all, and the part's only ten lines. But that's still infinitely better and nobler than pouring out tea five times a day and spying on the cook to see if she's been eating too much. But most important, Father must come and see that I'm capable of protesting.'

After tea she lay down on my bed and stayed there for some time with her eyes closed, looking very pale.

'How feeble,' she exclaimed, getting up. 'Vladimir said that all the women and girls in this town have become anaemic from laziness. How clever Vladimir is! He's right, so absolutely right. One must work!'

Two days later she went to a rehearsal at the Azhogins', notebook in hand. She wore a black dress with a coral necklace, a brooch that resembled puff-pastry from a distance, and large earrings, each with a jewel sparkling in it. I felt embarrassed looking at her and was shocked at her lack of taste. Others noticed too how unsuitably dressed she was, how out of place those earrings with the jewels were. I could see their smiles, and I heard someone laugh and say, 'Queen Cleopatra of Egypt!'

She had tried to be worldly, relaxed and assured, but she had only succeeded in looking pretentious and bizarre. Her simplicity and charm had deserted her.

'I just told Father that I was going to a rehearsal,' she began, coming over to me, 'and he shouted that he wouldn't give me his blessing and he even nearly hit me. Just imagine, I don't know my part,' she said, glancing at the notebook. 'I'm bound to mess it up. And so,' she went on, highly agitated, 'the die is cast. The die is cast . . .'

She felt that everyone was looking at her, that everyone was amazed at the decisive step she had taken, and that something special was expected of her. It was impossible to convince her that no one ever took any notice of such dull, mediocre people as she and I.

She didn't come on until the third act, and her part – a guest, a provincial scandalmonger – was merely to stand at the door as though eavesdropping and then make a short speech. For at least half an hour before her cue, while others strolled across the stage, read, drank tea, argued, she never left my side. She kept mumbling her lines and nervously crumpling her notebook. Imagining that everyone was looking at her and waiting for her to come on, she kept smoothing her hair with trembling hand.

'I'm bound to do it wrong,' she told me. 'If you knew how dreadful I feel! It's as if I'm being led out to execution, I'm so scared!'

In the end it was her cue.

'Cleopatra Poloznev, you're on!' the producer said.

She went out into the middle of the stage and she looked ugly and clumsy. Horror was written all over her face. She stood there for about thirty seconds as if in a stupor – quite still apart from the enormous earrings swinging on her ears.

'As it's the first time, you can use the book,' someone said.

I saw quite clearly that she was shaking so much that she could neither speak nor open the book, and that she wasn't up to it at all. I was just about to go over and speak to her when she suddenly sank on to her knees in the middle of the stage and burst into loud sobs.

There was general uproar and commotion. Only I stood still as I leant on the scenery in the wings, shattered by what had happened and at a complete loss what to do. I saw them lift her up and take her away. I saw Anyuta Blagovo come up to me. Until then I hadn't noticed her in the ballroom and now she seemed to have sprung out of the floor. She wore her hat and veil and, as always, looked as if she had only dropped in for a minute.

'I told her not to try and act,' she said angrily, snapping out each word and blushing. 'It's sheer madness! You should have stopped her!'

Thin and flat-chested, Mrs Azhogin hurried over in a short blouse with short sleeves – there was cigarette ash on the front.

'It's terrible, my dear,' she said, wringing her hands and staring me in the face as usual. 'It's terrible. Your sister's in a *certain condition* . . . she's . . . mm . . . pregnant! Take her away from here, I request you to.'

She was breathing heavily from excitement. Her three daughters, as thin and flat-chested as the mother, stood nearby, huddling together in terror. They were petrified, as if a convict had been caught in their house. How disgraceful, how terrible, they would have said! And yet this honourable family had been fighting prejudice and superstition throughout its existence. In their considered opinion, three candles, the thirteenth, unlucky Monday, constituted the entire stock of the superstitions and errors of mankind.

'I must re*quest* you . . .' Mrs Azhogin repeated, pursing her lips on the 'quest'. 'I must re*quest* you to take her home.'

XVIII

A little later my sister and I were walking down the street, and I protected her with the skirt of my coat. We hurried along side-streets where there were no lamps, avoiding passers-by as if we were fugitives.

She no longer cried, but looked at me with dry eyes. It was only about twenty minutes' walk to Makarikha, where I was taking her, and, strange to relate, in that short time we managed to recall the whole of our lives. We discussed everything, weighed up our position, thought of the best course of action.

We decided that we could stay no longer in that town and that as soon as I had a little money we would move somewhere else. In some houses the people were already in bed, in others they were playing cards. We detested and feared those houses and talked about the fanaticism, callousness and worthlessness of those worthy families, those lovers of dramatic art whom we had frightened so much. 'How are those stupid, cruel, lazy, dishonest people any better than the drunken, superstitious peasants of Kurilovka?' I asked. 'Are they any better than animals, which are similarly thrown into disarray when some random incident upsets the monotony of their lives that are bounded by instincts?' What would happen to my sister now if she continued to live at home? What moral torments would she have to endure, talking to Father, or meeting her friends every single day? I saw all this quite clearly and then I recalled all those people I knew who were slowly being hounded to death by their nearest and dearest. I remembered those tormented dogs that had gone mad, those live sparrows plucked bare by street urchins and thrown into water. And I remembered the long, long unbroken sequence of muted, protracted suffering that I had observed in that town since childhood. And I could not understand how those sixty thousand people coped, why they read the Gospels, prayed, read books and magazines. What good to them was all that had been so far written and spoken by mankind if they were still spiritually unenlightened, if they still had the same horror of freedom as a hundred, three hundred years ago?

A carpenter would spend all his life building houses in that town, but for all that he would go to his grave mispronouncing 'gallery'. Similarly, those sixty thousand inhabitants had been reading and hearing about truth, mercy and freedom for generations, yet to their dying day they would carry on lying from morning to night, making life hell for each other, and they feared and loathed freedom as if it were their deadly enemy.

'So, my fate is decided,' my sister said when we arrived home. 'After what has happened I can never go back *there* again. Heavens, that's good! I feel better now.'

She immediately went to bed. Tears glistened on her eyelashes, but her face was happy. She slept soundly and sweetly and I could see that she really was relaxed and able to rest now. It was simply ages since she had slept like that.

And so our life together began. She was always singing and telling me that she felt very well. Books borrowed from the library were returned by me unread, since she wasn't in the mood for reading now. Her only wish was to dream and talk of the future. While she mended my underwear or helped Karpovna at the stove, she would hum or talk about her Vladimir, praising his intellect, good manners, kindness, exceptional learning. I would agree with her, although I didn't like her doctor any more. She wanted to work and earn her own living, without any assistance. She said that she was going to be a teacher as soon as she was well enough and that she would scrub floors and do the washing herself. She loved her unborn child passionately – even though he had not entered this world yet. She knew already the colour of his eyes, what his hands were like, how he laughed. She loved talking about education, and since Vladimir was the best person in the world, all her thoughts on the subject centred around one thing – the son must be as fascinating as the father. We talked endlessly and everything she said filled her with keen joy. I felt glad too, without knowing why.

Her dreaminess must have infected me too. All I did was lounge about, and I too read nothing. For all my tiredness, I paced up and down the room in the evenings, hands in pockets, talking about Masha.

'When do you think she'll be back?' I would ask my sister. 'Towards Christmas, I think, no later. What *can* she be doing there?'

'She hasn't written, that means she'll be back soon.'

'That's true,' I would agree, although I knew very well that there was nothing in our town for Masha to come back to.

I missed her terribly and since I could no longer deceive myself, I tried to make others deceive me. My sister was waiting for her doctor, I was waiting for Masha, and we both talked and laughed incessantly without ever noticing that we were keeping Karpovna awake. She would lie over the stove in her room forever muttering, 'This morning the samovar was a-humming, oh, how it was humming! That means bad luck, my dears. Bad luck!'

The only caller was the postman, who brought my sister letters from the doctor, and Prokofy, who sometimes dropped in during the evening. He would look at my sister without saying a word and then go back into the kitchen.

'Everyone should stick to his calling,' he would say, 'and those what are too proud to understand will walk through a vale of tears in this life.'

He loved his 'vale of tears'. Once, around Christmas, when I was walking through the market, he called me to his butcher's stall and without shaking my hand declared that he had something very important to discuss. He was red in the face from frost and vodka. Next to him, at the counter, stood Nikolka of the murderous face, holding a bloody knife.

'I want to tell you what I think,' Prokofy began. 'This business here can't go on, because you yourself know this vale of tears can blacken our name. Of course, Ma's too sorry for you to tell you anything unpleasant – I mean, that your sister should move somewhere else because she's expecting, like. But I want no more of it, seeing as I can't approve of the way she's been carrying on.'

I understood and walked away from the stall. That same day my sister and I moved to Radish's. We had no money for a cab, so we walked. I carried our things in a bundle on my back, but my sister carried nothing. She kept gasping and coughing and asking if we would be there soon.

XIX

At last a letter from Masha arrived.

My dear, kind M. (she wrote), my kind, gentle 'guardian angel', as our old painter calls you. Goodbye. I'm going with Father to the Exhibition in America.[14] In a few days I shall see the ocean – it's so far from Dubechnya it frightens me to think of it! It's as distant and boundless as the sky and it's there I long to go, to be free. I'm exultant, as happy as a lark, I'm insane – you can see what a mess this letter is. My dear Misail, give me my freedom, please hurry and snap the thread which is still binding you and me. To have met and known you was like a ray of heavenly light that brightened my existence. But becoming your wife was a mistake, you understand that, and the realization of this mistake weighs heavy on me. I go down on my knees and beg you, my dear generous friend, to send me a telegram as quick as you can, before I travel over the ocean. Tell me that you agree to correct the mistake both of us made, to take away the only stone that drags my wings down. Father will make all the arrangements and he's promised not to trouble you too much with formalities. And so, am I as free as a bird? Yes? Be happy, God bless you. Forgive me for having sinned.

I'm alive and well. I'm throwing money away, I do many stupid things and every minute I thank God that a silly woman like me has no children. I'm having success with my singing, but it's no idle pastime, it's my refuge, my cell where I retire to find peace. King David had a ring with the inscription 'All things pass'. Whenever I feel sad those words cheer me up, but when I'm cheerful they make me sad.

I have a ring now with Hebrew letters and it's a talisman that will keep me from temptation. All things pass, and life itself will pass, which means one needs nothing. Or perhaps all one needs to know is that one is free, because free people need nothing, absolutely nothing. Break the thread. My fondest love to you and your sister.

Forgive and forget your M.

My sister was lying in one room; in another lay Radish, who had been ill again and was just convalescing. When the letter arrived my sister had quickly gone into the painter's room, had sat down and started reading to him. Every day she read Ostrovsky[15] or Gogol, and he would listen very seriously, staring into space. Now and then he would shake his head and mutter to himself 'All things are possible, all things!'

If something ugly, nasty was depicted in a play he would poke the book with his finger and start gloating, 'There's a pack of lies. That's what lying does for you!'

He liked plays for their plot, moral message and intricate artistic structure, and he always called the author *him*, *he*, never actually mentioning names. 'How skilfully *he*'s made everything fit together!' he would say.

This time my sister read only one page to him; she could not go on as her voice was too weak. Radish took her by the arm, twitched his dry lips and said in a barely audible, hoarse voice, 'The righteous man's soul is white and smooth as chalk, but a sinner's is like pumice stone. A righteous man's soul is like bright oil, but a sinner's is like tar. We must toil, endure sorrow, suffer illness,' he went on. 'But he who does not toil or grieve will never enter the kingdom of heaven. Woe to the well-fed, woe to the strong, woe to the rich, woe to the usurers. They will never enter the kingdom of heaven. Aphids eat grass, rust eats iron . . .'

I read the letter once more. Then the soldier came into the kitchen – the same soldier who twice weekly brought us tea, French rolls and grouse that smelt of perfume. Who the sender was remained a mystery. I had no work, so I had to stay at home for days on end, and whoever sent the rolls must have known that we were hard up.

I could hear my sister talking to the soldier and cheerfully laughing. Then she ate a small roll, lay on the bed and told me, 'From the very start, when you said you didn't want to work in an office and became a house-painter, Anyuta Blagovo and I knew that you were in the right, but we were too scared to say it out loud. Tell me, what is this strange power that prevents us from saying what we think? Take Anyuta Blagovo, for example. She loves you, she adores you, and she knows that you're right. She loves me like a sister and knows that I'm right as well. Perhaps in her heart of hearts she envies me. But something is stopping her from coming to see us. She avoids us, she's scared.'

My sister folded her hands on her breast and said excitedly, 'If only you knew how she loves you! She confessed it to me alone, and in secret, in the dark. She used to take me to a dark avenue in the garden and whisper how dear you are to her. You'll see, she'll never marry, because she loves you. Don't you feel sorry for her?'

'Yes.'

'*She* was the one who sent those rolls. She really makes me laugh. Why should she hide it? I was once funny and silly too, but now I've left that place I'm no longer scared of anyone. I think and I say what I like out loud and that's made me happy. When I was living at home I had no idea what happiness was; now I wouldn't change places with a queen.'

Dr Blagovo arrived. He had received his M.D. and was staying in town at his father's place for a little rest. He said that he would soon be off to St Petersburg again, as he wanted to do research in typhus and cholera inoculations, it seemed. He wanted to go abroad to complete his studies and then become a professor. He had resigned from the army and wore loose-fitting cheviot jackets, very wide trousers and superb ties. My sister was in raptures over the tiepins, the cufflinks, and the red silk scarf he sported in the top pocket of his jacket. Once, when we had nothing to do, we tried to remember how many suits he had and concluded that there were at least ten. He clearly loved my sister as much as before, but not once, even as a joke, did he suggest taking her with him to St Petersburg or abroad. I just couldn't imagine what would happen to her if she survived, what would become of the child. All she did was daydream, however, without giving any serious thought to the future: she said that he could go where he liked, even abandon her, as long as he was happy, and that she was quite content with things as they had turned out.

When he visited us he usually listened very carefully to her and insisted she had drops in her milk. And this time it was the same. He listened to her chest, then made her drink a glass of milk, after which our rooms smelled of creosote.

'That's my clever girl!' he said, taking her glass. 'You mustn't talk too much, you've been chattering ten to the dozen lately. Now, please don't talk so much!'

She burst out laughing. Then he went into Radish's room, where I was sitting, and gave me an affectionate pat on the shoulder.

'Well, how are you, old man?' he asked, bending over the invalid.

'Sir,' Radish said, quietly moving his lips. 'If I may be so bold as to inform you, sir . . . all of us are in God's hands, we all have to die some time . . . Allow me to tell you the truth, sir . . . *you* won't enter the kingdom of heaven!'

'What can I do about it?' the doctor joked. 'Someone has to go to hell.'

And then, suddenly, I seemed to lose consciousness and felt that I was dreaming: it was a winter's night and I was standing in the slaughterhouse next to Prokofy, who smelt of pepper-brandy. I tried to pull myself together, rubbed my eyes and seemed to be on my way to the Governor's, for the interview. Nothing like this has ever happened to me before or since and I can only put these strange, dream-like memories down to nervous strain. I lived through the scene at the slaughterhouse and my interview at the Governor's, vaguely conscious all the time that it wasn't real. When I came to, I realized that I wasn't in the house, but standing near a street-lamp with the doctor.

'It's sad, so sad,' he was saying, the tears running down his cheeks. 'She's cheerful, always laughing and full of hope. But her condition is hopeless, my dear friend. Your Radish hates me and keeps trying to drum into me how badly I've behaved towards her. In his way he's right, but I have my views as well and I don't regret what happened at all. One must love, we should all love, shouldn't we? Without love there wouldn't be any life and the man who fears love and runs away from it is not free.'

Gradually he turned to other topics – science, his thesis, which had a good reception in St Petersburg. He spoke very enthusiastically and quite forgot my sister, his own sorrows, and me. He was thrilled with life. 'She has America and a ring with an inscription,' I thought, 'and he has a higher degree and an academic career in front of him. Only my sister and I are in the same old rut.'

I said goodbye and went over to a street-lamp to read the letter again. And I remembered vividly how she had come down to the mill one spring morning to see me, how she lay down and covered herself with a sheepskin coat, trying to look like a simple old peasant woman. Another time, when we were pulling the fish-trap out of the water, large raindrops scattered over us from the willows along the bank and made us laugh.

Everything was dark in our house in Great Dvoryansky Street. I climbed the fence and went into the kitchen by the back door, as in former days, to fetch a lamp. No one was there. A samovar was hissing by the stove, all ready for Father. 'Who's going to pour Father's tea for him now?' I wondered. Taking the lamp, I went into my hut, made up a bed from old newspapers and lay down. The spikes on the wall looked as ominous as before and their shadows flickered. It was cold. I expected my sister to come in with my supper at any moment, but immediately I remembered that she was ill at Radish's. Climbing that fence and lying in my unheated hut struck me as bizarre. Everything seemed confused and my imagination conjured up the oddest things.

The bell rang. I remember those sounds from childhood: at first the wire rustling along the wall, then a short, plaintive tinkle. This was Father returning from his club. I got up and went into the kitchen. When Aksinya the cook saw me she clasped her hands and, for some reason, burst out crying.

'My dear boy!' she said softly. 'My dear! Oh, good heavens!'

She was so excited she began crumpling her apron. Half-gallon jars of berries in vodka stood in the window. I poured out a teacupful and gulped it down, I was so thirsty. Aksinya had just scrubbed the table and benches and there was that smell which bright, comfortable kitchens always have where the cook keeps everything clean and shining. This smell, with the chirping of crickets, always used to tempt us into the kitchen when we were children and put us in the mood for fairy tales and card games.

'Where's Cleopatra?' Aksinya asked, quietly and hurriedly, holding her breath. 'And where's your cap, dear? I hear your wife's gone to St Petersburg.'

She had worked for us when Mother was alive and used to bath me and Cleopatra in a tub. And for her we were still children who had to be told what to do. Within a quarter of an hour she had revealed to me, in that quiet kitchen, with all the wisdom of an old servant, the ideas she had been accumulating since we last met. She told me that the doctor ought to be forced to marry Cleopatra – he only needed a good fright, and that, if the application were made in the right way, the bishop would dissolve his first marriage. She said that it would be a good idea to sell Dubechnya without my wife knowing anything about it and to bank the money in my own name; that if my sister and I went down on bended knees before our father and begged hard enough, he would perhaps forgive us; and that we should say a special prayer to the Holy Mother.

'Well, off with you, dear, go and talk to him,' she said when we heard Father coughing. 'Go and talk to him, bow down before him, your head won't fall off.'

So I went. Father was at his desk sketching a plan for a villa with Gothic windows and a stumpy turret that resembled the watchtower of a fire-station – all very heavy-handed and amateurish. I entered his study and stopped where I could see the plan. I didn't know why I'd come to see Father, but when I saw his gaunt face, his red neck, his shadow on the wall, I remember that I wanted to throw my arms around his neck and go down on my bended knees as Aksinya had instructed. But the sight of that villa with its Gothic windows and stumpy turret held me back.

'Good evening,' I said.

He looked at me and immediately looked down at his plan.

'What do you want?' he asked after a while.

'I've come to tell you that my sister is very ill. She doesn't have long to live,' I added in an empty voice.

'Well, now,' Father sighed, taking off his spectacles and laying them on the table. 'As ye sow, so shall ye reap. As ye sow, so shall ye reap,' he repeated, getting up from the table. 'I want you to remember when you came here two years ago. In this very place I asked you, I begged you, to abandon the error of your ways. I reminded you of your duty, your honour, your debt to your ancestors, whose traditions must be held sacred. You ignored my advice and stubbornly clung to your erroneous ideas. What's more, you led your sister astray and made her lose her moral sense and all sense of decency. Now you're both paying for it. Well, then, as ye sow, so shall ye reap!'

He said all this pacing the study. Probably he thought that I'd come to apologize and probably plead for myself and my sister. I was cold, I shivered feverishly and spoke in a hoarse voice and with great difficulty.

'And I would also ask you to remember something,' I said. 'In this very room I begged you to try and understand my viewpoint, to think hard about what we're living for and how we should live. But your only answer was to talk about ancestors, about the grandfather who wrote poetry. Now, when you're told that your only daughter is hopelessly ill, all you can do is go on about ancestors and tradition. How can you be so thoughtless in your old age, when death is just round the corner and you have only five or ten years left?'

'Why have you come here?' Father asked sternly, clearly annoyed with me for calling him thoughtless.

'I don't know. I love you and can't say how sorry I am that we're so far apart. That's why I came. I still love you, but my sister's finished with you for good. She won't forgive you, she never will. The mere mention of your name fills her with revulsion for the past, for life.'

'And who's to blame?' Father shouted. '*You're* to blame, you scoundrel!'

'All right, I'm to blame,' I said. 'I admit that I'm to blame for many things. But why is the type of life you're leading – which you insist *we* have to follow – so boring, so undistinguished? In all the houses you've been building for thirty years now, why isn't there a single person who could teach me how to live the way you want? There's not one honest man in the whole town! These houses of yours are thieves' kitchens, where life is made hell for mothers and daughters and where children are tortured. My poor mother!' I went on despairingly. 'My poor sister! One has to drug oneself with vodka, cards, scandal, one has to cringe, play the hypocrite, draw up plan after plan for years and years to blind oneself to the horrors lurking in those houses. Our town has existed for hundreds of years and not once in all that time has it given one useful person to the country – not one! Anything at all bright and lively has been stifled at birth by you. This is a town of shopkeepers, publicans, clerks, priests. It's a useless town, no good to anyone. Not one person would be sorry if the earth suddenly swallowed it up.'

'I don't want to hear any more, you scoundrel!' my father said, picking up a ruler from the table. 'You're drunk! How dare you visit your father in that state! I'm telling you for the last time – and you can tell this to your slut of a sister – that you will get nothing from me. There's no place in my heart for disobedient children, and if they suffer for their disobedience and obstinacy they'll get no pity from me. You can go back to where you came from. It was God's will to punish me through you, but I endure this trial with all humility. I'll find consolation in suffering and never-ending toil, as Job did. You will never cross my doorstep again unless you reform. I'm a just person, everything I'm telling you is good sense. If you want to do yourself some good, remember what I said to you before and what I'm telling you now – remember it for the rest of your life!'

I gave up and left. I don't remember what happened that night or on the next day. People said that I staggered bare-headed through the streets, singing out loud, with crowds of boys following me and shouting 'Better-than-Nothing! Better-than-Nothing!'

XX

If I had wanted a ring I would have chosen the following inscription for it: 'Nothing passes'. I believe that nothing actually disappears without trace and that the slightest step we take has some meaning for the present and future.

What I have lived through has not been in vain. The people in the town have been touched by my misfortunes and my powers of endurance. No longer do they call me 'Better-than-Nothing', no longer do they laugh at me or pour water over me when I walk through the market. Now they are used to my being a workman and they see nothing strange in a gentleman like myself carrying buckets of paint and fitting window-panes. On the contrary, they willingly give me jobs to do and I'm considered an excellent workman and the best contractor after Radish. Although his health is better – he still paints church belfry cupolas without using scaffolding – he can no longer keep the men under control. I run around town now instead of him, looking for orders. I take men on, sack them, I borrow money at high interest. And now that I've become a contractor I can understand how a man can run round town for three days looking for roofers, for the sake of some lousy little job. People are polite to me, call me 'Mr', and in the houses where I'm working I'm given tea and asked if I want a hot meal. Children and girls often come and watch me, with sad, inquisitive looks.

One day I was working in the Governor's garden, painting a summer house to look like marble. The Governor was out strolling and came into the summer house. Having nothing else to do he started talking to me. I reminded him how once he had ordered me to his office for an interview. He stared into my face for a while, then he made an 'O' with his mouth, spread his arms out helplessly and said, 'I don't remember!'

I have aged and become taciturn, stiff and stern, and I rarely laugh. People say that I've come to resemble Radish, and I bore my workmen with useless moral exhortations.

My ex-wife Mariya Dolzhikov now lives abroad, and her father, the engineer, is building a railroad in some eastern Russian province and buying up estates there. Dr Blagovo is also abroad. Dubechnya has once again passed to Mrs Cheprakov, who bought it back after getting the engineer to cut twenty per cent off the price. Moisey now goes around in a bowler hat. He often comes into town on a racing droshky and stops near the bank. They say he's bought himself an estate on a mortgage and he's always inquiring at the bank about Dubechnya, which he intends buying as well. For a long time poor Ivan Cheprakov roamed around the town, doing nothing and drinking heavily. I had tried to fix him up with a job with us and for a while he worked with us, painting roofs and doing some glazing.

He even grew to like the work. Like any regular house-painter, he stole linseed oil, asked for tips and got drunk. But he soon grew sick and tired of it and went back to Dubechnya. Later on the lads confessed to me that he had been inciting them to help him kill Moisey at night and rob Mrs Cheprakov.

Father has aged terribly and become round-shouldered. In the evenings he takes a little stroll near his house. I never go and see him.

During the cholera epidemic Prokofy treated the shopkeepers with pepper-brandy and tar, and took money for it. As I later learnt from our newspaper, he was flogged for saying nasty things about doctors in his butcher's stall. Nikolka, the boy who helped him, died of cholera. Karpovna is still alive and, as ever, loves and fears her Prokofy. Whenever she sees me she shakes her head sadly.

'You're finished, you poor devil!' she says, sighing.

On weekdays I'm usually busy from morning to night. On holidays, when the weather is fine, I pick up my little niece (my sister was expecting a boy, but she had a girl) and walk, taking my time, to the cemetery. There I stand or sit down and gaze for a long time at the grave that is so dear to me, and I tell the little girl that her mother lies there.

Sometimes I meet Anyuta Blagovo at the graveside. We greet one another and stand in silence, or we talk about Cleopatra, about the little girl, and about the sadness of life. Then we leave the cemetery and walk silently – she walks slowly, so that she can stay next to me as long as possible. The little girl, happy and joyful, screws up her eyes in the bright sunlight and laughs as she stretches her small hands out towards me. We stop and together we fondle that dear little girl.

As we enter the town, Anyuta Blagovo becomes agitated and she blushes as she says goodbye and walks on alone, solemn and demure. And no one in that street looking at her now would have thought that only a moment ago she had been walking at my side and had even fondled that little child.

The Lady with the Little Dog

People said that there was a new arrival on the Promenade: a lady with a little dog. Dmitry Dmitrich Gurov, who had already spent a fortnight in Yalta[1] and who was by now used to the life there, had also begun to take an interest in new arrivals. As he sat on the terrace of Vernet's restaurant he saw a young, fair-haired woman walking along the Promenade, not very tall and wearing a beret. A white Pomeranian trotted after her.

And then he came across her several times a day in the municipal park and the square. She was always alone, always wearing that beret, always with the white Pomeranian. No one knew who she was and people simply called her 'The lady with the little dog'.

'If she's here without husband or friends,' Gurov reasoned, 'then it wouldn't be a bad idea if I got to know her.'

He was not yet forty, but already he had a twelve-year-old daughter and two schoolboy sons. He had been married off while still quite young, as a second-year student, and now his wife seemed about half as old again as he was. She was a tall, black-browed woman, plain-spoken, pretentious, respectable and – as she was fond of claiming – 'a thinking woman'. She was an avid reader, followed the latest reforms in spelling, called her husband Demetrius instead of Dmitry. But in secret he considered her not very bright, narrow-minded and unrefined. He was afraid of her and disliked being at home. He had begun deceiving her a long time ago, had frequently been unfaithful – which was probably why he always spoke disparagingly of women and whenever they were discussed in his company he would call them an 'inferior breed'.

He felt that he had learnt sufficiently from bitter experience to call them by whatever name he liked, yet, for all that, he could not have survived two days without his 'inferior breed'. He was bored in male company, not very talkative and offhand. But with women he felt free, knowing what to talk to them about and how to behave. Even saying nothing at all to them was easy for him. There was something attractive, elusive in his appearance, in his character – in his whole personality – that appealed to women and lured them to him. He was well aware of this and some power similarly attracted him.

Repeated – and in fact bitter – experience had long taught him that every affair, which at first adds spice and variety to life and seems such a charming, light-hearted adventure, inevitably develops into an enormous, extraordinarily complex problem with respectable people – especially Muscovites, who are so hesitant, so inhibited – until finally the whole situation becomes a real nightmare. But on every new encounter with an interesting woman all this experience was somehow forgotten and he simply wanted to enjoy life – and it all seemed so easy and amusing.

So, late one afternoon, he was dining at an open-air restaurant when the lady in the beret wandered over and sat at the table next to him. Her expression, the way she walked, her clothes, her hairstyle – all this told him that she was a socially respectable, married woman, that she was in Yalta for the first time, alone and bored.

There was a great deal of untruth in all those stories about the laxity of morals in that town and he despised them, knowing that such fictions are invented by people who would willingly have erred – if they'd had the chance. But when the lady seated herself about three paces away from him at the next table, those stories of easy conquests, of trips to the mountains came to mind; and the alluring thought of a swift, fleeting affair, of a romance with a strange woman whose name he didn't even know, suddenly possessed him.

Gently, he coaxed the dog over and when it came up to him he wagged his finger. The dog growled. Gurov wagged his finger again.

The lady glanced at him and immediately lowered her eyes.

'He doesn't bite,' she said, blushing.

'May I give him a bone?' he asked. And when she nodded he said affably:

'Have you been long in Yalta, madam?'

'About five days.'

'I've almost survived my second week here.'

There was a brief pause.

'The time passes quickly, but it's still so boring here!' she said, without looking at him.

'That's the done thing – to say it's boring there! Your average tripper who lives very nicely if you please in some backwater like Belyov or Zhizdra² never gets bored there, but the moment he comes here he says: "Oh, what a bore! Oh, all this dust!" You'd think he'd just breezed in from sunny Granada!'

She laughed. They both carried on eating in silence, like strangers. But after dinner they wandered off together and then there began that inconsequential, light-hearted conversation of people who have no ties, who are contented, who could not care less where they go or what they talk about. As they walked they talked about the unusual light on the sea. The water was the soft, warm colour of lilac and a golden strip of moonlight lay across it. They talked about how humid it was after the heat of the day. Gurov told her he was a Muscovite, a graduate in literature but working in a bank. At one time he had trained as an opera singer but had given it up; and he owned two houses in Moscow. From her he learnt that she had grown up in St Petersburg but had got married in S—, where she had been living for the past two years; that she intended staying another month in Yalta, after which her husband – who also needed a break – might possibly come and fetch her. She was quite unable to explain where her husband worked – whether he was with the rural or county council – and this she herself found very funny. And Gurov discovered that her name was Anna Sergeyevna.

Later, back in his hotel room, he thought about her. He was bound to meet her tomorrow, of that there was no doubt. As he went to bed he remembered that she had only recently left boarding-school, that she had been a schoolgirl just like his own daughter – and he remembered how much hesitancy, how much awkwardness there was in her laughter, in the way she talked to a stranger – it must have been the very first time in her life that she had been on her own, in such surroundings, where men followed her, eyed her and spoke to her with one secret aim in mind, which she could hardly fail to guess. He recalled her slender, frail neck, her beautiful grey eyes.

'Still, there's something pathetic about her,' he thought as he fell asleep.

II

A week had passed since their first encounter. It was a holiday. Indoors it was stifling and the wind swept the dust in swirling clouds down the streets, tearing off people's hats. All day one felt thirsty and Gurov kept going to the restaurant to fetch Anna Sergeyevna cordials or ice-cream. But there was no escaping the heat.

In the evening, when the wind had dropped, they went down to the pier to watch a steamer arrive. Crowds of people were strolling on the landing-stage: they were all there to meet someone and held bunches of flowers. Two distinguishing features of the Yalta smart set caught one's attention: the older women dressed like young girls and there were lots of generals.

The steamer arrived late – after sunset – owing to rough seas, and she swung about for some time before putting in at the jetty. Anna Sergeyevna peered at the boat and passengers through her lorgnette, as if trying to make out some people she knew, and when she turned to Gurov her eyes were sparkling. She talked a lot; her questions were abrupt and she immediately forgot what she had asked. Then she lost her lorgnette in the crowd.

The smartly dressed crowd dispersed, no more faces were to be seen; the wind had dropped completely and Gurov and Anna Sergeyevna still stood there, as if waiting for someone else to disembark. Anna Sergeyevna was silent now, sniffing her flowers and not looking at Gurov.

'The weather's improved a bit, now it's evening,' he said. 'So, where shall we go? How about driving out somewhere?'

She made no reply.

Then he stared at her – and he suddenly embraced her and kissed her lips. He was steeped in the fragrance, the dampness of the flowers and at once he looked around in fright: had anyone seen them?

'Let's go to your place,' he said softly.

And together they walked away, quickly.

Her room was stuffy and smelt of the perfume she had bought in the Japanese shop. Looking at her now Gurov thought: 'The encounters one has in life!' He still remembered those carefree, light-hearted women in his past, so happy in their love and grateful to him for their happiness – however short-lived. And he recalled women who, like his wife, made love insincerely, with too much talk, affectedly, hysterically, with an expression that seemed to say that it was neither love nor passion, but something more significant. And he recalled two or three very beautiful, cold women across whose faces there suddenly flashed a predatory expression, a stubborn desire to seize, to snatch from life more than it could provide . . . and these women were no longer young; they were capricious, irrational, domineering and unintelligent. And when Gurov cooled towards them their beauty aroused hatred in him and the lace on their underclothes seemed like fish scales.

But here there was that same hesitancy, that same discomfiture, that gaucheness of inexperienced youth. And there was an air of embarrassment, as if someone had just knocked at the door. In her own particular, very serious way, Anna Sergeyevna, that lady with the little dog, regarded what had happened just as if it were her downfall. So it seemed – and it was all very weird and out of place. Her features sank and faded, and her long hair hung sadly on each side of her face. She struck a pensive, dejected pose, like the woman taken in adultery in an old-fashioned painting.

'This is wrong,' she said. 'You'll be the first to lose respect for me now.'

On the table was a water-melon. Gurov cut himself a slice and slowly started eating it. Half an hour, at least, passed in silence.

Anna Sergeyevna looked most touching. She had that air of genuine, pure innocence of a woman with little experience of life. The solitary candle burning on the table barely illuminated her face, but he could see that she was obviously suffering.

'Why should I lose my respect for you?' Gurov asked. 'You don't know what you're saying.'

'May God forgive me!' she said – and her eyes filled with tears. 'It's terrible.'

'You seem to be defending yourself.'

'How can I defend myself? I'm a wicked, vile woman. I despise myself and I'm not going to make any excuses. It's not my husband but myself I've deceived. And I don't mean only just now, but for a long time. My husband's a fine honest man, but he's no more than a lackey. What does he do in that office of his? I've no idea. But I do know he's a mere lackey. I was twenty when I married him and dying from curiosity; but I wanted something better. Surely there must be a different kind of life, I told myself. I wanted to live life to the full, to enjoy life . . . to enjoy it! I was burning with curiosity. You won't understand this, but I swear that my feelings ran away with me, something was happening to me and there was no holding me back. So I told my husband I was ill and I came here . . . And ever since I've been going around as if intoxicated, like someone demented. So, now I'm a vulgar, worthless woman whom everyone has the right to despise.'

Gurov found all this very boring. He was irritated by her naïve tone, by that sudden, untimely remorse. But for the tears in her eyes he would have thought she was joking or play-acting.

'I don't understand,' he said softly. 'What is it you want?'

She buried her face on his chest and clung to him.

'Please, please believe me, I beg you,' she said. 'I yearn for a pure, honest life. Sin revolts me. I myself don't know what I'm doing. Simple folk say: "The devil's led me astray" – and I can honestly say that the devil's led *me* astray.'

'That's enough, enough,' he muttered.

He gazed into her staring, frightened eyes, kissed her and spoke softly and gently, so that gradually she grew calmer and her gaiety returned. They both started laughing.

Later, after they had gone out, there wasn't a soul to be seen on the Promenade and that town with its cypresses seemed completely dead; but the sea still roared as it broke on the shore. A small launch with its little lamp sleepily glimmering was tossing on the waves.

They took a cab and drove to Oreanda.[3]

'I've just discovered your name downstairs in the lobby. The board says "von Diederitz",' Gurov said. 'Is your husband German?'

'No. I think his grandfather was, but he's Russian.'

In Oreanda they sat on a bench near the church and looked down at the sea without saying a word. Yalta was barely visible through the morning mist; white clouds lay motionless on the mountain tops. Not one leaf stirred on the trees, cicadas chirped, and the monotonous, hollow roar of the sea that reached them from below spoke of peace, of that eternal slumber that awaits us. And so it roared down below when neither Yalta nor Oreanda existed. It was roaring now and would continue its hollow, indifferent booming when we are no more. And in this permanency, in this utter indifference to the life and death of every one of us there perhaps lies hidden a pledge of our eternal salvation, of never-ceasing progress of life upon earth, of the never-ceasing march towards perfection. As he sat there beside that young woman who seemed so beautiful at daybreak, soothed and enchanted at the sight of those magical surroundings – sea, mountains, clouds, wide skies – Gurov reflected that, if one thought hard about it, everything on earth was truly beautiful except those things we ourselves think of and do when we forget the higher aims of existence and our human dignity.

Someone came up – probably a watchman – glanced at them and went away. And even in this little incident there seemed to be something mysterious – and beautiful too. They could see the steamer arriving from Feodosiya,[4] illuminated by the sunrise, its lights extinguished.

'There's dew on the grass,' Anna Sergeyevna said after a pause.

'Yes, it's time to go back.'

They returned to town.

After this they met on the Promenade at noon every day, had lunch together, dinner together, strolled and admired the sea. She complained that she was sleeping badly, that she had palpitations and she asked him those same questions again, moved by jealousy, or fear that he did not respect her enough. And when they were in the square or municipal gardens, when no one was near, he would suddenly draw her to him and kiss her passionately. This complete idleness, the kisses in broad daylight when they would look around, afraid that someone had seen them, the heat, the smell of the sea and constant glimpses of those smartly dressed, well-fed people, seemed to transform him. He told Anna Sergeyevna how lovely she was, how seductive; he was impatient in his passion and did not leave her side for one moment. But she often became pensive and constantly asked him to admit that he had no respect for her, that he didn't love her at all and could only see her as a vulgar woman. Almost every day, in the late evening, they would drive out somewhere, to Oreanda or the waterfall.[5] The walks they took were a great success and every time they went their impressions were invariably beautiful and majestic.

Her husband was expected to arrive soon, but a letter came in which he told her that he had eye trouble and begged his wife to return as soon as possible. Anna Sergeyevna hurried.

'It's a good thing I'm leaving,' Anna Sergeyevna said. 'It's fate.'

She went by carriage and he rode with her. The drive took nearly a whole day. When she took her seat in the express train she said after the second departure bell:

'Let me look at you again . . . one last look. There . . .'

She was not crying, but she looked sad, as if she were ill, and her face was trembling.

'I shall think of you . . . I shall remember you . . .' she said. 'God bless you – and take care of yourself. Don't think badly of me. This is our final farewell – it must be, since we never should have met . . . Well, God bless you.'

The train swiftly drew out of the station, its lights soon vanished and a minute later its noise had died away, as though everything had deliberately conspired to put a speedy end to that sweet abandon, to that madness. Alone on the platform, gazing into the murky distance, Gurov listened to the chirring of the grasshoppers and the humming of the telegraph wires, and he felt that he had just woken up. So, this was just another adventure or event in his life, he reflected, and that too was over now, leaving only the memory . . . He was deeply moved and sad, and he felt a slight twinge of regret: that young woman, whom he would never see again, had not been happy with him, had she? He had been kind and affectionate, yet in his attitude, his tone and caresses, there had been a hint of casual mockery, of the rather coarse arrogance of a victorious male who, besides anything else, was twice her age. The whole time she had called him kind, exceptional, high-minded: obviously she had not seen him in his true colours, therefore he must have been unintentionally deceiving her . . .

Here at the station there was already a breath of autumn in the air and the evening was cool.

'It's time I went north too', Gurov thought, leaving the platform. 'It's time!'

III

Back home in Moscow it was already like winter; the stoves had been lit; it was dark in the mornings when the children were getting ready for school and having their breakfast, so Nanny would briefly light the lamp. The frosts had set in. When the first snow falls, on the first day of sleigh-rides, it is so delightful to see the white ground and the white roofs. The air is so soft and so marvellous to breathe – and at such times one remembers the days of one's youth. The old limes and birches, white with hoarfrost, have a welcoming look – they are closer to one's heart than cypresses or palms and beside them one has no desire to think of mountains and sea.

Gurov was a Muscovite and he returned to Moscow on a fine, frosty day. When he put on his fur coat and warm gloves, and strolled down the Petrovka,[6] when he heard the sound of bells on

Saturday evening, that recent trip and the places he had visited lost all their enchantment. Gradually he immersed himself in Moscow life, hungrily reading three newspapers a day whilst claiming that he didn't read any Moscow papers, on principle. Once again he could not resist the temptation of restaurants, clubs, dinner parties, anniversary celebrations; he was flattered that famous lawyers and artists visited him and that he played cards with a professor at the Doctors' Club. He could polish off a whole portion of Moscow hotpot straight from the pan.

After another month or two the memory of Anna Sergeyevna would become misted over, so it seemed, and only occasionally would he dream of her touching smile — just as he dreamt of others. But more than a month went by, deep winter set in, and he remembered Anna Sergeyevna as vividly as if he had parted from her yesterday. And those memories became even more vivid. Whether he heard in his study, in the quiet of evening, the voices of his children preparing their lessons, or a sentimental song, or an organ in a restaurant, whether the blizzard howled in the stove, everything would suddenly spring to life in his memory: the events on the jetty, that early, misty morning in the mountains, that steamer from Feodosiya and those kisses. For a long time he paced his room, reminiscing and smiling — and then those memories turned into dreams and the past merged in his imagination with what would be. He did not simply dream of Anna Sergeyevna — she followed him everywhere, like a shadow, watching him. When he closed his eyes he saw her as though she were there before him and she seemed prettier, younger, gentler than before. And he considered himself a better person than he had been in Yalta. In the evenings she would look at him from the bookcase, from the fireplace, from a corner; he could hear her breathing, the gentle rustle of her dress. In the street he followed women with his eyes, seeking someone who resembled her.

And now he was tormented by a strong desire to share his memories with someone. But it was impossible to talk about his love with anyone in the house — and there was no one outside it. Certainly not with his tenants or colleagues at the bank! And what was there to discuss? Had he really been in love? Had there been something beautiful, romantic, edifying or even interesting in his relations with Anna Sergeyevna? And so he was forced to talk about love and women in the vaguest terms and no one could guess what he was trying to say. Only his wife raised her dark eyebrows and said:

'Really, Demetrius! The role of ladies' man doesn't suit you one bit . . .'

One night, as he left the Doctors' Club with his partner – a civil servant – he was unable to hold back any more and said:

'If you only knew what an enchanting woman I met in Yalta!'

The civil servant climbed into his sledge and drove off. But then he suddenly turned round and called out:

'Dmitry Dmitrich!'

'What?'

'You were right the other day – the sturgeon *was* off!'

This trite remark for some reason suddenly nettled Gurov, striking him as degrading and dirty. What barbarous manners, what faces! What meaningless nights, what dismal, unmemorable days! Frenetic card games, gluttony, constant conversations about the same old thing. Those pointless business affairs and perpetual conversations – always on the same theme – were commandeering the best part of his time, his best strength, so that in the end there remained only a limited, humdrum life, just trivial nonsense. And it was impossible to run away, to escape – one might as well be in a lunatic asylum or a convict squad!

Gurov was so exasperated he did not sleep the whole night, and he suffered from a headache the whole day long. And on following nights too he slept badly, sitting up in his bed the whole time thinking, or pacing his room from corner to corner. The children bored him, he didn't want to go anywhere or talk about anything.

During the Christmas holidays he packed his things and told his wife that he was going to St Petersburg on behalf of a certain young man he wanted to help – and he went to S——. Why? He himself was not sure. But he wanted to see Anna Sergeyevna again, to arrange a meeting – if that were possible.

He arrived at S—— in the morning and took the best room in the hotel, where the entire floor was fitted from wall to wall with a carpet the colour of grey army cloth; on the table was an inkstand, grey with dust, in the form of a mounted horseman holding his hat in his uplifted hand and whose head had been broken off.

The porter told him all he needed to know: von Dodderfits (this was how he pronounced von Diederitz) was living on Old Pottery Street, in his own house, not far from the hospital. He lived lavishly, on the grand scale, kept his own horses and was known by everyone in town.

Without hurrying Gurov strolled down Old Pottery Street and found the house. Immediately opposite stretched a long grey fence topped with nails.

'That fence is enough to make you want to run away', Gurov thought, looking now at the windows, now at the fence.

It was a holiday, he reflected, and local government offices would be closed – therefore her husband was probably at home . . . In any event, it would have been tactless to go into the house and embarrass her. But if he were to send a note it would most likely fall into the husband's hands and this would ruin everything. Best of all was to trust to luck. So he continued walking along the street, by the fence, waiting for his opportunity. He watched how a beggar went through the gates and was set upon by dogs; and then, an hour later, he heard the faint, indistinct sounds of a piano. Anna Sergeyevna must be playing. Suddenly the front door opened and out came some old lady followed by that familiar white Pomeranian. Gurov wanted to call the dog, but his heart suddenly started pounding and he was too excited to remember the dog's name.

He carried on walking, hating that grey fence more and more. By now he was so irritated that he was convinced Anna Sergeyevna had forgotten him and was perhaps already dallying with someone else – which was only natural with a young woman forced to look at that damned fence from morning to night. He returned to his hotel room and sat on the sofa for a long time, not knowing what to do. Then he had dinner, after which he had a long sleep.

'How stupid and upsetting it all is!' he thought as he awoke and peered at the dark windows; it was already evening. 'Well, now that I've had a good sleep what shall I do tonight?'

He sat on the bed that was covered with a cheap, grey hospital-like blanket and in his irritation he mocked himself: 'So much for ladies with little dogs! So much for holiday adventures . . . Now I'm stuck in this hole!'

At the railway station that morning his attention had been caught by a poster that advertised in bold lettering the first night of *The Geisha*.[7] He remembered this now and drove to the theatre.

'It's very likely she goes to first nights', he thought.

The theatre was full and, as in all local theatres, there was a thick haze above the chandeliers; the gallery was noisy and excited. In the first row, before the performance began, the local dandies were standing with their arms crossed behind their backs. And in front, in the Governor's box, sat the Governor's daughter sporting a feather boa, while the Governor himself humbly hid behind the *portière*, so that only his hands were visible. The curtain shook, the orchestra took an age to tune up. All this time the audience were entering and taking their seats. Gurov looked eagerly around him.

And in came Anna Sergeyevna. She sat in the third row and when Gurov looked at her his heart seemed to miss a beat: now it was plain to him that no one in the whole world was closer, dearer and more important to him than she was. That little woman, not remarkable in any way, lost in that provincial crowd, with a vulgar lorgnette in her hand, now filled his whole life, was his sorrow, his joy, the only happiness that he now wished for himself. And to the sounds of that atrocious orchestra, of those wretched fiddlers, he thought how lovely she was. He thought – and he dreamed.

A young man with short side-whiskers, very tall and stooping, entered with Anna Sergeyevna and sat next to her. With every step he shook his head and he seemed to be perpetually bowing. Probably he was the husband whom she had called 'lackey' in Yalta in a fit of pique. And indeed, in his lanky figure, in his side-whiskers, in that slight baldness, there was something of a flunkey's subservience. He had a sickly smile and in his buttonhole there gleamed the badge of some learned society – just like the number on a flunkey's jacket.

In the first interval the husband went out for a smoke, while she remained in her seat. Gurov, who was also in the stalls, went up to her and forced a smile as he said in a trembling voice:

'Good evening!'

She looked at him and turned pale. Then she looked again, was horrified and could not believe her eyes, tightly clasping her fan and lorgnette and obviously trying hard to stop herself fainting. Neither said a word. She sat there, he stood, alarmed at her embarrassment and not daring to sit next to her. The fiddles and flutes began to tune up and suddenly they felt terrified – it seemed they were being scrutinized from every box. But then she stood up and quickly went towards the exit. He followed her and they both walked aimlessly along the corridors, up and down staircases, caught glimpses of people in all kinds of uniforms – lawyers, teachers, administrators of crown estates, all of them wearing insignia. They glimpsed ladies, fur coats on hangers; a cold draught brought the smell of cigarette ends. Gurov's heart was throbbing. 'God in heaven!' he thought. 'Why these people, this orchestra?'

And at that moment he suddenly remembered saying to himself, after he had seen Anna Sergeyevna off at the station that evening, that it was all over and that they would never see one another again. But how far they still were from the end!

On the narrow, gloomy staircase with the sign 'Entrance to Circle' she stopped.

'What a fright you gave me!' she exclaimed, breathing heavily, still pale and stunned. 'Oh, what a fright you gave me. I'm barely alive! Why have you come? Why?'

'Please understand, Anna, please understand,' he said hurriedly in an undertone. 'I beg you, *please* understand!'

She looked at him in fear, in supplication – and with love, staring at his face to fix his features more firmly in her mind.

'It's such hell for me!' she went on without listening to him. 'The whole time I've thought only of you. I've existed only by thinking about you. And I wanted to forget, forget. But why have you come?'

On a small landing above them two schoolboys were smoking and looking down, but Gurov didn't care. He drew Anna Sergeyevna to him and started kissing her face, her cheeks, her arms.

'What are you doing? What are you doing?' she cried out in horror, pushing him away. 'We've both gone out of our minds! You *must* leave tonight . . . you must go now . . . I implore you, by all that's holy, I *beg* you . . . Someone's coming . . . !'

Someone was coming up the staircase.

'You *must* go,' Anna Sergeyevna continued, whispering. 'Do you hear, Dmitry Dmitrich? I'll come and see you in Moscow. I've never been happy, I'm unhappy now and I shall never, never be happy! Never! Don't make me suffer even more! I swear I'll come to Moscow. But now we must say goodbye . . . My dear, kind darling, we must part!'

She pressed his hand and swiftly went downstairs, constantly looking back at him – and he could see from her eyes that she really was unhappy. Gurov stayed a while longer, listening hard. And then, when all was quiet, he found his peg and left the theatre.

IV

And Anna Sergeyevna began to visit him in Moscow. Two or three times a month she left S—, telling her husband that she was going to consult a professor about some women's complaint – and her husband neither believed nor disbelieved her. In Moscow she stayed at the Slav Fair Hotel,[8] and the moment she arrived she would send a messenger with a red cap over to Gurov. He would go to her hotel and no one in Moscow knew a thing.

One winter's morning he went to see her as usual (the messenger had called the previous evening but he had been out). With him walked his daughter, whom he wanted to take to school, as it was on the way. A thick wet snow was falling.

'It's three degrees above zero, yet it's snowing,' Gurov told his daughter. 'But it's only warm on the surface of the earth, the temperature's quite different in the upper layers of the atmosphere.'

'Papa, why isn't there thunder in winter?'

And he explained this too, conscious as he spoke that here he was on his way to an assignation, that not a soul knew about it and that probably no one would ever know. He was leading a double life: one was undisguised, plain for all to see and known to everyone who needed to know, full of conventional truths and conventional deception, identical to the lives of his friends and acquaintances; and another which went on in secret. And by some strange, possibly fortuitous chain of circumstances, everything that was important, interesting and necessary for him, where he behaved sincerely and did not deceive himself and which was the very essence of his life – that was conducted in complete secrecy; whereas all that was false about him, the front behind which he hid in order to conceal the truth – for instance, his work at the bank, those quarrels at the club, his notions of an 'inferior breed', his attending anniversary celebrations with his wife – that was plain for all to see. And he judged others by himself, disbelieving what he saw, invariably assuming that everyone's true, most interesting life was carried on under the cloak of secrecy, under the cover of night, as it were. The private, personal life of everyone is grounded in secrecy and this perhaps partly explains why civilized man fusses so neurotically over having this personal secrecy respected.

After taking his daughter to school, Gurov went to the Slav Fair Hotel. He took off his fur coat downstairs, went up and gently tapped at the door. Anna Sergeyevna, wearing his favourite grey dress, exhausted by the journey and by the wait, had been expecting him since the previous evening. She was pale and looked at him unsmiling; but the moment he entered the room she flung herself on his chest. Their kiss was long and lingering, as though they had not seen one another for two years.

'Well, how are things?' he asked. 'What's the news?'

'Wait, I'll tell you in a moment. But not now . . .'

She was unable to speak for crying. Turning away from him she pressed her handkerchief to her eyes.

'Well, let her have a good cry . . . I'll sit down in the meantime', he thought as he sat in the armchair.

Then he rang and ordered some tea. After he had drunk it she was still standing there, facing the window. She wept from the mournful realization that their lives had turned out so sadly. They were meeting in secret, hiding from others, like thieves! Surely their lives were ruined?

'Please stop crying!' he said.

Now he could see quite clearly that this was no short-lived affair – and it was impossible to say when it would finish. Anna Sergeyevna had become even more attached to him, she adored him and it would have been unthinkable of him to tell her that some time all this had to come to an end. And she would not have believed him even if he had.

He went over to her and put his hands on her shoulders, intending to caress her, to joke a little – and then he caught sight of himself in the mirror.

He was already going grey. And he thought it strange that he had aged so much over the past years, had lost his good looks. The shoulders on which his hands were resting were warm and trembling. He felt pity for this life, still so warm and beautiful, but probably about to fade and wither like his own. Why did she love him so? Women had never taken him for what he really was – they didn't love the man himself, but someone who was a figment of their imagination, someone they had been eagerly seeking all their lives. And then, when they realized their mistake, they still loved him. Not one of them had been happy with him. Time passed, he met new women, had affairs, parted, but never once had he been in love. There had been everything else, but there had been no love.

And only now, when his hair had turned grey, had he genuinely, truly fallen in love – for the first time in his life.

Anna Sergeyevna and he loved one another as close intimates, as man and wife, as very dear friends. They thought that fate itself had intended them for each other and it was a mystery why he should have a wife and she a husband. And in fact they were like two birds of passage, male and female, caught and forced to live in separate cages. They forgave one another all they had been ashamed of in the past, forgave everything in the present, and they felt that this love of theirs had transformed them both.

Before, in moments of sadness, he had reassured himself with any kind of argument that happened to enter his head, but now he was not in the mood for arguments: he felt profound pity and wanted to be sincere, tender . . .

'Please stop crying, my sweet,' he said. 'You've had a good cry . . . it's enough . . . Let's talk now – we'll think of something.'

Then they conferred for a long time and wondered how they could free themselves from the need to hide, to deceive, to live in different towns, to see each other only after long intervals. How could they break free from these intolerable chains?

'How? How?' he asked, clutching his head. '*How?*'

And it seemed – given a little more time – a solution would be found and then a new and beautiful life would begin. And both of them clearly realized that the end was far, far away and that the most complicated and difficult part was only just beginning.

In the Ravine

The village of Ukleyevo lay in a ravine, so that only the church belfry and the chimneys of calico-printing works could be seen from the main road and the railway station. When travellers asked its name they were told, 'It's that place where the lay reader ate all the caviare at a funeral.'

Once, during a wake at Kostyukov the manufacturer's house, an elderly lay reader had spotted some unpressed caviare among the savouries and immediately started gobbling it up. People nudged him, tugged his sleeve, but he seemed to be paralysed from the sheer enjoyment of it, which made him oblivious of everything, and he just continued eating, regardless. He scoffed the whole lot – and it was a four-pound jar! All this had happened many years ago and the lay reader was long since dead, but the story of the caviare was still fresh in everyone's mind. Whether it was because life there was so wretched or simply that the people could find nothing more exciting to talk about than that trivial little incident of ten years before, it was all you ever heard about Ukleyevo.

Swamp fever was still rife here and even in summer there were slimy patches of mud – especially under fences – which lay in the broad shade of old, overhanging willows. There was always a smell of factory waste, of the acetic acid they used for processing the cotton. The factories – three cotton-printing works and one tannery – were not in the village itself but a short distance away, on the outskirts. They weren't very large and the total workforce didn't amount to much more than four hundred. The waste from the tannery

239

made the water in the small river stink horribly, the meadows were polluted by the effluent, the cattle in the village suffered from anthrax, and so it was ordered to close down. However, although it was *supposed* to be shut, it was kept going on the quiet, with the full approval of the district police inspector and doctor, each receiving ten roubles a month from the owner. There were only two houses worthy of the name in the whole village, built of stone and with iron roofs. One of them was occupied by the council offices, while Grigory Petrov Tsybukin, a shopkeeper from Yepifan,[1] lived in the other, which was two storeys high and stood right opposite the church.

Grigory kept a grocery store, but this was only a cover for his secret business in vodka, cattle, hides, grain, pigs – in fact he sold anything that came his way. For example, when there were export orders for peasant women's bonnets (these were made into fashionable hats for ladies), he could earn himself thirty copecks a pair. He bought trees for sawing up, lent money on interest, and really the old man could turn his hand to anything. He had two sons. Anisim, the elder, was a police detective and seldom came home. The younger son, Stepan, had gone into the business to help his father. However, they could not expect any real help from him as he was in poor health and deaf as well. His wife, Aksinya, was a beautiful, well-built woman, who wore a hat and carried a parasol when she went to village festivals. She was an early riser, went late to bed and all day long kept rushing round the barn, the cellar or the shop with her skirts tucked up and her bunch of keys jangling. Old Tsybukin would cheer up as he watched her and his eyes would sparkle. At such moments he regretted that she had not married his elder son, but the younger one instead, who besides being deaf couldn't tell the beautiful from the ugly.

The old man always had a strong liking for domestic life and he loved his family more than anything else in the world – especially his elder detective son and his daughter-in-law. No sooner had Aksinya married the deaf son than she began to display an extraordinary head for business; in no time she got to know those who were credit-worthy and those she had to turn down. She always took charge of the keys, not even trusting her own husband with them, and she would click away at her abacus. Like a true peasant, she would look at a horse's teeth first and was always laughing or shouting. Whatever she did or said, it warmed the old man's heart and he would mutter, 'Well done, my daughter-in-law! That's the way, my beautiful girl!'

He had been a widower, but a year after his son's marriage he could bear it no longer and remarried. About twenty miles from Ukleyevo they found him a spinster called Varvara Nikolayevna, from a good family. Although she was middle-aged, she still kept her good looks. From the moment she settled into her little room on the first floor, everything in the house became shining bright, as though all the windows had suddenly been fitted with new glass. Icon-lamps were lit, tables covered with snow-white cloths, flowers with little red buds appeared on the window sills and in the front garden, and at mealtimes everyone had his own individual dish instead of eating from a communal bowl. Varvara Nikolayevna's warm, fetching smile seemed to infect the whole household. And then something quite out of the ordinary happened – beggars, wanderers and female pilgrims began to call at the house. The plaintive singsong voices of the Ukleyevo women and the guilty coughing of weak, haggard-looking peasants, sacked from the factory for drunkenness, came from outside, beneath the window-ledges. Varvara gave them money, bread, old clothes and, later on, when she was really settled in, brought them things from the shop. On one occasion the deaf son was most upset when he saw her taking away two small packets of tea.

'Mother's just pinched two packets of tea,' he told his father. 'Who's supposed to be paying for them?'

The old man did not reply, but stood there pondering and twitching his eyebrows; then he went upstairs to his wife. 'Varvara, dear,' he said affectionately, 'if ever you need *anything* from the shop, then help yourself. Take as much as you like, and don't feel guilty.'

Next day the deaf son shouted out to her as he ran across the yard, 'Mother, if you need anything, just *help yourself*!'

There was something fresh, cheerful and gay in her displays of charity, just like those brightly burning icon-lamps and the little red flowers. On the eve of a fast or on a saint's day festival (they usually took three days to celebrate them) when they used to fob the peasants off with rotten salt beef, which gave off such a revolting stench you could hardly go near the barrel; when they let the drunks pawn their scythes, caps, their wives' scarves; when the factory-hands, their heads reeling from cheap vodka, wallowed in the mud, so that the shamelessness of it all seemed to hang overhead in a thick haze – at these times it came as a relief to think that over there in the house lived a quiet, tidy woman who would have nothing to do with either salt beef or vodka. On such distressing, murky days her acts of charity had the effect of a safety-valve.

Every day at the Tsybukins' was a busy one. Before the sun had even risen, Aksinya puffed and panted as she washed herself in the hall, while the samovar boiled away in the kitchen with an ominous hum. Old Grigory Petrov, who looked so neat and small in his long black frock-coat, cotton-print trousers and shining jackboots, would pace up and down the house, tapping his heels like the father-in-law in the popular song. Then they would open the shop. When it was light, the racing droshky would be brought round to the front door and the old man would pull his large peaked cap right over his ears and jump into it with all the friskiness of a young man. To look at him no one would have guessed that he was already fifty-six. His wife and daughter-in-law used to see him off and on these momentous occasions, when he wore his fine clean frock-coat, when the enormous black stallion that had cost three hundred roubles was hitched to the droshky, the old man didn't like it if peasants came up to him asking for favours or complaining. He hated them and they disgusted him. If he happened to see one hanging around the gates he would shout furiously, 'What yer standing round here for? Clear off!' If it was a beggar he would yell, 'God'll feed yer!'

While he was away on business his wife, with her dark dress and black apron, would tidy the rooms or help in the kitchen. Aksinya served in the shop and one could hear bottles and coins clinking, the sound of her laughter or of offended customers getting cross. At the same time it was all too plain that the illegal vodka business was already running nice and smoothly. Her deaf husband would sit in the shop with her or walk up and down the street without any hat, hands in pockets, vacantly gazing at the huts or up at the sky. They drank tea six times a day in that house and had four proper meals at the table. In the evening they counted the takings, entered them in the books and then slept soundly.

All three cotton-printing works in Ukleyevo, as well as the owners' homes – the Khrymins' Senior, Khrymins' Junior and the Kostyukovs' – were on the telephone. The council offices had also been connected, but before long the telephone there was jammed with bugs and cockroaches. The chairman of the district council could barely read or write and began every word in his report with a capital letter; but when the telephone went out of order he remarked, 'Yes, it's going to be tricky without that telephone.'

The Khrymins Senior were perpetually suing the Khrymins Junior, and the Khrymins Junior sometimes quarrelled among themselves and sued each other – then their factory would stand idle for a month or two until they had patched things up: all this provided a source of amusement for the people of Ukleyevo, since each row provoked no end of gossip and malicious talk.

Kostyukov and the Khrymins Junior would go out driving on Sundays, running over calves as they tore through Ukleyevo. With her starched petticoats rustling and dressed to kill, Aksinya would stroll up and down the street near the shop; then the Khrymins Junior would swoop down and carry her off with them as though they were kidnapping her. Old Tsybukin would drive out to show off his new horse, taking his Varvara with him.

In the evening, when the riding was over and everyone was going to bed, someone would play an expensive-sounding accordion in the Khrymins' Junior yard; if the moon was shining, the music stirred and gladdened one's heart and Ukleyevo did not seem such a miserable hole after all.

II

Anisim (the elder son) came home very rarely – only for the principal festivals – but he often sent presents, which he handed to friends from the same village to take back for him, as well as letters written by someone else in a beautiful hand and invariably on good-quality paper, so that they looked like official application forms. They were filled with expressions that Anisim would never have used in conversation, for example: 'My dear Mama and Papa, I'm sending you a pound of herb tea for the *gratification* of your *physical requirements*.' At the foot of each letter the name *Anisim Tsybukin* was scribbled – with a cross-nibbed pen, it seemed – and beneath his signature, in the same beautiful handwriting, would appear the word 'Agent'. These letters were read out loud, several times, and afterwards the old man, deeply moved by them and flushed with excitement, would say, 'There you are, he wouldn't stay at home, wanted to be a scholar instead. Well, if that's what he wants! Each to his own, I say.'

Once, just before Shrovetide, there were torrential rainfalls and sleet. The old man and Varvara went to look out of the window, and lo and behold! – there was Anisim coming from the station on a sledge. This was a complete surprise. When he entered the room, he looked anxious, as though terribly worried by something; he stayed like this for the rest of his visit and he behaved in a rather free-and-easy, offhand way. He was in no hurry to leave, and it looked as though they had given him the sack. Varvara was glad he had come, eyed him cunningly, sighed and shook her head: 'Don't know what to make of it,' she said. 'The lad's turned twenty-seven and he's still running around like a gay bachelor! Oh, *dear, dear* me!' They could hear her quiet, regular speech – a series of '*dear, dear* me's' from the next room. Then she began whispering to the old man and Aksinya, and their faces took on that same cunning, mysterious, conspiratorial expression.

They had decided to marry Anisim off.

'Oh, dear, dear me! Your young brother was married ages ago,' Varvara said, 'but you're still without a mate, just like a cock in the market. What kind of life is that? If you did get married, God willing, you could do as you please, go back to work, while your wife could stay at home and be a help to you. It's a wild life you're leading, my boy, I can see you've really gone off the rails. Oh, dear, dear me, you lot from the town bring nothing but trouble!'

When a Tsybukin married, he could take the prettiest girl, as they were all very wealthy, and they found a pretty one for Anisim too. As for him, he was insignificant and uninteresting: while he was short and had a poorly built, unhealthy looking body, his cheeks were full and plump – as though he were puffing them out. He never blinked and his eyes had a piercing look. His beard was reddish and straggly, and he was always sticking it in his mouth and biting it when he was deep in thought. Moreover, he was very fond of the bottle – one could tell from his face and the way he walked. But when they told him that a very pretty bride had been found for him, he remarked, 'Well, I'm not exactly a freak. All of us Tsybukins are good-looking, that's for sure.'

The village of Torguyevo lay right next to the town. One half had recently been merged with it, while the other stayed as it was. In the town half there lived a widow, in her own little house. She had a very poor sister, who had to go out to work every day; this sister had a daughter called Lipa, who went out to work as well. Her beauty had long been a talking-point in Torguyevo, but her terrible poverty put everyone off. So they reasoned that perhaps some old man or widower might turn a blind eye to this and would marry her or would 'set her up' in his house – and if that happened the mother would not have to starve. When the local matchmakers told her about Lipa, Varvara drove out to Torguyevo.

After that, an 'inspection'[2] was arranged (as was proper) at the aunt's house, with snacks and drinks. Lipa wore a new pink dress made especially for the viewing and a crimson ribbon shone like a flame in her hair. She was a thin, pale-faced, fragile girl with fine, delicate features and her skin was tanned from working in the open air. Her face bore a perpetual sad, timid smile and her eyes were like a child's – trusting and inquisitive at the same time.

She was young – still a little girl in fact – with scarcely noticeable breasts. However, she was old enough for marriage. In actual fact she was a beauty, and the only objectionable thing about her was her large arms, just like a man's, which she allowed to dangle idly, so that they resembled two huge crab's claws.

'We're not in the least worried that there's no dowry,' the old man told the aunt. 'We took a girl in from a poor family for our son Stepan, and now we can't praise her enough. She's a wonderful help in the house and the business.'

Lipa stood by the door and it seemed she wanted to say, 'You can do what you like with me, I *trust* you,' while her mother, Praskovya, who had to go out charring, was overcome with shyness and shut herself away in the kitchen. Once, when she was still a young girl, a certain merchant (whose floors she used to scrub) suddenly stamped his feet at her in a fit of anger. She was terrified, went numb all over and the shock of it never left her for the rest of her life: her arms and legs were always trembling with fright – and her cheeks as well. From where she sat in the kitchen, she always tried hard to hear what visitors were saying in the next room, kept crossing herself, pressed her fingers to her forehead and peered at the icon. A slightly tipsy Anisim would open the kitchen door and breezily inquire, 'What you sitting out here for, my dearest Mama? It's so dull without you.' This would make Praskovya turn shy and she would clasp her small, wasted breasts and reply, 'But sir, you really *shouldn't*! I'm only too pleased . . . sir!'

After the inspection, the wedding day was fixed. Later on, when he was home, Anisim kept pacing up and down whistling; or something would suddenly spring to mind which made him think hard, look at the floor without moving an inch and stare so hard that it seemed he was trying to bore a hole deep into the earth with his eyes. He didn't show any pleasure at the fact that he was getting married, that it was going to be soon – the week after Easter – nor did he show any inclination to see his bride – all he did was whistle. Obviously he was marrying only because his father and stepmother wanted him to and because that was how things were done in the village: sons got married to have someone to help them in the house. He didn't hurry himself when the time came to leave and his behaviour during this last visit was quite different from the previous one – he was particularly free-and-easy with everyone and kept speaking out of turn.

III

Two dressmakers lived in the village of Shikalovo; they were sisters and belonged to the Flagellant sect. They got the order for the wedding dresses and came over very often for the fittings, when they would sit down for hours drinking tea. For Varvara they made a brown dress, with black lace and tubular glass beads, and Aksinya had a bright green dress, yellow in front and with a train. When they had finished, Tsybukin didn't pay them cash but in things from the shop, and so they went away very down in the mouth, carrying little packets of tallow candles and tins of sardines for which they didn't have any use at all. As soon as they were out of the village and in the fields, they sat down on a little mound and burst into tears.

Anisim turned up just three days before the wedding in a completely new outfit. He wore brilliantly glossy rubber galoshes and instead of a tie had a red lace with tassels hanging from it. A brand-new overcoat was draped over his shoulders like a cloak. After solemnly saying his prayers, he greeted his father and gave him ten silver roubles and ten fifty-copeck pieces; he gave Varvara the same, while Aksinya received twenty twenty-five-copeck pieces. The principal charm of these presents was that every single coin was brand-new, as though specially selected, and all of them glinted in the sun. In his effort to appear sober and serious, Anisim tensed his face muscles and puffed his cheeks out; he was reeking of drink.

Most likely he had dashed into every station bar during the journey. Once again there was that same free-and-easy attitude, something strangely exaggerated about his behaviour. After his arrival, Anisim drank tea and ate savouries with his father, while Varvara fingered the bright new roubles and asked him about her friends from the village, now living in the town.

'Everything's okay, thank God, they're all living well,' Anisim said. 'But there was a *certain occurrence* in Ivan Yegorov's *domestic* life: his old woman Sofya passed away. From consumption. The caterers charged them two and a half roubles a head for the *funeral repast* for the *repose of her soul*. There was wine too. Some peasants from our village were there – and they had to pay two and a half roubles for each of them! But they didn't eat a thing. You can't expect yokels to know anything about sauces!'

'Two and a half roubles!' exclaimed the old man, shaking his head.

'Well, what do you expect? It's not like the village. If you drop into a restaurant for a bite, you order this and that, friends come and join you, you have a few drinks and before you know what's happening it's dawn and you've run up a nice little bill of three or four roubles a head. And if Samorodov comes, he likes his coffee and brandy after a meal – and with brandy at sixty copecks a glass! I ask you!'

'He's all lies,' the old man said delightedly. 'Nothing but lies!'

'These days I'm always with him. He's the same Samorodov who does my letters for me. Writes excellently!'

Anisim turned to Varvara and continued cheerfully, 'If I told you, Mama, what kind of man he is, you'd never believe me. We all call him Mukhtar, as he rather looks like an Armenian – black all over. I can read him like a book, know everything he's up to, like the back of my hand, Mama. He knows it all right and he's behind me the whole time, doesn't leave me alone for one minute. Now we're as thick as thieves. Seems he's scared of me, but he can't do without me. Follows me everywhere. Now, I've very good eyesight, Mama. Just take the old clothes' market. If there's a peasant selling a shirt I say, "Hold on, that's been *stolen*." And as usual I'm always right. It *was* stolen!'

'But how do you know?' Varvara asked.

'I don't *know*, I've just got the eye for it. I didn't know anything about the shirt, but somehow I was drawn to it – it *was* stolen, and that was that. The detectives where I work just say the words, "Look, Anisim's gone shooting woodcock!" That means, "He's gone looking for stolen property." Yes . . . *anyone* can steal, but holding on to it's another matter! It's a great big world, but there's no hiding stolen goods!'

'But last week, in the village, the Guntorevs had a ram and two ewes stolen,' Varvara said, sighing. 'Only there was no one to go looking for them, oh, dear, dear me!'

'What? *Of course* you can go looking. It's really very easy.'

The wedding day arrived. Although the weather was cool, it was one of those bright and cheerful days in April. Since early morning, troikas and carriages and pairs had been driving round Ukleyevo with bells tinkling and their shaft-bows and horses' manes decorated with gaily coloured ribbons. Disturbed by all this commotion, rooks cawed in the willows and starlings sang incessantly, as hard as they could, so that it seemed they were overjoyed at the Tsybukins' wedding.

Back at the house, the tables were already laden with long fishes, stuffed legs of meat and gamebirds, boxes of sprats, different kinds of salted savouries and pickles, and a great quantity of vodka and wine bottles. One could smell the salami and soured lobster. The old man went hopping round the tables clicking his heels and sharpening the knives on each other. Time and again they called out to Varvara to bring them something. Looking quite bewildered and gasping for breath, she would run into the kitchen where the Kostyukovs' chef and the Khrymins Junior head cook had been slaving away since dawn. Aksinya, with her hair set in curls, wearing just a corset without any dress over it and squeaky new ankle-high boots, dashed round the yard like a whirlwind and all one could catch sight of were bare knees and breasts. It was all very noisy, with swearing and cursing. Passers-by stopped at the wide-open gates and everything indicated that they were preparing for something really special.

'They've gone for the bride!'

Harness bells rang out loud and then died away, far beyond the village . . . After two o'clock the villagers came running: they could hear the bells again, the bride was coming! The church was full, chandeliers shone brightly, and the choirboys sang from music-sheets, as the old man Tsybukin had specially requested this. The glare of the candles and the bright dresses dazzled Lipa, and the choirboys' loud voices seemed to beat on her head like hammers; her corset (it was the first time she had ever worn one) and her shoes were pinching her to death; from her expression it seemed she had fainted and was just coming to – she looked around without understanding anything.

Anisim stood there in that same black frock-coat, with a red lace instead of a tie; he was in a very thoughtful mood, kept staring at the same spot and crossed himself hastily whenever the choirboys sang very loud. He felt deeply moved and wanted to cry. He was familiar with this church from early childhood; his late mother had brought him there once to take the sacrament and once he had sung in the choir with the other boys. So he remembered every nook and cranny, every icon. Now he was being married, because that was the *right* thing to do; but he wasn't thinking about that at all and he seemed to have forgotten it completely. He could not see the icons for tears and his heart was heavy. He prayed and implored God to make those unavoidable misfortunes that were threatening to shower down on him any day now pass him by somehow, just as storm clouds pass over a village during a drought, without shedding a single drop of rain. So many sins from his past accumulated – so many, in fact, that it was impossible to shrug them off or expiate them now – that even to ask for pardon was ridiculous. But he *did* ask to be forgiven and even sobbed out loud; but everyone ignored him, thinking that he was drunk.

Then a frightened child started crying, '*Please*, darling Mama, take me away from here!'

'Be quiet over there!' shouted the priest.

On the way back from the church, villagers flocked after the couple. Outside the shop, at the gates and beneath the windows overlooking the yard, there were crowds too. The village women had come to sing in their honour. Hardly had the young couple crossed the threshold than the choirboys (already stationed in the hall with their music-sheets) sang as hard as they could, at the top of their shrill voices. Then the band, specially hired from the town, struck up. Sparkling Don wine was already being served in long glasses and Yelizarov, the jobbing carpenter – a tall lean man whose eyebrows were so bushy they nearly covered his eyes – turned to the young couple and said, 'Anisim – and *you*, my child – love one another, live like good Christians and the Holy Virgin will not forsake you.'

He fell on the old man's shoulder and sobbed. 'Grigory Petrov, let us weep, let us weep for joy!' he said in his thin little voice and then he suddenly laughed out loud and continued – this time lowering his voice, 'Oho! Your daughter-in-law's a real smasher. She's got everything in the right place, she's running nice and smooth, no rattling – all the machinery is in tip-top order – and there's plenty of screws.'

He came from around Yegoryevsk,[3] but he had worked in the Ukleyevo factories and local workshops since he was a young boy, and that's where his roots were. For as long as the people had known him, he had always been that same thin, tall old man – and he had always gone by the name of 'Crutchy'. Perhaps as a result of spending over forty years doing nothing else but repairs in factories, he judged everybody and everything solely in terms of soundness: did it need repairing? And even before he sat down at the table, he tested a few chairs to see if they were all right – and he also gave the salmon a poke.

After the sparkling wine, everyone sat down at the table. The wedding-guests talked and moved their chairs. The choirboys sang in the hall, the band played, and at the same time the village women sang out in the yard, their voices all at the same pitch, which produced such a horrible, wild jumble of sounds it made one's head reel. Crutchy fidgeted on his chair, elbowed the people sitting next to him, didn't let them get a word in, and cried and laughed out loud in turn. 'My children! My little *children* . . . little children!' he muttered swiftly. 'My dearest Aksinya, my sweet little Varvara, let's all live peacefully together . . . my darlings . . .'

He never drank very much and now one glass of strong vodka made him tipsy. This revolting brew, concocted from God knows what, made all who drank it so muzzy they felt they had been clubbed. Tongues began to falter.

The clergy was there, factory clerks and their wives, and inn-keepers from other villages. The chairman of the parish council and his clerk, who had been working together for as long as fourteen years now – during the whole course of which they had never signed a single document – and who never let anyone leave the office without first cheating and insulting him, had positioned their fat, well-fed selves next to each other. They had lived on lies for so long, it seemed that even the skin on their faces had taken on a peculiarly criminal complexion all of its own. The clerk's wife, a scraggy woman with a squint, had brought all her children along; just like a bird of prey she looked at the plates out of the corner of her eye and grabbed everything within reach, stuffing it away in her children's pockets and her own.

Lipa sat there like a stone and she looked the same as she did during the service. Not having exchanged a single word with her since their first meeting, Anisim still didn't know what her voice was like.

And now, even though he was sitting right next to her, he still didn't break the silence and drank vodka instead. But when he was drunk, however, he began to speak to his aunt, who was sitting on the other side of the table: 'I've a friend called Samorodov, he's a bit out of the ordinary, respected everywhere and a good talker too. But I can see right through him, Auntie, and he knows it. Will you please join me in toasting Samorodov's health, Auntie dear!'

Varvara went round the table serving the guests; she was worn out, confused, and clearly pleased that there were so many different dishes and that everything had been done so lavishly – *no one* could criticize her now. The sun had set, but still the dinner went on. Now they no longer knew what they were eating or drinking and it was impossible to catch a word they said. Only now and then, when the band stopped playing for a moment, could one hear – quite distinctly – a peasant woman outside shouting, 'You've sucked us dry, you rotten bastards. You can all go to hell!'

In the evening there was dancing with music. The Khrymins Junior arrived with their own drink and during the quadrille one of them held a bottle in each hand and a glass in his mouth, which everyone found highly amusing. Halfway through the quadrille they suddenly started dancing Cossack style. Aksinya flashed round the room, a green blur, and her train set up little gusts of wind. Somebody trod on one of her frills down below and Crutchy shouted, 'Hey, you've torn her skirting-board off! Oh, *children!*'

Aksinya had grey, naïve-looking eyes that seldom blinked and a naïve smile constantly played over her face. There was something snake-like in those unblinking eyes, in that small head and long neck, in that shapely figure. As she surveyed the guests in her green dress with its yellow front, she resembled a viper peering up out of the young spring rye at someone walking past – its body erect and head raised high. The Khrymins took liberties with her and it was glaringly obvious that she had been having an affair with the eldest for a long time now. But the deaf husband didn't notice a thing and he didn't even look at her. He merely sat there with his legs crossed, eating nuts, making such a racket as he cracked them with his teeth that it sounded like pistol shots.

And now old Tsybukin himself strode into the middle of the room and waved his handkerchief – a signal that he wanted to join in the Cossack dancing. A rumble of approval ran through the whole house – and through the crowd outside in the yard as well: 'It's the *old boy himself*. He's going to *dance*!'

In fact, only Varvara did the dancing, while the old man simply fluttered his handkerchief and shuffled his heels. In spite of this, the people out in the yard hung onto one another's back to get a good view through the windows, and they were absolutely delighted: for one brief moment they forgave him everything – his wealth *and* the insults they had suffered.

'That's me boy, Grigory Petrov!' someone shouted. 'Come on, have a go! You can still do it! Ha, ha!'

The celebrations finished late – after one o'clock in the morning. Anisim staggered over to the choirboys and the band and tipped all of them a new half-rouble piece. The old man, without tottering, but still hopping on one foot, saw the guests off and told everybody, 'That wedding cost two thousand.'

As they were leaving, the publican from Shikalovo discovered that his fine new coat had been exchanged for an old one. Anisim suddenly flared up and yelled, 'Hold on! I'll find it right away! I know who took it! Just wait a moment!'

He ran out into the street and chased after someone; they caught him, hauled him back to the house by the arms – he was drunk, red with anger and soaking wet – bundled him into the room where Auntie had been helping Lipa to undress and locked him in.

IV

Five days passed. When Anisim was ready to leave, he went upstairs to say goodbye to Varvara. All the icon-lamps in her room were burning and there was a strong smell of incense. She was sitting by the window knitting a red woollen sock.

'You didn't stay very long,' she said. 'Got bored, did you? Dear, dear me . . . We live well here, we've got plenty of everything, *and* we did the right thing by you and gave you a proper wedding. The old man said it cost two thousand. So I'll come straight to the point. We live in the lap of luxury here, only I find it all a bit boring. And how badly we treat the peasants! It plain makes my heart ache, dear, to think how we treat them. My God! Whether it's horse-dealing, buying, taking on a new workman – we do nothing but cheat . . . cheat . . . cheat. That butter we sell in the shop has turned rancid and rotten – some people's tar is better! Tell me, why can't we sell decent stuff, eh?'

'It's none of my business, Mama.'

'But we're all going to die one day, aren't we? You really should have a good talk with your father! . . .'

'No, *you* should talk to him.'

'Now, enough of that . . . I'll say my piece and then he'll tell me – just like you, without beating about the bush – that it's *none of my business*. They'll show you in heaven, they will, whose business it is! God is *just.*'

'Well of course, there's no chance of *that*,' Anisim said, sighing. 'There is no God anyway, Mama. So who's going to tell me what I should do?'

Varvara looked at him in amazement, burst out laughing and clasped her hands together. Her sincere astonishment at what he had just said, together with the way she was looking at him as though he were some kind of crank, deeply embarrassed him.

'Perhaps there is a God, but I don't believe in him,' he said. 'All through the wedding service I didn't feel myself at all. Imagine you just took an egg from underneath a hen while the chick's still cheeping inside it . . . Well, my conscience suddenly started cheeping and while we were being married I kept thinking that God does exist! But as soon as I was outside the church it had all gone from my mind! Anyway, how do you expect me to know if there's a God or not? We weren't taught about him, right from the time we were very young, and a young baby can still be sucking his mother's breasts and all they teach him is mind your own business. Papa doesn't believe in God either, does he? You said once that the Guntorevs had some sheep stolen . . . *I* found out it was that peasant from Shikalovo. He stole them, but it's Papa who's got the skins! There's religion for you!' Anisim winked and shook his head.

'The chairman of the parish council doesn't believe in God, either,' he went on, 'nor does the clerk, nor the lay reader. And if they do go to church to keep the fasts it's only so that people won't go saying nasty things about them – and just *in case* there *is* a Day of Judgement, after all. Now they're all talking as if the end of the world has come, because people have got slack in their ways, don't respect their parents and so on. That's a load of rubbish. Now, the way I see it, Mama, is that all unhappiness comes from people not having a conscience. I can see right through them, Mama, *I* understand. I can see if a man's wearing a stolen shirt or not. Take someone sitting in a pub – you might think all he's doing is just drinking tea. But tea or no tea, *I* can tell if he's got a conscience. You can go around all day and not find anyone with a conscience, all because people don't know if there's a God or not . . . Well, goodbye, Mama, I wish you long life and happiness – and don't think too badly of me.'

Anisim bowed very low. 'Thanks for everything, Mama,' he added. 'You're a real help to the family, a right good woman and I'm very pleased with you.'

Anisim felt deeply moved as he left the room, but he came straight back and said, 'Samorodov's got me mixed up in some deal: it'll make or break me. If the worst should happen, Mama, please comfort my Papa.'

'What are you on about now? Dear, dear me! God is merciful. And *you*, Anisim, should show that wife of yours a little affection or you'll be turning your noses up at each other. You should both smile a bit, really!'

'But she's such a strange one . . .' Anisim said with a sigh. 'Doesn't understand anything, never says anything. But she's still very young, I must give her a chance to grow up a little.'

A tall, well-fed white stallion, harnessed to a cabriolet, was already waiting at the front door.

Old Tsybukin came running up, leapt into it with the energy of a young man and grasped the reins. Anisim exchanged kisses with Varvara, Aksinya and his brother. Lipa was standing at the front door as well, quite still, and her eyes were turned to one side, as though she had not come to see him off at all but just happened to have turned up for some mysterious reason. Anisim went over to her, barely touched her cheek with his lips and said, 'Goodbye.' She didn't look at him and she smiled very strangely. Her face was trembling and everyone felt somewhat sorry for her. Anisim also leapt in and sat there with hands on hips, so convinced he was of his good looks.

As they drove up out of the ravine, Anisim kept looking back at the village. It was a fine warm day. For the first time that year, cattle had been led out to graze and young girls and women were walking round the herd in their holiday dresses. A brown bull bellowed, rejoicing in its freedom, and pawed the earth with its front hoofs. Larks were singing everywhere – on the ground and high up above. Anisim glanced back at the graceful church, which had recently been whitewashed, and he remembered that he had prayed there five days ago. And he looked back at the school, with its green roof, at the river where he once swam or tried to catch fish, and his heart thrilled with joy. He wanted a wall suddenly to rise up out of the ground to block his path, so that he could remain there, with only the past.

They went into the station bar and drank a glass of sherry. The old man started fumbling about in his pocket for his purse.

'Drinks on me,' Anisim said.

The old man clapped him affectionately on the shoulder and winked at the barman, as though wanting to say, 'See what a son I've got!'

'Anisim, you should really stay here with us and help in the business,' he said. 'You'd be priceless! I'd load you with money, from head to foot, dear boy!'

The sherry had a sourish taste and smelt of sealing-wax, but they both drank another glass.

When the old man got back from the station, he did not recognize his younger daughter-in-law any more. The moment her husband left, Lipa changed completely and became bright and cheerful. In her bare feet, with her sleeves tucked right up to her shoulders, she washed the staircase in the hall and sang in a thin, silvery voice. And when she carried the huge tub full of dirty water outside and looked at the sun with that childish smile of hers, she was like a skylark herself.

An old workman, who was passing the front door, shook his head and wheezed, 'Oh yes, Grigory Petrov, that's a fine daughter-in-law God's blessed you with. No ordernery girl, but a real treasure!'

V

On 8 July (a Friday), 'Crutchy' Yelizarov and Lipa were coming back from their pilgrimage to the village of Kazansk, where the Festival of Our Lady of Kazan had been celebrated. Lipa's mother, Praskovya, lagged a long way behind, as she was in poor health and short of breath. It was late afternoon.

As he listened to Lipa, Crutchy kept making startled 'ooh's and 'ah's.

'I just love jam, Ilya Makarych!' Lipa said. 'I like to sit in a little corner, all on my own, and just drink tea with jam in it. Or if Varvara drinks a cup with me, she tells me things that I find really touching. They've piles of jam, four jars in all, and they say, "Eat up, Lipa, don't be shy."'

'Aah! Four jars!'

'They live very well and give you white rolls with your tea and as much beef as you want. Yes, they live well, only it's a bit scary there, Ilya Makarych, ooh, so *scary*!'

'What's scary, dear?' Crutchy asked, as he looked back to see how far behind Praskovya was.

'To begin with, as soon as the wedding was over, I got scared of Anisim Grigorych. He'd done nothing nasty to me, but I had the shivers all over, in every bone, every time he came near. At night I couldn't sleep a wink and I kept shaking all over and prayed to God. But now it's Aksinya I'm frightened of, Ilya Makarych. She's all right really, always smiling. It's only when she looks out of the window, her eyes get so angry, all green and burning – just like a sheep in its shed. Those young Khrymins are always leading her astray. "Your old man's got a bit of land at Butyokhino, more than a hundred acres," they tell her. "There's sand and water, so you could build a brickworks there, Aksinya, and we'll go halves." Bricks are nearly twenty roubles a thousand now, could be a good thing. So yesterday Aksinya goes and tells the old man, "I want to start a brickworks at Butyokhino, I'll be in charge myself." She smiled when she said this, but Grigory Petrov gave her a blank look and didn't seem at all pleased. So he says, "While I'm alive, I'm not going to start dividing everything up, we must do everything together." But she looked daggers at him and ground her teeth . . . then we had pancakes, but *she* wouldn't touch them!'

'A-ah!' Crutchy said in amazement. 'Wouldn't touch 'em!'

'And you should just see the way she sleeps!' Lipa continued. 'She'll doze off for half an hour, then all of a sudden she'll jump up and start running round to see if the peasants have started a fire or stolen anything . . . It's *terrible* being with her, Ilya Makarych! Those Khrymin sons didn't go to bed after the wedding, but went straight off to town to bring the law on each other. And they say it's all Aksinya's doing. Two of the brothers promised to build her the brickyard, which made the third one mad. As the mill was shut down then for a month, my Uncle Prokhor had no work and had to go begging for scraps round people's backyards. So I said, "Look, Uncle, until it's open again, why don't you go and do some ploughing or woodchopping, why bring shame on yourself like this!" So he said, "Lost the 'abit of farm work I 'ave, can't do nothing, Lipa dear."'

They stopped by a young aspen grove for a rest and to wait until Praskovya caught them up. Yelizarov had been a jobbing carpenter for some time but, as he didn't have a horse, he used to go round the entire district on foot and all he took with him was a little bag of bread and onions. He took long strides, swinging his arms, and it was hard to keep up with him.

A boundary post stood at the entrance to the grove and Yelizarov tested it with his hands to see if it was sound. Then along came Praskovya, gasping for breath. Her wrinkled, perpetually anxious face beamed with happiness. That same day she had gone to church, like the others, and then she went along to the fair and had a drink of pear kvass.[4] This was so unusual for her that now she even felt – for the first time in her life – she was really enjoying herself. After they had rested, all three of them started off again together. The sun was already setting and its rays pierced the leaves and shone on the tree-trunks. They could hear loud shouting ahead – the girls of Ukleyevo had been out a long time before them but had stopped there in the grove, most probably to pick mushrooms.

'Hey, me gi-irls,' Yelizarov shouted. 'Hey, me beauties!'

He was answered by laughter.

'Crutchy's coming! *Crutchy*, you silly old fogey!'

And their echoing voices sounded like laughter as well. Now the grove was behind them. They could already see the tops of factory chimneys and the glittering cross on the belfry. This was the village, the same one where 'the lay reader ate all the caviare at a funeral'.

Now they were almost home and had only to go down into that great ravine. Lipa and Praskovya, who had been walking barefoot, sat down on the grass to put their shoes on and the carpenter sat down beside them. From high up, Ukleyevo looked pretty and peaceful with its willows and white church, its little river – a view spoilt only by the factory chimneys which had been painted a nasty dark grey: they had used cheap paint to save money. On the slope on the far side they could see rye lying in stooks and sheaves, scattered all over the place as if blown around in a storm; some of the rye lay in freshly cut swathes. The oats were ready as well and shone like mother-of-pearl in the sun. It was the height of harvest-time, but that day was a rest day. The following morning, a Saturday, they would be gathering in the rye and hay, and then they would rest again on the Sunday. Every day distant thunder rumbled; it was close and humid, and rain seemed to be in the air. As they looked at the fields, the villagers only thought about one thing – God willing, they would get the harvesting done in time – and they felt cheerful, gay and anxious all at once.

'Reapers cost money these days,' Praskovya exclaimed. 'One rouble forty a day!'

Meanwhile more and more people kept pouring in from the fair at Kazansk. Peasant women, factory-hands wearing new caps, beggars, children . . . A cart would rumble past in a cloud of dust, with an unsold horse (which seemed very pleased at the fact) trotting along behind it; then came an obstinate cow, which was being dragged along by the horns; then another cart rolled past, full of drunken peasants who let their legs dangle over the sides. One old woman came past with a boy who wore a large hat and big boots; he was exhausted by the heat and the weight of the boots, which didn't let him bend his knees, but in spite of this he kept blowing his toy trumpet for all he was worth. Even after they had reached the bottom of the ravine and turned down the main street, the trumpet could still be heard.

'Those factory owners ain't themselves at all,' Yelizarov said. 'Something shocking, it is! Kostyukov got mad at me. He says, "That's a lot of wood you've used for the cornices." "How come?" I says. "Only as much as was needed, Vasily Danilych. I don't eat them planks with me porridge." "*What?*" he says. "How dare you, you blockhead, you riff-raff!" Then he starts shouting away, "Don't forget, I made a contractor out of you." "So what?" I replies. "Before I was a carpenter, I still 'ad me cup of tea every day." And he replies, "You're crooks, the whole lot of you . . ." I says nothing and thinks to meself, "Oho! I may be a crook in this world, but you'll be doing the swindling in the *next*." Next day he changes his tune: "Now don't get mad at what I said. If I went a bit too far, it's only because I belong to the merchants' guild, which means I'm your *superior* and you shouldn't answer back." So I says to him, "Okay, you're a big noise in the merchants' guild, and I'm only a carpenter. But Saint Joseph was a carpenter as well. Our work is honest and is pleasing to God. But if you think you're superior, then that's all right by me, Vasily Danilych." After this – I mean after our talk – I starts thinking to meself, "Who *is* superior, really? A big merchant or a carpenter?" Well, of course, it must be the carpenter, children!'

Crutchy pondered for a moment and went on, 'That's how things are. It's those what work and doesn't give in what's superior.'

The sun had set and a thick, milk-white mist was rising over the river, the fences and the clearings near the factories. And now with darkness swiftly advancing and lights twinkling down below, when that mist seemed to be hiding a bottomless abyss, Lipa and her mother, who were born beggars and were resigned to staying beggars for the rest of their lives, surrendering everything except their own frightened souls to others – perhaps even *they* imagined, for one fleeting moment, that they mattered in that vast mysterious universe, where countless lives were being lived out, and that they had a certain strength and were better than someone else. They felt good sitting up there, high above the village and they smiled happily, forgetting that eventually they would have to go back down again.

At last they arrived home. Reapers were sitting on the ground by the gates close to the shop. The Ukleyevo peasants usually refused to do any work for Tsybukin and farmhands had to be taken on from other villages; and now, in the darkness, it seemed that everyone sitting there had a long black beard. The shop was open and through the doorway one could see the deaf brother playing draughts with a boy. The reapers sang so softly it was hard to hear anything; when they weren't singing, they would start shouting out loud for yesterday's wages. But they were deliberately not paid, to stop them leaving before the next day. Old Tsybukin, wearing a waistcoat, without any frock-coat, was sitting drinking tea with Aksinya on the front-door steps under a birch tree. A lamp was burning on the table. 'Grandpa!' one of the reapers called out teasingly from the other side of the gates. 'Grandpa, at least pay us half!'

Immediately there was laughter and then the singing continued, still barely audible . . . Crutchy joined them for tea.

'Well, I mean to say, there we were at the fair,' he began. 'Having a great time, children, God be praised, when something nasty happened. Sashka, the blacksmith, bought some tobacco, and paid the man half a rouble.' Crutchy took a look round and continued. 'But it was a *bad* one.' He was trying to keep his voice down to a whisper, but only managed to produce a hoarse, muffled sound which everyone could hear. 'Yes, it was forged all right. So the man asked, "Where did you get it?" And Sashka says, "Anisim Tsybukin gave me it when I was enjoying meself at his wedding . . ." So they calls the policeman, who takes him away . . . You'd better watch out, Grigory Petrovich, in case anybody gets to hear . . .'

Again came that teasing voice from behind the gates: 'Gra-and-pa!' Then all was quiet.

'Ah, me dear children,' Crutchy muttered rapidly as he got up – he was feeling very drowsy – 'thanks for the tea and sugar. Time for bed. I'm all mouldering, me timbers are rotting away. Ha, ha, ha!'

As he left, he said, 'It must be time for me to die!' and he burst out sobbing.

Old Tsybukin did not finish his tea, but still sat there thinking. From his expression it seemed he was listening to Crutchy's footsteps, although he was well down the street by then.

'That blacksmith, Sashka, was lying, perhaps,' Aksinya said, reading his thoughts.

He went into the house and emerged with a small packet, and when he undid it, brand-new roubles glinted. He picked one up, bit it and threw it onto the tray. Then he threw another . . .

'No doubt about it, they're forged,' he murmured and gave Aksinya a bewildered look. 'They're the same as those Anisim gave away at the wedding.'

Then he thrust the packet into her hands and whispered, 'Take them, go on, take them and throw them down the well, blast 'em. And don't say a thing, in case there's trouble. Clear the samovar away and put the lamps out . . .'

As they sat in the shed, Lipa and Praskovya saw the lights go out, one by one. Only upstairs, in Varvara's room, were there some red and blue icon-lamps still burning and their glow imparted a feeling of peace, contentment and blissful ignorance. Praskovya just could not get used to the idea of her daughter being married to a rich man and when she came to visit them she would cower in the hall and smile pleadingly – then they would send her some tea and sugar. It was the same with Lipa, and as soon as her husband went away she did not sleep in her own bed any more, but anywhere she could – in the kitchen or the barn; every day she scrubbed the floor or did the laundry and she felt she was being used as a charwoman. Now that they were back from their pilgrimage they drank tea in the kitchen with the cook, then went into the shed and lay down between the sledge and the wall. It was dark there and smelt of horse collars. All round the house lights went out and then they could hear the deaf brother locking the shop and the reapers settling down to sleep in the open. A long way off, at the Khrymin sons' house, someone was playing that expensive accordion . . . Praskovya and Lipa began to doze off.

When someone's footsteps woke them up everything was bright in the moonlight. Aksinya stood at the entrance to the shed with bed clothes in her arms. 'It's cooler out here, I think,' she murmured. Then she came in and lay down, almost on the threshold; she was bathed in moonlight from head to foot. She could not sleep and breathed heavily, tossed and turned from the heat, and threw off most of the bedclothes. How proud and beautiful she looked in the magical moonlight. A few moments passed and those footsteps could be heard again. The white figure of the old man appeared in the doorway.

'Aksinya,' he called. 'Are you here?'

'Well!' she answered angrily.

'Yesterday I told you to throw that money down the well. Did you?'

'What do you take me for, throwing good money into the water!'

'Oh, my God!' the old man muttered in terror and amazement. 'You're a real troublemaker . . . Oh, God in heaven . . .'

He wrung his hands and went away mumbling something under his breath. A few moments later Aksinya sat up and heaved a deep sigh of annoyance. Then she got up, bundled her bedclothes together and went outside.

'Mother, why did you let me marry into *this* family!' Lipa said.

'People have to get married, my dear daughter. It's not for us to say.'

And a feeling of inconsolable grief threatened to overwhelm them. At the same time they thought that someone was looking down on them from the very heights of heaven, out of the deep blue sky where the stars were, and that he could see everything that was happening in Ukleyevo and was watching over them. However much evil existed in the world, the night was still calm and beautiful, and there was, and always would be, truth in God's universe, a truth that was just as calm and beautiful. The whole earth was only waiting to merge with that truth, just as the moonlight blended into the night.

Both of them were soothed by these thoughts and they fell asleep, snuggling up close to each other.

VI

The news of Anisim's arrest for forging and passing counterfeit money had reached the village a long time ago. Months went by – more than half of the year: the long winter was past, spring arrived and everyone in the house and village was now used to the idea that Anisim was in prison. Whenever they passed the shop or the house at night-time they would be reminded of this. And the sound of the church bells, for some reason, also reminded them that Anisim was in prison awaiting trial.

A deep shadow seemed to be overhanging the yard. The house had grown dirty, the roof was rusty and the green paint on the heavy iron-bound shop door was peeling off and had become discoloured – or, as the deaf brother put it, had gone 'all scabby'. And old Tsybukin himself seemed to have turned a dark colour. For a long time now he hadn't trimmed his beard or his hair, which gave him a shaggy look, and no longer did he leap perkily into his carriage or shout, 'God'll feed yer!' to beggars. His strength was failing and everything he did showed it. The villagers were not so scared of him any longer and the local constable sent in a report about what was going on in the shop – although he still received his share of the money. Tsybukin was summoned three times to the town to stand trial for the secret dealing in spirits; but the case was always postponed because witnesses kept failing to turn up, and all this was sheer torture for the old man.

He frequently visited his son, hired lawyers, submitted appeals, and donated banners to churches. He bought the governor of Anisim's prison a silver glass-holder enamelled with the words: 'Moderation in all things', together with a long spoon.

'There's no one to help us, no one we can turn to,' Varvara said. 'Oh, dear, dear me . . . We should ask one of those gents to write to those what's in charge . . . If only they could let him out before the trial! It's wicked tormenting a young lad like that!'

Although she was very distressed, Varvara had put on weight, her skin was whiter, and as before she lit the icon-lamps in her room and made sure everything in the house was spotless, serving guests with jam and apple flans. The deaf brother and Aksinya worked in the shop. They had started a new business – the brickyard at Butyokhino – and Aksinya travelled out there nearly every day in a springless carriage. She drove herself and if she happened to pass friends on the way she would crane her neck, like a snake in the young rye, and give them a naïve and enigmatic smile. Meanwhile Lipa spent the whole time playing with her baby, who was born before Lent. It was a little boy, a skinny, pathetic, tiny thing, and it seemed strange that he could cry and could see, that he was a human being and even had a name – Nikifor. As he lay in his cradle, Lipa would walk over to the door, curtsey and say, 'Hullo, Nikifor Anisimych.' She would dash over and kiss him, and then go back to the door, curtsey again and repeat, 'Hullo, Nikifor Anisimych!' He would kick his little red legs up in the air and his cries mingled with laughter – just like Yelizarov the carpenter.

Finally the day of the trial was fixed and the old man left five days before it was due to start. Later they heard that some peasants from the village had been hauled in as witnesses. An old workman was summoned as well and off he went.

The trial started on a Thursday, but Sunday came and still the old man had not returned, and there was no news at all. Late on the Tuesday afternoon, Varvara was sitting at the open window listening out for the old man. In the next room Lipa was playing with her baby, tossing him up in the air and catching him in her arms.

'You're going to be such a big man, oh so big!' she told him in raptures. 'You'll be a farm worker and we'll go out to work together in the fields. We'll go out to work!'

'Well, well,' Varvara said in a very offended voice. 'What kind of work do you think you're going to do, you stupid cow. *He's* going to be a merchant like us! . . .'

Lipa began to sing softly, but soon stopped and told the child again, 'You're going to grow up into such a big, big man! You'll be a farm worker, we'll go out to work together!'

'Oh, so it's all arranged then!'

Lipa stopped in the doorway with Nikifor in her arms and asked, 'Mama dear, why do I love him so much?' Then she continued in a trembling voice, and her eyes glistened with tears, 'Why do I feel so sorry for him? Who is he? *What* is he, after all? He's as light as a feather or a crumb, but I love him, just like a real human being. He's quite helpless, can't say anything, but I can always tell what he wants from his dear little eyes.'

Varvara listened hard: in the distance she could make out the sound of the evening train drawing into the station. Was the old man on it? She no longer heard or understood what Lipa was saying, nor did she notice how the minutes ticked by: all she did was shake all over – not with fear but intense curiosity. She saw a cartful of peasants quickly rumble past: these were witnesses returning from the station. As the cart went by, the old workman leapt out and came into the yard, where she could hear people welcoming and questioning him.

'All rights and property taken away,' he said in a loud voice, 'and six years' hard labour in Siberia.'

They saw Aksinya coming out of the shop by the back door. She had just been selling some paraffin and she was holding the bottle in one hand and a funnel in the other. Some silver coins stuck out of her mouth.

'Where's Papa?' she lisped.

'Still at the station,' the workman replied. 'Said 'e'll be along when it's a bit darker.'

When the news about Anisim's sentence to hard labour reached the yard, the cook started wailing in the kitchen, like someone lamenting the dead – she thought that the occasion called for it – 'Oh, Anisim Grigorych, why have you left us, our very dearest . . .'

This frightened the dogs and they started barking. Varvara ran over to the window in a fit of despair and screamed out to the cook as hard as she could, 'Sto-op it, Stepanida, sto-op it! For Christ's sake, don't torture us!'

They forgot to put the samovar on and in fact they couldn't concentrate on anything. Only Lipa had no idea what had happened and she just carried on nursing her baby.

When the old man got back from the station, they did not ask him a thing. He greeted them and then wandered from room to room without saying a word. He didn't have any supper.

'We've no one to turn to . . .' Varvara said when she was alone with the old man. 'I asked you to go and see if any of them gents could do anything, but you wouldn't listen. We should have appealed . . .'

'But I *did* try,' the old man replied, waving his arm. 'As soon as they sentenced Anisim I went up to the gent what was defending him and he said, "There's nothing I can do, it's too late." Anisim says it's too late, as well. But the moment I got out of that courtroom I made a deal with a lawyer and gave him a little something in advance . . . I'll wait and see for another week, then I'll go and have another try. It's all in the hands of God.'

The old man silently wandered around the house, and then came back and told Varvara, 'I must be sickening for something. My head's going round and round, everything's all jumbled up.'

He shut the door so that Lipa couldn't hear and continued in a soft voice, 'There's trouble with that money. You remember the first week after Easter, just before the wedding, Anisim brought me some new roubles and half roubles? I hid one of the packets but somehow or other the others got mixed up with my own money . . . Now when

Uncle Dmitry Filatych, God rest his soul, was alive, he always went to Moscow or the Crimea to buy goods. He had a wife and once when he was away she started larking around with another man. She had six children. When he'd a drop or two he used to laugh. "Just can't sort 'em out," he says, "which ones are mine and which aren't." Now, I can't make out what money's real and what's forged. Looks like it's all forged.'

'Well, for heaven's sake now!'

'I goes and buys my ticket at the station, hands over three roubles and I starts thinking they're forged. Scared the living daylights out of me. That's why I'm feeling so bad.'

'Look, we're all in the hands of God,' Varvara murmured, shaking her head. 'That's something you should be thinking of, Grigory. Who knows what may happen, you're not young any more. Once you're dead and gone, they'll do your grandson an injury. Oh, I'm so frightened they'll do something to Nikifor! You might as well say he's got no father, and his mother's so young and stupid . . . You ought to put something by for him – at least some land. Yes, what about Butyokhino? Think about it!'

Varvara kept on trying to persuade him, adding, 'He's a pretty boy, it's such a shame. Now, there's no point in waiting, just go tomorrow and sign the papers.'

'Yes, I'd forgotten about my little grandson,' Tsybukin said. 'I must go and see him. You say there's nothing wrong with him? Well then, may he grow up healthy – God willing!'

He opened the door and curled his finger, beckoning Lipa over to him. She went up to him with the baby in her arms.

'Now Lipa, dear, you only have to tell me if there's anything you need,' he said. 'You can have whatever you like to eat, we won't grudge you anything. You must keep your strength up.' He made the sign of the cross over the baby. 'And look after my grandson. I haven't got a son any more, just a grandson.' Tears streamed down his cheeks. He sobbed and left the room. Soon afterwards he went to bed and fell into a deep sleep – after seven sleepless nights.

VII

The old man made a short trip into town. Someone had told Aksinya that he had gone to see a solicitor to make his will and that Butyokhino (where she was running the brickworks) had been left to his grandson Nikifor. She learnt this one morning when the old man and Varvara were sitting by the front door, drinking tea in the shade of the birch tree. Aksinya locked the front and back doors to the shop, collected as many keys as she could find and flung them at the old man's feet.

'I'm not working for the likes of you any more,' she shouted and suddenly burst out sobbing. 'Seems I'm your charwoman, not your daughter-in-law any more! Everyone's laughing at me and says, "Just look what a fine worker the Tsybukins have found for themselves!" But you didn't take me in as a housemaid. I'm not a beggar or a common slut, I have a mother and father.'

Without wiping her tears away, she glared at the old man; her eyes were brimming over with tears, had an evil look and squinted angrily. She shouted so hard her face and neck were red and taut from the effort. 'I'm not going to slave for you *any* more, I've worn myself to the bone! I'm expected to work all day long in the shop and sneak out for vodka at night, while you go and give land away to a convict's wife and her little devil. She's the lady of the house round here and I'm her slave. So give that convict's wife the lot and may she choke! *I'm* going home. Find yourself another fool, you damned bastard!'

The old man had never used bad language or punished his children and he just could not imagine one of his own family speaking rudely to him or being disrespectful. And now he was scared out of his wits. He rushed into the house and hid behind a cupboard. Varvara was so petrified she just could not stand up and she waved her arms in the air as though shooing a bee away.

'Oh, what's going on?' she muttered in horror. 'What's she shouting like that for? Oh, dear, dear me . . . The people will hear, please, please be quiet!'

'You've given Butyokhino to a convict's bird,' Aksinya went on shouting. 'Well, you can give her the whole lot, I don't want anything from you! You can all go to hell! You're a gang of crooks, all of you. I've seen enough now and I've had just about enough! You're just like bandits, you've robbed the old and the young, anyone who comes near! *Who* sold vodka without a licence! And what about the forged coins? You've stuffed your money-boxes full of them and now you don't need me any more!'

By now a crowd had gathered outside the wide-open gates and was staring into the yard.

'Let them look!' Aksinya screamed. 'I'll disgrace the lot of you. I'll make you burn with shame! You'll come grovelling!'

She called out to her deaf husband, 'Hey, Stepan, let's go home – and *this minute*! We'll go back to my mother and father, I don't want to live with convicts. Get ready!'

Washing was hanging on the line in the yard. She tore her skirts and blouses off (they were still damp) and threw them into her deaf husband's arms. Then, in a blind fury, she rushed round all the clothes lines and tore everything down, other people's washing as well, hurled it on the ground and trampled all over it.

'Good God, stop her!' Varvara groaned. 'Who does she think she is? Let her have Butyokhino, let her have it, for Christ's sake!'

The people standing by the gates said, 'What a wo-man, what a woman! She's really blown her top. It's shocking!'

Aksinya dashed into the kitchen, where they were doing laundry. Lipa was working there on her own, and the cook had gone down to the river to rinse some clothes. Clouds of steam rose from the tub and the cauldron by the stove, and the kitchen was dark and stuffy in the thick haze. A pile of dirty clothes lay on the floor and Nikifor was lying on a bench right next to it, so that he would not hurt himself if he fell off. He was kicking his little red legs up. Just as Aksinya came in, Lipa pulled her blouse out of the pile, put it in the tub and reached out for the large ladle of boiling water on the table.

'Give that to me!' Aksinya said, looking at her hatefully. Then she pulled the blouse out of the tub. 'Don't touch my things! You're a convict's wife and it's time you knew your place and who you *really* are!'

Lipa was stunned, looked at her and did not seem to understand. But when she suddenly saw how Aksinya was looking at her and the baby, she *did* understand and she went numb all over.

'You've taken my land, so take *that*!'

And she grabbed the ladle with the boiling water and poured it over Nikifor. A scream rang out, the like of which had never been heard in Ukleyevo and it was hard to believe it came from such a frail little creature as Lipa. Suddenly all was quiet outside. Without so much as a word, Aksinya went back into the house, with that same naïve smile on her face . . . All that time the deaf husband had been walking round the yard with an armful of washing and without hurrying or saying a word he started hanging it up to dry again. And not until the cook came back from the river did anyone dare to go and see what had happened in the kitchen.

VIII

Nikifor was taken to the local hospital, where he died towards evening. Lipa did not wait for the others to come and fetch her and she wrapped the body in a blanket and started walking home.

The hospital, which had just been built, with large windows, stood high up on a hill. It was flooded in the light of the setting sun and seemed to be burning inside. At the bottom of the hill was a small village. Lipa walked on down and sat by a pond before she reached it. A woman had brought her horse there for watering, but it would not drink.

'What do you want, then?' she was asking in a soft, bewildered voice. 'What else?'

A boy in a red shirt was sitting at the water's edge washing his father's boots. Apart from them, there wasn't a soul to be seen, either in the village or on the hillside.

'Won't drink, then?' Lipa said, looking at the horse.

But at that moment the woman and the boy with the boots went away and then the place was completely deserted. The sun lay down to rest under a blanket of purple and gold brocade, and long red and lilac clouds stretching right across the sky were watching over it. From somewhere far off came the mournful, indistinct cry of a bittern, sounding just like a cow locked up in a shed. Every spring this mysterious bird's song could be heard, but no one knew what it was or where it lived. Up by the hospital, in the bushes by the pond, beyond the village and in the fields all around, nightingales poured forth their song. A cuckoo seemed to be adding up someone's age, kept losing count and starting again. In the pond, frogs croaked angrily to each other, almost bursting their lungs and one could even make out something sounding like 'That's what you are! That's what you are!' What a noise! It seemed that all these creatures were singing and crying out loud on purpose, so that no one could sleep on that spring evening, and so that everything – even the angry frogs – should treasure and savour every minute of it. After all, we only live once!

A silver crescent moon shone in the sky and there were innumerable stars. Lipa could not remember how long she had been sitting by the pond, but when she got up and went on her way everyone in the village had already gone to bed and there wasn't a light to be seen. It was probably another eight miles back to the house, but all her strength had gone and she had no idea how she was going to get back. The moon shed its light first in front of her, then to the right, and that same cuckoo (its voice had grown hoarse by now) was still crying and its teasing laughter seemed to be saying, 'Oh, look out, you'll lose your way!' Lipa hurried along and her shawl fell off and was lost. She looked at the sky and wondered where her child's soul might be at that moment: was it following her or was it floating high up in the heavens, near the stars, and had forgotten its mother? How lonely it is at night out in the open fields, with all that singing, when you cannot sing yourself, amidst all those never-ending cries of joy when you can feel no joy yourself . . . when the moon, as lonely as you are, looks down from on high, indifferent to everything, whether it is spring or winter, whether people live or die . . . when the heart is heavy with grief it is hard to be alone. If only Praskovya, her mother, or Crutchy, or the cook, or any of the peasants were with her now!

'Boo-oo!' cried the bittern, 'boo-oo!'

Then suddenly she heard a man's voice, quite distinctly.

'Get those horses harnessed, Vavila.'

Right ahead of her to one side of the road was a bonfire. The flames had died down and there remained only smouldering embers. She could hear a horse munching and then she made out two carts in the darkness, one laden with a barrel and the other, which was slightly lower, with two sacks; and she saw the shapes of two men. One of them was leading the horse to be harnessed, while the other stood motionless by the fire with his hands behind his back. A dog growled near one of the carts. The man who was leading the horse stopped and said, 'Sounds like someone's coming.' The other one shouted at the dog, 'Sharik, be quiet!'

From the voice she could tell it was an old man. Lipa stopped and said, 'God be with you!'

The old man went up to her and after some hesitation said, 'Hullo!'

'Your dog doesn't bite, does he, Grandpa?'

'Don't worry, he won't touch you.'

'I've just come from the hospital,' Lipa said after a short silence. 'My little boy's just died there, I'm taking him home.'

The old man must have found this news unpleasant, as he moved away and said hurriedly, 'Don't worry, dear, it's God's will.' Then he turned to his companion and said, 'Stop dawdling, lad. Come on, look lively!'

'Can't find the shaft,' the boy replied. 'T'ain't 'ere.'

'You're a dead loss, Vavila!'

The old man picked up a smouldering ember and blew on it; in its light she could distinguish his nose and eyes. When they at last managed to find the shaft he went over to Lipa holding the burning wood and looked at her. His face was full of compassion and tenderness.

'Well, you're a mother,' he said. 'Every mother feels sorry for her child.'

With these words he sighed and shook his head. Vavila threw something onto the fire, stamped on it and suddenly there was nothing but darkness again. Everything disappeared and once more all Lipa could see were those same fields, the starlit sky; the birds were still making a noise, keeping each other awake, and Lipa thought she could hear a corncrake crying from the very spot where the bonfire had been. But a minute later she could see the carts again, the old man and the tall figure of Vavila. The carts creaked as they moved out onto the road.

'Are you *holy* men?' Lipa asked the old man.

'No, we're from Firsanovo.'

'When you looked at me just now, it made my heart go soft all over. And that boy's so well-behaved. That's why I thought you were holy men.'

'Got far to go?'

'Ukleyevo.'

'Get in, we'll take you as far as Kuzmyonki. From there you go straight on and we turn left.'

Vavila sat in the cart with the barrel, while the old man and Lipa climbed into the other. They moved at walking-pace, with Vavila leading the way.

'My little boy suffered all day long,' Lipa said. 'He'd look at me with his little eyes and say nothing – he wanted to tell me something, but couldn't. God in heaven, Holy Virgin! I just fell on the floor with grieving. Then I'd get up and fall down by his bed. Can you tell me, Grandpa, why little children have to suffer so before dying? When a grown-up man or a woman suffers, their sins are forgiven them. But why should a little child who's never sinned suffer so? Why?'

'*Who* knows!?' the old man answered.

They drove on in silence, for half an hour.

'We can't always know the whys and wherefores,' the old man said. 'A bird's got two wings, not four, just because two's enough to fly with. In the same way, man isn't meant to know everything, only half or a quarter. He just knows enough to get him through life.'

'Grandpa, I'd feel better walking now. My heart's pounding.'

'Don't be sad, just sit where you are.'

The old man yawned, then made the sign of the cross before his mouth.

'Don't be sad . . .' he repeated, 'your troubles aren't so terrible. It's a long life, and you'll go through good and bad, all kinds of things.'

He looked around him, then back, and went on, 'Mother Russia is so great! I've travelled all over it and I've seen everything, mark my words, dear. There's good to come, and bad. I've gone as a foot-messenger to Siberia, I've been on the Amur,[5] in the Altay.[6] I settled in Siberia, ploughed me own land. Then I pined for Mother Russia and came back to the village where I was born. Came back on foot, we did. I remember, I was on a ferry once,[7] not an ounce of flesh on me, all in rags, no shoes on me feet, frozen stiff, sucking away at a crust, when a gent what was crossing on the same ferry – if he's passed on, then God rest his soul – looks at me with pity in his eyes, and the tears just flowed. Then he says, "Your beard is black – and your life'll be the same too . . ." When I got back I didn't 'ave 'ouse nor 'ome, as the saying goes. I did 'ave a wife but she stayed behind in Siberia and she's buried there. So I goes and works as a farmhand. And what next? I'll tell you what – there was good and there was bad times. And now I don't want to die, me dear, I'd like to hang on for another twenty years. That means I must 'ave 'ad more good times than bad! Oh, Mother Russia is so big!' Once again he looked around as he said this.

'Grandpa,' Lipa asked, 'when someone dies, how long does the soul wander over the earth?'

'Well, who can say! Let's ask Vavila, he's been to school. Teach 'em everything these days.' The old man shouted, 'Vavila!'

'What?'

'Vavila, when someone dies, how long does the soul wander over the earth?'

Vavila made the horse stop first and then replied, 'Nine days. When my uncle Kirilla died, his soul lived on in our hut for thirteen days.'

'But how do you know?'

'There was a knocking in the stove for thirteen days.'

'All right. Let's be on our way now,' the old man said, clearly not believing one word of it.

Near Kuzmyonki the carts turned off onto the main road, while Lipa went straight on. Already it was getting light. As she went down into the ravine, the huts and church at Ukleyevo were hidden by mist. It was cold and she thought she could hear the same cuckoo calling.

Lipa was home before the cattle had been taken out to graze. Everyone was still sleeping. She sat on the front steps and waited. The first to come out was the old man. One look told him everything and for quite a while he couldn't say one word but just made a smacking noise with his lips.

'Oh, Lipa,' he said, 'you didn't look after my grandson . . .'

They woke Varvara up. She wrung her hands, burst out sobbing and immediately started laying the baby out.

'And he was the loveliest little boy . . .' she muttered again and again. 'Oh, dear, dear me . . . Her one and only child and still she couldn't look after it, the stupid girl!'

Prayers were said in the morning and evening. Next day the child was buried, and after the funeral the guests and clergy ate a great deal and with such enormous appetites it seemed they hadn't eaten for a long, long time. Lipa served them food at the table and the priest held up his fork with a pickled mushroom on the end of it and told her, 'Don't grieve for your child, for *theirs is the kingdom of heaven.*'

Only when everyone had left did Lipa fully realize that Nikifor was gone, would never come back and she began to sob. She didn't know which room to go into to have a good cry, since she felt that after her child's death there was no longer any place for her in that house, that she was no longer needed, that no one wanted her; and the others felt the same as well.

'Well, now, what's all this wailing for?' Aksinya suddenly shouted, as she appeared in the doorway. For the funeral she had specially put on a new dress and she had powdered her face. 'Shut up!'

Lipa wanted to stop but she just couldn't and sobbed even louder.

'Did you hear!' Aksinya screamed and stamped her feet furiously. '*Who* d'ye think you are, then? Clear off, and don't ever set foot in this house again, you convict's bird! Clear off!'

'Now now . . . come on . . .' the old man said fussily, 'calm down, Aksinya, dear, *please* . . . It's very understandable she's crying . . . she's lost her baby . . .'

'*Understandable* . . .' Aksinya said, mimicking him. 'She can stay the night then, but I want her *out* by the morning.' Again she mimicked him and said, '*Understandable!*', laughed and went off to the shop.

Early next morning Lipa went home to her mother at Torguyevo.

IX

These days the roof and the door of the shop are painted freshly and shine like new. Cheerful-looking geraniums are blossoming in their window-boxes as they used to do, and what happened three years ago at the Tsybukins' is almost forgotten.

Old Grigory Petrov is still looked upon as the master, but in fact Aksinya is in charge of everything. She does the buying and selling, and nothing is done without her permission. The brickyard is prospering – since bricks are needed for the railway, the price has risen to twenty-four roubles a thousand. Women and girls cart the bricks to the station, load the wagons and get twenty-five copecks for it.

Aksinya has gone into partnership with the Khrymins and the factory now bears the name: KHRYMIN SONS & CO. They have opened a pub near the station and it's there, not at the factory, that the expensive accordion is played now. Among the regulars are the postmaster, who has also started a business of his own, and the stationmaster. The Khrymin sons gave the deaf husband a gold watch, and he takes it out of his pocket every now and then and holds it to his ear.

There is talk in the village that Aksinya is very powerful now. And one can see this when she drives to the factory in the mornings, looking pretty and happy (she still has that same naïve smile), and starts giving orders. Whether at home, in the village or in the factory, everyone is afraid of her. When she drops in at the post office, the postmaster leaps to his feet and says, 'Please, do take a seat, Kseniya Abramovna!'

Once, when a rather elderly landowner, who was a bit of a dandy and wore a fine silk coat and high lacquered boots, was selling her a horse, he was so carried away that he sold her the horse at whatever price she wanted. He held her hand for a long time as he gazed into her gay, cunning, naïve eyes and told her, 'I would do *anything* to please a woman like you, Kseniya Abramovna. Just tell me when we can meet again, without anyone disturbing us.'

'Whenever you like!'

Since then the elderly dandy has been driving to the shop almost every day for some beer, which is plain revolting and has the bitter taste of wormwood. But the landowner just shakes his head and drinks it up.

Old Tsybukin doesn't have anything to do with the business now. He doesn't handle money any more, as he just can't distinguish counterfeit coins from good ones, but he never says a word to anyone about this failing of his. He's become rather forgetful and if no one gives him food, then he doesn't ask for any – indeed, all the others are used to eating without him and Varvara often says, 'My old man went to bed yesterday again without a bite to eat.'

And she says this from force of habit, as though she could not care less.

For some odd reason, the old man wears a heavy coat whether it's winter or summer and he stays indoors only when it's very hot. Well wrapped up in his fur coat, with the collar up, he strolls round the village, along the road to the station, or else he'll sit on a bench by the church gates all day long. He'll just stay there without budging. People greet him as they walk past, but he ignores them, as he dislikes peasants as much as ever. If they ask him a question he'll give them an intelligent, polite but curt reply. There's talk in the village that his daughter-in-law has thrown him out of his own house and refuses him food, so that he has to rely on charity. Some of the villagers are glad, others feel sorry for him.

Varvara is even fatter now and she looks paler too. She still does her good deeds and Aksinya keeps out of her way. There's so much jam that they can't get through it all before the next crop of berries is ready. It crystallizes and Varvara is almost reduced to tears, not knowing what to do with it. And they have almost forgotten all about Anisim. A letter did come from him once, written in verse, on a large sheet of paper – just like an official appeal and in that same lovely handwriting. Clearly, his friend Samorodov was doing time in the same prison. Beneath the verses there was one line, in ugly writing that was almost impossible to decipher: 'I'm always ill in this place, it's terrible, please help me, for the love of Christ.'

One fine autumn day, in the late afternoon, old Tsybukin was sitting near the church gates, his collar turned up so high that only his nose and the peak of his cap were visible. At the other end of the long bench Yelizarov, the carpenter, was sitting next to Yakov, the school caretaker, a toothless old man of seventy, and they were having a chat.

'Children should see that old people have enough to eat – *honour thy father and thy mother*,' Yakov was saying with great annoyance. 'But as for *her*, that daughter-in-law, she threw her father-in-law out of 'is own 'ouse. The old man has nothing to eat or drink – and where can 'e go? 'Asn't eaten nothing for three days.'

'Three days!' Crutchy exclaimed.

'Yes, all 'e does is just sit and say nothing. He's very weak now. Why should we keep quiet about it? She should be sent for trial – they wouldn't let her off so lightly in court!'

'*Who* did they let off lightly in court?' Crutchy asked, not catching what the other had said.

'What?'

'His old girl's all right, a real worker. In their kind of business you can't get far without hard work . . . not without a bit of fiddling, I mean . . .'

'Thrown out of his own 'ouse,' Yakov said as irritably as before. 'You earns money to buy your own 'ouse, then you have to clear out. She's a right one, eh? A real pest!'

Tsybukin listened and didn't move an inch.

'What does it matter if it's your own house or someone else's, as long as it's warm and the women don't start squabbling?' Crutchy said and burst out laughing. 'When I was a young lad, I 'ad a real soft spot for my Nastasya. Quiet little woman she was. She kept on telling me, "Ilya Makarych, buy a house, buy a house! Buy a house!" When she was dying, she still kept saying, "Ilya Makarych, buy a nice fast droshky, so's we won't have to walk." But all I ever bought her was gingerbread, nothing else.'

'That deaf husband of 'ers is an idiot,' Yakov went on, as though he hadn't been listening. 'A real clot, like a goose. Expect *him* to understand anything? You can bash a goose on the 'ead with a stick but it won't understand.'

Crutchy got up to make his way back to the factory. So did Yakov, and they both set off together, still chatting away. When they had gone about fifty paces, old Tsybukin stood up and shuffled off after them, stepping very gingerly, as though walking on slippery ice.

The village had already sunk deep into the dusk and the sun was shining now only on the highest stretch of the road, which twisted down the slope like a snake. Old women and their children were returning from the forest and they carried baskets full of coral milkcap and agaric mushrooms. Women and young girls crowded back from the station where they had been loading bricks onto wagons and their noses and cheeks – just below the eyes – were caked with the red dust. They sang as they came. Lipa walked on in front of everybody and her thin voice broke into overflowing song as she looked up at the sky, and it was as if she were celebrating some victory and rejoicing that the day, thank God, was at an end, and that now she could rest. Her mother, Praskovya, was in the crowd, carrying her little bundle in her hand and – as always – gasping for breath.

'Good evening, Ilya Makarych!' Lipa said when she saw Crutchy. 'Hullo, my poppet!'

'Good evening, darling Lipa,' Crutchy joyfully replied. 'My dear women and girlies, be nice to the rich carpenter! Oho, my dear little children, my children,' (he started sobbing), 'my darlings!'

The women could hear Crutchy and Yakov talking as they walked away. Immediately they had disappeared, old Tsybukin came towards the crowd and everything went quiet. Lipa and Praskovya were lagging a little way behind the others and when the old man caught them up Lipa made a deep curtsey and said, 'Good evening, Grigory Petrov!'

And the mother curtseyed as well. The old man stopped and looked at them without saying a word. His lips were trembling and his eyes full of tears. Lipa took a piece of buckwheat pie out of her mother's bundle and handed it to him. He took it and started eating.

Now the sun had completely set and its light was gone even from the high stretch of road. It became dark and cool. Lipa and Praskovya continued on their way and kept crossing themselves for a long time afterwards.

Disturbing the Balance

I

Evening service was in progress at the house of Mikhail Ilich Bonda-rev, a man of some distinction in the county. Officiating was a young priest, plump and fair-haired, with long curls and a broad nose – rather like a lion. The only singers were the sacristan and parish clerk.

Mikhail Ilich, a very sick man, was sitting motionless in his armchair, pale-faced and with eyes closed, just like a corpse. His wife, Vera Andreyevna, stood by him, her head leaning to one side in the lazy, modest pose of someone indifferent to religion but obliged to stand and make the occasional sign of the cross. Aleksandr Andreich Yanshin, Vera Andreyevna's brother, and his wife Len-ochka, stood behind the armchair, close by. It was Whit Sunday Eve. The trees in the garden softly rustled and a magnificent sunset flamed exuberantly, flooding half the sky.

Whether they could hear the ringing of the city and monastery bells through the open windows, or the peacock crying in the courtyard, or someone coughing in the hall, none of them could help thinking that Mikhail Ilich was seriously ill, that the doctors had ordered him to be taken abroad as soon as he felt a little better. But he felt better one day and worse the next – this they were at a loss to understand – but as time passed the uncertainty began to try everyone's nerves. At Easter Yanshin had come to help his sister take her husband abroad, but he and his wife had already spent two whole months here and this was about the third service that was being held for him – but still the future was as hazy as before, and it was all a big mystery. Besides, there was no guarantee that this nightmare would not drag on until autumn.

Yanshin was feeling disgruntled and bored. He was sick and tired of getting ready every day to go abroad and he wanted to go back home, to his own place at Novosyolki. True, it wasn't very cheerful at home, but at least there wasn't this vast drawing-room with the four columns in the corners, none of these white armchairs with gold upholstery, no yellow door curtains, no chandeliers, none of this parade of bad taste with pretensions to grandeur, no echoes that repeated your every step at night. But above all there was no sickly, sallow, puffy face with closed eyes . . . At home one could laugh, talk nonsense, have a heated argument with one's wife or mother – in brief, you could live as you pleased. But here it was just like boarding-school: you had to tiptoe around and talk only in whispers, say only clever things. Or you had to stand there and listen to an evening service that was held not from any religious feeling, but, as Mikhail Ilich himself said, because 'tradition dictated it'. And there's nothing more wearisome or degrading than a situation where you have to kowtow to a person you consider – in your heart of hearts – a nobody, and to fuss over an invalid for whom you don't feel sorry.

And Yanshin was thinking about something else: last night his wife Lenochka had announced that she was pregnant. This piece of news was of interest for the sole reason that it made the problem of the journey abroad even more vexed. What should he do now? Take Lenochka with him – or send her to his mother at Novosyolki? But it would not be wise for her to travel in her condition. However, she wouldn't go home for anything, since she didn't get on with her mother-in-law and she would never agree to live in the country on her own, without her husband.

'Or should I make this an excuse to go home with her?' Yanshin thought, trying not to listen to the sacristan. 'No, it would be awkward leaving Vera here on her own,' he decided, looking at his sister's shapely figure. 'What shall I do?'

As he pondered and asked himself this question, his life struck him as an extremely complicated muddle. All these problems – the journey, his sister, his wife, his brother-in-law – each one of them taken separately might possibly be resolved very easily and conveniently, but they were terribly jumbled up and it was like being stuck in a swamp from which there was no climbing out. Only one of them had to be solved for the others to become even more of a tangle.

When the priest turned and said 'Peace be with you' before reading from the Gospels, the sick Mikhail Ilich suddenly opened his eyes and started fidgeting in his armchair.

'Sasha!' he called.

Yanshin quickly went to him and leant down.

'I don't like the way he's taking the service,' Mikhail Ilich said in an undertone, but loud enough for his words to clearly carry through the room. His breathing was heavy, accompanied by whistling and wheezing. 'I'm leaving! Help me out of here, Sasha.'

Yanshin helped him up and took his arm.

'You stay here, dear,' Mikhail Ilich feebly begged his wife, who wanted to support him from the other side. 'Stay here!' he repeated irritably, looking at her indifferent face. 'I'll manage without you.'

The priest stood with his Gospels open, waiting. In the ensuing silence the harmonious singing of a male voice choir could be clearly heard: they were singing somewhere beyond the garden, by the river, no doubt. And it was so delightful when the bells in the neighbouring monastery suddenly pealed and their soft, melodious chimes blended with the singing. Yanshin's heart seemed to miss a beat in sweet anticipation of something fine and he almost forgot that he was supposed to be helping an invalid. The sounds from outside that floated into the room somehow reminded him how little freedom and enjoyment there was in his present life and how trivial, insignificant and boring were the tasks with which he so furiously grappled every day, from dawn to dusk. When he had led the sick man out, while the servants made way and looked on with that morbid curiosity with which village people usually survey corpses, he suddenly felt hatred, a deep, intense hatred for the invalid's puffy, clean-shaven face, for his waxen hands, for his plush dressing-gown, for his heavy breathing, for the tapping of his black cane. This feeling, which he was experiencing for the first time in his life and which had taken possession of him so suddenly, made his head and legs go cold and his heart pound. He passionately wanted Mikhail Ilich to drop dead that very minute, to utter a last cry and slump onto the floor, but in a flash he pictured that death for himself and recoiled in horror. When they left the room no longer did he want the sick man to die, but craved life for himself. If only he could tear his hand from that warm armpit and run away, to run and run without looking back.

A bed had been made up for Mikhail Ilich on an ottoman in the study, as the sick man felt hot and uncomfortable in his bedroom.

'He can't make up his mind whether he's a priest or an officer in the hussars!' he said, settling himself heavily on the ottoman. 'How pretentious! God, I'd demote that fop in priest's vestments to grave-digger if I had my way!'

As he looked at his wilful, unhappy face Yanshin felt like answering him back, saying something impertinent, admitting his hatred for him, but he remembered the doctors' orders that the patient wasn't to be upset, so he held his peace. However, the problem wasn't to do with doctors. He would have really told him a thing or two if his sister's fate hadn't been so permanently, so hopelessly bound up with that hateful man.

Mikhail Ilich was in the habit of constantly sticking out his tightly pressed lips and moving them from side to side, as if he were sucking a boiled sweet. And this pouting of fleshy lips set in a clean-shaven face irritated Yanshin now.

'You ought to go back now,' Mikhail Ilich said. 'You're indifferent towards the church, it seems. You couldn't care less who officiates . . . Go now . . .'

'But aren't you indifferent towards the church too?' Yanshin softly murmured, trying to control himself.

'No, I believe in Providence and I recognize the church.'

'Precisely. It strikes me that you don't need God or truth in religion, but words like "Providence" and "from on high".'

Yanshin felt like adding: 'Otherwise you wouldn't have offended that priest the way you did this evening', but he said nothing. He had already allowed himself to say more than enough.

'Please go!' Mikhail Ilich said impatiently – he disliked it when anyone didn't agree with him or talked personally about him. 'I don't want to cramp anyone's style . . . I know how difficult it is to sit with an invalid . . . I know, my friend! As I've always said and will keep on repeating: there's no harder or saintlier work than a nurse's. Now, do me a favour and go.'

Yanshin left the study. After going downstairs to his room he put on his hat and coat and went out into the garden through the front door. It was already past eight o'clock. Upstairs they were singing the Consecration. Making his way between flowerbeds, rose bushes, the initials V and M (that is, Vera and Mikhail) formed from blue heliotrope, and past a profusion of magnificent flowers which gave no one on the estate any pleasure, but simply grew and blossomed – most probably because it was as 'tradition dictated' – Yanshin hurried, afraid that his wife might call him from upstairs. But now, cutting through a park, he came out onto a long, dark avenue of firs, through which one could see the sun set in the evenings. Here the ancient, decrepit firs always produced a light, forbidding rustle, even in calm weather; there was the smell of resin and one's feet slipped over the dry needles.

As Yanshin walked on he thought that he would never shake off that hatred which had so unexpectedly taken hold of him during the service that day and it was something that could not be ignored. It introduced into his life a further complication and promised little that was good. But peace and a sense of grace wafted from these firs, from that calm, distant sky and that exuberant sunset. With pleasure he listened to his own footsteps that gave out a solitary, hollow ring in the dark avenue and no longer did he wonder what to do.

Almost every evening he would go to the station to fetch news-papers and letters – while living with his brother-in-law this was his only diversion. The mail train arrived at a quarter to ten, just when the unbearable boredom of evening had set in at home. There was no one to play cards with, no supper was served, he didn't feel like sleeping and therefore, whether he liked it or not, he was forced either to sit with the invalid or read out loud to Lenochka novels in translation, of which she was very fond. It was a large station, with buffet and bookstall. One could have a bite to eat, drink beer, look at some books. Most of all Yanshin liked meeting the train and envying the passengers who were travelling somewhere and were apparently happier than he was. When he arrived at the station people whom he had grown used to seeing there every evening were already strolling along the platform, waiting for the train. They were the owners of summer cottages who lived near the station, two or three officers from the town, a certain landowner with a spur on his right foot and with a mastiff that followed him, its head sadly bowed. The cottage owners, male and female, who evidently knew each other very well, were noisily chatting and laughing. As always, an engineer cottage owner – a very corpulent gentleman of about forty-five, with whiskers and a broad pelvis, with a cotton shirt over his belt, and wide velveteen trousers – was liveliest of all and laughed louder than anyone else. When he walked past Yanshin, his large belly sticking out, stroking his whiskers as he amiably glanced at him with his oily eyes, Yanshin thought that here was a man with a very healthy appetite. The engineer even wore a distinctive expression which one could only interpret as saying: 'Aha! How very tasty!' He had an absurd triple-barrelled surname and the only reason Yanshin remembered it was because the engineer, who was very partial to ranting about politics and engaging in quarrels, would often swear and say:

'If I weren't Bitny-Kushle-Suvryomovich!'

He was said to be a very convivial fellow, a generous host and a fanatical whist player. Yanshin had long wanted to make his acquaintance, but he never ventured to go up and talk to him, although he guessed that he was not averse to making friends with him . . . As he wandered on his own down the platform and listened to the holiday-makers, for some reason Yanshin remembered that he was thirty-one now and that, from the age of twenty-four, when he graduated, not one day of his life had ever given him the slightest pleasure: either there was a lawsuit with the neighbours over boundaries, or his wife miscarried, or his sister appeared unhappy. And now Mikhail Ilich was ill and had to be taken abroad. He imagined that all this would continue and be endlessly repeated, in one way or another, and that at forty or fifty he would be plagued with precisely the same worries and preoccupations as at thirty-one. In brief, he wouldn't escape from that hard shell until his dying day. In order to view things differently he needed to be able to deceive himself. And he wanted to stop being an oyster – at least for one hour. He wanted to look into someone else's world, to be involved in things that did not concern him personally, to talk to people who were strangers to him – if only to that fat engineer, or to the female holiday-makers in the twilight who all looked so pretty, gay and, above all, young.

The train arrived. The landowner with the single spur met a fat, elderly lady who embraced him and repeated several times in an emotional voice: 'Alexis!' It was probably his mother. With great ceremony, like a *jeune premier* in ballet, jingling his spur, he offered her his hand, telling the porter in a cloying, velvety baritone: 'Please be so good as to take our luggage!'

Soon the train left. The holiday-makers collected their papers and letters and went home. It became quiet. Yanshin strolled a little further down the platform and then entered the first-class waiting-room. He didn't feel hungry, but he ate a piece of veal all the same and drank some beer. Those ceremonious, affected manners of the landowner with the spur, his sickly sweet baritone and that politeness which was so artificial produced a morbid impression that was very hard to shake off. He recalled his long whiskers, his kind and quite intelligent face which was somehow strange and inscrutable, his habit of rubbing his hands as if it were cold, and he concluded that if that plump, elderly lady were in fact that man's mother, then she was probably most unhappy. Her excited voice said but one word – Alexis – but her timid, distracted face and loving eyes said all there was left to be said . . .

I I

Vera Andreyevna had looked out of the window and seen her brother leave. She knew that he was going to the station and visualized the whole avenue of firs from start to finish, then the slope down to the river, the broad vista, and the feeling of peace and simplicity that the river and water meadows always evoked – and beyond them the station and the birch forest where the summer cottage owners lived, and far away to the right that small provincial town and the monastery with its golden onion domes. Then again she visualized that avenue, the darkness, her fear and shame, those familiar footsteps and everything that might be repeated, even that same day perhaps. And she left the room for a moment to see to the priest's tea. When she was in the dining-room she took from her pocket a letter folded in two, in a stiff envelope, bearing a foreign stamp. This letter had been handed to her five minutes before the service and she had already managed to read it twice.

'My dearest, my darling, my torment, my anguish,' she read, holding the envelope in both hands and letting them both be intoxicated at the touch of those dear, ardent lines. 'My dearest,' she began again right from the beginning:

my dearest, my darling, my torment, my anguish, you write convincingly, but I still don't know what to do. At the time you said that you would *definitely* go to Italy and like a madman I dashed on ahead to meet you here and to love my darling, my joy . . . Here, I thought, you wouldn't be afraid of your husband or brother seeing my shadow from the window on moonlit nights. Here you and I could stroll along the streets and you wouldn't be afraid of Rome or Venice finding out that we love one another. Forgive me, my treasure, but there are two Veras: one is timid, faint-hearted, indecisive; and there's an indifferent Vera, who's cold and proud, who addresses me formally in front of strangers and pretends she hardly notices me. I want this other Vera – the proud and beautiful one – to love me . . . I don't want to be an eagle that can enjoy itself only in the evening and at night. Give me some light! The dark oppresses me, my precious, and this fitful, clandestine love of ours keeps me half-starving . . . I'm irritated . . . I'm suffering, I'm going out of my mind . . . Well, to cut it short, I thought that *my* Vera – not the first but the second, here abroad, where it's easier to escape from prying eyes than at home – would grant me at least one hour of total, unstinting, true love, without the need for caution, so that I might at least once be entitled to feel that I'm a lover and not a smuggler. And so that when you embrace me you don't say: 'It's time I left!' These were my thoughts, but then a whole month went by since I was living in Florence, you weren't there, and there was no news of you. You write: 'This month we'll hardly get out of this mess.'

What *is* this? My despair, what are you doing to me? Please understand that I can't go on without you. I can't! I *can't*! They say that Italy is beautiful, but I'm bored. It's as if I'm an exile and my powerful love grows weary, as if it were in exile. You'll say this joke isn't funny, but then, I do have a clownish sense of humour. I rush first to Bologna, then to Venice, then to Rome and the whole time I keep trying to see if there's a woman in the crowd like you. Out of sheer boredom I've visited all the art galleries and museums – five times each – and all I see is you in the paintings. In Rome I clamber breathlessly up Monte Pincio[1] and from there I survey the Eternal City. But eternity, beauty, the sky – all these things blend with your face and dress into a single image. Here, in Florence, I visit all the shops where they sell sculptures and when there's no one there I embrace the statues and I feel as though I'm embracing *you*. I need you this very minute, this very minute . . . Vera, I'm behaving like a madman, but please forgive me, I cannot cope any more, I'm coming to see you tomorrow . . . This letter isn't really necessary, but what of it! So, my precious, it's all decided. I'm coming tomorrow.

The Bishop

It was the eve of Palm Sunday and night service had begun at the old convent of St Peter. By the time they had started giving out the willow branches, it was nearly ten, lights had burnt low, wicks needed snuffing and everything was obscured by a thick haze. The congregation rocked like the sea in the gloomy church and all those faces, old and young, male and female, looked exactly alike to Bishop Pyotr, who had not been feeling well for the past three days; to him they all appeared to have exactly the same look in their eyes as they came forward for palms. The doors couldn't be seen through the haze and the congregation kept moving forward in a seemingly never-ending procession. A woman's choir was singing and a nun was reading the lessons.

How hot and stuffy it was – and the service was so long! Bishop Pyotr felt tired. He was breathing heavily and panting, his throat was dry, his shoulders ached from weariness and his legs were shaking. Now and then he was unpleasantly disturbed by some 'God's fool' shrieking up in the gallery. Then, all of a sudden, just as though he were dreaming or delirious, the bishop thought that he could see his mother, Marya Timofeyevna (whom he had not seen for nine years) – or an old woman who looked like her – make her way towards him in the congregation, take her branch and gaze at him with a cheerful, kindly, joyful smile as she walked away and was lost in the crowd. For some reason tears trickled down his cheeks. He felt calm enough and all was well, but he stood there quite still, staring at the choir on his left, where the lessons were being read, unable to make out a single face in the dusk – and he wept. Tears glistened on his face and beard. Then someone else, close by, burst out crying, then another a little further away, then another and another, until the entire church was gradually filled with a gentle weeping. But about five minutes later the nuns were singing, the weeping had stopped and everything was normal again.

Soon the service was over. As the bishop climbed into his carriage, homeward bound, the whole moonlit garden was overflowing with the joyful, harmonious ringing of heavy bells. White walls, white crosses on graves, white birches, dark shadows, the moon high above the convent – everything seemed to be living a life of its own, beyond the understanding of man, but close to him nonetheless. It was early April, and after that mild day it had turned chilly, with a slight frost, and there was a breath of spring in that soft, cold air. The road from the convent to the town was sandy and they had to travel at walking pace. In the bright, tranquil moonlight churchgoers were trudging through the sand, on both sides of the carriage. They were all silent and deep in thought; and everything around was so welcoming, young, so near at hand – the trees, the sky, even the moon – that one wished it would always be like this.

The carriage finally reached the town and rumbled down the main street. The shops were already closed, except Yerakin's (a merchant millionaire), where electric lighting was being tested, violently flashing on and off while a crowd of people looked on. Dark, wide, deserted streets followed, then the high road (built by the council) on the far side of town, then the open fields, where the fragrance of pines filled the air. Suddenly a white, crenellated wall loomed up before the bishop, with a lofty belfry beyond, flooded by the moonlight, and with five, large gleaming golden 'onion' cupolas next to it – this was Pankratiyev Monastery, where Bishop Pyotr lived. And here again, far above, was that same tranquil, pensive moon. The carriage drove through the gates, crunching over the sand, and here and there he caught fleeting glimpses of dark figures of monks in the moonlight; footsteps echoed on flagstones.

'Your mother called while you were out, your grace,' the lay brother announced as the bishop went into his room.

'My mother? When did she come?'

'Before evening service. First she asked where you were, then she drove off to the convent.'

'So I *did* see her in the church then – goodness gracious!' The bishop laughed joyfully.

'She asked me to inform your grace that she'll be coming tomorrow,' the lay brother went on. 'There's a little girl with her, her granddaughter, I suppose. They're staying at Ovsyannikov's inn.'

'What's the time now?'

'Just past eleven.'

'Oh, that's a shame.'

The bishop sat meditating in his drawing-room for a little while, hardly believing that it was so late. His arms and legs were aching all over, and he had a pain in the back of his neck; he felt hot and uncomfortable. After he had rested, he went to his bedroom and sat down again, still thinking about his mother. He could hear the lay brother going out and Father Sisoy coughing in the next room. The monastery clock struck the quarter. The bishop changed into his nightclothes and began to say his prayers. As he carefully read those old, long-familiar words he thought of his mother. She had nine children and about forty grandchildren. Once she had lived with her husband, a deacon, in a poor village. This was for a long, long time, from her seventeenth to her sixtieth year. The bishop remembered her from his early childhood, almost from the age of three, and how he had loved her! Dear, precious, unforgettable childhood! It had gone for ever and was irrevocable. Why does this time always seem brighter, gayer, richer than it is in reality? How tender and caring his mother had been when he was ill as a child and a young man! And now prayers mingled with his memories, which flared up even brighter now, like flames – and these prayers did not disturb his thoughts about his mother.

When he had finished his prayers, he undressed and lay down. The moment darkness closed in all around him he had visions of his late father, his mother, his native village of Lesopolye . . . Creaking wheels, bleating sheep, church bells ringing out on bright summer mornings, gipsies at the window – how delightful it was thinking about these things! He recalled the priest at Lesopolye – that gentle, humble, good-hearted Father Simeon who was very short and thin, but who had a terribly tall son (a theological student) with a furious-sounding bass voice. Once his son had lost his temper with the cook and called her 'Ass of Jehudiel', which made Father Simeon go very quiet, for he was only too ashamed of not being able to remember where this particular ass was mentioned in the Bible. He was succeeded at Lesopolye by Father Demyan, who drank until he saw green serpents and even earned the nickname Demyan Snake-eye. Matvey Nikolaich, the village schoolmaster, a former theological student, had been a kind, intelligent man, but a heavy drinker as well. He never beat his pupils, but for some reason always had a bundle of birch twigs hanging on the wall with the motto in dog Latin underneath: *Betula kinderbalsamica secuta*.[1] He had a shaggy black dog called Syntax.

The bishop laughed. About five miles from Lesopolye was the village of Obnino with its miracle-working icon, carried in procession round the neighbouring villages every summer, when bells would ring out all day long – first in one village, then in another. On these occasions the bishop (who was called 'Pavlusha') thought that the very air was quivering with joy and he would follow the icon bare-headed, barefoot, smiling innocently, immeasurably happy in his simple faith. Now he remembered that the congregations at Obnino were always quite large, and that the priest there, Father Aleksey, had managed to shorten the services by making his deaf nephew Ilarion read out the little notices and inscriptions pinned to the communion bread – prayers 'for the health of' and 'for the departed soul of'. Ilarion read these out, occasionally getting five or ten copecks for his trouble, and only when he had gone grey and bald, when life had passed him by, did he suddenly notice a piece of paper with 'Ilarion is a fool' written on it. Pavlusha had been a backward child, at least until he was fifteen years old, and he was such a poor pupil at the church school that they even considered sending him to work in a shop. Once when he was collecting the mail from Obnino post office, he had stared at the clerks there for a long time, after which he asked, 'May I inquire how you're paid, monthly or daily?'

The bishop crossed himself and turned over in an effort to stop thinking about such things and go to sleep.

'Mother's here,' he remembered – and he laughed.

The moon peered in at the window, casting its light on the floor, where shadows lay.

A cricket chirped. In the next room Father Sisoy was snoring away, and there was a solitary note in his senile snoring, making one think of an orphan or a homeless wanderer. At one time Sisoy had been a diocesan bishop's servant and he was called 'Father ex-housekeeper'. He was seventy, and now lived in a monastery about ten miles from the town. But he stayed in town whenever he had to. Three days before, he had gone to the Pankratiyev Monastery, and the bishop had taken him into his own rooms, so that they could have a leisurely chat about church affairs and local business.

At half past one the bell rang for matins. The bishop could hear Father Sisoy coughing and mumbling ill-humouredly, after which he got up and started pacing up and down in his bare feet.

The bishop called out, 'Father Sisoy!', upon which Sisoy went back to his room, reappearing a little later in his boots, with a candle in his hand. Over his underclothes he was wearing a cassock and an old, faded skullcap.

'I can't get to sleep,' the bishop said as he sat down. 'I must be ill, I just don't know what's wrong! It's so hot!'

'Your grace must have caught a cold. You need a rubdown with candle grease.'

Sisoy stood there for a few minutes and said to himself with a yawn, 'Lord forgive me, miserable sinner that I am.'

Then he said out loud, 'Those Yerakins have got electric lights now, I don't like it!'

Father Sisoy was old, skinny and hunchbacked and he was always complaining. His eyes were angry and bulging, like a crab's.

'Don't like it,' he repeated as he went out, 'don't want nothing to do with it!'

II

Next day, Palm Sunday, the bishop celebrated Mass in the cathedral, after which he visited the diocesan bishop, called on a very old general's wife, who was extremely ill, and finally went home. After one o'clock he had some rather special guests to lunch – his aged mother and his eight-year-old niece, Katya.

Throughout the meal the spring sun shone through the windows overlooking the yard, glinting cheerfully on the white tablecloth and in Katya's red hair. Through the double windows they could hear the rooks cawing in the garden and the starlings singing.

'It's nine years since we last saw each other,' the old lady was saying. 'But when I saw you yesterday in the convent – heavens, I thought, you haven't changed one bit, only you're thinner now and you've let your beard grow. Blessed Virgin! Everyone cried at the service, they just couldn't help it. When I looked at you I cried too, quite suddenly, just don't know why. It's God's will!'

Although she said this with affection, she was clearly quite embarrassed, wondering whether she should address him formally or as a close relative, whether she could laugh or not. And she seemed to think she was more a deacon's widow than a bishop's mother. All this time Katya looked at her right reverend uncle without blinking an eyelid, apparently trying to guess what kind of man he was. Her hair welled up like a halo from her comb and velvet ribbon; she had a snub nose and cunning eyes. Before lunch she had broken a glass and her grandmother kept moving tumblers and wine glasses out of her reach during the conversation. As he listened to his mother, the bishop recalled the time, many, many years ago, when she took him and his brothers and sisters to see some relatives, who were supposed to be rich. Then she had her hands full with the children. Now she had grandchildren, and here she was with Katya.

'Your sister Barbara has four children,' she told him. 'Katya's the eldest. Father Ivan – your brother-in-law – was taken ill, God knows with what, and he passed away three days before Assumption. Now my poor Barbara has to go round begging.'

The bishop inquired about Nikanor, his eldest brother.

'He's all right, thank God. He doesn't have much, but he makes ends meet, thank God. But there's just one thing: his son Nikolasha, my little grandson, didn't want to go into the church and he's at university, studying to be a doctor. He thinks that's better, but who knows? It's the will of God.'

'Nikolasha cuts up dead people,' Katya said, spilling water over her lap.

'Sit still, child,' her grandmother said calmly, taking a tumbler out of her hands. 'You must pray before you eat.'

'It's been such a long time since we met,' the bishop observed, tenderly stroking his mother's arm and shoulder. 'When I was abroad I missed you, Mother, I really missed you!'

'That's very kind of you!'

'I used to sit during the evenings by an open window, all on my own, when suddenly I'd hear a band playing and then I'd long for Russia. I felt I would have given *anything* just to go home, to see you . . .'

His mother beamed all over but immediately pulled a serious face and repeated, 'That's very kind of you!'

Then he had a sharp change of mood. As he looked at his mother, he was puzzled by this obsequious, timid expression and tone of voice. What was the reason? – it wasn't at all like her.

He felt sad and irritated. And now he had the same headache as yesterday, and a killing pain in the legs. Moreover, the fish was unappetizing, had no flavour at all and it made him continually thirsty.

After lunch two rich landowning ladies arrived and they sat for over an hour and a half without saying a word, making long faces. The Father Superior, a taciturn man, who was rather hard of hearing, came on some business. Then the bells rang for evensong, the sun sank behind the forest and the day was over. As soon as he came back from the church, the bishop hurriedly said his prayers, went to bed and tucked himself up more warmly than usual.

The thought of the fish at lunch lingered very unpleasantly in his mind. First the moonlight disturbed him, then he could hear people talking. Father Sisoy was most likely talking politics in the next room, or the drawing-room, perhaps.

'The Japanese are at war now and fighting. Like the Montenegrins they are, ma'am, the same tribe, both were under the Turkish yoke.'

Then the bishop's mother was heard to say, 'Well then, after we said our prayers, hum – and had a cup of tea, we went to see Father Yegor at Novokhatnoye, hum . . .'

From those continual 'had a cup of tea's or 'drank a drop's, one would have thought that all she ever did in her life was drink tea. Slowly and phlegmatically the bishop recalled the theological college and academy. For three years he had taught Greek in the college, and then he could no longer read without spectacles; afterwards he became a monk and then inspector of schools. Then he took his doctorate. At the age of thirty-two he was appointed rector of the college and made Father Superior. Life was so pleasant and easy then, that it seemed it would continue like that for ever. But then he was taken ill, lost a lot of weight and nearly went blind. As a result he was obliged, on his doctors' advice, to drop everything and go abroad.

'And then what?' Sisoy asked in the next room.

'Then we had tea,' the bishop's mother replied.

'Father, you've got a green beard!' Katya suddenly exclaimed with a surprised laugh. The bishop laughed too, remembering that grey-haired Father Sisoy's beard actually did have a greenish tinge.

'Heavens, that girl's a real terror,' Sisoy said in a loud, angry voice. 'Such a spoilt child! Sit still!'

The bishop recalled the newly built white church, where he had officiated when he was abroad. And he remembered the roar of that warm sea. He had a five-room flat there with high ceilings, a new desk in the study and a library. He had read and written a lot. He remembered feeling homesick for his native Russia and how that blind beggar woman who sang of love and played the guitar every day under his window had always reminded him of the past. But eight years had gone by, and he was recalled to Russia. By now he was a suffragan bishop, and his entire past seemed to have disappeared into the misty beyond, as though it had all been a dream. Father Sisoy came into the bedroom carrying a candle.

'Oho, asleep already, your grace?'

'What's the matter?'

'Well, it's still quite early, ten o'clock – even earlier perhaps. I've brought a candle so I can give you a good greasing.'

'I've a temperature,' the bishop said and sat up. 'But I really must take something, my head's terrible . . .'

Sisoy took the bishop's shirt off and started rubbing his chest and back with candle grease.

'Yes, that's it, there, that's it. Oh Christ in heaven! There . . . I went into town today and called on Father – what's his name? – Sidonsky and I had tea with him. Don't care for him much. Lord save us! No, I don't care for him . . .'

III

The diocesan bishop, old, very stout, and afflicted with rheumatism or gout, had been bedridden for over a month. Bishop Pyotr called on him almost every day and himself saw to the villagers who came for his advice and help. But now *he* was ill he was struck by the futility and triviality of their tearful petitions. Their ignorance and timidity infuriated him and the sheer weight of all those petty, trifling matters they came to see him about depressed him. He felt that he understood the diocesan bishop, who, in his younger days, had written *Studies in Free Will*, but who seemed now to be completely obsessed by these trifles, having forgotten everything else, never giving any thought to God. While he was abroad, the bishop must have lost touch completely with Russia and things were not easy for him now. The peasants seemed so coarse, the ladies who came for help so boring and stupid, the theological students and their teachers so ignorant and sometimes so uncivilized, like savages. And all those incoming and outgoing documents – they could be counted by the thousand – what documents! The senior clergy, all over the diocese, were in the habit of awarding good-conduct marks to junior priests, young or old, even to wives and children, and all this had to be discussed, scrutinized and solemnly recorded in official reports. There was never any let-up, not even for a minute, and Bishop Pyotr found this played on his nerves the whole day long: only when he was in church could he relax.

He found it quite impossible to harden himself against the fear he aroused in people (through no desire of his own) despite his gentle, modest nature. Everyone in the province struck him as small, terrified and guilty when he looked at them. Everyone – even the senior clergy – quailed when he was around, all of them threw themselves at his feet. Not so long before, an old country priest's wife, who had come begging some favour, was struck dumb with fear and left without saying one word, her mission unaccomplished. As the bishop could never bring himself to say a bad word about anyone in his sermons, and felt too much compassion to criticize, he found himself flying into tempers, getting mad with his petitioners and throwing their applications on the floor. Never had anyone spoken openly and naturally to him, as man to man, during the whole time he was there. Even his old mother seemed to have been transformed – now she was *quite* a different person! And he asked himself how she could chatter away to Sisoy and laugh so much, while with *him*, her own son, she was so withdrawn and embarrassed – which wasn't like her at all. The only one to feel free and easy and who would speak his mind in his presence was old Sisoy, who had spent his whole life attending bishops and who had outlived eleven of them. This was why the bishop felt at ease with him, although he was, without question, a difficult, cantankerous old man.

After Tuesday morning service the bishop received parish petitioners at the episcopal palace, which upset and angered him no end: afterwards he went home. Once again he felt ill and longed for his bed. But hardly had he reached his room than he was told that a young merchant called Yerakin, a most charitable man, had come on a most urgent matter. He just could not turn him away. Yerakin stayed for about an hour, and spoke so loud he nearly shouted, making it almost impossible to understand a word he said.

'God grant – well, you know,' he said as he left. 'Oh, most

certainly! Depending on the circumstances, your grace. I wish you — well, you know!'

Then the Mother Superior from a distant convent arrived. But by the time she had left, the bells were ringing for evensong and he had to go to church.

That evening the monks' singing was harmonious and inspired; a young, black-bearded priest was officiating. When he heard the 'bridegroom who cometh at midnight'[2] and 'the mansion richly adorned', he felt neither penitent nor sorrowful, but a spiritual peace and calm as his thoughts wandered off into the distant past, to his childhood and youth, when they had sung of that same bridegroom and mansion. Now that past seemed alive, beautiful, joyful, such as it most probably had never been. Perhaps, in the next world, in the life to come, we will remember that distant past and our life on earth below with just the same feelings. Who knows? The bishop took his seat in the dark chancel, and the tears flowed. He reflected that he had attained everything a man of his position could hope for, and his faith was still strong. All the same, there were things he did not understand, something was lacking. He did not want to die. And still it seemed that an integral part of his life, which he had vaguely dreamed of at some time, had vanished; and precisely the same hopes for the future which he had nurtured in his childhood, at the college and abroad, still haunted him.

'Just listen to them sing today!' he thought, listening intently. 'How wonderful!'

IV

On Maundy Thursday he celebrated Mass and ritual washing of feet in the cathedral. When the service was over and the congregation had gone home, the weather turned out sunny, warm and cheerful, and water bubbled along the ditches, while the never-ending, sweetly soothing song of the skylarks drifted in from the fields beyond the town. The trees, already in bud, smiled their welcome, while the fathomless, vast expanse of blue sky overhead floated away into the mysterious beyond.

When he arrived home the bishop had his tea, changed, climbed into bed and ordered the lay brother to close the shutters. It was dark in the bedroom. How tired he felt, though, how his legs and back ached with that cold numbing pain – and what a ringing in his ears! He felt that it was ages since he last got some sleep, absolutely ages, and every time he closed his eyes there seemed to be some little trifling thought that flickered into life in his brain and kept him awake. And, just like yesterday, he could hear voices and the clink of glasses and teaspoons through the walls of the adjoining rooms. His mother, Marya, was cheerfully telling Father Sisoy some funny story while the priest kept commenting in a crusty, disgruntled voice, 'Damn them! Not on your life! What for!' Once more the bishop felt annoyed, then offended, when he saw that old lady behaving so naturally and normally with strangers, while with him, her own son, she was so timid and inarticulate, always saying the wrong thing and even trying to find an excuse to stand up, as she was too shy to sit down. And what about his father? Had he been alive, he would probably have been unable to say one word with his son there.

In the next room something fell on the floor and broke. Katya must have dropped a cup or saucer, because Father Sisoy suddenly spat and said angrily, 'That girl's a real terror, Lord forgive me, miserable sinner! She won't be satisfied until she's broken everything!'

Then it grew quiet except for some sounds from outside. When the bishop opened his eyes, Katya was in his room, standing quite still and looking at him. As usual, her red hair rose up above her comb like a halo.

'Is that you, Katya?' he asked. 'Who keeps opening and shutting that door downstairs?'

'I can't hear anything,' she replied, listening hard.

'Listen – someone's just gone through.'

'That was your stomach rumbling, Uncle!'

He laughed and stroked her head.

'So Cousin Nikolasha cuts dead bodies up, does he?' he asked after a short silence.

'Yes, he's studying to be a doctor.'

'Is he nice?'

'Yes, he's all right, but he's a real devil with the vodka!'

'What did your father die of?'

'Papa was always weak and terribly thin, then suddenly he had a bad throat. I became ill as well, and my brother Fedya too – all of us had bad throats. Papa died, but we got better, Uncle.'

Her chin trembled and tears welled up in her eyes and trickled down her cheeks. 'Your grace,' she said in a thin little voice, weeping bitterly now, 'Mama and I were left with nothing . . . please give us a little money, please Uncle, dear!'

He burst out crying too and for a while was so upset he couldn't say a word. Then he stroked her hair, touched her shoulder and said, 'Never mind, little girl, it's all right. Soon it will be Easter Sunday and we'll have a little talk then . . . Of course I'll help you . . .'

Then his mother came in, quietly and timidly, and turned and prayed to the icon. Seeing that he was awake she asked, 'Would you like a little soup?'

'No thanks, I'm not hungry.'

'Looking at you now, I can see you're not well. And I'm not surprised. On your feet all day long. Good God, it really hurts me to see you like this. Well, Easter's not far away and you can have a rest then, God willing. But I won't bother you any more with my nonsense. Come on, Katya, let the bishop sleep.'

He could recall her talking to some rural dean in that mock-respectful way a long, long time ago, when he was still a small boy. Only from her unusually loving eyes and the anxious, nervous look she darted at him as she left the room could one tell that she was actually his mother. He closed his eyes and appeared to have fallen asleep, but twice he heard the clock striking, then Father Sisoy coughing in the next room. His mother came into the room again and watched him anxiously for a minute. He heard some coach or carriage drive up to the front steps. Suddenly there was a knock and the door banged: in came the lay brother, shouting, 'Your grace.'

'What's the matter?'

'The carriage is ready, it's time for evening service.'

'What's the time?'

'Quarter past seven.'

He got dressed and went to the cathedral. Throughout the entire twelve lessons from the Gospels he had to stand motionless in the centre; he read the first, the longest and most beautiful, himself. A lighthearted mood came over him. He knew that first lesson ('Now is the Son of Man glorified')[3] by heart. Now and again he raised his eyes as he read and he saw a sea of lights on both sides of him, heard the candles sputtering. But he could not make any faces out as he used to do in years gone by, and he felt that this was the very same congregation he had seen when he was a boy and a young man, and he felt that it would be the same year after year – for how long God alone knew. His father had been a deacon, his grandfather a priest, and his great-grandfather a deacon. In all likelihood his entire family, from the time of the coming of Christianity to Russia,[4] had belonged to the clergy and his love of ritual, of the priesthood, of ringing bells was deep, innate and ineradicable. He always felt active, cheerful and happy when he was in church, especially when he was officiating, and this was how he felt now. Only after the eighth lesson had been read did he feel that his voice was weakening, he could not even hear himself cough and he had a splitting headache; he began to fear he might fall down any moment. In actual fact his legs had gone quite numb, there was no longer any feeling in them. He just could not make out how he was managing to keep on his feet at all and didn't fall over.

It was a quarter to twelve when the service finished. The moment he arrived home, the bishop undressed and went to bed without even saying his prayers. He was unable to speak and thought his legs were about to give way. As he pulled the blanket over him he had a sudden urge, an intolerable longing to go abroad. He felt that he could even sacrifice his life, so long as he didn't have to look at those miserable cheap shutters any more, those low ceilings, and he yearned to escape from that nasty monastery smell.

For a long time he heard someone's footsteps in the next room, but he just could not recollect whose they could be.

Finally the door opened and in came Sisoy with candle and tea cup.

'In bed already, your grace?' he asked. 'I've come to give you a good rubdown with vodka and vinegar. It'll do you the world of good if it's well rubbed in. Lord above! There, that's it . . . I've just been to the monastery. Don't like it there! I'm leaving tomorrow, master, I've had enough. Oh, Jesus Christ!'

Sisoy was incapable of staying very long in one place and he felt as though he had already spent a whole year at the Pankratiyev Monastery. But the hardest thing was making any sense out of what he said, discovering where his home really was, whether he loved anyone or anything, whether he believed in God. He did not really know himself why he had become a monk – he never gave the matter any thought – and he had long forgotten the time when he had taken his vows. It was as if he had come into this world as a monk.

'Tomorrow I'm off, damn it all!'

'I'd like to have a talk with you, but I never seem to get round to it,' the bishop said softly and with great effort. 'But I don't know anyone or anything here.'

'I'll stay until Sunday if you like, but after that I'm off, damn it!'

'Why am I a bishop?' the bishop continued in his soft voice. 'I should have been a village priest, a lay reader or an ordinary monk. All of this crushes the life out of me . . .'

'What? Heavens above! Now . . . there! You can have a good sleep now, your grace. Whatever next! Good night!'

The bishop did not sleep the whole night. At about eight o'clock in the morning he had rectal bleeding. The lay brother panicked and rushed off, first to the Father Superior, then he went to the monastery doctor, Ivan Andreyevich, who lived in town. This doctor, a plump old man with a long grey beard, gave the bishop a thorough examination, kept shaking his head and frowning, after which he said, 'Did you know it's typhoid, your grace?'

Within an hour of the haemorrhage, the bishop had turned thin, pale, and he had a pinched look. His face became wrinkled, his eyes dilated and he seemed suddenly to have aged and shrunk. He felt thinner and weaker and more insignificant than anyone else, and it seemed the entire past had vanished somewhere far, far away and would never be repeated or continued.

'How wonderful!' he thought. 'How wonderful!'

His old mother arrived. She was frightened when she saw his wrinkled face and dilated eyes, and she fell on her knees by the bed and started kissing his face, shoulders and hands. And somehow she too thought that he had become thinner, weaker and more insignificant than anyone else; she forgot that he was a bishop and kissed him like a much-loved child.

'Darling Pavlusha,' she said. 'My own flesh and blood . . . my little son . . . What's happened to you? Pavlusha, answer me.'

Katya stood there, pale and solemn, unable to understand what had happened to her uncle and why her grandmother had such a pained expression, why she spoke so sadly and emotionally. But the bishop just could not articulate a simple word, understood nothing that was going on and he felt that he was just an ordinary, simple man walking swiftly and cheerfully across fields, beating his stick on the ground, under a broad, brilliant sky. Now he was as free as a bird and could go wherever he liked!

'Pavlusha, my angel, my son!' the old lady said. 'What's the matter, dear, *please* answer!'

'Leave him alone,' Sisoy said angrily as he crossed the room. 'Let him sleep, there's nothing you can do . . . nothing . . .'

Three doctors arrived, consulted together and left. That day seemed never-ending, unbelievably long, and then came a seemingly endless night. Just before dawn on the Saturday, the lay brother went up to the old lady, who was lying on a couch in the drawing-room, and asked her to come to the bedroom as the bishop had just departed this world.

Next day was Easter Sunday. There were forty-two churches in the town and six monasteries and the sonorous, joyful, incessant pealing of bells lay over it, from morn till night, rippling the spring air. Birds sang and the sun shone brightly. The big market square was noisy, swings rocked back and forwards, barrel organs played, an accordion squealed and drunken shouts rang out.

In the afternoon there was pony-trotting down the main street. In brief, it was all so cheerful, gay and happy, just as it had been the year before and as it probably would be in the years to come.

A month later a new suffragan bishop was appointed. No one remembered Bishop Pyotr any more and soon they forgot all about him. Only the old lady (the late bishop's mother) who was now living with her brother-in-law, a deacon in an obscure provincial town, talked about her son to the women she met when she went out in the evening to fetch her cow from pasture; then she would tell them about her children, her grandchildren, about her son who had been a bishop. And she spoke hesitantly, afraid they would not believe her. Nor did they all believe her, as it happened.

The Bride

I

It was ten o'clock in the evening and a full moon was shining over the garden. At the Shumins' the service held at Grandmother's request had just finished. Nadya had gone out into the garden for a moment and now she could see them laying the table for supper, with Grandmother fussing about in her splendid silk dress. Father Andrey, a cathedral dean, was chatting to Nina Ivanovna, Nadya's mother. In the window, in the evening light, her mother looked somehow very young. Father Andrey's son (also called Andrey) was standing nearby listening attentively.

The garden was quiet and cool, and deep, restful shadows lay on the earth. Somewhere, far, far away, probably on the other side of town, she could hear frogs croaking. May, beautiful May, was all around! She could breathe deeply and she liked to imagine that somewhere else, beneath the sky, above the trees, far beyond the town, in the fields and forests, spring was unfolding its own secret life, so lovely, rich and sacred, beyond the understanding of weak, sinful man. And she felt rather like crying.

Nadya was twenty-three now. Since the age of sixteen she had longed passionately for marriage and now, at last, she was engaged to that Andrey Andreich whom she could see through the window. She liked him, the wedding was fixed for 7 July, and yet she felt no joy, slept badly and was miserable. Through an open window she could hear people rushing about, knives clattering, a door banging on its block and pulley in the basement where the kitchen was. There was a smell of roast turkey and pickled cherries. She felt that life would go on for ever like this, never changing.

Just then someone came out of the house and stopped on the steps. It was Aleksandr Timofeich, or Sasha for short: he was one of the guests who had arrived from Moscow about ten days before. Once, a long time ago, a distant relative of Grandmother's by the name of Marya Petrovna – an impoverished, widowed gentlewoman, small, thin and in poor health – used to call on her and be given money. Sasha was her son. People said for some mysterious reason that he was a fine artist, and when his mother died Grandmother sent him off to the Komissarov School in Moscow, for the good of her soul. About two years later he transferred to the Fine Arts Institute, where he stayed almost fifteen years, just managing in the end to qualify in architecture. But he did not practise architecture and worked for a firm of lithographers in Moscow instead. Seriously ill most of the time, he would come and stay at Grandmother's nearly every summer to rest and recuperate.

He was wearing a buttoned-up frock-coat and shabby canvas trousers that were ragged at the bottoms. His shirt had not been ironed and on the whole he looked somewhat grubby. Although very thin, with large eyes, long gaunt fingers, a beard and swarthy complexion, he was still a handsome man. He was like one of the family with the Shumins and felt quite at home with them. The room in which he stayed had been known as Sasha's for years.

As he stood in the porch he caught sight of Nadya and went up to her.

'Nice here, isn't it?' he remarked.

'Why, of course. You ought to stay until the autumn.'

'Yes, I might have to. Yes, I may well stay until September.'

For no reason he laughed and sat down next to her.

'Here I am sitting watching Mother,' Nadya said. 'She looks so young from here!' After a brief silence she added, 'Mother does have her weak points. Despite that, she's a remarkable woman.'

'Yes, she's a good woman,' Sasha agreed. 'In her own way your mother's very kind and charming of course, but . . . how can I put it? . . . early this morning I popped into the kitchen and four of the servants were asleep on the bare floor. They don't have beds; instead of bedding all they have is rags, stench, bugs, cockroaches. It's all exactly the same as twenty years ago – nothing's changed. Well, don't blame your grandmother, it's not her fault. But your mother speaks French, doesn't she? She takes part in amateur dramatics. You would have thought that *she* would understand.'

When Sasha spoke he would point two long, emaciated fingers towards the person he was talking to.

'When you're not used to it here it all seems a bit primitive,' he went on. 'No one does a damned thing! Your mother spends the whole day running around enjoying herself like some duchess. Your grandmother doesn't do anything either, nor do you. The same goes for your fiancé Andrey.'

Nadya had heard all this last year and the year before that, she thought. She knew that Sasha just could not think in any other way. This was amusing once; now it rather irritated her.

'That's all old hat, so boring,' she said, getting up. 'You might try and think of something new.'

He laughed as he too got up and both of them walked towards the house. Tall, pretty, with a good figure, she looked so healthy, so attractive next to him. She sensed this and felt sorry for him and somewhat embarrassed. 'You're always going too far!' she said. 'Just now you said something about my Andrey, for example. But you don't know him, do you?'

' "*My*" Andrey! Blow *your* Andrey! It's your *youth* I feel sorry for.'

As they entered the large dining-room, everyone was already sitting down to supper. Grandmother, known as 'Grannie' by everyone in that house, was a very stout, ugly woman with bushy eyebrows and whiskers. She spoke loudly and it was plain from her voice and manner who was head of the house. She owned rows of stalls in the market, and this old house with its columns and garden, but every morning she asked God to spare her from bankruptcy, crying as she prayed. And then there was her daughter-in-law Nina Ivanovna (Nadya's mother), a fair-haired, tightly corseted woman with pince-nez, and diamonds on every finger. There was Father Andrey, a skinny toothless old man, who always seemed about to tell some very funny story. And there was his son Andrey Andreich, Nadya's fiancé: he was stout, handsome, with curly hair, and he looked like an actor or an artist. All three of them were discussing hypnotism.

'One week here with me and you'll be better,' Grannie told Sasha. 'But you must eat more – what do you look like!' she sighed. 'Really awful, a true Prodigal Son.'

'He wasted his substance with riotous living,'[1] Father Andrey observed slowly, with laughter in his eyes. 'He filled his belly with the husks that the swine did eat.'

'I do love that dear old father of mine,' Andrey said, touching his father's shoulder. 'He's wonderful – so kind.'

No one said a word. Sasha suddenly burst out laughing and pressed a serviette to his mouth.

'So you believe in hypnotism?' Father Andrey asked Nina Ivanovna.

'I wouldn't venture to assert, of course, that I believe in it,' Nina Ivanovna replied, assuming a deadly serious, almost grim expression. 'But I must admit that nature is full of mysterious, incomprehensible things.'

'I agree entirely, only I would add that religion significantly reduces the domain of the Mysterious.'

A large, extremely plump turkey was served. Father Andrey and Nina Ivanovna carried on talking. The diamonds sparkled on Iavnovna's fingers, then tears sparkled in her eyes. She was excited.

'I daren't even argue with you,' she said. 'Still, you must agree that life has so many insoluble puzzles.'

'Not one, may I assure you.'

After supper Andrey Andreich played the violin and Nina Ivanovna accompanied him on the piano. Ten years ago he had taken a degree in modern languages, but he had never worked anywhere and had no fixed occupation apart from occasionally participating in charity concerts. In town he was called 'The Musician'.

They all listened in silence as Andrey Andreich played. The samovar quietly bubbled on the table – only Sasha drank tea. Then, when twelve o'clock struck, a violin string suddenly snapped. Everyone burst out laughing, rushed around and began to say farewell.

After she had seen her fiancé out, Nadya went upstairs, where she and her mother lived (Grandmother occupied the lower floor). Downstairs, in the dining-room, they had started putting the lights out, but Sasha still sat there drinking his tea. He always took a long time over it, Moscow style, and would drink seven glasses at one sitting. For a long while after she had undressed and gone to bed, Nadya could hear the servants clearing away downstairs and Grannie getting cross. Finally, everything was quiet, except for the occasional sound of Sasha's deep cough from his room downstairs.

II

It must have been about two in the morning when Nadya woke up. Dawn was breaking. Somewhere in the distance a nightwatchman was banging away. She did not feel sleepy. The bed was uncomfortable – much too soft. As she used to do on May nights in the past she sat up in bed to take stock. Her thoughts were just the same as last night's – monotonous, barren, obsessive thoughts about Andrey Andreich courting her and proposing, about her accepting him and then gradually coming to appreciate the true worth of that kind, clever man. But now, with the wedding less than a month away, she began to feel scared for some reason, uneasy, as if something vaguely unpleasant lay in store for her.

Once again she heard the watchman lazily beating his stick.

Through the large old window she could see the garden and then, a little further away, the richly blossoming lilac bushes, sleepy and lifeless in the cold. A dense white mist was drifting towards the lilac, wanting to envelop it. Drowsy crows cawed in far-off trees.

'God, why am I so miserable?'

Perhaps every bride felt like this before her wedding – who knows? Or was it Sasha's influence? But hadn't he been saying the same old thing for years now, as if reciting from a book? He sounded so naïve, so peculiar. Then why couldn't she get Sasha out of her head? Why?

The watchman had long stopped banging. Birds began to chirp beneath the window, and in the garden the mist disappeared and everything around was illumined in the smiling spring sunlight. Soon the whole garden, warmed and caressed by the sun, came to life, and dewdrops glittered on leaves like diamonds. That morning the old, long-neglected garden seemed so young, so decked out.

Grannie was already awake. Sasha was producing his deep rough cough. She could hear them downstairs putting on the samovar and moving the chairs.

The hours passed slowly. Nadya had been up and taken her garden stroll long ago, but still the morning dragged on.

Then Nina Ivanovna came out with a glass of mineral water, her eyes full of tears. She practised spiritualism and homoeopathy, read a great deal and liked talking about the doubts that were plaguing her – all this (so she thought) had some profound, mysterious meaning. Nadya kissed her mother and walked along with her.

'What were you crying about, Mother?' she asked.

'Last night I started reading a story about an old man and his daughter. The old man was working somewhere and his boss fell in love with his daughter. I didn't finish it, but there was one part you couldn't help crying over.' Nina Ivanovna took a sip from her glass. 'I remembered it this morning and started crying again.'

'I've been feeling so miserable recently,' Nadya said. 'Why can't I sleep at night?'

'I don't know, my dearest. Whenever I can't sleep I close my eyes ever so tight – like this – and imagine Anna Karenina walking and talking. Or I think of something from history, from the ancient world.' Nadya felt that her mother did not and could not understand her – this she felt for the first time in her life, and it really frightened her. She wanted to hide, so she went up to her room.

They had lunch at two. As it was a Wednesday – a fast day – Grandmother was served borsch and then bream with buckwheat.

To tease Grandmother, Sasha ate both the borsch and some meat broth of his own concoction. All through lunch he joked, but his clumsy, moralizing witticisms misfired. When he lifted those long, emaciated, corpse-like fingers before launching some joke and you could see how very ill he was – not long for this world perhaps – the effect was far from funny, and you felt so sorry you could have cried.

After lunch Grandmother went to her room to lie down. Nina Ivanovna played the piano for a short while and then she too left.

'Oh, my dear Nadya,' Sasha said, embarking on his customary after-lunch speech. 'If you would only, if you would only . . . listen to me . . .'

She was deep in an antique armchair, eyes closed, while he slowly paced the room.

'If you would only go away and study!' he said. 'The only interesting people are the educated and idealistic, they're the ones we need. The more there are of these people, the quicker God's kingdom will come on earth – agreed? Very gradually, not one stone of your town will be left on another, everything will be turned upside down, everything will change as if by magic. And then there will be magnificent, huge houses, wonderful gardens, splendid fountains, remarkable people. But that's not the most important part of it. The main thing is, the mob, as we know it, as it exists now – that evil will be no more, since every man will have something to believe in, everyone will know what the purpose of his life is and no one will seek support from the masses. My dear, darling girl, get away from here! Show everyone that you're sick of this vegetating, dull, shameful existence! At least show *yourself*!'

'I can't, Sasha. I'm getting married.'

'That's a fat lot of good! You can't mean it!'

They went out into the garden and walked a little.

'You can say what you like, my dear,' Sasha continued, 'but you must try and realize how squalid and immoral this idle existence of yours is. You must see that! If you, your mother and that Grannie of yours, for example, never do a stroke of work, it means others are doing the work for you, you're ruining the lives of people you've never even met. Isn't that squalid, dishonourable?'

Nadya felt like saying, 'Yes, that's the truth.' She wanted to tell him that she understood, but her eyes filled with tears, and she suddenly grew quiet, hunched her shoulders and went to her room.

Andrey Andreich arrived in the late afternoon and gave his usual lengthy performance on the violin. On the whole he was rather taciturn and perhaps he liked playing the violin because then he didn't have to talk. After ten o'clock, when he was preparing to leave and had already put on his coat, he embraced Nadya, hungrily kissing her face, shoulders and hands. 'My dear beautiful darling!' he muttered. 'Oh, how happy I am! I'm going mad with ecstasy!'

Nadya thought that she had heard all this long, long ago – or that she had read it somewhere, in an old, dog-eared, long-abandoned novel.

Sasha was sitting at the dining-room table drinking tea with the saucer balanced on his five long fingers. Grannie was playing patience, Nina Ivanovna was reading. The icon-lamp sputtered and everything seemed serene and happy. Nadya said goodnight and went up to her room, got into bed and fell asleep immediately. However, as on the previous night, she awoke at the first glimmer of dawn. She wasn't sleepy and felt uneasy and depressed. Her head on her knees, she sat thinking about her fiancé, about the wedding. For some reason she recalled that her mother hadn't loved her husband (he had died), that now she had nothing, being completely dependent on Grannie, Nina's mother-in-law. However hard she thought about it Nadya just could not understand why, up to now, she had looked on her mother as someone special, unusual. Why hadn't she realized that she was just a very simple, ordinary, unhappy sort of woman?

Downstairs, Sasha couldn't sleep either. She could hear him coughing. He was a strange, naïve person, thought Nadya, and there was something absurd in those dreams of his, in all those marvellous gardens and extraordinary fountains. But somehow, in that very naïvety – even in his absurdity – there was so much that was fine that the mere thought of going away to study was enough to send a cold shiver through her heart and breast, and flood her whole being with joy and rapture.

'But it's best not to think about it,' she whispered. 'I mustn't think about it.'

Far off she could hear the nightwatchman's knocking.

III

In the middle of June, Sasha suddenly felt bored and prepared to leave for Moscow.

'I just can't live in this town,' he said gloomily. 'There's no running water, no drains. And I'm a bit squeamish about eating meals here – that kitchen's positively filthy!'

'Now, wait a minute, Prodigal Son,' Grandmother urged, whispering for some reason. 'The wedding's on the seventh!'

'I don't want to stay any longer.'

'But I thought you'd be here until September!'

'Well, I don't want to stay now. I have work to do.'

Summer had turned out cold and damp, the trees were soaking wet and the whole garden looked miserable and uninviting: it really did make you feel like working. In the upstairs and downstairs rooms unfamiliar women's voices rang out. The sewing-machine in Grandmother's room rattled away – they were hurrying to get the trousseau finished. There were no fewer than six fur coats and the cheapest was costing three hundred roubles, according to Grandmother. All this fuss irritated Sasha, who stayed in his room getting very cross. All the same they persuaded him to stay on and he gave his word not to leave before 1 July.

Time flew. On St Peter's Day,[2] after lunch, Andrey Andreich went to Moscow Street with Nadya to have another look at the house that had been rented and prepared for the young couple a long time before. There were two floors, but so far only the upper one had been decorated. There was a glittering floor painted to look like parquet in the lounge, bentwood chairs, a grand piano and a violin-stand. The room smelt of paint. A large oil painting of a naked lady with a broken-handled, violet-coloured vase by her side hung in its gilt frame on the wall.

'Marvellous!' Andrey Andreich said with a respectful sigh. 'It's a Shishmachevsky.'[3]

After that came a sitting-room, with a round table, sofa and armchairs upholstered in a bright blue material. A large photograph of Father Andrey, in priest's hat and wearing decorations, hung over the sofa. Then they entered the dining-room, with its sideboard, and then the bedroom. Here in the half-light, two beds stood side by side, giving the impression that the room had been furnished with the intention that everything there would always be perfect and could never be otherwise. Andrey Andreich led Nadya through the whole house, keeping his arm around her waist all the time. But she felt weak and guilty, hating all those rooms, beds and armchairs, and nauseated by that naked lady. Now she clearly understood that she no longer loved Andrey Andreich and that perhaps she never had. But how could she put it into words, whom could she tell and what good would it do? This was something she did not and could not understand, although she had thought about it for days and nights on end. He was holding her round the waist, talking to her so affectionately, so modestly – he was happy walking around his new house. But all she saw was vulgarity, stupid, fatuous, intolerable vulgarity, and that arm round her waist seemed as hard and cold as an iron hoop. Every minute she was on the verge of running away, sobbing, throwing herself out of the window. Andrey Andreich led her to the bathroom, where he placed his hand on a tap set in the wall – and suddenly water flowed.

'What do you think of that?' he said, laughing. 'I had a two-hundred-gallon tank put in the loft. Now you and I shall have water.'

They strolled around the yard and then went out into the street, where they took a cab. Thick clouds of dust blew about, and it looked like rain.

'Don't you feel cold?' Andrey Andreich asked, screwing up his eyes from the dust.

She did not reply.

'Do you remember how Sasha told me off yesterday for doing nothing?' he asked after a short silence. 'Well, he's absolutely right! I never do a thing, I just can't. Why is it, my dear? Why does the mere thought of pinning a cockade on my hat and entering government service repel me so much? Why do I feel so edgy when I see a lawyer, a Latin teacher or a local councillor? Oh, Russia, Russia! What a lot of useless idlers you carry on your shoulders! My dear, long-suffering native land, there's so many like me you have to tolerate!'

He was trying to turn the fact that he did nothing into a general truth, seeing it as a sign of the times.

'When we're married,' he continued, 'we'll both go into the country and we'll work! We'll buy a small plot of land with a garden, near a river, we'll slave away and observe the life all around us. Oh, that will be so wonderful!'

He took off his hat and his hair streamed in the wind. As she listened she thought, 'Good God, I want to go back home!'

They were almost back at the house when they overtook Father Andrey.

'There's Father!' Andrey Andreich said, joyfully waving his hat. 'I'm so fond of my old man, I really am,' he said as he paid the cab-driver. 'He's such a kind old boy.'

Nadya entered the house feeling angry and unwell. She thought about the guests she would have to entertain all evening – she would have to smile, listen to that violin and all sorts of rubbish, and talk of nothing except that wedding.

Impressive and splendid in her silk dress, Grandmother was sitting by the samovar. She looked haughty, as she invariably did to her guests. Father Andrey came in, smiling his crafty smile.

'I have the pleasure and inestimable satisfaction of seeing you in good health,' he told Grandmother, and it was hard to tell if this was meant seriously or as a joke.

IV

The wind beat against the windows and roof. There was a whistling noise and the hobgoblin in the stove sang its song, plaintively, mournfully. It was past midnight. Everyone in the house had gone to bed, but no one slept and Nadya fancied she could hear someone playing the violin downstairs. Then there was a sharp bang – a shutter must have been torn off its hinges. A minute later Nina Ivanovna entered in her nightdress, with a candle.

'Nadya, what was that bang?' she asked.

With her hair done up in a single plait and smiling timidly, her mother looked older, uglier and shorter on that stormy night. Nadya recalled how, not long ago, she had looked on her mother as an extraordinary woman and had listened proudly to her every word. But now she could not remember those words: everything that came to mind was so feeble and useless.

Suddenly, several deep voices began droning in the stove and she could even make out the words, 'O-oh! Good Go-od!' Nadya sat up in bed, suddenly clutched her head and burst out sobbing.

'Dearest Mother,' she sobbed, 'if only you knew what's happening to me! I beg you, implore you, let me go away from here. Please!'

'But where?' Nina Ivanovna asked, not understanding. 'Where to?'

Nadya wept for a long time, and could not say one word. 'Please let me leave this town!' she said at last. 'There can't be any wedding, there shan't be any wedding, so there! I don't love that man and I can't bear talking about him.'

'No, my darling, no,' Nina Ivanovna said quickly, absolutely horrified. 'Please calm down. You're not yourself at the moment, it will pass. These things happen. You've probably had a little argument with Andrey, but love's not complete without a quarrel.'

'Please leave me alone, Mother. Please!' sobbed Nadya.

'Yes,' Nina Ivanovna said after a brief silence. 'Not long ago you were a child, just a little girl, and now you're going to be married. This transmutation of matter is constantly taking place in nature. Without even noticing it, you'll be a mother yourself, then an old lady – and then you'll have a stubborn little daughter like I have.'

'My sweet darling, you *are* clever, but you're unhappy,' Nadya said. 'You're very unhappy, but why say such nasty things? In heaven's name why?'

Nina Ivanovna wanted to speak, but she was unable to utter one word. Sobbing, she went to her room. Those deep voices began droning in the stove again and Nadya suddenly felt terrified. She leapt out of bed and dashed to her mother's room. Nina Ivanovna was lying under a light blue quilt, book in hand; her eyes were filled with tears.

'Mother, please hear what I have to say!' Nadya said. 'Now think and try to see my point of view. Just look how petty and degrading our lives are. My eyes have been opened, I can see everything clearly now. What's so special about Andrey? He's not very clever, is he, Mother? Heavens, can't you see that he's stupid!'

Nina Ivanovna sat up abruptly. 'You and your grandmother are torturing me,' she sobbed. 'I want some life . . . some life!' she repeated, striking herself twice on the chest with her fist. 'Give me my freedom. I'm still young, I want some life, but you two have made an old woman out of me.'

She wept bitterly, lay down and curled up under the quilt – she seemed so small, pathetic, stupid. Nadya went to her room, dressed, and sat by the window to wait for morning. All night long she sat there brooding, while someone seemed to be banging the shutter from outside and whistling.

In the morning Grandmother complained that the wind had blown all the apples off the trees during the night and broken an old plum tree. Everything was so grey, dull and cheerless, it seemed dark enough for lighting the lamps. Everyone complained of the cold, and the rain lashed the windows. After her morning tea, Nadya went to Sasha's room. Without a word she knelt in the corner by his armchair and covered her face in her hands.

'What's the matter?' Sasha asked.

'I can't stand it any more,' she said. 'I just don't understand how I could ever have lived in this place. It's beyond me. I despise my fiancé, I despise myself and I despise this idle existence.'

'It's all right now,' Sasha said, not yet realizing what was wrong. 'It's all right. Everything's fine.'

For a minute, Sasha looked at her in amazement. Finally he understood and was as happy as a little boy. He waved his arms and delightedly performed a tapdance in his slippers.

'Wonderful!' he said, rubbing his hands. 'God, that's wonderful!'

Like one enchanted, her large eyes full of love, she looked at him unblinking, expecting him to tell her something vitally, immensely important there and then. He had not told her anything yet, but she felt that a new, boundless world that she had never known was opening up before her. She watched him, full of expectation and ready for anything – even death.

'I'm leaving tomorrow,' he said after a moment's thought, 'and you can come to the station, so that it looks as if you're seeing me off. I'll put your luggage in my trunk and get your ticket. When the departure bell rings, on you get and off we go. Come with me as far as Moscow, then travel on to St Petersburg on your own. Do you have a passport?'[4]

'Yes.'

'You won't be sorry, I swear it. You won't have any regrets,' Sasha said enthusiastically. 'You'll start your studies and then it's all in the hands of fate. Drastically alter your way of life and then everything else will change too. The most important thing is to make a completely fresh start, the rest doesn't matter. So, we'll leave tomorrow then?'

'Oh yes, for God's sake yes!'

Nadya felt very agitated, more depressed than ever before – and now there was the prospect of going through sheer mental hell until the time came to leave. But the moment she went upstairs and lay on her bed she fell asleep. And she slept soundly, right until the evening, and there was a smile on her tear-stained face.

V

A cab had been ordered. With her hat and coat on, Nadya went upstairs for one more look at her mother, at all that had been hers. In her own room she stood by the bed – still warm – looked around and then went to her mother's room without making a sound. Nina Ivanovna was asleep and it was quiet there. Nadya kissed her mother, smoothed her hair and stood still for a couple of minutes. Then she slowly went downstairs.

It was pelting with rain. The cab's top was up and the driver was standing near the porch, soaking wet.

'There won't be enough room for you, Nadya,' Grandmother said when the servants started putting the luggage in. 'Fancy seeing someone off in this weather! You should stay at home! Heavens, just look at that rain!'

Nadya wanted to say something, but she couldn't. Sasha helped her to sit down, covered her legs with a rug and sat beside her.

'Good luck! God bless!' Grandmother shouted from the porch. 'Mind you write to us from Moscow, Sasha.'

'Of course. Cheerio, Grannie.'

'May God protect you!'

'What lousy weather,' Sasha said.

Only now did Nadya begin to cry. Only now did she realize that she was actually leaving – even when she had said goodbye to Grandmother and looked at her mother she still hadn't believed it. Farewell, dear old town! Suddenly she remembered everything: Andrey, his father, the new house, the naked lady with the vase. None of these things frightened or oppressed her any more – it all seemed so mindless and trivial, and was receding ever further into the past. When they climbed into the carriage and the train moved off, all that past existence which had seemed so large, so serious, now dwindled into insignificance, and a vast, broad future opened out before her, a future she had hardly dreamt of. The rain beat against the carriage windows and all she could see was green fields, with glimpses of telegraph poles and birds on the wires. Suddenly she gasped for joy: she remembered that she was travelling to freedom, that she was going to study – it was exactly the same as running away to join the Cossacks, as it was called long, long ago. She laughed, she wept, she prayed.

'Don't worry!' Sasha said, grinning. 'Everything's going to be all right!'

VI

Autumn passed, winter followed. Nadya felt very homesick. Every day she thought about Mother and Grandmother, and about Sasha. The letters from home were calm and affectionate and it seemed that all had been forgiven and forgotten. After the May examinations she went home feeling healthy and cheerful, stopping at Moscow on the way to see Sasha. He looked just the same as last summer: bearded, hair dishevelled, with the same frock-coat and canvas trousers, the same big, handsome eyes. But he looked ill and worn out, and he had aged, grown thinner and was always coughing. Somehow he struck Nadya as dull, provincial.

'Good God, Nadya's here!' he said, laughing cheerfully. 'My dear little darling!'

They sat in the smoky printing-room with its suffocating, over-whelming smell of Indian ink and paint. Then they went to his room, also full of the smell of stale tobacco, and with saliva stains. On the table, next to a cold samovar, lay a broken plate and a piece of dark paper. Both table and floor were covered with dead flies. Everything showed what a slipshod existence Sasha led – he was living any old how, with a profound contempt for creature comforts. If someone had spoken to him about his personal happiness, his private life, about someone being in love with him, he wouldn't have understood – he would have just laughed.

'It's all right, everything's turned out nicely,' Nadya said hurriedly. 'Last autumn Mother came to St Petersburg to see me. She told me that Grandmother isn't angry, but she keeps going to my room and making the sign of the cross over the walls.'

Sasha looked at her cheerfully, but he kept coughing and spoke in a cracked voice. Nadya watched him closely, unable to tell whether he really was seriously ill or if she was imagining it.

'Dear Sasha, you really *are* ill, aren't you?' she asked.

'No, it's nothing. I'm ill, but not terribly . . .'

'Good God,' Nadya said, deeply disturbed. 'Why don't you go and see a doctor, why don't you look after your health? My dear, sweet Sasha!' The tears spurted from her eyes. For some strange reason, Andrey, that naked lady with the vase, her entire past which now seemed as remote as her childhood – all this loomed in her imagination now. She wept because Sasha did not seem as abreast of things, as intellectual, as interesting as last year.

'Dear Sasha, you are very, very ill. I would do anything in the world to stop you being so pale and thin. I owe you so much. You can't imagine how much you've done for me, my good Sasha! Really, you're my very nearest and dearest now.'

They sat talking for a while. But now, after that winter she had spent in St Petersburg, everything about Sasha – his words, his smile, his whole presence – seemed outmoded, old-fashioned, obsolete and lifeless.

'I'm going down to the Volga the day after tomorrow,' Sasha said, 'and then I'll be taking the fermented mare's milk cure – drinking *koumiss*.[5] A friend of mine and his wife are coming with me. The wife's quite amazing. I've been trying to win her over and persuade her to go and study. I want her life to be transformed.'

After their talk they went to the station. Sasha treated her to tea and some apples. As he stood there smiling and waving his handkerchief while the train pulled out, one could tell just by looking at his legs that he was desperately ill and did not have long to live.

Nadya arrived at her home town at noon. As she drove from the station, the streets seemed very wide, but the houses small and squat. No one was about, except for a German piano-tuner in his brown coat. All the houses seemed covered in dust. Grandmother, who was really quite ancient now and as plump and ugly as ever, flung her arms round Nadya and wept for a long time, pressing her face to her shoulder and unable to tear herself away. Nina Ivanovna also looked a great deal older and had deteriorated considerably. She had a hunched-up look, but was still as tightly corseted as before and diamonds still sparkled on her fingers.

'My darling!' she exclaimed, trembling all over. 'My darling!'

They sat down, silently weeping. Grandmother and Mother plainly sensed that the past had gone for ever, that nothing could bring it back. No longer did they have any position in society, reputation, the right to entertain guests. It was rather like when, in the midst of a life without cares, the police raid the house suddenly one night and the master turns out to be an embezzler and forger – then it's goodbye for ever to any carefree, untroubled existence!

Nadya went upstairs and saw that same bed, those same windows with their simple white curtains, that same cheerful, noisy garden bathed in sunlight. She touched her table, sat down and pondered. Then she ate a fine lunch and drank tea with delicious rich cream. But something was missing, however – the rooms seemed empty and the ceilings low. That night, when she went to bed and pulled up the blankets, it was somehow rather funny lying in that warm, very soft bed again.

Nina Ivanovna came in for a moment and sat down guiltily, timidly glancing around her.

'Well, how are you, Nadya?' she asked after a brief silence. 'Are you happy? Very happy?'

'Yes I am, Mother.'

Nina Ivanovna stood up and made the sign of the cross over Nadya and the windows.

'As you see, I've become religious. You know, I'm studying philosophy now and I think a great deal. Many things have become as clear as daylight now. Filter your whole life through a prism – that's the most important thing.'

'Tell me, Mother, how's Grandmother's health these days?'

'Not too bad, it seems. After you left with Sasha and your telegram arrived, Grandmother collapsed when she read it. She lay for three days without moving. Then she kept praying and crying. But she's all right now.'

She stood up and paced the room.

That knocking could be heard again – it was the night watchman.

'Your whole life must be filtered through a prism, that's what's most important,' she said. 'In other words, one's perception of life must be broken down into its simplest elements, like the seven primary colours, and each element must be studied separately.'

Whatever else Nina Ivanovna said, Nadya didn't hear. And she didn't hear her leave either, as she was soon fast asleep.

May passed, June began. Nadya had grown used to that house again. Grandmother fussed over the samovar, heaving deep sighs, and Nina Ivanovna talked about her philosophy in the evenings. She was still in the ignominious position of hanger-on in that household and had to turn to Grandmother for every twenty-copeck piece. The house was full of flies and the ceilings seemed to get lower and lower. Grannie and Nina Ivanovna never went out into the street, for fear of meeting Father Andrey, or Andrey his son. Nadya would walk around the garden, down the street, look at the houses, the grey fences. Everything in that town struck her as ancient, obsolete – either it was awaiting its own demise or perhaps some fresh beginning. Oh, if only that bright new life would come quickly, then one could face one's destiny boldly, cheerful and free in the knowledge that one was right! That life would come, sooner or later. Surely the time would come when not a trace would remain of Grandmother's house, where four servants were forced to live in one filthy basement room – it would be forgotten, erased from the memory. The only distraction for Nadya was the small boys from next door. Whenever she strolled in the garden they would bang on the fence, laugh and taunt her with the words, 'And she thought she was going to get married, she did!'

A letter came from Sasha – from Saratov.[6] In that sprightly, dancing hand of his he wrote that his trip on the Volga had been a huge success, but that he hadn't been well in Saratov, had lost his voice and had been in hospital for two weeks. Nadya understood what this meant and felt a deep foreboding that was very similar to absolute certainty. But her forebodings and thoughts about Sasha did not trouble her as much as before, and this she found disagreeable. She passionately wanted a full life and to go to St Petersburg again, and her friendship with Sasha seemed a thing of the far distant past, even though she still cherished it. She lay awake the whole night and next morning sat by the window listening. And she did hear voices down below – Grandmother, highly agitated, was asking one question after another.

Then someone began to cry. When Nadya went downstairs she

saw Grandmother standing in a corner praying, her face tear-stained. On the table lay a telegram.

Nadya paced the room for a long time listening to Grandmother crying, then she picked up the telegram and read it. The news was that yesterday morning Aleksandr Timofeich (or Sasha for short) had died of tuberculosis in Saratov.

Grandmother and Nina Ivanovna went to church to arrange a prayer service, while Nadya kept pacing the house, thinking things over. She saw quite clearly that her life had been turned upside down, as Sasha had wanted, that she was a stranger in this place, unwanted, and that there was nothing in fact that *she* needed from it. She saw how her whole past had been torn away, had vanished as if burnt and the ashes scattered in the wind.

She went to Sasha's room and stood there for a while.

'Goodbye, dear Sasha!' she thought, and before her there opened up a new, full and rich life. As yet vague and mysterious, this life beckoned and lured her.

She went upstairs to pack and next morning said goodbye to her family. In a lively, cheerful mood she left that town – for ever, so she thought.

PUBLISHING HISTORY
AND NOTES

The House with the Mezzanine

First published in *Russian Thought* in 1896. On 29 December 1895 Chekhov wrote to A. S. Suvorin: 'I'm writing a short story and I just cannot finish it: visitors keep disturbing me. Since 23 December people have been knocking around all over the place and I long for solitude. But when I'm on my own I get angry and feel revulsion for the day that has passed. All day long nothing but eating and talking, eating and talking.'

Chekhov's first reference to this story is in his *First Notebook* (1891–1904) for February 1895, where he writes: 'Missy: I respect and love my sister so dearly that I would never offend or hurt her.' The first mention of actual work on the story is in a letter of 26 November 1895 to Yelena Shavrova: 'I'm writing a little story now, "My Fiancée". I once had a fiancée, she was called Missy. That's what I'm writing about.'

The story's setting – and possibly prototypes for the characters – is largely derived from Chekhov's stay at Bogimovo, Kaluga province, during the summer of 1891, where he rented part of a large country house on the estate. Chekhov's brother Mikhail states that the owner of Bogimovo, Ye. D. Bylim-Kosolovsky and his wife Anemaisa were possibly the prototypes for Belokurov and Lyubov Ivanovna.

Chekhov described the rented house (clearly the house in the story) in a letter to Suvorin on 18 May 1891: 'If only you knew how charming it is! Huge rooms . . . a wonderful garden with avenues of which I've never seen the like, a river, pond, church . . . and every comfort.' And Chekhov's brother Mikhail writes: 'Anton Pavlovich occupied the large drawing-room in Bogimovo, a vast room with columns and a couch of such improbable size that you could sit twelve men on it side by side. He slept on that couch. When a storm passed over at night those huge windows were illuminated in the lightning.'

The main theme of Lida's quarrel with the artist – the state of the peasantry – had become particularly topical since the famine and cholera epidemic of 1891–2.

Chekhov's attitude to the peasant (exemplified in the artist's speeches in the story) echoes some of Tolstoy's pronouncements at the time, especially the articles *What Then Must We Do?* (1886) and *On Famine* (1891), where, like the artist in the story, Tolstoy stresses that the condition of the suffering peasants cannot be improved without changing one's own life.

1. *Amos stoves*: A special kind of stove invented by Major-General Nikolay Amosov (1787–1868).

2. *Lake Baikal*: So-called 'pearl of Siberia', seventh largest lake in the world and the deepest.

3. *Buryat*: A Mongol people, forming a large indigenous group in south-eastern Siberia, living near Lake Baikal and in Irkutsk district.

4. *Ryurik's*: Ryurik was a Varangian prince of Kiev, traditionally said to be the founder of the Russian state (AD 862). The Varangians were Viking warriors.

5. *Gogol's Petrushka's*: Chichikov's comically inept (and bibulous) manservant in Gogol's *Dead Souls* (1842), renowned for reading with little comprehension.

6. *Vichy*: Famous spa in central France.

7. *'God sent a crow a piece of cheese'*: from the fable *The Crow and the Fox*, by I. A. Krylov (1769–1844).

Peasants

'Peasants' was first published in *Russian Thought* in 1897 and subsequently in a separate edition (1897), together with 'My Life', with Suvorin the publisher. The story was written at Melikhovo and, according to Chekhov's brother Mikhail, 'every page reflects Melikhovo scenes and characters', particularly the fire of 1895 (*Around Chekhov*, Moscow/Leningrad, 1933, p. 280). Later, when explaining to Suvorin his intention of selling Melikhovo, he wrote: 'From a literary point of view, after "Peasants" Melikhovo ran dry and it lost its value for me' (letter of 26 June 1899).

Writing to Yelena Shavrova on 1 January 1897 Chekhov mentions his work on 'Peasants': 'I'm up to my eyes in work. I write and cross out, write and cross out . . .' On 1 March that year he wrote to Suvorin: 'I've written a story about peasant life, but they say it won't pass the censors and I'll have to cut it by half.' Later that month Chekhov went to Moscow to check the proofs but on the day of his arrival suffered a severe lung haemorrhage and had to stay in the Ostroumovsky Clinic until 10 April. At his request, Lidiya Avilova took the proofs from V. A. Goltsev, editor of *Russian Thought*, to the clinic for Chekhov to correct.

Whether from his own instincts or following the advice of the editors of *Russian Thought*, Chekhov deemed it prudent completely to drop the chapter describing the peasants' conversation about God and the authorities, for censorship considerations. The text of this chapter is unknown.

'Peasants' was severely mutilated by the censors – particularly because, according to them, it painted far too dark a picture of peasant life. One censor complained: 'On first impressions this is something highly suspect' and a telegram from St Petersburg to the Moscow Censorship Committee stated in no uncertain terms: 'Omit p. 193 of the Chekhov. To be arrested if in disagreement.' Accordingly, Goltsev dropped this particular page where the drunkenness of the peasants is described.

Other sections, some substantial, were excised and on 16 April 1897 Chekhov wrote to M. O. Menshikov (editor of the monthly magazine *The Week*): 'The censors have taken quite a large chunk out of "Peasants".' However, in later editions, sections were reinstated. Some of the most 'offensive' passages, depicting the general depravity of the peasants, were toned down when published in Suvorin's edition. In effect, so true to life were the descriptions of the downtrodden, exploited peasants that the censorship committee looked upon the story as a documentary article.

In a letter to his brother Mikhail, Chekhov states that the fire in the story was based on an actual occurrence at Melikhovo, his country estate, two years previously. Mikhail writes in his memoirs most revealingly: 'These five years in Melikhovo were not wasted by Anton. They laid their special imprint on his works of this period, influenced his literary activity and made him a profounder and more serious writer.' Chekhov's brother categorically states that Chekhov's direct dealings with peasants on the estate had a strong influence on both 'Peasants' and 'In the Ravine'. As one would expect, Chekhov was a good master and life at Melikhovo was peaceful. Chekhov's picture of the peasants' sad lot contrasts sharply with Tolstoy's idealization of the peasant with his 'unsullied virtues', and in both 'Peasants' and 'In the Ravine' he shows up the cardinal error of regarding these poor creatures as the living embodiment of God-like purity and true guardians of Christian morality.

The unfinished continuation of 'Peasants' (chapters X and XI) has survived in draft form, but it is difficult to date precisely – possibly 1900. However, the idea of a continuation probably arose earlier, since Goltsev wrote to Chekhov in March 1897: 'I need your "Peasants" and their continuation . . .' These final two chapters considerably broaden the canvas, describing the further lives of Olga and her daughter Sasha in Moscow, after leaving the village. Although Chekhov possibly intended continuing the story with a portrayal of low city life, as intimated in the Introduction (p. xiii), he may have come to feel that this would clash with the harrowing depiction of the peasantry in preceding chapters.

1. *Slav Fair*: (Slavyansky Bazaar) Famous Moscow hotel and restaurant, frequently mentioned in Chekhov's stories. Chekhov often stayed there.

2. *'But whosoever shall smite thee . . .'*: Matthew 5:39.

3. *'Come unto me . . .'*: Matthew 11:28.

4. *Vladimir*: Ancient city about 120 miles east of Moscow, formerly the capital of central Russia.

5. *Hermitage Garden [or Variety] Theatre*: In Karetny Ryad (Coach Row) where Stanislavsky first achieved success with the Moscow Art Theatre's production of Chekhov's *The Seagull* (1898). This Hermitage has no connection with either the Hermitage Museum in St Petersburg or the Hermitage restaurant in Moscow.

6. *Aumont's*: Well-known amusement house.

7. *'And when they were departed . . .'*: Matthew 2:13.

8. *Exaltation of the Cross*: 14 September.

9. *I lo-ove the flowers that bloom . . .* : According to Chekhov's sister Masha, Chekhov had often heard the village girls at Melikhovo singing this song.

10. *Fast of the Assumption*: One of the strictest fasts, a two-week period preceding the Feast of the Assumption which took place on 15 August.

11. *kasha*: A kind of porridge or gruel made of cooked grain or boiled groats. Staple peasant food.

12. *the serfs were emancipated*: The serfs were officially emancipated in 1861.

13. *used to ride out with wolfhounds . . .* : The skilled hunters were from Pskov province. They would work in threes and drive the wolves or foxes from cover for the huntsmen.

14. *Tver*: Large town on the Volga, about 100 miles north-west of Moscow. Known as Kalinin in Soviet era (after Stalin's puppet president).

15. *freedom*: Marya means freedom from serfdom.

16. *portrait of Battenberg*: Alexander of Battenberg, Prince of Bulgaria (1879–86), forced to abdicate by Alexander III of Russia, after being kidnapped by Russian officers and deported to Russian territory. W. H. Bruford, in his *Chekhov and His Russia* (1948; 1971), states: 'These details

... indicated perhaps the elder's ignorance, for one so loyal would not otherwise have given the place of honour to an enemy of his Tsar.'

17. *Elijah's Day*: 20 July.

18. *Patriarch's Ponds*: Actually one large pond formed from three fishponds that were dug out of the medieval Goat's Marsh. Patriarch's Ponds is where two literary hacks meet the Devil in the first chapter of Bulgakov's *The Master and Margarita*.

19. *Filippov's*: Moscow's most fashionable coffee house before the Revolution, richly decorated with stuccoed ceiling and caryatids. Founded by the court baker Filippov.

20. *Tversky Boulevard*: Long thoroughfare in west central Moscow, stretching from Nikitsky Gates to Pushkin Square.

21. *Little Bronny*: A Moscow street frequented by prostitutes.

Trilogy: Man in a Case, Gooseberries, About Love

That 'Man in a Case', 'Gooseberries' and 'About Love', all published in *Russian Thought*, 1898, were to be considered a cycle, or trilogy, was stressed by Chekhov in a letter to a female translator of his stories into English, O. R. Vasilyeva, who for some reason decided to translate only the second two stories: 'Do as you please, but if you leave out "Man in a Case" it will be unclear who's talking and why' (5 January 1899). Chekhov had intended continuing the trilogy – this is clear from a letter to the publisher A. F. Marks: 'The stories "Man in a Case", "Gooseberries" and "About Love" are a part of a series which is far from finished . . .' (28 September 1899). But this projected series was never written, possibly because of mental exhaustion at the time. After the trilogy was completed he wrote to Lidiya Avilova: 'Writing revolts me and I don't know what to do' (23–27 July 1898). This mood soon passed, but with the coming of autumn Chekhov was forced to go south for health reasons. From Yalta he wrote to P. F. Iordanov (a Taganrog doctor): 'I'm unsettled and hardly working. This enforced idleness and wandering around resorts is worse than any bacilli' (21 September 1898). Eventually he started writing again – but independent stories such as 'A Case History' and 'On Official Duty'.

These three stories are the only case of interconnectedness in Chekhov's work. The ideas for the stories had long been fermenting in his mind: this is clear from notes made in Paris and Nice and from his *First Notebook*. On 2 July he wrote to N. A. Leykin[6]: 'As you know, I spent the winter in the South of France, where I was bored without snow and couldn't work. In the spring I was in Paris, where I spent about four weeks. Now I'm at home and writing. I've sent my story to [*The*] *Cornfield* and another to *Russian Thought*.' This second story was 'Man in a Case'. Separate publishing histories and notes for each of the three stories in the trilogy now follow in the order in which they appear in this volume.

In early June 1898 'Man in a Case' was prepared for the press and on the 12th of that month Chekhov wrote to Suvorin: 'I'm fussing about and doing a little bit of work. I've already written a long and a short story.' These were 'Ionych' and 'Man in a Case'.

Chekhov's brother Mikhail states that the prototype for the main character, Belikov, was a certain Dyakanov, an inspector at the Taganrog Gymnasium where Anton had studied (this attribution is now disputed), adding that his brother also drew on events at the school – the annual spring outing, for example (*A. P. Chekhov and His Subjects*, Moscow, 1923). It is also possible that the prototype could have been the journalist M. O. Menshikov, editor of the journal *The Week*, as Chekhov refers to him in his diary for 1896: 'Menshikov goes around with galoshes in dry weather, carrying an umbrella so as not to perish from sunstroke and is scared of washing in cold water . . .' In addition, Professor Serebryakov in *Uncle Vanya* never ventures out without umbrella and galoshes. Clearly, Chekhov was fascinated by this type of encapsulated, cocooned individual and 'Man in a Case' is his fullest portrayal of this strange manifestation of extreme eccentricity. However, it is likely that Belikov is an amalgam of various characters Chekhov had known.

The second story in the trilogy, 'Gooseberries', links the first and last and contemporary critics were quick to see the similarity of the thematic material running through the three stories: lack of will, moral cowardice, pettiness and bigotry generated by a complacent society. Chekhov thought that all these defects could be pinned on his own generation.

The story was written at Melikhovo in July 1898 and published the following month in *Russian Thought*. On 20 July Chekhov wrote in mock-serious tone to Goltsev, editor of *Russian Thought*: 'Nine tenths of the story for the August issue are ready and if nothing prevents the happy conclusion of the aforementioned story you will receive it from my own hands on 1 August.'

According to Mikhail Chekhov, several features of the estate of Bakumovka, owned by S. I. Smagin, are incorporated in the story – for example, swimming in the river. Chekhov's brother interestingly relates the origin of the extraordinary surname Chimsha-Gimalaysky: 'When Anton Pavlovich travelled right across Siberia to Sakhalin, somewhere, on the very edge of the world, a local gentleman came forth and wanted to make his acquaintance. He gave him his card on which was written: "Rymsha-Pilsudsky". Anton Pavlovich took this card away and for a long time laughed at a name you couldn't invent even if you were drunk, and decided to use it when the opportunity arose' (*A. P. Chekhov and His Subjects*, Moscow, 1923).

The third story in the trilogy, 'About Love' was first published in *Russian Thought* in 1898. The plot for the story is outlined in Chekhov's *First Notebook*. Like the other two stories in the trilogy, 'About Love' was written at Melikhovo in the summer of 1898 and was prepared for the August issue of *Russian Thought*. The first version of the story ended with a matter-of-fact dialogue about Ivan Ivanych's departure, but in the *Collected Edition* of 1903 it ends on a lyrical note, with poetic descriptions of Nature and sad reflections about those who had heard Alyokhin's story.

In her memoirs, *A. P. Chekhov in My Life: A Love Story* (London, 1950), Lidiya Avilova wrote: '"About Love" concerned me, I had no doubt about it . . .' According to her, her relations with Chekhov are reflected in the story and she refers to a ten-year relationship. After reading the story she sent Chekhov a hostile letter in which she 'thanked him for the honour of figuring as a heroine, even if only in a little story'. However, Avilova's memoirs are now considered highly suspect and mainly based on delusion.

Man in a Case

1. *Shchedrin*: M. E. Saltykov-Shchedrin (1826–89), Russia's greatest satirical novelist.

2. *Henry Buckles*: Henry Thomas Buckle (1821–62), English social historian whose *History of Civilisation* (1858, 1861) was extremely popular in Russia.

3. *'Breezes of the South . . .'*: From a popular Ukrainian folksong.

4. *Gadyach*: Small Ukrainian town, in Poltava province.

5. *Mr Creepy-Crawly*: (Ukrainian) Lit. *The Bloodsucker or Spider*, a four-act drama by M. L. Kropivnitsky, written for the actress M. K. Zankovetsky, whom Chekhov had first met at the Suvorins in 1892.

6. Nikolay Aleksandrovich Leykin (1841–1906), journalist, novelist and writer of satirical short stories. He was publisher and editor of the highly popular comic magazine *Oskolki* (*Fragments*), to which Chekhov contributed more than 200 short stories between 1882 and 1887.

Gooseberries

1. *only six feet of earth*: A possible allusion to Tolstoy's famous story 'How Much Land Does a Man Need?'.
2. *'Uplifting illusion . . .'*: Inaccurate quotation from the poem *The Hero* (1830). The original reads: 'Uplifting illusion is dearer to me than a host of vile truths.'

About Love

1. *European Herald*: Liberal monthly journal that published works by leading writers (Ostrovsky, Turgenev, Goncharov). It was published from 1866 to 1918.

A Visit to Friends

First published in the journal *Cosmopolis*, 1898, and written at the request of F. D. Batyushkov (1857–1920; literary historian and critic, editor of Russian section of *Cosmopolis*. Author of interesting memoirs and articles about Chekhov). From Nice, Chekhov wrote to Batyushkov: 'I promise to write a story for *Cosmopolis* at the first opportunity and if nothing gets in the way I'll send it in December.' (letter of 9 November 1897).

In December he wrote a highly interesting letter from Nice to Batyushkov which throws much light on his creative methods: 'I'm writing the story for *Cosmopolis*, slowly, in fits and starts. I usually write slowly, with much effort, but here, in a hotel room, at a strange table, in good weather, when I yearn to go out, I write even worse . . . and therefore I can't promise the story earlier than in two weeks. I'll send it before 1 January . . . You expressed the wish . . . for me to send an international story, with a subject from the local life here. I can only write such stories in Russia, from memory. I can write only from memory and have never written direct from nature. My memory has to sieve the subject so that only what's important or typical is left on it, as on a filter' (letter of 15 December 1897).

Early the following year he wrote to the sociologist M. M. Kovalevsky: 'I sent a story to *Cosmopolis* and have already received a thank-you telegram from the editor, although the story isn't quite right – rather poor, I think' (letter of 8 January 1898).

'A Visit to Friends' was the only late story of Chekhov's to be excluded from the *Collected Edition* – for some reason he took a dislike to it.

1. *Tula*: Large town about 120 miles south of Moscow, famous for the manufacture of guns and samovars. Peter the Great established a small-arms factory there in 1712. The gunsmiths were renowned for the quality of their workmanship.

2. *Slav Fair*: See 'Peasants', note 1, p. 333.

3. *Hermitage*: Restaurant in Trubny Place in Moscow.

4. *Little Bronny Street*: See 'Peasants', note 21, p. 334.

5. *Is something rotten in the state of Denmark?*: Cf. *Hamlet*, Act I, Scene 4, 'Something is rotten in the state of Denmark'.

6. *Ufa*: Capital of Bashkir Autonomous Republic, on Belaya River, near the Urals.

7. *Perm*: Large city on River Kama, in western Urals. An important cultural and industrial centre.

8. *The line runs straight* . . . : From N. A. Nekrasov's *The Railway* (1865); also the following excerpts. The poem is full of strong civic protest.

9. *Before he had time to groan* . . . : From the fable *The Peasant and the Workman* (1815), by I. A. Krylov.

10. *'And thou shalt be que-een of the world'*: From the opera *The Demon*, by A. G. Rubinstein, based on Lermontov's famous narrative poem (1841).

Ionych

'Ionych' was first published in the *Monthly Literary Supplement to the Journal The Cornfield* in 1898. Chekhov completed this story at Melikhovo in about one month. Previously it had been thought that 'Ionych' had originally been intended for *Russian Thought* and then taken back, but this has been shown to refer to another story.

On 13 March 1898 Chekhov wrote from Nice to Y. O. Gryunberg, managing editor of A. F. Marks' publishing house and of the journal *The Cornfield*: 'I'll send the story without delay, but not before I return home. Here I can't write, I've grown lazy. I'm going to Paris around 5–10 April and then back home . . . in May or June probably I'll be able to write for *The Cornfield*.'

According to Mikhail Chekhov the cemetery in the story is based on that in Taganrog, together with other details from Chekhov's earlier life in the provincial town (*A. P. Chekhov and His Subjects*, Moscow, 1923).

*

1. *'Ere I had drunk from life's cup of tears*: From the poem *Elegy* (1821) by Anton Delvig (1798–1831), a close friend of Pushkin. The poem was set to music by M. L. Yakovlev, a friend of Delvig's.

2. *'Die now Denis, you'll never write better!'*: Words attributed to Prince Potyomkin after seeing the first performance of Denis Fonvizin's satirical comedy *The Minor* (1782). The same quotation also appears in Dostoyevsky's *Winter Notes on Summer Impressions* (1863).

3. *Thy voice for me is dear and languorous*: Line from Pushkin's *Night* (1823), slightly altered. The original reads: 'My voice for thee is dear and languorous.' The poem was set to music by A. G. Rubinstein, Rimsky-Korsakov and Mussorgsky.

4. *Pisemsky*: Aleksey Feofilaktovich (1821–81). Novelist. His *A Thousand Souls* (1858) is an entertaining satirical novel about the rise and fall of an ambitious young man from the provinces. The requisite number of serfs for a landowner to be considered wealthy was one thousand. The shortened version of the patronymic is conversational.

5. *The cemetery*: Possibly the cemetery in Chekhov's native town of Taganrog, or Feodosiya. Chekhov was very fond of wandering around cemeteries.

6. *'The hour is coming when . . .'*: John 5:28. The full verse is: 'For the hour is coming, in the which all that are in the graves shall hear his voice.'

My Life

'My Life' was first published in the *Monthly Literary Supplement to the Journal The Cornfield* in 1896 and subsequently published by Suvorin as a separate volume (together with 'Peasants') in 1897.

On 11 July 1895 Chekhov was invited by the editor of *The Cornfield*, A. A. Tikhonov (pseudonym A. Lugovoy), to contribute to the journal and he accepted. The first definite indication that work on the story had begun is given in a letter to I. M. Potapenko (1856–1928; writer and close friend of Chekhov after 1893): 'I'm writing a novel for *The Cornfield* . . .'; and shortly afterwards he added: 'I think it will be called "My Marriage" . . . I can't say for certain yet . . . the subject's from the life of the provincial intelligentsia.' On 16 June he sent the first nine chapters to Lugovoy, which he did not consider as final, for he asked for them to be returned after being read: 'I'll have to correct a great deal, since it's not a story yet, only a crudely constructed framework that I'll whitewash and paint when I finish the building.' On 11 July he told Suvorin that the story was nearly finished and it was sent to the editors on 10 August. The following day Chekhov confessed to M. O. Menshikov: 'A big story, exhausting, and hellishly boring.'

After the Coronation of Nicholas II there had been a great increase in the number of workers' strikes and Lugovoy expected a more oppressive regime, with a harder line from the censors. Moreover, at this time a new censor had been appointed, which did not bode well. Therefore Lugovoy suggested that the first and 'safest' five chapters be printed in the October issue of *The Cornfield*, hoping to 'lull the censor's vigilance'. As it happened nothing was excised in these chapters. Lugovoy, however, foresaw problems with the continuation, especially in the sixth chapter with its discussion about social progress, and told Chekhov to 'tone down' a few details – for example, the father beating the son, and the son of a general's wife fighting with her lover. In particular, Lugovoy, who had great experience of the censors' methods, advised Chekhov to be especially careful with the last chapter.

When the completed story was submitted to the censors, in galley form, it was severely mutilated: they cut the scene with the Governor and the son's final humiliation with his father. These were later restored. The publication was sorrowfully greeted by Chekhov and in letters to Lugovoy, Suvorin and T. L. Tolstaya (Tolstoy's eldest daughter) he voiced his distress, complaining to Tolstaya: 'Toward the end of summer I had a story ready . . . "My Life" – I couldn't think of any other title and I was counting on bringing it with me to Yasnaya Polyana, in page proof form. But it's now being printed in the *Supplement* and I feel revulsion for it, since the censors have gone over it and many parts are unrecognizable' (letter of 9 November 1896). He was particularly shocked at the rough censorial treatment of the last chapter, writing to Suvorin: 'It's horrible, just horrible! They've turned the last chapter into a desert.'

Chekhov never liked the final title (Lugovoy had persuaded him to retain the present title, with the subtitle 'A Provincial's Story'), which struck him as 'revolting' – especially the word 'My', preferring to call it 'In the Nineties', which Lugovoy thought pretentious.

It was the mutilation at the hands of the censors that prompted Chekhov to have the story published as a separate book, together with 'Peasants', but in accordance with conditions laid down by A. F. Marks' publishing house this could not be published until one year later.

The background of the story is most probably Taganrog, Chekhov's birthplace, and there are several features linked to the author's childhood. Like Chekhov, the story's hero, Misail Poloznev, has a loathing for Greek and suffers humiliating beatings from a tyrannical father.

*

1. *Borodino*: Village about eighty miles west of Moscow, scene of the bloody battle in 1812 between Napoleon's army and the Russians under Kutuzov. In about fifteen hours more than a third of each army had perished, totalling over 100,000 soldiers. After the battle Napoleon marched into Moscow.

2. *Dubechnya*: Name of actual village where Chekhov lived for a time; it was close to Melikhovo.

3. *Kimry*: Small town in Tver province on left bank of the Volga and centre of shoe-making industry.

4. *Tula*: See 'A Visit to Friends', note 1, p. 337.

5. *pig-faced freaks*: Reference to the human 'monsters' in Gogol's *Dead Souls*. Lit. 'swinish snouts'.

6. *Serfdom has been abolished*: Serfdom was officially abolished in 1861.

7. *'Make to yourselves . . .'*: Luke 16:9.

8. *vegetarian*: Vegetarianism, widespread among opposition circles (e.g. Tolstoyans), was deeply frowned upon by the official church.

9. *Zalegoshch*: Village in Tula province, east of Oryol.

10. *Khlyst*: Member of religious sect practising flagellation.

11. *Russia began . . .*: AD 862 is the traditional date of the foundation of Russian statehood, when the Varangian (Viking) Ryurik was established as Prince of Novgorod. See also 'The House with the Mezzanine', note 4, p. 331.

12. *'Holy Virgin, Intercessor'*: Hymn in honour of Our Lady of Kazan.

13. *'Why do I love thee, O radiant night?'*: From *Night* (1850), a poem by Ya. P. Polonsky, set to music by Tchaikovsky.

14. *Exhibition in America*: The World's Columbian Exposition, Chicago, 1893.

15. *Ostrovsky*: A. N. Ostrovsky (1823–86), major Russian playwright; his chief plays are *The Storm* (1860) and *The Forest* (1875).

The Lady with the Little Dog

Chekhov began writing 'The Lady with the Little Dog' in Yalta, in August or September 1899. In a letter of 15 September that year he wrote to V. A. Goltsev, editor of *Russian Thought*: 'Forgive me for not sending the story, because it's not ready yet. Parquet floor layers and carpenters are banging away from morning to night and stop me from working. And the weather's very good, so it's difficult sitting indoors.' The story was published in the December issue of *Russian Thought* and for the *Collected Edition* of 1903 Chekhov made significant changes, chiefly in elimination of superfluous detail and material in the depiction of Gurov and Anna Sergeyevna. In the later version Chekhov gave much greater emphasis to Gurov's capacity for abstract thought and analysing his own actions. Similarly, lengthy description of the heroine's married life and her life in S— was eliminated.

At the time of writing this story Chekhov's relationship with Olga Knipper was deepening. Together they made many excursions around Yalta, which are reflected in the story.

1. *Yalta*: Crimean town on the Black Sea, a major health resort from the 1880s. Chekhov built a villa there in 1899 and lived chiefly in Yalta until his death in 1904. 'The Lady with the Little Dog' is his only story set in Yalta. In the summer of 1899 Chekhov had a meeting at Vernet's restaurant with the young writer Yelena Shavrova, who was infatuated with him.

2. *Belyov or Zhizdra*: Small, insignificant towns to the south and south-west of Moscow respectively.

3. *Oreanda*: Picturesque viewpoint about three miles west of Yalta, formerly a royal estate. A summer residence was built there by Nicholas I, but burnt down in 1881. A beautiful park leads down to the sea from the ruins.

4. *Feodosiya*: Fashionable resort on the south-eastern Crimean coast, about seventy miles from Yalta.

5. *the waterfall*: Uchasu Waterfall, a beauty spot about five miles from Yalta and very popular for excursions.

6. *Petrovka*: One of the most aristocratic streets in Moscow and a major thoroughfare.

7. *The Geisha*: An operetta by the English composer Sidney Jones (1861–1946), written in 1896. This very popular work was performed in Paris, London, Berlin, Vienna, etc., and enjoyed great success in Russia, with more than 200 performances in Moscow. Chekhov had possibly seen this operetta in Yalta in 1899, where it was performed by a local opera group. Impressions of the Yalta and Taganrog theatres are no doubt reflected in the theatre in the town of S—. In a letter of 15 December 1898 Chekhov wrote to his sister: 'I'm writing this in the theatre, in a fur coat, sitting in the gallery. This lousy little orchestra and gallery remind me of my childhood.'

8. *Slav Fair Hotel*: See 'Peasants', note 1, p. 333.

In the Ravine

'In the Ravine' was published in the journal *Life* in 1900. Chekhov had begun work on the story in Yalta, in November–December 1899, widely using random material from his *First Notebook* (1891–1904). The close ties with 'Peasants' are evident from these preliminary notes. 'In the Ravine' was written at the persistent request of V. A. Posset, editor of *Life*, and of Maxim Gorky, who took part in the literary section of the journal. From December 1898 both Posset and Gorky had repeatedly invited Chekhov to contribute to *Life*.

Chekhov mentions the forthcoming story in a letter to his sister (14 November 1899): 'I'm writing a big story. I'll finish it soon and begin another.' On 19 November 1899 he had written to Posset: 'I'm writing the story for *Life* and it will soon be ready, probably by the second half of December. There's only three sheets in all, but masses of characters, a real crush. It's very cramped and I'll have to take great care so that the crush doesn't become too apparent. Whatever, it'll be ready around 10 December and can be typeset. But the trouble is – I'm afraid the censors might start plucking it. Please return my story if you feel that certain places won't pass the censorship . . .' (After 'Peasants', Chekhov was understandably apprehensive about the reception this new story might have at the hands of the censors.) On 6 December Chekhov wrote to V. I. Nemirovich-Danchenko[8] about his work on the story. However, it was not sent to *Life* until 20 December, with Chekhov repeatedly apologizing to Posset for the delay.

On 26 December he wrote to M. O. Menshikov (editor of the magazine *The Week*): 'I've written a lot recently. I've sent my story to *Life*. In this story I depict factory life, I discuss how sad it is . . .' On 2 January 1900 he wrote amusingly to Olga Knipper about 'In the Ravine': 'My story will appear in the February issue of *Life* – it's very strange. Many characters – and a landscape too. There's a crescent moon, a bird called a bittern, which makes a booming noise far off somewhere, like a cow locked in a shed. There's *everything*.' And in a letter to G. I. Rossolimo (Professor of Neuropathology at Moscow University and once a medical student with Chekhov) he called the story 'my last from the life of the common people'.

On 11 January Chekhov complained bitterly to Posset (on receipt of the page proofs) that lines had been left out, with chaotic punctuation. For all that, the story appeared in *Life* with numerous misprints. The exasperated Chekhov concluded the letter with the words: 'Such an abundance of misprints is something I've never encountered before and it strikes me as a veritable orgy of typographical slovenliness. Please forgive my irritation.'

From the memoirs of Chekhov's brother Mikhail (*A. P. Chekhov and His Subjects*, Moscow, 1923, p. 146) we learn that an incident from Sakhalin is incorporated in the story and that the scene is set near Melikhovo. S. N. Shchukin, a Yalta teacher and man of letters, who has left interesting memoirs of Chekhov, records his saying of 'In the Ravine': 'I'm describing life as it is encountered in the provinces of Middle Russia. I know them best. And the Khrymin merchants really do exist. Only, in actual fact they are worse. From the age of eight their children start drinking vodka, and from childhood they lead dissipated lives. They have infected the whole area with syphilis. I don't mention this in the story, because I don't consider that kind of thing very artistic. Lipa's baby being scalded to death with boiling water is nothing out of the ordinary. Local doctors often meet with such cases.' The writer Ivan Bunin (1870–1938) stated that he told Chekhov of an incident involving a parish priest consuming two pounds of caviare at his father's name-day party, altered by Chekhov and used at the beginning of 'In the Ravine'.

1. *Yepifan*: Large village about 140 miles south-east of Moscow.

2. *'inspection'*: Old Russian peasant ceremony when the prospective bride was 'viewed'.

3. *Yegoryevsk*: Small town about seventy miles south-east of Moscow.

4. *kvass*: Fermented drink made from malt, rye or different kinds of fruit, in this case pears.

5. *Amur*: Siberian river, 800 miles of which form the boundary between Russia and China. It flows into the Tatar Strait.

6. *Altay*: Mountainous region in southern Siberia.

7. *I was on a ferry once*: This is reminiscent of an incident recorded by Chekhov in his *Out of Siberia* (prologue to *The Island of Sakhalin*) where he describes meeting a freezing peasant when crossing the Kama River on his way to Sakhalin.

8. Vladimir Ivanovich Nemirovich-Danchenko (1858–1943), co-founder, with Konstantin Stanislavsky, of the Moscow Art Theatre. He was one of the first to recognize the merits of *The Seagull*, with which he launched the Moscow Art Theatre in 1898. Olga Knipper, who played Arkadina in the play, was one of his prize pupils.

Disturbing the Balance

The text of this unfinished story is based on a manuscript, in Chekhov's writing, in the Lenin State Library in St Petersburg. Probably written in 1902–3, it was published in 1905, after Chekhov's death, in *Everybody's Magazine*, a popular St Petersburg monthly. On the manuscript there are signs of editing by V. S. Mirolyubov, editor of the magazine.

1. *Monte Pincio*: Hill in the north of Rome, linked to the park of the Villa Borghese, with a superb view, especially at dusk.

The Bishop

First published in *Everybody's Magazine*, 1902. In the autumn of 1899 Chekhov promised to send a new story to *Everybody's Magazine*, at the persistent request of V. S. Mirolyubov, its editor, who required the story for the January 1900 issue: he had to wait two years for it. There are many mentions of a story in his letters on this subject that point to a much earlier conception of the main idea. In a letter of 16 March 1901 to Olga Knipper he refers to the subject as 'already being in my head for fifteen years'. However, work on the story was exceedingly spasmodic, protracted, constantly interrupted by ill health. No story cost Chekhov so much effort.

In November 1899, when he was working on 'In the Ravine', Chekhov told his sister: 'I'm writing a big story. I'll finish it soon and begin another' (letter of 14 November 1899). There is no doubt that the second story referred to here is 'The Bishop'. Although work on the story was interrupted by ill health, Chekhov returned to it after completion of *Three Sisters*. But work was slow, interrupted by idle visitors, creative self-doubts, as well as by bad health. In January 1901 he wrote to Olga Knipper: 'I'm writing of course, but without any desire at all. It seems *Three Sisters* has worn me out – or, simply, that I'm bored with writing, grown old. I don't know. I should stop writing for five years, travel for five years and then return and sit down to work.'

Mirolyubov, who was in Yalta in February and March 1901, again urged Chekhov to finish the story for his journal. But for reasons of health Chekhov could only return to work at the end of August; despite this he still went to Moscow in the autumn, from where he wrote to the frantic Mirolyubov: 'Forgive me, dear chap, for not sending the story before. It's because I broke off work and I've always found it difficult to take up interrupted work again. But the moment I'm home I'll start from the beginning and send it. Don't worry!' (19 October 1901).

Replying to Olga Knipper's request to send V. I. Nemirovich-Danchenko a new story to be read at a charity concert, Chekhov wrote: 'I'd send a story to Nemirovich-Danchenko with the greatest pleasure, but really, what I'm writing now would hardly pass the censors – that is, it's hardly permissible for a public reading.' The very mention of censors shows almost without doubt that the story in question here is 'The Bishop'. At the time the censors were increasingly wary of works where representatives of the clergy were depicted. In early December Chekhov was again forced to break off work owing to a worsening of his illness and on the 17th of that month he wrote to Mirolyubov: '. . . I'm ill – or not quite healthy . . . and I can't write. I've coughed blood, now I feel weakness and malice, I sit with a hot compress on my side, take creosote and all kinds of rubbish. Whatever, I shan't cheat you with "The Bishop", I'll send it sooner or later.' Only two weeks later was he able to resume work on the story and on 20 February 1902 wrote to Mirolyubov: 'Forgive me for dragging it out for so long. I finished the story some time ago, but it was difficult copying it out. I'm ill the whole time . . . send me the page proofs without fail. I'll add a short phrase or two at the end. But I shan't change one word for the censors, please take that into consideration. If the censors throw out only one word, then send the story back and I'll send you another in May.'

Therefore the story was written in seven periods, starting from the end of December 1899 up to the first part of February 1902, partly in Yalta, partly in Nice, partly in Moscow.

The short story writer A. I. Kuprin (1870–1938), astonished at the accuracy of observation, stated that the characters must have been based on real people – monks from the monastery near Melikhovo. But Chekhov's brother Mikhail said that the prototype for the bishop was a Stepan Petrov, student at Moscow University, who knew Chekhov when he was living in Moscow. This student later took holy orders and became Father Sergey; when he later went to Yalta, suffering from a nervous disorder, he often called on Chekhov. Mikhail Chekhov goes on to say that the frequent meetings Anton had with Father Sergey provided the basic material for the story. However, according to S.N. Shchukin (1873–1931; a Yalta priest, teacher and minor man of letters), Chekhov happened to see a photograph in a Yalta shop window of a certain Bishop Gribanovsky: Chekhov was intrigued, made inquiries and the present story was the result. Whatever the prototype (and there are autobiographical elements too) 'The Bishop' is all the more remarkable for its essential unity and compression in the light of the dreadful burden of ill health Chekhov had to bear during its composition.

1. *Betula kinderbalsamica secuta*: A linguistic hotchpotch, ostensibly meaning 'curative birch for beating children'.
2. *'bridegroom who cometh at midnight'*: Cf. Matthew 25:6, 'And at midnight there was a cry made, Behold, the bridegroom cometh.'
3. *'Now is the Son of Man glorified'*: John 13:31.
4. *the coming of Christianity to Russia*: In about AD 988, when Vladimir, Grand Prince of Kiev, was converted to Christianity, which he made the official religion.

The Bride

Chekhov's last story, 'The Bride', was first published in *Everybody's Magazine* in 1903. Chekhov revised the text many times – no fewer than five versions exist. It was written at the same time as *The Cherry Orchard*.

At the time he was corresponding with V. S. Mirolyubov at the beginning of 1902, about 'The Bishop', Chekhov twice wrote that in the event of trouble with the censors he would send 'another story' (letters of 20 February and 8 March). There is no doubt that this other story was 'The Bride': after 'The Bishop' had been printed Mirolyubov persistently reminded Chekhov of the promised story. The variants show that the story was very carefully constructed, with particular attention to the style, which became increasingly tightened. Even the names of the main characters were changed; with each version Chekhov tried to put more emphasis on Andrey Andreich's smugness and self-satisfaction, on Nina Ivanovna's lachrymose sentimentality and alienation from her daughter, and so on. If the rough drafts are compared with the final version it is evident that Chekhov introduced substantial changes into the characters of both Sasha and Nadya.

He began work on the story in October 1902, writing on the 16th in reply to a telegram from Mirolyubov about the title: 'I'll send you the title as soon as it's possible – that is, when I settle on a theme . . .' and 'If you need a title so much, which can be changed later, here it is: "The Bride".'

Chekhov began work on the story immediately on his return to Yalta. After telling Olga Knipper several times that he was hard at work, a cooling-off soon set in: 'At the moment I'm at work on a story that is fairly uninteresting – for me at least. I'm bored with it' (14 December 1902).

However, work went well, with no interruptions from visitors or because of illness. However, the following month he is complaining of ill health and slow progress on the story.

At the end of January 1903 Chekhov wrote to his wife: 'I'm writing a story for *Everybody's Magazine*, in the antiquated style of the seventies. I don't know how it will turn out.' And: 'I'm writing a story, but very slowly, a tablespoonful an hour . . . possibly because there's a lot of characters or because I've lost the knack. I must recover it' (letter of 30 January 1903). And in early February he writes to Olga Knipper: 'Although it's going slowly, nevertheless I'm writing. Now I'm going to sit down to write, I shall continue the story, but I'll probably write badly, limply, since there's still a strong wind and it's insufferably boring in the house.' Soon after he tells Olga he is writing only six or seven lines a day. All the same, work progressed and, in reply to repeated urgings from Mirolyubov, told him that he would finish 'The Bride' by 20 February or earlier, depending on his health: wary of the censors, he had written to Mirolyubov on 9 February: 'I'm writing "The Bride", I aim to finish it by 20 February or earlier, or rather later . . . However, don't worry, I'll send it. But there's one thing: I'm afraid "The Bride" might catch it from those bachelor-gentlemen who are watching over the chastity of your journal!' Chekhov made repeated requests for proofs to be sent to him for correction and the story was not published until December.

1. *'He wasted his substance . . .'*: Luke 15:13–16.
2. *St Peter's Day*: 29 June.
3. *Shishmachevsky*: This name is untraceable. Most probably invented by Chekhov.
4. *passport*: A passport was needed for internal as well as foreign travel.
5. *koumiss*: Chekhov himself went on such a diet, for his tuberculosis. This milk was supposed to have generally restorative powers. Tolstoy also took the cure.
6. *Saratov*: Large city on the Volga; an important trading and industrial centre.